PURCHASE

a novel

CHRISTOPHER K. DOYLE

Blank Slate Press | Saint Louis, Missouri

Blank Slate Press
St. Louis, MO
an imprint of Amphorae Publishing Group

This is a work of fiction. Any resemblance to actual events or locales or persons, living or dead, is merely coincidental, and names, characters, places, and incidents are either the products of the author's imagination or are used fictitiously.

Cover design Blank Slate Communications
Interior design by Kristina Blank Makansi

Library of Congress Control Number: 2017952355
ISBN: 9781943075409

PRINTED IN THE UNITED STATES OF AMERICA

To my daughter Nico
and wife Angela
(who've endured my singing long enough)

PURCHASE

Oh, have you seen those mournful doves
Flying from pine to pine
A-mournin' for their own true love
Just like I mourn for mine
—Carter Family

I

Runnymede McCall and the Piedmont Pipers ⁓ Hemlines of
the ladies ⁓ A cracked looking glass ⁓ Of Faustus ⁓
Bookcases and shelves ⁓ The words ⁓ Parmenides thinks not

HE HAD HEARD THE NAME WHISPERED in the shadows: Runnymede.
There was music in its naming, in its repetition. A music that spilled out of the
warehouses on Lombard Street, that sung from the docks lining Baltimore's
gray harbor, that hung in the placards and posters strung about the city: Runnymede McCall. Singer Extraordinaire. Lately of the Piedmont Pipers. There
was a performance scheduled that night at the Peabody, and as the people waiting to enter filed up, A.D. heard in the tapping canes of the gentleman, and
swishing hemlines of the ladies, a symphony already begun. Before Runnymede
even took stage. It was happening, he would later tell me. The element in him
had been finally raised; the excitement reaching such a peak, that he did not see
himself as a derelict anymore, as a porter of detritus, wandering in his home-
lessness. But saw himself in the music—as the music—the music he'd hummed
now for weeks outside each dance hall and soda fountain, marketplace and saloon. So that leaning up to the windowsill, he craned the cracked looking glass
he'd scavenged from a trashcan just so he could see.

There were chandeliers above the stage. Green and gold confetti drifted in
airy profusion. The Peabody was renowned for steeping its students in a tradition, and Runnymede certainly had his tradition down pat. Being once a
student of Juilliard in New York and later the Oberlin Conservatory in Ohio,
he sung from the Don Giovanni flawlessly. Then acted out a scene of Faustus
with such urgency and wit that when he took a wide sweeping bow and the

multitude cheered for more, it sparked such a bolt of jealousy in the boy, he suddenly wanted the life of the great man held before him. But then the Piedmont Pipers stepped from their hidden places in the wings and played a music with such pulse and feeling, the notes filtering down as if tripping from a mountain stream, that he just stood there rapt and centered, and forgot about everything else.

All the classical stuff, the high-ranging notes and lilting voice from before hadn't moved him like these bold, bright sounds. During the previous performance he'd fixated on the lights instead. On the wide wooden stage. On the way Runnymede had of gathering in the crowd and settling them down beside him with the smooth currency of his voice. So that when Runnymede bowed again and the Piedmont Pipers—two brothers and a sister—raised their arms and waved their instruments, A.D. had to reconsider his life in accordance to this fierce new sound.

Runnymede was older than A.D., by maybe only a dozen years, but already he'd been accomplished, and celebrated as such. A.D. looked at the raggedness of his own clothing, pondered the scavenged nature of his food, and pictured a day not too far removed when he, too, might grace the boards above the crowd and serenade them with his art. Yes, his art, he muttered, for what was his art if not a singing? Or a moving forward? Moving, he thought, and listening, cataloging the complete Earth. He'd done nothing but these last four years, hearing scraps of conversation dropped here and there, picking up what others left behind. Things they only saw fit to hand him when he raised his hollowed-out eyes long enough to stare. The boy, just eighteen by 1926, learned all he could as he walked the city, pounding his shape into the solemn lines hidden beneath cotton and corduroy, denim and thread. He'd learned to become so close with his surroundings, it was easy for him to slip inside unseen as the people poured out of the performance. He wanted nothing less than to look for this Runnymede himself.

It was quiet inside the marble hall. A few stragglers purchased tickets, while still a few ushers hauled out great tattered stacks of programs with Runnymede's smiling face on the cover. But A.D. was not interested in surveying the theater. Nor the grand arcade. Already he saw balconies in the heavens. Then he heard a single voice, lilting above bookcases and shelves with such an inflection it compelled the listener for more, holding some unutterable charm. And before A.D. could consider his intrusion, his grubby boots tiptoed his pale thin frame to the doorway to see.

It's shit, Runnymede said, bellowing above a man whose monocle dangled to his waist.

It's what's agreed to in the contract. Nothing more. Nothing less.

For future returns, man. Future. Returns. In so much as to my weighted decision for returning to your fine establishment. For showcasing the prodigious vocal stylings of one Runnymede McCall. For bringing myself back to this odious establishment. The extra money is for me, my good man. How can you be so obtuse?

Runnymede was taller than A.D. thought. His rich black hair was swept up above his high pale forehead, and as A.D. looked, he couldn't see a line or crease in the man's whole face. It was almost as if he'd been swept and wiped clean with a mason's quick edge. His blue suit was frosted with white piping about the sleeves, and it must have been the same one he'd worn onstage because bits of confetti drifted in the folds whenever he shook his finger in the smaller man's face. (The Peabody's director, A.D. would later understand, a man of much distinction in Baltimore, if not the shrewdest negotiator.)

I'll have to check with Agnes, the man said, before hurrying past A.D. But we've never even had hillbilly music in here before. You should at least acknowledge that.

Acknowledge that? Runnymede turned his granite jaw to follow the man. Acknowledge that it was as transcendent as God's green gospel? That it was more resplendent than any opera of note? That your theatergoers ate it up as if served the last supper? But the director was gone, and as Runnymede's oratory ceased, he smiled when he saw A.D. in the doorway. The thin urchin of a boy stared at the great man and band behind, huddled in that hallowed space, the George Peabody Library. The moonlight a slight pulse in the upper windows. A frail trace of brightness and time. Something A.D. must have seen and thought upon, wondering where he might sleep that night, and if the park across the street was safe. The citizens should have that man taken out and shot, Runnymede declared. What say you about it—man? Student? Pope? How do your classmates stand that fool?

A.D.'s eyes were moist. He was so seldom spoken to—and usually only by someone telling him to move—that he suffered to hear Runnymede's voice. How it shook the very firmament about him. How it sent up shivers in the light. Friend, Runnymede said, as he stepped closer, turning his broad-barreled chest to the boy; it's not enough to witness the world. It's not enough to even lead the world, I can assure you that.

Runnymede peered down into A.D.'s eyes as the air between them became close, and a scent of ash wafted up. Wind? Did A.D. hear a rush of wind stir between them?

Change, Runnymede finally spoke, as the sounds of life and death and even breathing ceased inside the room. It's the one true force upon Earth.

Parmenides thinks not. A.D. said, and the great man fell silent. A.D. had even silenced himself. He hadn't seen the words rising up from inside, from all the books he'd built his life upon these years, finding them at food stalls and streetcars and in the trash heaps of the city. But there they were. They flew out into the face of what Runnymede pontificated, and as the man turned to the Piedmont Pipers, as if to persuade them to his argument, they were suddenly elated. Even stirred by A.D.'s words. As if they'd found in the boy the first instance to wound the great man they'd trudged beneath for so long. The two brothers blinked at each other like stunned owls, while the girl, the one who hadn't even looked at A.D. before, shook her gold-hued hair at him, before turning down her face. But there was more. The great man drew himself up as if to pontificate further when A.D. cleared his throat. Parmenides the Greek, he said. That which truly is has always been.

Runnymede's mouth gaped open, his hand wavering in air. He had reared up on his lustrous, black loafers to meet this particular challenge, but slumped down now as if taken aback by the balance of the thin odorous mold before him, this boy with a complexion like bubbled wax paper and a mealy gloss about his teeth. The man's lips clenched in a cruel and decided crease, but he said nothing as the harried director stepped back, another fistful of twenties in his hand. Runnymede grabbed the bills and, without another word, stalked out into the street.

II

The librarian ~ Ms. Mary Frick Garret Jacobs ~ My red
guitar ~ Hawthorne and Poe ~ His first impromptu
performance ~ Our daily bread ~ A visitation in sunlight
~ What we need and what we leave ~ Singing honey

IT WAS THE LIBRARIAN, GOD HELP HER, who saved him. Even if I
did give her a nudge in the right direction, mentioning in whispers about the boy
speaking on Parmenides right there in front of her, since all she'd heard was A.D.
stifling the swagger of old Runnymede. She caught A.D. by the sleeve after he'd
watched, silent and forlorn, as the great man burst off from the scene, followed by
the Piedmont Pipers, hustling through the grand arcade with their baggage and
instruments, and A.D. thought he'd been the cause for their leaving in such a hurry.

There's a place for someone like you, she said. Programs for which you
qualify, that the great philanthropist Ms. Mary Frick Garret Jacobs put in place
years ago. Being childless herself, she's particularly fond of wayward students,
and I think she'll listen to you very well. I think she'll help.

Now, Ms. Mary Frick had married Robert Garrett in 1872, when she was but
21 years old (and then Dr. Henry Jacobs after Robert died in 1902). But before
all that, Robert's father owned that great silver line spreading out east and west
across the gathered states—the B & O Railroad—and also that red sandstone
mansion right up the street. And all A.D. had to do was go with her one day
to see, the librarian said. She never once asked questions about his particulars,
like where he slept or what he ate, for she was known to have premonitions
on students in such straights. So he sloughed off his earlier inclination toward
loneliness and silence, and thought about Runnymede instead. O he thought
on him and wondered how else he could ever become like that man. How else

could he ever sing those songs and tread those boards, if he didn't go see? If he didn't try? So he did. The very next day. He looked upon Ms. Mary Frick's gray and wizened face and repeated his story of Parmenides and Runnymede until she laughed and coughed into her hand, and that was it. He found himself on a cot that very same night, right next to mine, in the Peabody's boiler room.

Isaiah, I said and pointed at my chest.

A.D., he said and looked at my old, beat-up red guitar before setting down a grimy bag of possessions out of which a dozen books spilled around his feet. You play?

I do. I eyed him. I'd my evening mopping to do, but was told to meet the new maintenance apprentice, as he was dubbed, before starting my rounds. Though I'd not thought to see such a one as him, all scruffed up and sooted over from head to foot, from his days spent hovelling and begging and whatever else he did. I'd not thought they'd bring me one so white neither. I mean, white as to not even look white the more I spied him, the more I considered. Meaning he didn't have that same general whiteness as all the other white folks I'd known. That same sense of authority or standing, and probably never would. Being as he'd looked up from the bottom like me for so long. Thin as a rail, the boy had a mind on him that saw every little thing, for he noticed my stack of phonographs forthwith. Even took off the blue shirt I'd hung over my bookcase so he could assess my library in accordance to his own scattered about the floor.

I do not like that Hawthorne, he said. I do not like him at all. He looked at me and blinked, his face not moving. The cunningness of his thin nose had become amplified in the fading light. The single window looked above street level to the sky, and as the clouds darkened above us, it made me pause to see him so concentrated, almost furious in his opinion. I mean, the notion of it, he continued, that a letter, a simple stitched letter might burn on a woman's chest for all time, designating her, that it would separate her from man and child alike. Just imagine!

Taking the canvas hat from my head, I wiped my high kinky hair and trailed a hand across my whiskered cheek and thought on him. O I thought on him and leaned to one side before finally stirring enough to address him. Designating nothing, I said. Have you read his stories?

He was quiet. Shuffling in his dirty boots, he picked through another few books before he saw one he liked and lifted it. Then he shook it out as if some certain aspect of it might flutter between us. Something he alone could detect or interpret and must have thought on for some time to say to somebody and now had the chance. Now that Poe is something else, he said. That Poe means business. He don't fuss with all that foolishness like that other Jakes there. With all that symbolizing.

Symbolizing?

Sure.

But symbols is all they is, I said and pointed to the blue stars on the flag above my cot, and to the white bird on a poster pasted to the wall, and to a delicate few notes I'd written for a song I'd just started on a treble clef in G. Stepping closer, he studied the notes and even creased his brow before pressing his skinny finger to the paper. He sort of danced along with it then, humming with the melody that I followed in my head and stomped along to with my foot. And friends, we carried on like that for a few measures, and didn't say a word until he stopped, humming his way to the end.

You wrote that?

I looked at him straight then. I sure did, and I rubbed my hands together as if performing some magician's rite.

What's it mean?

Why everything, son. It's mine. Mine alone.

He was quiet then and looked at the notes humming his own tune, before touching the lines. Almost as if deciphering some alien landscape, something written long ago and left to dust. Something renounced henceforth from other names of people in other places. Mine, was what he heard. A word he probably hadn't spoken since before his father had started on his long decline into drinking and drugs, like his mother before him, and what ultimately spat the boy out into the world in the first place. Mine, he finally whispered, lifting his eyes. Because I could hear it was something that stirred in him some outpouring, some idea or premonition that lingered in him even after his humming had ceased. His face was red, and as he stared at me, I suppose I was meant to know this information about him entire, that I should be informed of it for all time: Who he was. What he was. And what he meant to make with his own sound, with his incessant humming. Mine. A word he took in and ate up as sustenance itself, as another rung to incorporate into the half-won ladder of his life.

Okay, I said. That's my music, and this here's your mop.

IT WAS ABOUT THIS TIME WE BEGAN BORROWING books from one another, me and A.D., and singing. It wasn't easy, I assure you. He kept to himself in the beginning, and always followed at a distance, whispering some lyrics or such nonsense, humming a tune only he knew. I had to ask him about it many times, but he'd just hush up the instant I started in on him and turn his mop in the bucket, or shine another doorknob, and it was as if I hadn't heard anything at all.

Well, I wouldn't have none of that in my own school, mind you, where I was maintenance supervisor, so I devised one day to catch him at it. It went something like this: He filled the buckets in the utility closet with the hot water and I mopped the hallway outside it. There were a few classrooms thereabouts, and all I had to do was get him in there with a dozen buckets to scrub and inside a minute he was crooning away behind the bolted door. Well, what he didn't know was that I had the key! And I had a way of attracting most any student with a two-step I'd sometimes do Fridays. Or before a holiday or semester break. Soft-shoeing it for the kids who thought nothing more of it than sunshine, and anyways I didn't feel too denigrated by it. Considering I was happy to see the young people smile by my antics, for I missed that entire, the lightness of children's laughter, that innocent charm. (Why? I'll touch on that directly). What's important now is the crowd I'd gathered for him, and the single key I jingled when my performance had ended, when A.D. sung out in his highest register. All I had to do was unlatch the lock and take my bow, for there he stood—singing for all his worth—before dozens of his own age, who laughed and applauded at the show.

I know, I know. It wasn't the nicest thing to do, but it certainly wasn't the meanest neither, and it did knock the starch out of his lonesomeness routine. For if he wanted to know everything about the music surrounding him, I did too, and thought since we were working together, it was natural enough to sing while we worked, and be friends in the process. To play back and forth with the melodies we heard in the studios and hallways that we swept through, and that ended up forming the daily ramblings of our lives. Our daily bread, so to speak. Because this was the way of the blues, I told him, when I felt he was ready. Just by looking at him I could tell he needed a good dose of the blues himself, even if he seemed to have enough of it in spades. Even if he didn't have the first clue what to do with them.

The blues? he said and looked down queer at its mentioning, considering he wasn't sure of my meaning, so I had to explain. I had to tell him the blues was a whispering away, really, that it was a dying down, too, and a rising up. That it was everything and nothing at once.

A dying down?

Well, sure, I said. And it's a name you cannot speak, not entire. It's something made of bone and ash and smoke. And it blows out your fingers and toes, from your eyes and teeth. Blowing out in song and chanting across the sad salt sea, when it first made its way here to mark us from the beginning. This is my prayer, son. And I say it every night to the darkness. And every day to the brightness. And you got it, too, I swear. You got it through and through.

Got what?

In your bones and teeth and throat. And you can go ahead and call it a song or poem or whatever you want, whatever you're always humming. But you've got to make it your own one day, to deal with it no matter what.

He was silent then and not sure of any of it, and I might have lost him entire with my soliloquy, of turning him on to the blues side of life. But the universe has a way of bringing you what you need at exactly the right moment, even if it can take everything away, too. All I had to do was sit there and watch as a gaggle of girls stepped around the corner. O we were hushed then because of it, and always reminded of our place when the students happened on us in our reveries and administrations, but that was all I needed. As A.D. watched them go by, I seen a small spark flirt about his lips as a certain young thing dropped some sheet music, before bending down in a flurry of spangles and rose-printed dressings to retrieve it, and then I knew he'd got it. The blues, for sure. He'd felt it as she hurried off.

Well, now, he finally said, not looking at me in the least, not budging from his broom neither, but just watching her go. Shoot, he whispered. The blues. The boy must not have seen women his whole time roaming the city. At least, not like the ones at the Peabody—Southern belles and rich Northern ones alike—girls who might make him forget about all the troubles that had been set upon him from the beginning. Sent out shivering into the darkness as he was, after his father burned down their house with him in it. The fire. A.D. was always remembering that fire, and how he'd hid on the raw edge of it. Watching as the water wagons appeared and the folks from town mumbled about the remains of the family they'd found inside, which only filled one measly flour sack. The memory of it all, smoldering in the center of him, a moment that had both contained him for what he'd lost, a cruel and inattentive father, but released him for what he'd gained—his freedom. Considering everyone thought he'd been burned up, too, before walking the twenty miles into Baltimore, leaving behind as much as he could of his sad, damaged self. So he just stood there whispering the blues, the blues over and over, even with the sunlight falling in the high upper windows that we still had to wash. I think the word might of rearranged him in some sense. Even if I knew it was probably just that girl that had done it, moving him toward the blues side of life, toward the feelings and desires he'd hid in his smoldering shell for so long.

The blues, I said after I let him linger there long enough. That's what that is and I need it every day to remind me. And every night to sing. We all need it to remind us.

Remind us of what?

Of what we had and want to have again. Of what we still need.

Need, he said and looked at me, but didn't say anything as he turned to the empty hallway and seemed to sniff something. Or waft his hand up slow and steady, churning the fragrance of the girl's departed air, before looking back as if the essence of what he wanted was out there somewhere. Just out of reach. Tantalizing him. For here he was with the luxury to ponder inside himself finally, to absorb sight and sound unseen, all at his leisure—even if he did have to push a mop for the privilege of it—and the boy didn't know how to begin. So I just listened to him. I listened as he was quiet, and quiet some more, until finally I outlasted him and another bit of his shell came chaffing off as he cleared his throat. That's funny, he said.

What is?

Need. Because I never thought I needed anything before this, and he nodded to the hallway, the windows, to the bucket and mop and invisible path the girl had taken, before shaking his head. I thought I just had to move. That it was all I was, that it was all I'd ever be, and he shook his boots out to show me the strength of him, for his muscles practically pulsed at the end of his long skinny legs. He was a specimen, truly, of moving, of walking miles and miles untold, of the sheer perseverance he'd made of himself (and which probably served him well later driving night after night through the mountains and farms to find his songs, all the precious songs he needed). But as he looked at his feet and relished them a moment longer, I watched as something new seemed to take hold. As if all that packed muscle and bone had flowed up inside him, spreading over his thoughts and mind and dreams—which were still bathed in blackness as far as I could tell—or streaked with the flames from living as fast and easy as he had before this. But which seemed contained now all a sudden. Caged even.

Moving's the easy part, son. It is. For I know what you're thinking: Where's this been my whole life? And: Why now? and other such things as that. Well, don't fight it. Not a bit. Fightin's the easy part, too. It's all anyone can do. It's the staying and accepting that takes some doing. It's the staying that really matters. That makes up who you are. That proves it.

That proves what?

That you're real. With real feelings and needs. And then I watched as he mouthed the word twice for he seemed to be trying out the notion of it even as I spoke it. Even as he knew his whole life had been the exact opposite in nearly every way.

Real, he finally whispered. That's a word I thought I didn't need. Not a once. I just thought I'd move and always move and that'd be it. That nothing would ever take hold of me. That nothing would ever last except the moving, the freedom.

But it does last, son. It does. It lasts longer than you could ever know, and I had to turn my eyes then and wipe them, for I was thinking on my wife and baby girl then. The ones I used to sing and dance for down in Bristol, Virginia, but had to leave years past (and so of course, that was why I loved dancing for the kids here, too). But I didn't tell him none of that. Not with him being just a boy, and one who thought his whole life would be a movement away from something, from whatever he felt was dragging him down. His sadness? His lonesomeness? Who could say? I had the same sadness in me and the moving hadn't helped no matter how far I went. No matter how hard I tried to get it back and right the wrong I'd done, and so I just looked on him instead. I looked and thought of the only thing that might make him listen for once, that might make the idea take hold. You'll see, I finally said, and shook my head to show him I meant it, that the words mattered, that they were true. Because it stays with you, no matter what you do. No matter how far you move. Your life—it's always there, always watching you—that much I know.

He looked at me and nodded as if he'd truly heard it, but then sung out real soft and slow, Honey, so I knew that was the refrain I was meant to sing back. So I sang Honey in the hallway until he sang again. There you go away. There you go. Then I didn't say nothing, because it sounded like the song was finished. And I watched instead as he mopped the same spot for the next half hour, mopping around the puddle of his life that was, and the fast glistening streaks he thought it might soon become.

III

Ms. Clara May Staunton ~ Dumbstruck in the wide
rows ~ Guitar lessons and composition ~ The true
chord and metronome ~ John Hill Carter ~ On the
James River ~ Cataloging his affections ~ White
perfect circles ~ A birdcage ~ The canaries

SHE WAS FROM NORFOLK, VIRGINIA he found out soon enough. Ms.
Clara May Staunton, and I did not like it one bit, I told him, even as he changed
himself so the girl might notice him when everyone else in the school either
walked past or couldn't have guessed his intentions. Each morning he stood at
the sink and combed his brown hair. The same shag I'd cut after he'd first seen
her, considering he'd come in all curled up and wavy and you'd a thought he
was something Poseidon mighta dragged in from the salt sea to glimpse him. O
he was adding all kinds of flourishes to his appearance, and even fiddled with
his belt buckle too, shining it up with a tin of old Brasso I had lying about for
instruments and door handles and other surfaces in a school such as that. The
good old librarian even brought all sorts of hand-me-downs and holdovers from
her own nephews and kin, so that in no short order he had a wardrobe that beat
out mine all the way through.

Of course, he spent most of his free and working time in the library, as did
I. And often, he saw her reading there or combing through the great books and
stood beside her as if poised in the midst of his stated occupation—polishing up
floors and tabletops or straightening the card catalog. Though more often than
not, he'd succumb to a more tortuous and pressing anticipation and creep up as
close to her as he could get. It was agonizing to watch, but humorous, too. He'd
often hover there on the other side of the shelves, watching through the cracks.
But after a spell of waiting that might of burst his young cleaving heart, he'd

kind of curl his paper-thin self up closer to listen. While on the other side, she was so entranced with whatever she was reading, she couldn't have known the drama unfolding in his soul as he stood there on the precipice of connection, of being noticed by her in the slightest. This went on for weeks, I assure you, and months—and even past his nineteenth birthday. He was so affected by the trials of worship he put to her appearance, it began to keep me from my own guitar playing, and the lessons I'd taken to teaching him each evening, even though he didn't prove to be such an easy study as I'd hoped.

Relax, I told him. You're young yet, son. Move your hands like you want them to. Let them flow. Let it all go. He set beside me and had gotten his own beat up guitar, a Lyon & Healy we'd found stowed away in a practice studio and whose silky strings were much easier to finger than the steel ones on my guitar. It was something we didn't mention to our supervisor, Mr. Vickers, or to the Peabody director, Dr. Alpionaire, the one old Runnymede had shook down for money all those months ago. We just let it pass as sometimes I often would during my years in such matters. So that when nobody raised a fuss about a missing instrument, we'd play each evening when we had some time of our own to devote to it.

O he was devoting all sorts of time to other things as was set down by Ms. Mary Frick Garret Jacobs in her sponsorship of his employment, consigned as he was to a rigor of courses over the semesters. He'd taken a drawing class offered at the Peabody, and an English class for the classics (which he'd already mostly read), and a music composition class that he so hemmed and hawed over, before finally deciding on what he hoped to accomplish with it, that I never saw him so concentrated, so charged. As for Runnymede, I should say it now, as it's most likely obvious to anyone with eyes, he still loomed over everything A.D. did. The boy still thought on emulating that great man he held so highly in esteem, for he was determined now to do it, to raise himself up to those great heights, to reach some higher purpose. And I didn't disbelieve him in anything he set himself to, except maybe his guitar, which was a terrible thing to listen to, truth be told. But still I held out hope.

I can't do it like you, he said, I can't, and he set his guitar aside. We were working on chords, for he'd found a few to his liking, but the fingering had caused him a considerable strain, and I was thinking of showing him a barre chord instead. Something to much easier approximate the sounds he saw me conjure and that delighted him most nights into a mimicry of my technique.

It's practice, son, that's all it is. Practice them and then you'll get them and you won't have to think about it as you play. You won't even have to look. It'll just be like you're walking down the street, moving over the land, and often you might rise up your foot without even noticing a stump or crack in the sidewalk. It's just something that comes to you. Like moving up through your body. A feeling, as they say.

Sure, he said, a feeling, and he looked at his feet.

That's right, look at those feet. Look at everything that keeps you balanced and moving because it's part of you now. It's something that flows out of you all natural and easy and it's all just practice, son. Practice for anybody. Even me.

Shoot, he said, anybody but you, and stretching his long fingers, he pressed on the strings strumming, but the vibrations buzzed up as he played. He hadn't pressed hard enough on his smallest finger and the note wasn't true, and thus the chord wasn't true. Jesus Christ, he fumed and stood as if he might smash the instrument to the floor and fling the splinters into the furnace that had flared up just then as if on cue. It was a terrible winter that year, and the sleet and ice kept up such a steady ticking as of a metronome on the greased window, that I thought it was the noise itself causing his frustrations.

What? What is it, son? I said as he stood with his back to me. I was on my cot, my foot tapping the worn floor. We'd the rest of the night off and it was close to Christmas anyways and the long marble hallways were quiet and sad, and it gave me pause to think on my wife and daughter then for whole hours some days. Thinking on what they could be doing so far away from me after so many years. And I did not like it one bit, I told him, this idleness to consider things. I did not like it in the least.

I seen her today, he said.

So. You see her every day.

No, he said, and still he hadn't looked at me. He'd set his guitar down and plucked now so quietly on the fretboard, the plinking of his fingers echoed with the skittering icedrops against the window. I seen her with a fellow, he said, and then he turned to me. His face moist beneath his eyes. His cheeks drawn and red. His hands shaking white.

O, a fella, I said, and was quiet as I bowed my head.

JOHN HILL CARTER WAS NOT WHO I EXPECTED to find consorting with Ms. Clara May Staunton, I assure you. But considering A.D.'s luck in things thus far in life, I figured it pretty much held in line with all the other things that generally conspired against a man's very notion of right and wrong.

John Hill Carter was one of the older students at the Peabody, and one of its most distinguished composers. And a first class ass to boot. I cannot say it any other way. It's as soft as it gets. I did not like him ever since I seen him that first day his big granddaddy dropped him off out front, stepping as they did from their horse-drawn carriage. The one they'd hired special at the train station to carry them in with all of John Hill's accoutrements and furnishings. Old Dr. Alpionaire was out there himself to greet him, and Mr. Vickers, my boss, mentioned I should help too as we both descended the steps and unloaded the various suitcases and trunks John Hill pointed to as if I were too black to understand their importance for his grand arrival at our backwash of a town.

He was from one of the oldest tobacco families in Richmond and made it plain to hear how much money he'd brought to spend on the frivolous little things he'd need to keep himself satisfied in a northern outpost such as this. He said all of this to Mr. Vickers as I hauled up crate after crate of what all I know not—lead most likely, it felt like to me on my back—and then took out the slickest silver lighter I'd ever seen and lit up cigarette after cigarette describing the strain of the plant, and the gross of the yield, and the general conditions that comprised the flavor he now gloried in. He just stood there pontificating as he smoked. As if he were still on the James River, enjoying a warm summer's day, drinking mint juleps and cavorting with the pretty young things there in their silk parasols, transporting in the earthly light as if it was all his in its making. He did all this as I dried my forehead and cussed him under my breath and then watched as he blew out the smartest white smoke rings I'd ever seen.

John Hill is not the man to truck with, I said, and that seemed to shake A.D. from his moping. It was January, late afternoon, and the students had been back a few weeks, but he'd not seen Ms. Clara May yet, though he'd been thinking of her all break. He'd even taken the notion of writing her a love song to win her affection from this John Hill Carter. This man who'd just unwrapped the finest silk sheets for her that he then paraded through the grand arcade. Or the rosewood bookcases, delivered from a boutique in New York City, and that Mr. Vickers had A.D. and me carry up to Ms. Clara May's room. So in this way A.D. finally saw where she slept and memorized all she had in case John Hill brought in any more belongings or had them delivered to her door. Now I didn't think A.D. meant to stop John Hill from bringing in more treasures for Ms. Clara May, only to find out what he was up against, to somehow steel himself to the wealth of it. To use it as ballast upon which to build the song he'd started crafting slowly at first, over the Christmas holidays, but then faster the more John Hill and the students were awash with the excitement of his latest exploits.

O he knew he was poor, A.D. did, and that he couldn't possibly compete in that line of wealth. But was it too much to ask for it to stop, he moaned at night as he hemmed and hawed over a chord progression, or the few scant lyrics he felt aright themselves beneath the anguish of his tongue. For surely all his emotions tumbled to the page as he scribbled with the pencil nubs he'd found sweeping the hallways, as the great wadded paper littered his side, and then the floor. Before stuffing it all into the furnace as it shot up a dark blue flame. Is it too much to ask? he repeated.

No, son, it isn't, I said. It's just gonna be hard like I told you, fixating on one of them students like that. On one we're only ever entrusted with sweeping up after and to serve practically from the get go.

Practically? He was thinking on John Hill Carter, on all the things we'd carried in with him always lighting up another damn cigarette as he watched. Snapping open his silver lighter. Saying his own daddy made this batch just two months before with the niggers on their land still called niggers, working back-breaking in the barns where they kept the crop stored all winter and where you'd a thought the Civil War hadn't just ended fifty years before to hear them toiling away for all that white man's business. There's no practically about it, A.D. said. He burns me. The thought of John Hill standing above me, puffing away with them white perfect circles falling around Ms. Clara May's face. He burns me to no end.

I know, I said. I know it, because you're of two worlds now, both of you. But he didn't listen. He was so far in it already—in his worship of her and his despising of him—that he couldn't hear me go on about them being so far above us, and even over everyone else we knew, that it was always fire that would end it like that between them. Fire in the belly of man that would flare up when the two worlds met, when they collided. But he didn't mind me at all. He was fixated on other things. On plans he'd made. On visions he saw set in his mind and revolving. Images even of Runnymede high up in the air. Floating above it all. Floating in the ether.

A birdcage, he finally said, after he'd watched silent and forlorn all week as deliverymen of every variety stopped off with their silver paper weights for Ms. Clara May, and a gold statue of a goose, and a red mahogany table adorned with brass handles and a copper frontispiece with the woodwork of a primitive etched on the side, and a porcelain tea set from Japan, and jade collection of geometries that hung from the wires of a bamboo sculpture that was so wide and unruly that

A.D. and I had to take the doors off the hinges in the dormitory just to get it up the staircase because John Hill insisted the little silver screws couldn't be touched for their perfect escapement and alignment. And of course that had A.D. reeling and red-faced when he saw the final article arrive at the end of this cavalcade on a Sunday, when the high upper windows of the Peabody were thrust open and lovely with voices lilting in the midst of arias and solos as violins lowed softly in the dirty Baltimore dusk.

A birdcage, I said. So where are the birds?

He didn't say. He touched his mop and then set it down with a wet thump in his bucket. There were voices approaching from a far corner, and as we stepped to the side of the hallway (as Mr. Vickers had advised us in doing, steering clear of the students at all times), Ms. Clara May herself appeared out of a bright slant of sunlight and leaned her delicate little head down as she passed with a gaggle of friends all delighting and giggling in their way. Conversing about their lives as if it couldn't be more natural to pass two men mopping for all they were worth just for them to step foot on immaculate floors. But I swear—and I swear to this day—I seen her glance at A.D. as he looked at her, focusing like none other on her face. Leaning up closer, she raised her head and blinked at him and said, Thank you, in the sweetest kind voice you ever heard. Then leaning forward in the light, she touched his shoulder, and sort of just kept it there, her perfect hand, because I suppose she'd heard about his singing. Or seen him hauling in all her treasures and trinkets over the last week, and needed him to know she saw him not just as the hired help, but as a man besides. A man to touch. A man to look at and to know, and when he was about to reply, when he'd tilted his head just so and opened his mouth to speak, she was gone, and A.D. stood looking at the space her figure had vacated. Almost as if he couldn't believe anything else was as purely divine in the whole world.

Did you see it? I said as I stepped closer and nudged him back to the land of the living.

I did, he said, and she was perfect.

No, I said, in her hand, the one at her side. Didn't you see what she carried?

What?

The answer.

The answer to what?

To all your worries, son. To your mind.

My what?

Why the birdcage, of course? Didn't you see the canaries?

IV

The giant keychain ~ Crows in the eaves ~ Perfectionists and obsessives all of them ~ Motifs and themes ~
From Morgan Park to Sandtown ~ On picnic tables
and chairs ~ The incident in the courtyard ~ A small
glinting trophy ~ His great silver lighter ~ The fire

A.D. WENT TO SEE THE CANARIES AT NIGHT. This I know because
I seen him and warned him not to. But he did it anyway and couldn't help
himself when it came to her, and besides, he knew her schedule like the back
of his hand. She had choir practice Monday and Wednesday afternoons, and
then solo rehearsal Thursday nights. And when A.D. wasn't sitting outside the
choir room listening to the thrill of her high-arching soprano, he was sorting
through the giant keychain he kept in his pocket as he hurried up the staircase
to her room. Mr. Vickers had been so pleased with A.D.'s work he'd promoted
him to full janitor after six months. A promotion that brought with it the added
responsibility of the keychain and the myriad doorways he could open in that
almost full city block of a campus.

He would open her door and step in when she wasn't there and just stare. I'd
crept up to it once, following him, and held my ear to the cold edge listening
as he snapped off the white handkerchief she draped over the birdcage so the
canaries would sing out as you'd never heard with such a triumph of awakening,
I could only imagine A.D.'s face in that moment: the furtive darkness of it lifting, his eyes and ears raised up as if breaching the top of a white cresting wave.
He'd told me before about his years spent in the city hovelling in basements,
how the crows had cackled in the eaves and he'd thought it the sound of death
itself. Death incarnate and black. Death tolling away the hours. But now there
were only these bright yellow canaries to consider. They were unlike anything

he'd ever seen. As he listened to them, he watched their cage sway as they moved on their thin wooden perch, and something inside him must have moved too. Some sense of life must have lifted above all the darkness always falling around him, because I could hear him singing louder to their call, singing to their sweet voice. But of course when her choir class was almost through, he'd slide her handkerchief back over the cage and glide out into the hall, locking the door, and then smell his hand all the way down into the courtyard because he knew she'd touched the handkerchief too. That she'd held it near her cheek, and that it felt like he was caressing and holding her close. That he was with her. Together.

Surely he said all those words in the darkness of the boiler room as the sounds of tubas and violas echoed down through the ventilation, careening from the lips of some insomniac student practicing for something—an audition, a recital, a solo—practicing habitually as the students there did, perfectionists and obsessives all of them. Sometimes it inspired A.D. to sit up and touch his guitar, gathering it to his chest, before moving his fingers down through a key. His composition class had been going well, and he'd felt in the midst of his studies an idea for words, for a repetition that might approximate the motifs and themes the great composers had woven throughout their music. He was still struggling to write her song though. He hadn't found the hook yet, as he called it, the theme to wind his words around. O he'd scoured books and books, looking at words, pointing at ideas and characters that might better represent what he had in his mind to say to her. But none of it rang true. None of it was real, he said, and paused on the sensation of saying that word again, for still the elusive nature of the song vexed him.

More and more he went to her room to search for inspiration, an inkling to her life, a knowingness that might inform his music. Even during the daylight hours this persisted, and I worried for him and told him so. But he would not hear me, and only ever offered a low haughty laugh whenever I inquired. Something I'd not heard before, but which gave me pause and had me wondering that this course could only ever lead to confusion and pain, as far as I was concerned. And to maybe somewheres else that I did not want to go.

It was easy to understand why, of course. It was the music. The heady strains of it were everywhere in the Peabody. The music of great sorrows and tragedies echoed in every hallway and classroom, and for months it was all he heard, and I think it finally enthralled him, or swallowed him up entire. So that when he first saw Ms. Clara May as a flirtation, as a movement in his cold breast toward something warmer after all his years spent wandering and surviving, by the close of spring, the feeling burned into something much brighter that only he could see. Something made real by his persistence to feel something—to feel anything—and in his heady fervor he might have believed she loved him as much as he loved her. I cannot say for sure. But what I can say is that he wasn't the only one with eyes. Not by a long shot.

I'd seen John Hill Carter on more than one occasion standing idle and inquisitive on a faraway corner when we'd clean the high windows of the director's office. O we'd sing there, and play back and forth with ideas and lyrics as we watched the water fountain in the park trickle down, and the city's pigeons bathe their blue- and green-mottled feathers in the clay-rimmed waters, as maybe a mother pushed a sleeping baby past in a rickety pram. But as I noticed John Hill watching us, there was something else in his demeanor, a haughtiness or contempt—even more so than his usual contempt for those around him—that led me to believe he'd been clued into A.D.'s feelings on Ms. Clara May. That he knew.

For seven years I'd been at the Peabody and had done little else than work and send money to the Honorable Reverend Michael Williams at the Faith Baptist Congregation in Bristol, Virginia, where my wife and I'd gone often enough when I was there, and where I still hoped she returned. But I'd also watched the students. I'd studied them as much as they'd studied their music, and I could tell from a hundred yards what they were thinking. Very rarely had I let myself stray to the east and west neighborhoods where my color eased my visits, from Morgan Park to Montebello Terrace, Upton to Sandtown. Or even—in my weakest moments—when thinking on my wife and baby girl had plunged me into fits of drunkeness and dejection, to the Bottom or Mercer's Row, where the real downhearted colored folks congregated in slums. Drinking poormans in paper sacks. Raising mudcaked hands to fireblackened barrels. Whispering spirituals from time immemorial, from when the blues had been passed down across the cotton, when we'd been scattered as little more than property. The men more so than the women. With the loss of family and dignity our only recompense, of what we could not hope to keep. It was this same indignation I saw on John Hill's face now whenever he thought on what A.D. represented, with his intentions for Ms. Clara May. So for the next few weeks as A.D. watched Ms. Clara May, I watched John Hill, and the circle repeated itself.

Of course this helped our playing considerable. The more A.D. focused on monitoring Ms. Clara May, the more he dug into his emotions. He still hadn't written his song yet, but in the chords he played and the notes I sometimes got to string over his progressions, there were a few dizzying moments where there was only the sound of us striving together. Only the sound of our music rising in the stillness of the boiler room, before echoing out into the larger world. Often I'd heard footsteps outside our doorway. When we'd finish a particularly inspired session, one in which the feeling of lifting ourselves into the sound had taken over everything, I'd hear something stir as of a flushed heartbeat or breathing, and it wasn't mine or A.D.'s. We'd already alighted into the sound, as it sometimes happened, when you'd find yourself floating up from everything you knew, that the music could even do that when it was right, when it wanted to. Of course it never lasted, those heights, and as we descended again to our lives in the boiler room, I'd bring my attention back to the Peabody and its minute movements, as that footstep or heartbeat slunk away. And I'd remember with a dark, heavy heart the course A.D. had set in motion with his behavior.

He's watching you, I told him, after a particularly inspired night of playing had buoyed our spirits. The winter had given way to April, and in a little less than a month there would be a recital for the students who'd finished their studies, and old John Hill was one of them. The most celebrated, in fact. It was even rumored he'd conduct a sonata he'd penned as part of his final studies, one receiving rave reviews from his professors. The box office had already strung up posters; the excited word had gone out by various newspaper and print outlets. So that A.D. felt a darker burning to complete his song for Ms. Clara May, even though he still hadn't found the ease of expression he thought would flow from his thinking and feeling on her. O his feeling on her. He found it had only grown the more his lonesomeness persisted. The more it lingered and was enflamed by the music of the place, by the very reverberations of the walls.

Well, I'm watching him, too, he finally said, and blinked his cold blue eyes so I could gauge his seriousness. So I guess that makes the two of us, now don't it.

I guess it does.

He was jangling his keychain as we sat in the courtyard, out where the students often sprawled on a summer's day, lounging on picnic tables and folding chairs, singing or huddled in groups with their instruments. A.D. had taken to lingering in the shadows as if completing the sweeping he was meant to do, but I knew he was really only watching for Ms. Clara May. For sure enough, he'd gauged her entrance to the second. As if on cue, she appeared with a sandwich and glassful of milk and sat on a faraway table with her pretty strawberry head buried in her music. She was reading something intently, perfecting each note as she moved her mouth soundlessly to the accents and pitches of the score.

And as I turned to A.D., to let him know I was on to what he'd planned, he was already up before I could blink or nod a reproach. Moving across the courtyard, he set his keychain in his back pocket before pulling out a crumpled sheet of notepaper he held now as he sidled up beside her.

Miss? he said, taking a step closer. Ms. Clara May Staunton? whispering her name, as behind him in the daylight a stunning violin echoed his aching approach.

Yes? she said, and though she hadn't raised her head to see him, she'd raised her white perfect hand as if to stay him, to still his voice. She was still lingering amidst the last notes of a measure that captured her entire, and I've often wondered what symphony so gathered her in to remove her bodily from the day and moment—from this moment above any other—after the days and months had spent themselves, clanking away in their calibrations to arrive at this one instant for A.D.

Yet as softly as she'd raised her hand, she let it fall. She'd reached the end of her aria and looked up at him and had to shade her eyes for the sunlight fell at such an angle to leak a spangled aura across his combed brown hair. It was a halo of brightness surely, for she seemed suddenly struck by the thunderbolt of his appearance, and arched her face back as a rosy flush flooded her cheeks. It was obvious to see why. Throughout his time at the Peabody, A.D. had grown considerable. So that his thinness, that defining emblem that had so followed him until that moment—was much leaner and stronger now—as if transforming his body into the kind seen on men of work, with a much hardier disposition, and I don't believe she mistook it. Not in the least. Maybe she'd noticed it all along? Maybe she looked up at him then and smiled at this boy she'd said thank you to before in the hallway, touching his shoulder. This boy who looked now as if he was composed to raise their earlier flirtation into a higher, singular resonance.

Don't.

Pardon?

John Hill had appeared at A.D.'s shoulder and with one great hand spun A.D.'s body so that he faced away from Ms. Clara May, who now stood not knowing what to do. Don't, he said, whatever it is.

I will do it, said A.D., I will, and he shook John Hill's hand from his shoulder.

You will not, John Hill said and smiled. He took the cigarette from his lips and blew a white smoke ring in A.D.'s face. He was shorter than A.D. by a few inches but had sixty pounds on him if an ounce and knew it. Leaning his meaty finger into A.D.'s ribs, he nudged him back. You seem very much like a nigger to me now. Do you know that? he said. In your ignorance you are just like one of them. So why don't you just go on back to your nigger friend there like a good boy. Go on, John Hill said and shooed at A.D. with his big strong hands, and the courtyard, which was very loud till then, with students singing and playing, had grown quiet as A.D. looked on at Ms. Clara May Staunton, who only touched John Hill's shoulder and said something so that John Hill smiled as he watched A.D. a moment longer. Go on, he said. Get. Then the two of them, Ms. Clara May, quiet and confused, and John Hill, fulsome and smiling, walked back toward the dorm.

THERE WERE NO WORDS AFTER THAT FROM A.D., for one week, two, three. He'd touch his guitar before setting it down in a huff, and the crumpled paper he'd hoped to read to Ms. Clara May was in pieces. But then he'd pick it up in a rash of pasting and rearranging, before tearing it up again the next instant, so that he was useless in his duties from then on and I had to hide him from Mr. Vickers. Who as far as I could tell, had not heard one word of the incident in the courtyard between A.D. and John Hill. If he had, he hadn't let on because he was of a mind like me in not caring one ounce for that John Hill Carter who lorded over A.D. now whenever he saw him in the hallways, or in the courtyard, trudging through his duties. It was the damndest thing. John Hill wouldn't say a word. He'd just smile and open his silver lighter, before clacking it shut with a loud slapping sound, as he watched and waited—for what, I know not—a sign in A.D., a premonition of the rage he'd stirred in him, a conflagration of the strife set in motion now between them?

For his part, A.D. kept his head down throughout all of this and was as dark and foreboding as I could remember. I believe his considerable brain was singularly focused on formulating curses to scald the heavens, and the more I watched him, the more apprehensive I grew. He would pause now in the hallways and touch the posters with John Hill's name upon them. Mumbling certain invectives, he'd then peel down one of the top corners, and I'd have to shuffle up behind him so he knew I was on to what he meant to do, to tear down each trace of that John Hill Carter for what A.D. believed in his delusion John Hill had taken from him.

He's taken her from me, he said. As surely as I stand here, he's taken her when she was not his to take. When she was not his at all.

The grand recital was the next afternoon and we'd spent all week arranging chairs in the courtyard. O we'd strung up bunting and streamers from the balustrades and balconies, from the hallways and doorframes. The whole campus was delightful and effusive, as if it floated within a flowing wind of enchantment. Soft crinoline sheets and votive candles were everywhere so that if you hadn't set your eyes upon it before, the great cheerfulness of the decorations would have eased your weary heart. All except A.D.'s, of course, whose heart was still black and burning in its leaden pit as he paced and jangled his keychain even after I told him to quit it, that it was over. That hadn't I told him it would only come to this, to no good from the beginning? Hadn't I had my misgivings?

It is not over, he said and turned to me with poison in his throat before storming off, so that I had to follow him to stay his demon mind. I knew where he was headed, and only wondered what I could do to keep the venom inside him, to stop whatever plan he'd set in motion now that he'd come full circle in his mind to this night of fruition.

The birds, I said, hurrying up behind him. What are you going to do with the birds?

There was a cry above me in the stairwell, and then a great sundering of wood. When I reached the third floor, A.D. was inside her dorm room holding the birdcage as Ms. Clara May herself looked dumbstruck and incredulous from her bedside as John Hill Carter stood buttoning his shirt.

Take your hands off them this instant, John Hill said and stepped toward A.D., a half-drunk whiskey bottle in his hand. The brown bottle leaked its rich perfume as he twisted it like so much incense sprinkled about the air. As a few drops caught A.D. on the cheek, he smiled to see John Hill come for him as he'd hoped, because his legs were long and he held one out catching John Hill in the gut.

John Hill slumped forward with a sound like a gashed tire. His eyes were red and watery as he lurched up trying to grab A.D., but A.D. just laughed and brought the birdcage down on the back of John Hill's head. As John Hill fell to one knee, the whiskey bottle shattered on the carpet. I knew it, John Hill said, I knew it, as he leaned up and watched as A.D. prepared to bring the birdcage down again on its target. What'd I tell you, Clara May? You give a nigger an inch and he takes the whole world.

Boys! Boys! Ms. Clara May said, but she was nothing to them now. A small trophy at the edge of their entanglement. A trinket that could only stand there as the canaries fluttered up in their cage and cried out against whatever malevolence had been brought against them. For myself, I'd have rushed in to help, but the general commotion had raised voices in the hallway, and straining to look, I feared for Mr. Vickers at any moment (with maybe even the constables to boot), and sort of froze there in the doorway, a colored man suspended in a white world run amok.

There ain't no boys about it, John Hill shouted. There's just niggers, and the ones who tame them. John Hill was grinning now in his devilment, holding the cage up with one strong hand as A.D. pushed down with it again, while in the same instant eyeing the broken bottle below him. The shards were drenched and glistening, and where the whiskey-soaked rug ran between A.D.'s boots, John Hill lit his great silver lighter and tossed it out toward him. Before you could blink, the flames shot up and danced all blue and hypnotic, and for a moment we stood in a strange sort of abeyance. Felled, I think, by the notion of the world spiraling away from us. A.D.'s boots were black and afire and as he shook them in an odd sort of dance, Ms. Clara May stepped toward him through the smoke to take the cage.

Come on, A.D. said, holding his hand out to her, practically begging her to leave, for John Hill had already pushed his way blindly from the room. There was only A.D. now to pull Ms. Clara May from the smoke. But she would not move. Flat out refused. It was confounding to see. How she kind of just shrugged her shoulders and A.D.'s sweating hands were no match for her discomfort. As A.D. and I watched then, she wrapped her arms tighter around the cage as if she'd done the same thing every Sunday, as if it were nothing at all to her, before kneeling down, overcome by the heat. I had to drag A.D. out after that from the end of my arm, while Ms. Clara May only seemed to teeter beneath that great awkward cage as we watched. The smoke rose up fierce and black, with her soft strawberry head already sweating and soaked by the moisture, and she seemed strangely at ease. As if she were doing nothing more than wading out into a tepid lake and settling herself down in the water. So that in our last glimpse of her, there was only her face—her soft sad face framed by the great orange flames—and then the yellow birds singing, singing, singing out their song.

V

An overseer of sorts ~ The blues through and through
~ The bartender's glasses ~ A.D.'s conspiring ~ No killing tonight ~ Guns and songs and Jessico ~ The boxcar ~
Killers and fugitives ~ Old Hackett and what transpired
there ~ A fog descending ~ Reaching Bladen Street

THE FLAMES SHOT UP AND THE SIRENS called out so that A.D. told
me later, after we'd made it to a saloon I knew on the south side of town, that
he'd thought it was his childhood all over. That he was watching his father smol-
der again in their house and had felt the overwhelming urge to crouch behind a
tree and watch the dormitory burn from the park. I'd not let him, of course. Instead, I'd led him in a sort of trance really, grabbing his shoulders and marching
him through the side streets and alleys where we might not be found, for there
was already the fear of discovery about us. John Hill Carter had certainly made
it out and even in the chaotic few moments after everyone realized what was
happening, I'd heard him calling out my name and A.D.'s as the perpetrators of
this most heinous act.

Sitting at the bar then, with the whiskey poured before us, I thought on
all the articles and implements, books and sheet music I'd accumulated in my
seven years at the Peabody, and knew I couldn't go back for it. It was gone, and
I was with A.D. now, and felt like an overseer of sorts. Considering he was so
dismayed about leaving Ms. Clara May as we had—burnished in the flames,
sweating down to the sweet center of her being—that I thought he might try
something rash in his state, like suicide or some other infernal decision. Maybe
even confessing to a crime he didn't commit, just for the guilt he felt in him, for
the downright wretchedness of it. The blues, I guess you could say. He had 'em
all over for sure. The blues through and through.

A.D.? I said. But he didn't move. Didn't answer neither. I held a whiskey to his lips and made him take a few sips just so the life might be restored to him, so his mind might descend from its high pale lonesomeness. But he didn't respond. Didn't even blink. So I tried again. A.D.? Before shaking his arm and patting his back, as if trying to force the air back into him physically, as after a drowning or flogging. But it weren't no use. He just sat there as cold as ice. It's okay, son. It is. Truly.

What's okay? He turned his cold burning eyes on me, eyes that were lit with a fire whenever he turned his head to scowl at the bar, or the wall, irradiating the world as he looked upon it with his hatred and anguish. That I killed her? That I did it with my own damn ignorance? Is that what's okay? Is that it? Before I could write her one damn song? The flush had returned to his cheeks and his eyes fluttered up quickly and were shut as he played his fingers over his chin and lips, as if engaged in some physical or religious inventory of his few remaining possessions.

No, son, I said. Not at all, and I looked to see what other patron might have heard his eruption. This was an establishment known to be raided on occasion with prohibition instituted not six years earlier. Though with it being a colored place, and tucked beside the trolley line, I was not as anxious as I might have been elsewhere. There were just a few old timers at the bar, and they seemed wholly caught up in their own ineptness. Littered amongst the tables, a few groups conversed while others played poker by the light of a paraffin lamp that sent a black cloying soot over everything, and the whole scene made me lonesome to be pursued like this, lonesome to no end. Out there in the darkness I knew I was labeled a killer, a fugitive, and in the thunderous noise of the trolley clamoring by, and soft shoes scuffling peanut shells across the floor, the accusations and forces marshalling against us rose in my mind to confront me. And I hoped upon hope A.D.'s words hadn't been heard by anybody—let alone the bartender—who was the only one left to consider.

I looked at him and he looked away as if something gnawed at him, before feigning to scour his fogged-up little spectacles. He wiped them again before drying the few bottles near the register, chewing all the while on a cinnamon toothpick he tucked inside the edge of his lip. He was mumbling something too. Some such prayer I never quite caught the gist of. Something about misericordia or a beatitude perhaps.

She didn't deserve it, A.D. whimpered. Nobody did. Except maybe that old John Hill Carter bastard, and he stood for a second so that I had to grab his waist and set him back beside me on the stool, holding him close.

Son, son, I said and touched A.D.'s arm as the bartender watched me from the shadows, rubbing his chin.

All I need now is to end it for him, A.D. said, not modulating his volume in the least, nor his intentions. Just to find that good old boy and skin him up for what he done to her. Leaving her like that with her cage. Burning up to nothing but smoke and sadness in her abandonment. Hell, and he turned to me as he said it, remembering her and the sad singing voices of those canaries. His blue glassy eyes implored me to speak, to appease him somehow—or the world perhaps—for the fate of every last one of us in our anguish, something I could not do. Something no one could. I watched his hands shake as he said it, and then his fingers fiddled with the empty glass in front of him. But it weren't no good. Nothing he did could appease his dejection, and pushing himself back on his barstool, he looked me straight in the eye. I left her, Isaiah. I did. As sure as I'm sitting here. When I could have changed everything. When I could have sung to her. When I could have sung.

Friend, I looked up and the bartender was there. He looked at me and folded his rag into a damp little square before setting his sharp black elbows on the bar. You talking about killing a white man?

I looked at him for a long moment and didn't shift my eyes as I thought I might have to drag him out physically if he were to talk any louder and alert everyone to A.D.'s conspiring. Why? I finally said.

It's okay, he said and winked his dark beady eyes at me. I don't care none about it. Not at all, and he shook his gray dusted afro before leaning back and spitting to the floor.

Then how do you know? A.D. said, and with it I could see A.D. was finally starting to come out of his depression enough to realize he'd been a fool to speak about what he proposed. Even if it was just a colored bar and talk about white folk usually erred to the violent and reprehensible side anyways.

Hell, ain't nobody talk about killing a nigger. They just goes out and kills him.

A.D. looked at me as the bartender leaned in closer. I smelled cinnamon on the man's breath. He was skinnier than I first thought, and cinched his belt as he watched us and kept tucking his thumbs into his belt as if to suggest it was alright to conspire with him, that it happened nearly every day.

Well, there ain't no killing going on tonight, I finally said, and rested my hands on the bar as if that settled it. But he only kept looking at A.D. because A.D. was a sight to see and anybody with eyes could have known something much darker tormented his soul. Something even I couldn't fathom.

You sure? he said and smiled at A.D., his bright teeth luminous in the dim chamber, hovering like white-heated coals before us. Because I knows a nigger selling guns not too far from here, and he don't care who comes for 'em. He's even got songs too. 'Cause you said you wanted to sing for her now, didn't you? Didn't you?

A.D. didn't blink. He stared at the bartender, concentrating on what the man was saying, for the bartender had heard everything, and probably heard worse from others all the time. I had to chuckle to think I could a brought A.D. anywheres without his intentions laid bare for the world to see. We weren't fooling anybody, that's for sure.

A gun? A.D. said

Well, sure, the bartender said. Old Jessico's got all kinds. And he's givin' everything away, too—for the right price. That's all he talked about. Was here just the other night. He's got his religion back, too, and says the good lord makes him give up such foolishness when he can't take the aggravation no more. When he can't take the guilt.

A.D. was quiet and bowed in his thoughts, for he must have looked inside himself and seen the guilt he felt too and had held onto in his darkened state, before raising up his heavy head. Where? he finally said, and looked on the bartender as if he were a gift delivered by the fates themselves. I could see he was determined now to carry out whatever curse implored him on in his hunger to right the wrong of Ms. Clara May Staunton.

Annapolis, the bartender said. On Bladen Street. All I knows is if he don't drive up he takes the trolley as far as Washburn and then rides the train. Catches a freighter or boxcar as it rolls. Finding his way. You boys can do it. Just tell him old Montague sent you. He knows me. Get you a gun and set your business straight. Especially if he's white.

I glared at Montague, but it didn't do no good. He'd already spoken and A.D. was up and running for the trolley.

THE FIRST BOXCAR WE JUMPED WAS ROLLING TOO FAST and A.D. fell face first to the tracks and stones and came up spitting splinters and sedge. I had to laugh to see him like that, but he weren't in the mood so I boosted him up the next chance we had which wasn't long coming. We jumped to catch one heading south just as easy as could be. Inside we found crates of sacked sugar rolling down from Baltimore and slumped hard on them as we were tired and drunk from our night spent wandering. As we watched the rolling marshland and crab shacks far out on the Chesapeake, A.D. spoke again about the gun and of killing John Hill Carter, and I knew I had to tell him my own reasons for being so dead set against it.

It don't change nothing, I said. It don't. I know.

He turned and sort of sneered at me, content in his new boldness. How do you know? All you do is mop.

The night seemed to fall down and push all its mystery and vagueness upon us. The warm spring air carried the dusky scent of coal fire and fish kills and the reeds buzzed with beetles and cicadas and the sounds vibrated up louder through every part of us. So that it seemed to step right in line with the rhythm of the rails we rode until we fell into a kind of connection with everything around us. Like in the boiler room, I guess. In rising up above it, from our bodies, when we played guitar, and I felt like I didn't have to hold nothing back no more. Not from him. That we were together. The two of us. Killers and fugitives alike. One black and the other white and no color mattered in those circumstances. Even if they'd be coming for me just a little bit more than for him, I thought that was okay just as long as they got him, too. So I breathed out low and long and let him have it. All of it. Why I'd been gone from Bristol to begin with.

I killed a man, I said. So I knows why, okay? I knows all about it, son.

You? He turned to me, his mouth agape, his body almost set to rise up on his feet to shake himself free of his disbelief, the notion of it so farfetched to his mind. Where?

In Virginia, I said and nodded in the direction we were headed. With my own hands, and I looked at them as if they had their own significance, their own part to play in all this. And it ain't no good, son. I tell you. That's why I had to leave Bristol to begin with. After all the unpleasantness and hate it changes nothing, and you still feel the same and even worse when you think it's a release of everything boiling up inside you. But it ain't. It only ever ends up piling on more of the same, with the guilt and shame.

You killed a man?

Is it that hard to figure? and I stared at him with such a cold glare, he turned away and whistled to himself, and finally fell into believing me because he looked over his shoulder now and then and shook his head as he considered it. Well, there wasn't nothing I could a done to stop it, I said, as if to assure him. It was just part of the plan, I guess.

What plan?

The universe's plan. Of them great black skies up there, which had done got sick of seeing me get on as an honest and loving family man for over five years, and kept turning me over till it found a soft spot to test, to poke and prod to see if I'd cave like what it thought I might. Like what they all thought. All of them. To this day. About us.

The white man?

Sure. The white man. Who else? But this one I'm talking about was low-down even for a white man and none wanted to be called his friend and so none probably were surprised he ended up the way he did. Maybe that's why they didn't chase after me as much as I thought they would. They already knew everything had been taken from me, and that I couldn't come back for it.

I took a deep breath and A.D. waited for me to continue. It'd been many a year since I'd spoken the man's name, and I didn't relish having the taste of it on my tongue.

His name was Hackett, and he was an ornery humpbacked man who worked overseer for the farm I sharecropped with my little wife Annie and our daughter Lucy—who was nothing more than a blackberry of a thing Annie wrapped in a shawl each morning and slung over her shoulder as we worked our parcel. O it was ours, for sure, for five good years, but then Hackett had a notion for the good work we done and wanted more than his share entitled. We grew corn and sorghum for silage, but we had considerable yields. And he desired them. He also developed a taste for nigger as they say, the white men. For he come around most sharecropper shacks after conspiring to have the men called away for whatever inventory or review he could fabricate. With all the other smiling and doddering fools he paid for the convenience, laughing away the whole lot of them like it was the funniest damn thing they'd ever done their whole misbegotten lives, assisting in the outright cruelty of that man.

Now I was hot, warmed up by the telling of my tale, and shook the jacket from my shoulders as I thought on those lost years. I turned to A.D., who now kept watch on the night and maybe imagined a small piece of my life for once, and saw me in a different way.

Annie was beautiful, I said. My wife. She was of free stock but had moved south even though her own kind told her not to. But she had a head of ideas and her own notion of renewal and truth, and so it was I met her in Bristol on a hot summer's day, at the open market. Her with her brown wicker basket full of potatoes and pigs feet wrapped in butchers' paper; me standing stock-still and dumbfounded to see such a beauty as that with her white kerchief about her head and her face so brown and smooth. I couldn't of guessed where she was headed, even though I just started following her anyways until I recognized the church that had been mine and my peoples since before emancipation. We were wed the next summer. After considerable courting, for sure, but I don't want to go into all that, as it's still mine, those memories, all of them.

A.D. had been quiet till then and immobile, but he moved as I said this last part, which I hadn't felt coming up in me until I spoke. I hadn't realized I still needed something for myself, even though I'd never told anyone this before. But A.D. seemed to understand and shifted toward me slightly as a gust of air billowed in. Traces of sugar swirled up then in little white puffs coating everything anew, till the sweetness gleamed on our teeth and skin, and it was all delicious again for a moment—the world—and we sat together as the land rolled by, dangling our legs. Did he touch her? A.D. finally said, as outside a steel trestle towered up and the moonlight shined down, sending a woven pattern that thatched us like a weave until we passed over and there were just fields again, and water far out and endless.

He did. I'd been called away for some reprimand but knew this was his pattern by then, speaking as I had to the other sharecroppers who'd all sworn vengeance on the humpbacked man. A form we'd sometimes see silhouetted at night, creeping through the fields, when we thought him the incarnation of the devil himself. Sneaking between the lives of man. Taking what was not his to take. Touching what was not his to touch.

Just like old John Hill Carter, A.D. said and perked up considerable to hear the parallel I'd drawn between the two.

Sure, just like your John Hill Carter, I echoed. For this Hackett stood much as the one that torments you, with a bluster and fulsomeness that all was his, ever last possession. When I realized what he'd done to conspire against me, and then seen them smiling faces of the men who knew, I hurried out of the barn as fast as I could and come up on that old humpback as he had Annie down on the kitchen floor. Her dress pulled up over her waist. With him trying to force his way inside her with his rank little pizzle athrob and gorged as it was, that it was easy to stomp down on it after I turned him over. Annie was fierce and clawed him considerable and didn't cry out none. But instead took the occasion to stuff her kitchen rag in his mouth so that the others weren't alerted to the pain I laid in on him then. And I swear, A.D., I swear to this day, I was other than myself in that moment. I don't know from where that man came, nor where he went, but it was as a fog descending upon me. I seen him only in his littleness, as if looking upon an animal left discarded in the chaff. He peered up at me out of his red narrow eyes and pleaded forgiveness from his suffocated mouth. But I didn't hear him and neither did Annie as she herself stepped down on his eye with her heel and blinded it as the blood spurted over his cheeks and I knew then it was over for him and reached down with my hands to squeeze the life from him entire.

A.D. looked at me and breathed. He didn't speak a full minute. She did that for you?

She did. And I had to protect her for it too, and didn't say a word as I hauled his body on a mule to Holston Mountain not too far off where I found a tree and hung him from it. From the very same one I'd seen the white devils hang so many of my kind all those years hence, and where I knew they'd find it, a hunter or some such picking through the berries. I didn't have time to think on what I should a done, in hiding him proper. But I was fulsome then myself, too, I guess, fulsome and proud. Proud to have righted some wrong in the world, proud to have thwarted some evil, for I thought it a power in myself then to have done it. When really, it weren't no power at all. It only ever made me have to run from then on and to shrink from my own life and to fail, son. For surely, I failed my Annie. I had to leave her that same night, and Lucy just a blackberry flower at that. Never to know my smell nor sound nor touch of hand no more. Never to know my touch. My Lucy. My girl.

The train had stopped. The brakes had sung out. We could hear water lapping away as of an echo of something—our arrival or incidence—and the strung lines of the boats and sails creaked far off in the wind carrying sounds and voices, and also the last light of the lanterns still blazed as it was just past midnight on a Saturday and the quiet of the world seemed ours alone. As if shaking A.D. from his stupor, from the dumbstruck sense that had since scrawled its sign across his face, a sense of relief finally arrived. For we'd found our way to Bladen Street easy enough, and A.D. had to breathe then real soft and calm to find himself standing before Jessico's door.

VI

A siren blaring ~ Disciples and prophets for the truth
~ Glass pipettes and such ~ Old Jessico Ayles ~ The
unmasking of the spirit ~ In among the moneychangers
~ Mr. Mavis Mathey and his obvious bootlegging ~
You My Calvary ~ The boats far off in their offing

WE KNEW IT WAS JESSICO'S DOOR because of the continuous singing
we heard that was muffled and low. But the closer we leaned, the clearer we
heard him, like a siren blaring out his gospel for all to hear from his high up
window. A.D. rapped lightly on the door, and I thought I'd have to ask him
to rap harder or try myself, but lo, old Jessico was in the doorway in a moment with a smile on his deep black face as wide and clear as a looking glass,
and there was nothing we knew to say to begin with or entreat him for our
appearance. We just stared, for there were very few teeth on display in that
face and his great pink tongue lolled about as he spoke with a faint slur for us
to enter. To come in. To speak. Why didn't we speak? Didn't we know he was
almost with the lord already? That it was his time?

Time? A.D. finally managed.

Why, yessir, Jessico said. It ain't but time that brings you here neither, I
suppose. Because only He brings me those who know it's time enough for me
to go.

To bring you who?

Why, disciples, of course, Jessico said and shook his broad, teetering head.
He was almost as tall as A.D. and to look on him was to look at A.D.'s shadow
for sure, and I had to blink to send the notion away before accepting it entire.
What else is there, man, Jessico said, but disciples? And his great deep voice
rattled against the smudged up windows, before echoing into the basement.

Disciples through and through, he said, thundering aloud again. Disciples stretched out across the whole Earth.

A.D. shook his head then and looked down shuffling his boots before looking back at him. You mean disciples like as in prophets? he finally said.

Well, sure, Jessico said, but in the true way. Prophets for the truth, that is, and he stood near his sink looking on A.D. and smiled. Then as if to prove something to the boy, or to prove his own righteousness, Jessico picked up a full whiskey bottle, cracked it on the sink, and poured it all out on the floor. Pouring its brown liquid out smiling all the while as if it was something he'd been planning on doing since before we arrived, since before maybe even kingdom come was ordained and ordered in its mysteriousness. Just to do it, I guess. To change himself.

A.D. looked on Jessico and then me as if he'd never seen such a thing his whole life. I looked back blank-faced and still because I knew this was hardly the beginning for a man in a state such as Jessico, and Jessico had to laugh to see us so quelled.

Shoot, he said, I've been pouring them out for days, boys. For days. He pointed to a pile on a pallet in a corner with innumerable bottles of all shapes and sizes, and which A.D. had to shake his head on and whistle to calculate all the drunkenness he could a got into with all that. I ain't sellin' it no more and I ain't makin' it neither. So sayeth the lord.

We could smell the beech wood smoke from the basement. The fire was dying but the scent remained and as Jessico saw us look he took us down to see the complexity of it all, with the pot and wash stills and cisterns and glass beakers and charred white oak casks. There were wooden mixing spoons and glass pipettes and mortars and pestles, with the peeled potatoes and corn and molasses and other fermenting crops that must have been slopped in there for months but which he stepped over now and shoveled into a corner. All the brown and clear bottles stood with labels too, with brand names I recognized, while others appeared beneath a canvas blanket that I hadn't ever heard of before as he spread it all out bare in its unveiling. Some even had Old Jessico Ayles scrawled across the top, as I seen now a small printing press and pots of ink and a copper plate with moveable type that he must of surely poured over with his considerable talents counterfeiting ever last label he saw fit to emulate. The basement went on considerable and sacks of barley and yeast heaved up and the sweet smell of mash in the tuns and grist competed with the dying smoke and had A.D. and I, and most assuredly old Jessico himself, lightheaded and otherworldly as if galloping upon the fumes. (And I submit as well that old Jessico must have been long gone before this time, working and distilling and mixing his wares. So that I could see why he thought his time was up, as he had no earthly idea what time it was anymore, not with his own wits since drifted as a wind between the aroma and unmasking of the spirit.)

You ain't making what no more? A.D. said and smiled as he dipped his fingers into a bucket of malted barley. As he brought them up, he let the fine grains drift down so that another sweetened wave wafted up. Jessico had to grin to know his talents were so esteemed.

I ain't making myself false, he said. This—and he pointed at the whole get-up, at the casks and stills and crops and bottles, waving even to the upstairs that was outlandish and heaped with hordes of fabrics and materials that he'd procured with his ill-gotten gains—this, he said, is all false. All of it. It's a delusion and an unbecoming, and the lord will come in upon the moneychangers again and again as He has throughout time to show them what is what. Because I'm the moneychangers now, I say. And ye are the moneychangers, too, he said. And even that one there is the moneychangers too, he said, pointing his long finger at me. And any man who has not come into the lord in his own weakness and time after sloughing off his delusion is a moneychanger for sure. A moneychanger just sifting through time again and again for them to use. For them to reap and abuse. For them to bend civilization between the dark and alighted souls in the sweetness of the air. To take and spend everyone as they see fit.

He was quiet then, and so were we. It had taken considerable effort to enumerate his charge and yet I felt another round of it in him and almost out of my own lament for hearing him continue in this nonsensical way, I came to rest my hand on the polished stock of a long barrel rifle. It was beautiful and clean and leaned against the basement wall, and in touching it, I hoped it might refocus A.D. in his desires of enacting his vengeance on that John Hill Carter. Now I didn't want to redirect him in this pursuit, I assure you. I was just worried that A.D., as pitiful and impressionable as he was, and with such sorrowful words emanating from that strange and forceful Jessico—with his wild green eyes and slick lurid wealth—that his fever might spread if left unchecked to my youthful charge. That it might flourish.

So you know Montague? A.D. said as he'd seen my hand lay casual and obvious on the smooth birch stock, stroking it back and forth as I could, before touching the walnut handgrip. A.D. stepped over and before Jessico had time to respond, he touched it too. Is this here then going away too? A.D. said and nodded to the rifle, before raising the stock to his eye and blinking as he attempted to sight in on some imaginary John Hill Carter striding across the world. A John Hill tall and innumerable and who shook his great silver lighter at him and blinked his cold tobacco eyes for all the world to see what he'd done. Though I suppose A.D. in his rage couldn't quite shake clear of this image for he aimed all weak and wobbly against the wall, and I wondered if he'd ever in his life held a gun or fired a single bullet?

Of course, Jessico said, as he watched us look over all his earthy materials, at everything that had brought him to such heights. It goes too. It all does. Ever last thing has got to go back out into damnation before being consumed by the all and all. Truly, he said and then hummed something cheerful and shook his head smiling as if we strolled about a summer's day, the three of us, wading knee high through the daisies. I'm giving it all away and have already handed some considerable tracts to Mr. Mavis Mathey, my good friend and confidante gone to Roanoke just this morning. Jessico smiled and tilted his head as if listening to some otherworldly choir or emanation from afar, something only he could hear. For his voice gave up a sudden and most dolorous call, the lyrics of which I'd not occasion to follow nor remember for the sweetened singing of it was such that I had to lean against the wall to compose myself.

A.D. was even more taken aback by the harmonious sound emanating from the man. Jessico hadn't as much turned and ascended the steps to his living room, that A.D. wasn't already hard on his heels. What was it you just sang? A.D. blurted out. We were all three gathered again upstairs and I started to eye the material abundance upon display.

I hadn't noticed it before as Jessico's demeanor and dramatic posturing had captured my attention. But now that his obvious bootlegging had been set aside, there was nothing to mistake for the stunning opulence surrounding us. There was a mahogany Queen Ann table near the door, and a few Wilton rugs stretched below everything. One with the design of some long lost kingdom or insignia upon it, the other with a most somber and oriental elaboration, as of a mountain pagoda etched in stitches. Several wrought iron lamps wavered their gloomy luminescence above everything and outlined a beautiful powder green sofa that rested against the back wall near the staircase. It was the perch Jessico himself lounged on as the smell of the poured liquor sopped and squished about the floor.

What did I say? Jessico said and smiled beatifically before running his gnarled fingers across the silk cushion he rearranged at his hip. You mean concerning my articles of document? Because I've given Mavis everything: my last will and testament, my certificates and deeds of material, everything about the distillation of the spirit and my other apothecary pursuits. My entire song catalog and journal, alphabetized, of course, with all the recipes of my most favored concoctions written out—my whole legacy—as it were. A sinful list I did not want to see no more and that Mavis took and promised not to publish in part nor in its entirety until twenty-four years hence my demise.

Your demise? I said and tilted my head. What the hell are you talking about? But A.D. waved away my impatience. He had crept across the room toward Jessico and I could tell by the red flush rising along his neck that his mind had succumbed to a brighter burning fever. His skin glistened with a blood color and glowed so that I stayed back and kept quiet in the shadows as he spoke.

That song. A.D. said. What was the song you just sang? Just now. In the basement. Stepping closer, he hovered above Jessico, who looked up at him confused. I'd not seen such an intense concentration on the boy's face since he'd perched on his cot in the boiler room working on his song for Ms. Clara May, and I was as stunned as Jessico to see the turn in the boy's demeanor, in his temper. I had not seen his hands clench into fists even when old John Hill Carter had knelt below him in Ms. Clara May's room and lit the rug beneath his boots. But as he stood there as resolute as a statue, and swung his knotted fists at his side, I didn't know what he meant to do, but leaned in just the same to watch. Even as old Jessico, in his hallucinatory state, seemed to pause and appraise the boy before sliding out from his comfortable perch.

Why? he finally said.

Because I need it, A.D. said. I need it as sure as the sun, and he shook his fists and swayed there as Jessico made his way across the room, all the while watching the boy.

Jessico was at the sink in a moment and pulled a full whiskey bottle from a crate as if to redirect his mind from the force of A.D.'s internal fire. He appraised the broad-labeled bottle, raised it to a lantern, and stared for a long moment at the brown liquor. It was a motion I imagined he must have often delighted in before his turn again to religion, admiring his own craftsmanship and yearning for the spirit. But now I could see him reconsider this decision beneath the considerable strain of A.D.'s gaze. He pulled the cork out with a soft plop and sniffed the vaporous aroma as he tilted the bottle to his nose and looked at A.D. with vacant eyes. A euphoria graced Jessico's face then, as if he'd forgotten there were any other human beings left in the world to watch his behavior, for he seemed taken aback by the muscle memory of uncorking, of tipping up and imbibing. Yet he paused amidst his single pursuit—paused before drinking from his past wares and numerous faults.

Boy, why you vex me like this? he said, and his hands shook as the liquor trembled at his lips. Who sent you?

I don't vex you at all, A.D. said. And no one sent me. A.D. hadn't moved. Hadn't blinked an eye as Jessico seemed to shrink now in the lamplight, sweating something profuse as the beads drew glistening lines like a spider's web along his cheeks before dripping to the floor.

You the devil then who's gonna bring me back to drinking? After all this time? You the devil who's gonna bring me back to all that foolishness I put down weeks and weeks ago?

I ain't no such kind, A.D. said. Not a one. I hadn't noticed before, but A.D. had carried up the rifle from the basement, and as he picked up the long barrel and clacked the butt end against the floor, Jessico gave out a slight shiver. He then touched the bottle to his lips and hesitated before singing out sharp and clear with a sad whispering of words. Tilting his head, A.D. listened, but straightened back up when Jessico had finished, before shaking his head amidst the wondrous silence. That ain't it, A.D. said.

I knowed, I knowed it, Jessico said, as soon as I sung it, and then he took a long drink before closing his eyes. After gulping low and lean, he sighed and sung out again, keeping his eyes closed all the while, swaying as he got into it soulfully. I had to sit on the staircase because I was so taken by the sweet misery of his tale, of the voice and wandering melody, of the whole tragedy of it, that I hoped its harmony might never end.

Well, that ain't it neither, A.D. said.

Jessico stopped and opened his eyes for his tears were now mixed with sweat. He looked at A.D. and wiped his mouth and smiled his diminished smile as he shook all over to feel it, the spirit coursing through him, coursing wild and free and entire.

Again, A.D. said and set down to watch, leaning his head against the couch. As he did, old Jessico sung out with a different tune, something about a graveyard or horse thief, and the song was so pretty and so choice, even A.D. seemed to waver now exhausted by the full day of emotion and wandering.

Though as Jessico finished up and looked at A.D. he knew it weren't it neither, and surely felt the same tiredness in him, too, in trying to rack his brain for the song he'd sung in the basement, the same one that had A.D. so hot and forged on finding it. Of maybe even claiming it as his own, for he still wished to give Ms. Clara May Staunton a song. Even though he knew as well as I that she was gone and that she'd never hear what he'd found for her.

Again, A.D. said.

I knowed it. I knowed it as soon as I seen you. I knowed it was my own final test and deliverance come back to me for sure, Jessico moaned. My Calvary. You my Calvary, son! You been sent here to do this to me. And at the very end at that, at my very end. And he started again, wavering a bit and halting, but as his deep rich baritone rose and crackled louder on the higher notes, he had to drink to soothe his burning throat, pouring through the whiskey as it slobbered down his chin and neck and chest as he sang again along another divergent line. Along another set of tales and fractured tunes, and it happened this way for an hour or more. And either the fear in Jessico's soul, or the liquor washing through his skin kept him from remembering that particular song A.D. so desired, and as I left, creeping up the stairs, they were still occupied upon that manic pursuit.

I HADN'T SLEPT ALL DAY AND THE TRIALS AND TRAVELS of the night poured through me as I slumped onto Jessico's brass bed, swallowed up amongst his silk and satin finery. Closing my eyes was a gift I hadn't expected, and I don't think I heard another peep from them nor the world the whole night. My sleep was so dark and my mind so heavy that even in the morning when the sunlight swept across the lintel and splashed upon my skin, I didn't want to acknowledge where I was and what I'd done. O but as soon as I felt the soft rich sheets and puffed up pillows, I knew it had not been a dream at all. None of it. I was here. I'd had to run from my life again as I'd done in Bristol, and I was sorry for it all over again. I shook my head and rubbed my eyes and wondered where A.D. and Jessico had ended in their pursuit of that song, the one A.D. so desired. Yet as I sat up and turned to the window, and heard the first faint birds singing, and the call of the hands on the boats far off in their offing, with the strung lines and sails fluttering in the first sharp breeze—and then as all of Annapolis come muttering back to life, to a new life and day upon the cold, slick bay—I almost didn't want to know where they'd ended up for fear of their conclusion.

VII

A hung man ~ His bare black feet ~ Your dark universe ~ An advertisement for a show ~ Runnymede's domain ~ A raid ~ An escape ~ Keys ~ Blue boys in the street ~ Jessico's coupe ~ On to Roanoke and the rising sun ~ He watches me drive

JESSICO HUNG FROM A RAFTER BY A ROPE that swayed as A.D. touched his bare black feet. I stood on the steps disbelieving my eyes and the quiet, almost curious tone A.D. had struck in looking on the man. There seemed not a touch of sadness in him nor anger and when he turned to me, his face blank and long from the night of searching for that song in Jessico's mind, he wiped his mouth and seemed struck by something else entire than the vision of the man hanged above him. Something that I could not grasp, nor likewise incline, nor hope to ever think or know.

Do you see it? he said.

How can I not? I said and took another slow step into the room. Did he do this?

Well, it sure weren't me, he said, and his face went dark and ominous as he watched me come closer, stepping softly on the rug before touching my hand to a chair. I swear it, he said and mumbled something low and hoarse to himself and turned again to Jessico's legs, holding them steady before sending them out again swaying with a gentle push into the room. I'd swear on whatever you want—a Bible, your dark universe, his whiskey, he said—and he watched the man turn a soft circle in the air. I was asleep and heard the dripping of it and just knew, he said. He pointed to Jessico's right foot where a yellow stain stretched a dried line before dripping to the floor. I heard it and then smelled it. He pointed to the man's pants and I knew what he meant in often hearing a hanged man evacuates his body in both regards, so that if there were urine then there was sure to be the other mess, too.

Did he tell you?

Tell me what? A.D. was still looking up and as I come beside him, I wanted to touch his shoulder to see if he was as hard and cold as I thought he was in looking upon such a thing and not feeling anything at all. But I held back. For I knowed now what he meant in first asking me if I'd seen it because he wasn't talking about old Jessico. Not in the least.

Well, I'll be, I said, because behind Jessico's swinging legs, as they moved back and forth before me, moving from shadow to lightness, a poster came into focus. It was pasted to the wall and was the thing A.D. couldn't stop staring at. Couldn't stop figuring for the life of him. It was of Runnymede and the Piedmont Pipers. An advertisement for a show just commenced in Annapolis in a pavilion of distinguished repute nigh upon the water. Then another line detailed a performance to be held the past night in the old state house.

In the goddamned state house, A.D. said as if following my mind entire, for the governor. He clicked his teeth and pushed Jessico's feet out a ways so we could step closer and see the announcement in its entire. My Runnymede, A.D. whispered as his finger swept along the raised letters of that sinewy-sounding name: Runnymede McCall. Singer extraordinaire. I didn't see it until I stepped closer to gauge Jessico and then couldn't see nothing else, he said. He shook his head and as I reached to grab the poster he made a deep noise in his chest as if to state it should not be touched nor moved in the slightest, this poster, as it was now an artifact in Runnymede's domain, as I believed he later called it. A domain of his own that we should not encroach upon. O he still thought considerable of that man and saw him as the poster depicted, as if raised from a beam of light. Smiling, singing unto the masses, cavorting as a prince for all to see, and must have stood long and serene envisioning himself in Runnymede's place, leader of his own such pipers. Commensurate to the king. Revealed for what he knew he was—a star, a noble, an artiste—but in seeing me again on the stairs, he must have remembered he was no such thing. We were no kings or pipers. We were scoundrels. Runaways at best, and I could see where his eyes had been rubbed red from crying to know what had befallen him since he'd first spied old Runnymede onstage. I could even hear the hurt in his voice as he straightened himself up and spoke to me, all low and desperate like, but with a feeling I hadn't heard. What have I done to get myself here? he said, as I pushed him away from fixating on Runnymede's smiling face. What have I done?

You've done what you've had to, I said. You've learned.

Learned what? To run? To hide? Truly—what have I learned? And he turned with such a collapsed face I had no idea what to tell him nor how to assuage his concern. And yet, as sure as we were standing there, upon the door behind us, a great lurking shadow rose into shape. Then a strange shuffling of feet murmured as of a rushing tide not six inches from where we stood. While in the next instant, a thunderous rattling shook the wall and window and all my thoughts fell to dust.

Jessico? A voice bellowed from the street. Jessico Ayles? I know you're in there! I know you're in there this instant!

Well, it didn't take long to realize old Jessico hadn't just hung himself to be with the good lord. Looking out the front door's little brass window, I seen not a few blue boys gathering in the street with their guns and batons raised as if planning to do what they could to bust in on Jessico's distilleries. They probably meant to roust him out of the ranks of the living too, if they could have managed (though I suspected they'd be disappointed in that regard). Course I about froze to see the mean-set faces on display and to realize in just a second they'd find two fugitives to boot to bring back to Baltimore to hang for whatever we were accused of doing, and my mind felt constricted to think on it. It was as if the whole world had narrowed, and yet, when I looked on A.D., I seen his cool calm face and the way he grabbed the rifle from the wall, raising it from where he'd leaned it the night before, and I wondered if he meant to shoot our way out. But then he made the slightest motion with his arm and I heard a jingling in his fingers and knew it was something else entire that had come over him, a plan for our escape.

Keys, A.D. said and he raised his hand to show me the brass set before turning down the back hallway. I got the keys to Jessico's coupe.

WELL, I'D THOUGHT HE'D START FOR BALTIMORE straight away, to get at that old John Hill Carter with the gun. But after we climbed out the back and hurried a few blocks to where Jessico must have assured A.D. his coup was parked, I understood more perfectly what he'd figured.

The song, I said as I eyed him and he watched behind as I headed out through a maze of muddy streets.

That's right, he said, the song, and he relaxed a bit and stopped watching now that he thought it was clear enough to breathe again. Since he figured the police hadn't thought we'd be there to begin with and wouldn't of missed us anyways with us headed south instead of north. To Roanoke, he said, where Mavis has it. At least, that's what Jessico professed and was insistent.

I watched him then as I had occasion to for we were the only car in sight and the road was still empty that early. What? I finally said. What was he insistent about?

About everything. Every last thing, and then he paused to touch the door, smoothing his hand along the leather insides before touching the seat again.

What things?

The truth, he said, mostly, and he looked at me and then out on the road, searching for something he thought would appear laid before us. The answer to whatever Jessico had meant for him, perhaps. Or something else that I do not know. Something strange and furtive that I'd never thought of or hoped to find. Jessico wanted to tell me the truth, A.D. said, after I'd put the car in full and plunged on the accelerator. At least, as he saw it, he continued, leaning to one side, pushed by the speed. To have someone listen to him for once was all he wanted. And yet after all that singing and carrying on he still couldn't find it no more, what I wanted. He couldn't reach in to get it no more. That song.

But he tried?

O he tried, A.D. said and shook his head thinking, before tapping his hand on the rifle's long black barrel still clutched in his hands. I suppose I didn't help much being so enchanted by it, or fixated, as it were. So I told him, Relax, and set the gun against the wall. But I don't think that helped. The drink was in him by then, after being so long without, and the last thing he remembered was he gave it in a bundle to old Mavis, with all his other writings. That's why he gave me this by way of appeasement, and he nodded to the keys and car and rifle. Which he set down on the floor all casual and simple like, and I wondered again if he'd ever in his life carried one. He had the barrel pointed up at me, so I had to reach over and face it toward the passenger side door instead.

Appeasement, I muttered, and looked at him and thought on it. O I knew he was still a kid. Sure. He was just as green as could be, even though he'd lost all that he'd lost, read all that he'd read, and thought all that he'd thought, and I didn't even need to ask why. Why this traveling? Why such a fuss over one song? I already knew what he meant to do with it once he found it. Why it meant so much to hear it and then to give it away in the next second to the dead and gone Ms. Clara May Staunton, since he'd never had the chance to give her anything before, anything but his heart and soul. He needed that connection, with all the emotion he still had left for her. He needed to give her the song. And yet, as we raced on, and drove down into the blazing sun, I wondered if he did find that song, if that would be the end of it for him? Or if it would only open up something else inside him, something I couldn't imagine. Like another passion or need that I hadn't yet considered, so I just set it aside awhile and drove.

O I drove and drove, because he had no clue as to how or what driving even was. He'd never done it and was as quiet and focused as I'd ever seen him. Watching as I fooled with the clutch when I had to shift, or my hands, as I turned the wheel when a tree trunk sprung up in the way, or when an apple cart was turned over in the road. Or my feet, when I pushed the pedals and accelerated or braked. It was something to truly behold. I'd never seen his mind so hard at work, configuring the operation of another man's actions as he was with mine and that automobile. All, of course, except for the guitar, when he watched me play, when I'd first learned him how at the Peabody. And as I thought on it, I got a feeling then very deeply in my bones to strum those strings. To play a chord or two, to pass my fingers though a slow progression and be back in my element, in the music, to get this road back into Virginia behind us. Because I knew that it not only went into the heart of A.D.'s current needs and aspirations and fears, but that it also drove straight through my own store of sorrow and neglecting and dreaming. That it led us on into every last thing I'd once hoped to find and to finally flee. That it led straight into the heart of the blues and covered us up in it, drowned us in it. But still we kept driving. Still we kept moving faster and faster, trying to swallow it all up.

VIII

Richmond and its heaventree of stars ~ Tobacco
barns and maypoles ~ Popes Creek and a man of
my color ~ Old John Hill's ancestral home ~ I give
him his chance ~ Another suspicion entire ~ The
flames ~ The moths ~ The world's fevered passing

NOW? HE TAPPED HIS FOOT AND WATCHED ME. Now can I try?

No, I said and pushed on into the darkness, driving down on Richmond,
which was lit up and expansive. Like a heaventree of stars. It was something I
hadn't expected. As if the town, which was big enough as it was, had a carnival
or grand revival or something going on at this late hour to make it even bigger
and grander in its illumination, so that I wasn't sure what to focus on. With
the lights of it reflected up into the air, and the wind lifting voices and music
as harmonious and dreamy as you could imagine, it seemed we drove on a
world turned upside down and reflected in the ether. It was so otherworldly and
strange that even A.D. had to pause in his excitement to watch the wonder of
it, leaning his head out all the while looking up.

Old John Hill Carter might be here, A.D. said as his mouth gaped to see it
all with the tobacco barns and maypoles and street signs spread out as we come
around and started eastward away from it. He tapped his foot again for he'd
wanted to try driving. But I'd refused for fear for our general safety and didn't
let up till Richmond was thirty miles behind and we were on the outskirts of
Gum Spring past midnight.

It was a small bit of a town and not so far from Annapolis as a map was
concerned, but we'd lost considerable time crossing the Chesapeake near Popes
Creek where there was once a horse ferry but that now took cars across for a
dollar. I knew it was there because I'd passed over it seven years before and

was amazed I'd recollected it at all in the diverse paths and circuits I'd taken in getting out of Bristol to begin with. It was a mystery that was stored up inside me, I suppose, in each thought and doubt, and I swore even as we done it, as I moved through the same motions, but in reverse this time. As if retracing those thoughts and memories now but backwards was all we could do, and I had to shiver to think on it the farther we went.

I had taken us in a not altogether haphazard way, steering clear of the straight route east through the City of Washington where I thought they might be laying for us. Going south wouldn't of hurt none as they probably thought our inclination was to head north anyways, where it was a bit easier for a man my color. This path didn't entirely satisfy me, obviously, but it didn't entirely un-satisfy me neither. Still, it did trouble me, I assure you, and I guess A.D. might have seen this a little (if he saw anything of the kind, the fellow, who was still so dead set on killing old John Hill Carter, that I wondered if anything distracted him in the least), for it strained him to think on any other agitation. Of course, he still remembered my stories on Bristol, even though he said it couldn't of been helped coming this way. Not since Roanoke was where we had to go to get Jessico's song, and in this comment alone he seemed to consider my needs just a bit, and I thanked him quietly, nodding my head.

But even for all this, I couldn't abide his idea for driving up on old John Hill's ancestral home and shooting away at it. He'd been enamored with this design ever since crossing the Chesapeake. Then with us creeping down all the while on it, I could just smell the blood lust rising in him the more he thought on it, and his eyes sort of glazed over the closer we come as the fog I'd seen in him with Jessico was raised up again. Of course, it was mad, the idea, and I'd railed against it from the start and only determined to let him drive once we was far enough away and low enough on gas he couldn't get anywheres anyways, forfeiting whatever plan he still had devised in him. So here we were. Outside Gum Spring, and I slid over finally to give him his chance.

Easy now, I said, as I kept my hand on the wheel while he steered sort of wobbly and all over the road for it was mainly just pocked dirt anyways and the wheels skidded ever which way as he was so undetermined in the path he meant to follow. Soon enough we were heartened to see the lights blazing from an Esso gas station still open at that late hour. (Now forgive me if I repose here a moment and mention it is awful difficult recalling what to tell straight and honest, especially with it being my Virginia we was driving into the heart of. I don't want to overplay too much my reluctance in traveling this way in the least, nor undersell it neither, even if it pains me to paint a picture of the vagaries of my home state. But I know it must be done, and it's not in the least a surprise to anyone now, surely. For I still loved her, my Virginia, and still called her home and knew all about her positives and negatives, and at first, we thought seeing that gas station so open and bright was about as positive as could be. But when we coasted up to the pump and stopped there with a sad little squeak of the brakes, not a soul was to be had, and I got another suspicion entire in my mind. And that's the sad truth of it.)

As A.D. leaned out and listened to the engine tick, we noticed the road going off into blackness as the shadows from some vast brightness threw down its wavering shape from some great height beyond us, something swirling and free behind the stark white-washed walls of the station. It was just a shack really, raised up on red bricks as most stations were then, with one pump out front on one side and a bucket and metal spigot rusted over on the other. But as I stepped out of the car to implore the station master or serving boy or whoever might appear at that late hour, something come to me a sudden. It was as a wind. Or a great ripping strain. Something hovering high above the trees, and it shook me tolerable to hear it and to know I had to creep closer to see it. Just to know.

There was a clearing out back. A few picnic tables were scattered in the tall grass and just before the woods started in earnest sloping into the hills, there it was, as stark and undisguised as you could believe. It towered over everything, some thirty feet high, blazing as tall and clear as the polestar—the biggest and brightest burning cross I'd ever seen. Standing stock still and alone as if a sentry to the unrecovered night. The line of trees flared up, singed and smoking, as the flames rose and swirled and it looked as if all the spirits of the world were being summoned up together and consumed by it. A thousand million white thumb-prints fluttered by in the air. They even brushed against my cheek the closer I crept, and were taken up into the howling swirl, into that white hot vortex of heat. As I seen them levitate and rise up before me, alighting and twisting and curling, I couldn't help but take another step closer and then another to hear the snapping, sizzling, fizz of all them gathered in by the flames, as of the dead to their unimagined pyre.

Moths.

So many moths I'd never seen and they were being snatched up by the millions as the blaze sucked the very marrow from the mountains. A.D. stood beside me and touched his head and was sweating and I didn't see another person for my eyes began to blur and blink and yet I felt the eyes of the hills upon me surely. It was as if they'd been on me my whole life, marking and tracking my kind as if we were nothing more than cattle or hogs. And as I gathered up my wits again, and hurried to the car, we filled her up as fast as we could and left a shiny new quarter on the pump as if to spell our efforts—as an appeasement perhaps, or settlement that I could not know—and I let him drive all the rest of that night as I lay in the back and just watched it all go by. O I watched it and felt it and interred it for what it was, and what a night it was to watch! To see how it all lurched past. Here is how it went:

In great chunks it rose up, the road. There would be nothing for stretches. Just landscape or an occasional barn sketched in silhouette, etched with its dark geometry of sides. Or a long skeletal fence would stretch off for miles. Cattle would then low way out in their lament as raw and mean as the echoing Earth. Then a mangy pack of dogs would slink away from the sound of the engine and all the gleaming green eyes would glint in the sweeping yellow lights as I alone slumped back in my seat and seemed to keep vigil on the world's fevered passing, for I thought about all those moths rising up again and again. All the little moths spinning into the night, swirling into their infinite demise as A.D. spoke to me at first about the wheel and the gears and the route, but there were no words for me to reply with. Then he spoke to me not at all, as he'd finally acquired the rhythm of the road and the world raced by. Pale muddy sheets drifted in the open windows as he slowed on the main streets of Charlottesville and Lynchburg and Bedford before turning down. Maneuvering through the starkness of souls and towns and sleeping history to slow from the queasy blur of forty miles per to a creeping ten or even five as the eyes of vagrants and drunkards watched slack-jawed and astonished as a white one drove a black one along the ridge in the predawn light.

IX

Norfolk and Western Railway ~ This grand elusive thing ~
Dangling in his stupor ~ The fog descends ~ So far
down in Dixie already ~ A.D. has no idea of the
situation ~ The flames of Hades ~ I was the Mabry
he mentioned ~ My little Lucy girl ~ Mine

MAVIS GAVE US THE SONG STRAIGHT AWAY. It was easy. We found
him after we stopped near an open market with the vendors just setting out their
wares and all A.D. had to do was inquire to some of the folks gathering there
if they'd seen Mavis or knew his kind. Sure enough they looked at one another
and then dropped their heads in the naming of it before looking back up at him
and directing him to the closest and most frequented colored saloon in town.
We weren't but three blocks from it. Tucked away as it was on the right side of
Patterson Ave. between the Roanoke River and the Norfolk and Western Railway.

It weren't nothing to me, he said, as we found him half-lit and still drinking
even with the sunlight already cresting the Blue Ridge and the bartender
himself half asleep but still pouring shots, still pouring ale to whoever wanted
it or inquired. Old Mavis was broad in the belly and smiled all the while,
with his eyes so swallowed up in that rich black face of his I can't rightly say
if he did or didn't have eyes. But I sure never seen them. Almost at once he
up and says old Jessico was half-crazed and mad and for all those rantings and
ravings he'd made about his last will and testament and other such documents
he didn't have but one notebook of nonsense to give Mavis anyways. And a
few scrawled on napkins with words and little pencil doodles of hens and
chickens on them. So that when he laid it all out in front of A.D. all he had
to do was buy Mavis another shot to take away the pages he found with the
words Jessico had sung and that A.D. was in such a fever to get.

O it was a beautiful song, surely. A tale of the most unrequited love A.D. had ever read and so sweated over to compose but couldn't. As it was probably his first ever love to begin with, so he didn't have the words yet in him to know what it was nor what it meant. But there it all was for him in its entirety and A.D. held the pages to his breast and stood silent near the bar and mumbled something as he scanned all of it again. He had to wipe his eyes as he recited the lines and then hummed the tune he remembered Jessico had strung to it with his deep rich baritone.

I was so happy for him to finally see it, and to end this mad search for this grand elusive thing—which was nothing more than a paltry little scrap of paper anyways with the inklings of that drunken lunatic on it—though I knew it was probably just the beginning of what it could mean for A.D., and for us, I guess you could say. For I'd never seen such a startling change in a man to hold a thing so meek—and so quick!

He practically set on the floor as I kept it up with Mavis to pump him for any information now that he'd been in Roanoke a spell and knew most the folks and had come and gone as much as half-a-dozen times the last few weeks traveling and delivering his wares as he called them. Though I knew rightly well what it was he delivered—Jessico's crates of bootleg whiskey. I also sought to leach out any news he might have heard from Annapolis before he left. Anything about the Peabody in Baltimore and the fire there recently consumed. O I needed to get my bearings. I was already in the land of my birth, a land where I stood accused of murder and was just now returning with another murder hovering above me and arson to boot and needed to know if they'd sent out my name. If they'd broadsheeted it to the hills. If there were any pictures of me and A.D. and sworn affidavits from maybe old John Hill Carter, Mr. Vickers, and Dr. Alpionaire all typed out in brash, smudgy ink.

Lucky for me, the bartender stirred from his slumber just then because Mavis hadn't heard a word I'd said. In fact, he'd slumped over after the last shot and was dangling from his stool and would probably fall to the floor in another minute. Well, of course, I seen Mavis had the *Sun* in his back pocket and that it was from only two days ago printed up in Baltimore and that it couldn't help us none anyways to have the news from then. So I straightened him back up and put his brown derby over his eyes and took the *Roanoke World News* instead that the bartender was just then throwing out. With it, I followed A.D. into the fresh air of the new day as he was intent on moving us on into the heated direction of his needs.

Because wasn't that just like him? Always on the go for his needs, always in a sweat. I hadn't even spread out the front section along the dash before he was driving through the streets as if he'd lived in Roanoke his whole life. I looked on him and seen that sort of blaze in his eyes again. That fog falling down when he got so concentrated and charged in his pursuits, and knew he must have talked to someone in there even though I hadn't seen him consort with none except maybe old Mavis. And even then he didn't seem to have the occasion to do so or the ability to comport himself with any other in that respect. And yet, he seemed to know just where he wanted to go. The whole while he didn't speak nor turn his head, but just hummed as if he had a tune he'd just learned and needed to repeat to the end of him so as not to lose it. The car responded beautifully now to his attentions for his hands were of the wheel and his feet of the pedals, and as I sat back and scanned the news I didn't run across anything untoward, and certainly nothing concerning our names or general description, and rested easy to know it. That had me backing off considerable in my mania of being collared by the law so far down in Dixie already. Yet when we turned the next corner, and he brought the car up to the curb, I had to sweat again to consider our present predicament.

He'd parked right in front of the local police station. I don't think he knew it nor cared in the least, he was in such a state. As he got out, he grabbed the rifle and was hefting it aloft when I leaned over from inside to grab at his belt loop to stop him. But he was already racing off without even looking back to hear me in my anguish. For sure enough here comes a police cruiser pulling up not three feet from where we sat and a tall man with dark sunglasses and a waxed mustache was leaning out with his mean white face.

The officer said something to A.D. I couldn't hear. But as the man's engine shut and his car door opened, I certainly heard his Chippewa boots grind the gravel as he sauntered all slow and steady as if reconnoitering our position. He was taller than A.D. by a spell, and that took some doing, and had the rifle from him in an instant because I suppose he'd asked for it and A.D. complied. All the while I wanted to slink down into the seat curling up on the floorboards into a little ink spot so he wouldn't see me nor inquire as to our purposes. I didn't rightly know what to say. Only A.D. knew that (if he ever did). But I guess he must have told him something because the officer laughed and lifted his dark sunglasses to his forehead and then sighted far off on a fencepost. He breathed then slow and steady for what seemed like ages before sure enough *CRACK CRACK* there goes the rifle and the fencepost blusters up into dust at the top and that old boy laughs again and pats A.D. on the back. Setting his sunglasses back down on his nose, he pointed to a shack then that A.D. hadn't seen before. Well, I seen right away it was open because it had a bright little blue light out front and realized A.D. was only taking me to a pawn broker right next to the police station to trade something for the rifle.

To think, I bore all that anxiety over something as trivial as a pawn shop. I had a mind to tell A.D. about it when I stepped out of the car after he called me, but felt right away that good old boy watching me as sure as Sunday and just knew. Don't they always? Don't they? They get the scent of something suspicious as any bloodhound, and I guarantee he watched me, peering through them dark portals over his eyes the whole while I caught up to A.D. Because I could still feel that officer's gaze penetrating the walls to watch a nigger in his own town chase after a white man with a rifle. I hadn't missed that at all up in Baltimore, no sir. Not in the last seven years, and I wanted to tell A.D. about it, too, and ask him what they'd said to each other, carrying on as they had. But he was already hefting the rifle to the countertop where a potato-looking man was running his fingers over the stock, squinting his eyes up to smell the freshly-singed gunpowder.

Was that you just now shooting the fencepost? he said, and lifted the sight to see, aiming through the shack at a display of bicycles and baby prams all missing wheels or handlebars or gears.

No, sir, A.D. said. Officer just took it and wanted to see. Thought he might want to buy it his own self, but he just fired it and walked off.

Hmmpf, the man said and I wasn't sure if that was a good hmmpf or a bad hmmpf, and neither did A.D. But already A.D. was checking out the instruments arranged along one side of the store. In particular, he eyed a red Martin guitar that had a beautiful rosewood fret board and ivory-tipped tuning pegs that I so wanted to touch and strum, but surely I didn't do it. I didn't move an inch so that old potato-looking man couldn't question me nor ask nothing least he confers with that old officer out there about me and something truly untoward starts to gather around us. That was how it happened, for sure. That was how it always happened down here, and I knew it and stood stock-still and played dumb and would have only talked if talked to, even if I seen A.D. had no idea as to the situation.

He was touching that red guitar, and then moved on to a black shiny Stella that was dinged up a bit about the body, but serviceable. He strummed his hands along the strings and a sharp twang raised up in the air and the potato-looking man stopped his fiddling long enough to listen to the twangy tinny sound. It was so obviously off a half step, I had a notion to raise up my hand to go tune it but then here comes that old officer stomping in through the door as if he held the whole world in his hand. He still had on his sunglasses, and looked at me and just leveled his head and stared and I didn't turn an inch to feel him interrogating me with that hidden gaze of his turned up like the flames of Hades. As he did, a soft pitiful. No, *sir* rose up in the center of me as clear as day. Even though I hadn't said it. Even though I hadn't spoken a word. It was just there, from time immemorial, and was something my body must have felt deep in its muscles and needed to express because it was all it knew how to do, and that made me flinch to feel it. To still feel so abused and low inside after all those years. Well, then the potato-looking man stopped for sure since he seen me flinch, and with the officer already so close, I thought he'd heard me, too, though it might have only been my heartbeat that alerted A.D. to any trouble. Even though I knew he couldn't have possibly heard it though it nearly ruptured my ears.

That's okay, Mabry, A.D. said, not looking up. He was strumming another guitar, something I hadn't seen before. Something almost like a steel body shining in the light like a beacon, and so I could see straight away how taken A.D. was with it. Though he must of seen my face in the reflection, for I was already sweating considerable and melting to be so inspected like that, so close to those two men. You can wait in the car, he said. This here won't take but a minute.

I looked up at him then and seen the slightest smirk on his lips and knew that I was the Mabry he was speaking of and that he was meant to be in charge of me. Turning slow and solemn then, with my head bowed like a good nigger, I walked past that officer's gaze not once turning nor looking up and it all dripped by like molasses, the time. For surely it felt like I was sliding my hand across a razor blade, the process was such a torture and wreck. That even when the walk to the car seemed to take another half-day at least, and the air was burdensome and syrupy, I still felt inspected by them old boys. But finally I made it to the driver's side and breathed out my sorrow and torment. Even though I probably only set there another five minutes, it felt like five years till A.D. finally comes out smiling and laughing as if nothing untoward in the whole world had transpired, and lo, what is dangling from his hands—not one but two guitars in their worn leather cases.

I DROVE AFTER THAT. From then on A.D. sat in the back and was on his guitar (the red one) nonstop, and had that song beside him scribbling and working it, searching for a way to string a tune to it that he didn't even notice when I left Roanoke behind. To never feel that officer's gaze no more was all I wanted, it had unsettled me so, and so I started thinking of my old home. How I'd lived there free and unfettered with my family, at least before all that Hackett mess, and damned if I didn't get a need to see it again, after all those years. For Bristol was my intention now. Bristol my home and torment, my loss and gain, for I figured even Bristol would have been better than that old Roanoke. In Bristol, I knew I was an outlaw, and wouldn't have to wonder who else knew it or cared. And yet, in seeing how it was another 150 miles down the ridge, and I had nothing to occupy me, as A.D. might have only spoken one more word in all that time, he was so concentrated on that song, I got to thinking about Annie again. And my sweet Lucy.

O my little Lucy. I had time to consider their faces, or what used to be their faces, the ones I remembered. The soft sweet lips of my wife. The dark curious eyes of my baby girl. And I remembered my life then and how it had all flowed quiet and simple and sweet, like I'd always hoped, with Annie teaching me to read at church Sundays, and at night by the lantern. Then at home, us making dinner together and settling little Lucy on our laps as we listened to the woods and crickets and wind crossing the fields, soughing the crops. And as I considered it all, I realized I'd never allowed the sounds of that life to return to me before. Hell, I'd never had the occasion. At the Peabody there was always music to mend my mind, to take it off into heights and pursuits unseen. But I guess my leaning now was for seeing all that I'd lost return to me, to feel that perfect center of my life again, a center I'd never really left behind, even after all those years.

The land certainly wasn't something I couldn't leave behind. The land was just fine, and had fit me all those years just right, and as I thought about it now, I seen it still fit me. As I watched the fields and valleys slip past, I drove without thinking. It was so familiar. I drove and A.D. played and it was as a dream, the scenery and his music, like something buzzing at the edge of my mind. I drove in the shadow of the mountains right into Bristol without stopping. Then right on through State Street that was still as sharp and busy as I remembered. Till I come out the western end of it a few miles toward the parcel I'd kept with my beautiful wife, and which was still stretched out as it had been before I left.

Though it was changed, of course, from that time, from that life.

The place was lonesome now, and weedy. The small weather-rotted shack had sunk into a sad compilation of boards and busted-out windows. But as A.D. kept right on playing, I stepped out to see it in its entirety and to remember. Ah, mine, I muttered, and watched a patchwork of fields stretch off for miles beneath the blue hazy ridge. Always above me. Always there. Watching. The mountains never too big nor beyond your thinking, and yet never too small nor meddling neither. I remembered how it often felt when you walked with the land, that you took it with you wherever you went. How the land did not overpower me none in its making, nor underwhelm me neither in its silence. Rather it fit me just right and always whispered and eased my mind to know I could be so entwined with such a thing of beauty and strength. With how the leaves burned through their colors come fall. Or how the snow swept soft amongst the sorghum. With all the pretty birds chirping away as you stretched out into it with your life, and how the land was poised upon each wayward thought. Always still and waiting and true.

When I thought of it all, I recalled how difficult it was for me to know I was a black man in a state with white people who refused my kind. Even as the land held me and gave me all it had to give, and more—so much more—and another solemn wave of sadness stole through me like a breeze.

O but I loved it. I did, and loved it still as I looked upon it. Because it was mine. Even if Annie and Lucy had long since gone and the house had been worn to dust and the crops tilled under, with the echo of all those sharecroppers folded into one long stitch in the soil. I still loved it and felt it all anew as I followed the crumbled stone wall I'd built with my own hands—for it was mine.

But then listening to A.D. tinkle on with his song, with the sentiment and loss that tale wove, the sound swept through me and pushed against the whole of my heart, and before I even noticed it, I'd picked up the other guitar (the black one, dinged a bit, but serviceable) and stepped through my front door's ruined jamb. Standing in my soured drawing room, I gazed upon the open sky, at a collection of dusty birds' nests strung where the rafters once hung, and I could hear A.D.'s song as a refrain of the land even as I watched the stars fall out one by one in the dusk. I could hear him singing and playing and the notes that lifted from my own strings were not of me anymore. They weren't from my hand nor hope nor sorrow, but from my own sweet Annie and Lucy girl gone away now for sure. They were from my girls, from when I was here—when we were here—and as I played and carried on with A.D.'s sad strumming, I wept for wherever my girls could have gone.

X

In the relics ~ To his own satisfaction ~ The dream
was of the land ~ The last carnival of Revelation ~
Auditioning in the hat factory ~ There ain't but one
other ~ Covered in moonlight and dust ~ Mr. Jimmie
Rodgers ~ Heaven then the sound ~ The pearls

A.D. WAS GONE IN THE MORNING. When I turned over in the grass and
looked, I couldn't see one trace of him. I called out and heard nothing, only the
sound of the cicadas in the early dawning. We'd set up camp right there on my
old land, but not in the house as it was too close to the road, and I feared someone driving by and suspecting something in seeing us sprawled out in the relics
of that broken down frame. So instead, I'd hefted our few things and guitar
cases and a bucket of well water still fine enough to drink to a stand of stunted
oak a ways off from the road where I thought we might better hide ourselves
and where me and A.D. kept at it for three solid hours playing. O we went on
into the darkness and the hooting of owls, before sitting down together by the
edge of the fire to rest.

I'd meant to ask him about the guitars then and why these were the ones
he wanted for the rifle, when I knew all along he wanted to kill old John Hill
Carter, but I'd already listened and knew. That song was in him now and it
wouldn't leave and he didn't need anything else since he'd found it and worked
on it to his own satisfaction. Hell, he hadn't even eaten any of the potatoes I'd
found growing wild from the edge of my old garden. I'd roasted half a dozen
on hickory sticks and eaten my fair share, and hoped to dream that night of
something particular, of my family perhaps, and their freedom, but it weren't
no good. The dream was of the land and always had been. Now here we were
and what I wanted to tell A.D. filled my whole heart concerning my Annie and

Lucy girl, and where we should start looking for them. But he was already gone. I seen the car gone, too, from where we'd stashed it behind some old paving brick and barrel staves, and it made me lonesome to feel myself on my own land again without anyone to appreciate it, to walk with me and recollect all that had happened here. But after a moment, I figured right where he'd went. He'd only been bellyaching all night about getting some fancy new paper and a pen to commit his new song to posterity, and of course an envelope to carry it all around official like so he could address it to his dearly departed, to Ms. Clara May Staunton (as sad and misbegotten as that sounds). So grabbing my guitar, I slung it over my shoulder, and played my whole way into town on the walk.

It was only three miles and I figured in my happiness now, in returning home, that if they were to arrest me here, then I could at least play myself up to the gallows and be done with it for good. So I kept at it the whole time and even as I graced the sidewalks and kept playing, the people milling about and bustling from store to store with their arms full of packages eyed me and my coloredness and just smiled to hear me play, and I was confused to be such a pleasurable sight for them. It was unusual and suspicious, and I had a mind I was in the wrong town to begin with, that somehow I'd walked down another street entire, into some other Bristol in another part of the world. Until of course I seen the poster in the window of the local Mercantile. Then it was easy enough to figure out. It was all there in black letters:

AN AUDITION:
FOR THE VICTOR TALKING MACHINE COMPANY
TWO WEEKS ONLY!

I couldn't hardly believe my eyes to see such a thing and know we'd just come across a song as powerful and alive as that, and all the while it was just setting on the edge of A.D.'s fingertips—and mine—since I'd played along with him enough to know it by heart. And by the dates displayed, I figured it was already the second week of an open tryout so that a feeling like a fiery excitement grew in me to see it. Well, I knew right away A.D. had seen it too, and that he was already there probably waiting to play. For it seemed a Mr. Ralph Peer was auditioning musicians of all kinds for the rights of publishing. And as the townsfolk streamed past and stared at me, working the strings and sweating as I set to my music, they must of thought I was just more of the musical kind traipsing through their town to make their mark and didn't think nothing of it.

Shoot, they must of thought it most natural to see me there, too, and it eased my mind to think of my past deeds going unnoticed and unseen, that I could set right out in public and play as I wanted. My fingers practically flew across the frets then teasing out the lead I wanted to play for A.D.'s re-working of that song. And sure enough, some folks even give me a few nickels they liked it so much, and I would have tipped my hat to them if I'd had one, but knew right away where to find my A.D.

THERE WAS AN OLD HAT COMPANY on the edge of town near the state line (in fact, right on State Street), where Tennessee started south and west of the state of Virginia and made up its own version of a city named Bristol, picking up right where the city of Bristol, Virginia left off, if you can believe it. It was something to see. How those two cities divided themselves, almost as of a heart cleaved in two. But the warehouse when I come up on it was on this side, in Virginia, and lined outside with the craziest acts you'd ever seen. There were great ragged yodelers and flatpickers from down the piedmont as far as the Carolinas and inside Tennessee, and of course all kinds of great ma and pa hillbilly acts from the most remote Appalachian towns. Even little groups of children swarmed about a central singer with them all going choral style and as loud and furious as can be because maybe they'd only ever sung in their own church in the hills for the good lord they whooped it up so fierce and biblical. Then of course there were the more formal, city-styled ladies, the heavy-set ones who'd changed up the opera they must have learned into a hillbilly song that the commoner might take to heart, but it weren't no use. None of them was gonna hack it. Old moonshine jugmen and queer looking harpists, bass men and fiddlers, squeezebox men and drummers, trumpeters and poets—it sounded as if the last carnival of Revelation had arrived it got so confusing and loud that the whole lot of them was enough to drown out every last thought you could of conjured. It took me a full five minutes to spot A.D. with his red guitar near the main entrance. There he stood, all thin and composed, strumming away as if he hadn't heard a sound in the world, he was so concentrated and stoic. He might not have even noticed me if I hadn't touched his shoulder to begin with, nodding at all those surrounding us.

There ain't but one other here, he said when he spied me.

One other what?

Real deal, he said and winked before nodding through the double doors to one man kind of set apart from the rest. Leaning against a wall, he was thin and had a small-cropped head of brownish-red hair and coughed once into his hand before he twirled his guitar with the other.

Him? I said and stepped toward A.D. all casual like and quiet as I looked at him and A.D. kept his head down strumming soft and concentrated on his strings.

Calls himself a brakeman or something. Had a band supposedly. From right over in Bristol, Tennessee. But then I heard they all just fell apart. Had an argument, I guess. Now it's just him.

And us, I said.

A.D. smiled and heard me just then as I was running along my notes, running down an accompaniment to the song he'd worked out. That's right, he said. It's just him and us from what I can hear. Cause there ain't no Runnymedes in this whole lot. Not one damn Runnymede at all.

THERE WERE VOICES ON THE OTHER SIDE of a small door. Then we'd hear a man say something and the singing would start or it would end and another act would stroll out quiet and red-faced, as if they'd just lost their first newborn, they looked so sad and defeated. But then the voice would holler Next from the open doorway and another act would hustle in so excited and jubilant that the whole miserable thing would start all over again, and we'd trudge up another spot. It was intolerable waiting like that, but A.D. didn't say nothing. He just sang under his breath until that other fellow went in and then all of us—everyone in the whole hallway—leaned forward and was astonished to hear what he sung and how he sung it and how it went on and on so light and full and perfect rising up—like he'd just been rustled in from the open range or something. Covered in moonlight and dust. Well, we finally found out the name of this fellow, of the other real deal in A.D.'s mind, when he reemerged, because he was kept inside for nearly an hour, when most everyone else wasn't in for more than three minutes.

Jimmie Rodgers, he said and shook A.D.'s hand when he come out. For he shook all the hands of all the acts after he come out at the end of his session just as if he'd been pumped full of sunshine he sparkled so much in his smiling. He coughed and stood beside A.D. and was shorter than him and smiled his glowing smile and winked at A.D. with his red droopy eyes looking us over.

What? A.D. said when he seen that quick wink and took offense to it, though I don't think Jimmie meant nothing by it in the least.

You alright, he said and pursed his lips before wiping them with the back of his hand. I got my eye on you, he said. I got it set.

We didn't rightly know what that meant, but Jimmie sort of drifted off then without explaining. He was the most curious kind. He just sort of floated on his own euphoria and glee (and on the sweet charms of whatever he'd been smoking). Because he'd just lit his own handrolled cigarette and the sugary aroma wafted above everything else and then he was gone and it was almost our time to shuffle on through.

Well, what'd he mean by that? A.D. said. He's got something set?

It's nothing, I said. Maybe he just heard you before and liked it. Maybe he just liked it.

Sure, A.D. said, he liked it. But I don't think he was sure about anything other than that song. I'd never seen him so concentrated with how he set his eyes forward after that. He looked at the last one to go in before us and then as that one come slumping out after only a minute of the most god-awful cackling, sounding more like a cat being dragged over a pincushion, the voice called out Next and A.D. was in before I even realized it sauntering up to Mr. Ralph Peer and pumping his hand in greeting. Hi, hi, A.D. said and he was smiling like I never seen him smile so that his whole body seemed to be smiling. Mr. Ralph Peer was much smaller than A.D. and there weren't anything but one blond-haired lady in there with a clipboard and two other fellows crawling around on the floor looking over a host of wires and readjusting a microphone. So that finally I pulled A.D. away to where I thought Mr. Peer wanted us to stand because he was holding up both palms as if to push A.D. back.

Fine, fine, Mr. Peer said and readjusted his black-rimmed glasses as he looked over the two of us, for we were as disheveled and homely as you'd think. A.D. was covered in the dust from our travels and the campfire soot was in the creases of his sleeves, while I was just as rumpled as a potato sack. But I felt better seeing A.D.'s energy and the general setup of all those wires and microphones. The excitement had built up inside us so, I could almost feel it permeating the walls and covered-up windows. Until Mr. Peer shook his hand in the direction of those two fellows who had to flip a few switches to get something rolling. Then Mr. Peer just looked at us and nodded. Well, that was all A.D. needed, for he knew exactly what to do and started up the introduction with a few notes, and it was heaven then the sound. After one and then two strummed chords, I come in under him all smooth and sparse with my lead just as he starts the first lyric, and it all went perfect. There weren't any other motion in the room. Just the swaying of our bodies so that I didn't even hear the song, or anything else for that matter. It was just like we were driving down the ridge in the light, with the mountains all blue and misty above us, just a motion of substance blurred into their beauty. Just a shape hovering there. I looked at A.D. and his eyes were closed and his neck arched so that I knew he was singing, even if I couldn't hear him. Even if I couldn't hear anything but my own heart—but by then I couldn't even hear that! It was just a softness. The world, the room, even Mr. Peer's sharp face dissolved from view so that there was only my Annie and Lucy girl in the air. I swear, I seen them! As if swaying beyond me in the dusted-up windows, they smiled down at me, it was so golden the sound. It resonated beyond my hearing and knowing and glowed as if pearls themselves were being pulled one by one from our fingers and throats. O and I didn't even know what to do with my hands when we finished and the last sad note resonated into the stillness. But when I seen Mr. Ralph Peer reach back to a wooden folding chair without looking, as his small little fish mouth kind of opened and closed without speaking—all while searching with his hand for something to support himself—I looked at A.D. to know we'd done it. We'd set that old boy back on his heels in his silence to hear us.

XI

Nothing but whiskey ~ The pressing into grooves of
voice and guitars ~ The radio ~ A blind trace in the
larch ~ The anonymity of their art ~ The Hardy Family
~ Up into the ridge ~ Into the ghostworld then ~ Some
dark idea or order ~ Their echoing conclusion

WELL IT WEREN'T NOTHING BUT WHISKEY AFTER THAT. All night
I followed A.D. from bar to bar as we heard Jimmie Rodgers was out somewheres stalking the Bristol streets and that he had a habit of moving on and
through if you weren't sharp enough to see. So when we finally did catch up
with him, it was in one of the last places we looked. Though as we shuffled towards him all quiet and reverent, as if approaching some newfound god in the
wilds of Africa or Arabia, we realized it weren't even him to begin with. But only
another fellow who only looked like him, and who'd been at the auditions too,
and who'd already taken up in styling himself after Jimmie and everything he
did. Sure, he had the look down pat. He had the same short brownish-red hair
and scruffy wide boots, the same half-smirk on his face and rumpled up shirt.
Wobbling up to us, he yodeled all the while with a whiskey bottle in his hand
and a rolled up cigarette on his lips.

Well, it sure was something to stand there and watch this feller try to fid-
get and move and shuffle his feet about as if the whole Earth was too hot and
rolling away for him to stand because that was all we'd ever heard Jimmie did.
But then he slapped A.D. on the back and said Jimmie had just been in there.
That he'd waved a handful of bills that Mr. Ralph Peer gave him for recording
and counted it all out for everyone to see and set it at $100 worth. When A.D.
looked down at his own handful and knew it to be $50 worth he smiled to
know Mr. Ralph Peer had picked out Jimmie and us over all the others to give

the top pay—and this was before they even pressed and played the things, the fellow reminded him.

Pressed what? A.D. said.

Well, the records, of course. Didn't he tell you? Up in Camden, New Jersey. That's where they make them from the original. At the Victor Talking Machine Company. Pressing into grooves your voices and guitars and everything else as thin as can be. Then he lit another handrolled cigarette in a special way with his lighter, snapping it open against the palm of his hand, because he must have seen Jimmie do that, and leaned up to the bar to grab the bottle he'd bought to pour out another shot for each of us and for any other person who happened to be standing nearby. O he certainly had a way, this young fellow, and if I hadn't known, I would of said it was Jimmie Rodgers standing there before us, for there was something about this fellow that pulled you into the fire of his life. Something burning away as swift as the smoke he shot up out of his mouth and nostrils, trailing away with the sweetened aroma of whatever he offered around. Till even A.D. slumped against the bar as this young fellow—Burl I believe his name was—turned in his Tennessee boots and smiled at us shaking his head. Radio, was all he said then, and waved a half-empty whiskey bottle in A.D.'s face.

Radio? A.D. said and scratched his head.

Sure, Burl said smiling, radio, and his high forehead was grease-stained from where he rubbed it with his corduroy sleeve. Jimmie was talking all about it before he left. Radio radio radio. He said it's changing everything. Even my granddaddy, old Burlhead Mathers—that's Eck Burlhead to you, you under-stand (you might have heard of him)—even he said the same thing the other night when we played. And since he was the one that wrote all the songs I sang, and with Mr. Ralph Peer giving me $15 for the lot of them, I tend to believe him mostly. He swaggered then a bit, teetering before us. My old granddaddy sings sweeter than dandelion wine, he said, if you haven't heard. But then he got quieter as he thought on his granddaddy and shot back his whiskey, slurping it down with a hitch in the back of his throat. My granddaddy, he said again, as the room sort of spun around him, he just can't come down the mountain no more. That's all, and he put a sweaty hand on A.D.'s cheek. Cause of the rheumatism, he said. In his hips, and as he pointed to his waist, I could see the fire burning in him again from the whiskey. That's why he sent me here to sing. Though he sings better than me by a long shot and anyone else here, and he spun around with his hand in the air, pointing from the chairs to the tables to the wall, before wiping it across the bar in one last grand sweeping gesture.

You don't say? A.D. said and stared at him through the blue haze of the room. The boy was tilting from his stool now that he'd finally set down after I think he'd forgotten all about keeping up his Jimmie Rodgers routine. He just swayed now side to side and then slumped forward into one sad heap. His head was down in the crossed pyramid of his arms. His boots dangled from his feet, and I couldn't hear it, but A.D. was inching closer and then whispering in his ear as the young feller said something that I couldn't quite make out—something about a blind trace in the larch, and a shed high up on a bluff. But I lost the train of it entire as the bar had just then ratcheted up as the bartender clanged the bell saying it was closing time for everyone and for all of them to Git. Well, this was particular hard to hear as most the folks left were musicians and had been turned down by Mr. Ralph Peer that day or the last. So they'd been drinking since then to wash away the sadness of their anonymity. The anonymity of their art, which was their souls, I suppose, and I think the bartender knew it and had a bit of sympathy left for them after all, for he eased off on the bell and set up another round of drinks all free on the till.

It was awful kind of him and I had a notion to grab another drink myself even if we didn't find Jimmie traipsing through town as we'd hoped. I was happy enough anyway with something A.D. had done at the end of our audition, after Mr. Ralph Peer needed to support his body physically in hearing us play. You remember. How he'd reached back to his seat easing himself down, and set still for another full minute taking it all in as his technicians scurried about his feet, turning knobs and switches, reconfiguring something with the recording device before whispering up to Mr. Peer who just touched his thick black glasses as A.D. and I watched. We were swaying there before him, our shoulders touching, the meek light coming in the covered up windows. The motes of dust like rays of sun spidered in the hushed space about us, with the light now rising all golden and glorious and impossibly perfect in our minds for what we'd just accomplished. When, in no uncertain terms, Mr. Peer shifted in his brown leather loafers, cleared his throat, and asked in his high-nasal twang: Well, fellas, what do you call yourselves?

The Hardy Family, A.D. said and he didn't even hesitate. It was right there on the tip of his tongue as if all he'd ever wanted the whole time was to say it and confirm it, our presence to the man, of who we were. And I looked on him after that because it was my last name and the last name of my Annie and Lucy girl. A name I hadn't heard spoken since back in the basement of the Peabody, when I might have mumbled it in my sleep, or when Mr. Vickers come down to reprimand me for something. But hearing it said this time was different. This saying stirred something deeper in me with how sure A.D. was and confident in its proclamation. As of an oath or assurance of some kind. A truth, maybe, to be commended. I can't say, but whatever it was stirred something in me considerable. Something whole and warmer than I'd felt in years being who I was, and working how I'd worked, and I thought on A.D. then with such dignity and trust, as on no other white man I'd ever encountered, and still feel that way, and you can take that to whoever you want to verify it with, too.

Well, okay, Mr. Peer said, and the blonde-haired woman beside him was already scribbling in black ink our name across a brown envelope and licking the flap shut with all our precious information tucked inside.

THE NEXT MORNING MY MIND WAS A FOG. My thoughts were like rusty nails in a glass jar. Or copper pennies. I turned my head and the squelch of it all rattled my eyeballs. When I gathered the nerve to peek from beneath my eyelids, I saw the road rise into the Blue Ridge parting smoky treetop clouds into the heavens. We had wound our way up considerable from Bristol, but when we dropped back in a switchback, crossing down along the ridge, I could see the town laid out far below like a smudge of haze and zigzags and tiny church spires. I turned to A.D. and all I seen was the whiskey bottle in one hand and the steering wheel gripped in the other. His eyes were such a mess of red cracked lines I had to touch the wheel myself to make sure we were still living and breathing.

It's alright, A.D. said, not looking at me, his eyes unblinking from the maze of road winding down and up and around and through that blessed ridge. I got it set, he said. I got everything set.

Well, I knowed right away that was what old Jimmie Rodgers had said to us at the audition and that A.D. had taken it to heart as something meant for him, as of an insult or slander, though I never understood why. But here he was in the early dawn driving into the back country past even the parts I used to know, and still he drove and only looked on occasion at the back label of his whiskey bottle where he'd scribbled some directions that was taking us farther into the blueness.

But I didn't mind. Not in the state I was in. I just leaned my head against the seat and looked mournful at the blueness of the air, at how it changed and moved and flowed off those mountains the closer we came in to them. Or, when a random assortment of dales and glens would spring up as if out of nowhere when we turned the next hill. It just went on and on and was perfect, and I remembered how it had all looked like such a vagueness my whole life, how it had hovered as a distillation of some faraway color or spirit. But right up close it was something else entire. Something as a creature that stole through you and set your sights reeling. A creature that could nestle down and turn inside till the color you felt for yourself was washed out and drained away and there was only blue left behind. Only the blue left through and through. For surely it was a lonesome and exalted and perishable thing, all of it, and I had to wipe away the tears to see it as he sped on before finally stopping below the slightest bit of trail-head that poked out from some thick briar. A particular patch must have been worked back over the years by mules or horses or such, for there were strands of the faintest fur hanging in the thorns that swayed in the breeze. Strands that would not shake loose for anything as A.D. pointed and looked intently at the back of his whiskey bottle.

There, he said and as he got out I hadn't realized it yet, but he'd slung his guitar over his shoulder as he took another long pull from the bottle.

There what? I said and slumped out of the car myself. My eyes were splintered and cracked but thankful that the blue mist hung low and wet. I could rub it into my pores and sockets to feel the wetness as a relief for all the dryness the whiskey had left in me.

That's where we've set ourselves to go, he said and smiled his thin-lipped smile, slapping my shoulder. I had no earthly notion as to what he meant, nodding as he did to the loose-swaying hair on the briar. But I started up after him anyways, and stuffed a few wet fern leaves into my cheeks to keep from feeling that slow watery drip that begins and never stops in your mouth after an all-night drunk like the one we'd just had. But then he was off. Up up up into the fog, and it was as if we strode through a ghostworld then. One I knew and had grown up in but which was now changed by my mind and age and by the light that bent and refracted in that strange mixture of heat and mist.

Wait, I said, but he didn't hear and took another step forward and wisps were all there were. Wisps of light and sound. I could hear a thwack thwack thwack echoing up farther, moving away from me, and took a step toward it. But it was gone and when I returned to my starting point it dissolved until I stood lonesome and lost and closed my eyes. For it was just as easy to orient myself with them closed as keeping them open to all that emptiness. A.D.? I said. But there was nothing. A.D.? I repeated, and a breath of that ghostworld arose and caressed my face, and for a moment I saw the trail stretch out before me though I could not tell if it rose or fell. I was buffeted on both sides by fog and could not orient myself otherwise but went on, balancing as if on the precipice of the universe itself. Something formless and hazy felt strung below me, like a ribbon tied between two poles. Stretching out my arms, I may have walked like that for half-an-hour, though truly I cannot say. Time had slowed into something imperceptible that you could not count on nor begin to fathom. It was nothing but the ridge and fog now, the beauty and strength of it, having constructed its own sense entire out there, its own sense of world and power and peace.

It was only when I heard the voices that I stopped—for it was the only human thing I could hear besides my racing heart. A swinging screen door slapped shut and then A.D.'s boots shuffled along a porch. I was below it but listening to the voices and then the guitar strings brought me in closer to their origin. They started out slow and disjointed and I knew it was A.D. starting on something low, some dark idea or order. But then another brighter hand began and the tune lifted up and tilted over and wove shimmering through the fog as if it had attached itself to my very ears to tug me along, guiding my feet. O it was a racing and silvery sound like rushing water in a mountain stream, and then the voice of the man A.D. played with started low and gravely before rising through a series of twists and pitches to stand outside of the whole harmony, before mounting up against the notes falling and rising as the mist tugged and swirled against my face. He chanted about an ocean the closer I crept, and it was sad to hear him cry out for the waters of the world he would never see. It was a renunciation. Or lament. As if he was renouncing himself and his entire life, even as he cried that much more to be part of a world he could not touch. Nor touch his love. O it was most lonesome and awful to hear, and the tears welled in my eyes to learn of the storm that besieged the boat he sailed upon, sweeping it full of sea wrack and foam as it was dragged into the cold dark depths. O the ocean, I heard and it echoed in my heart and I could not help it. But I looked at the mist-shrouded hands I held up then because I was strumming along in the mist to the song, stringing notes as even A.D. and the man strummed louder and raced off toward their echoing conclusion. Of course it was then that the mist finally lifted, for as I stood below the porch in the front yard, tears streaming down my face, the man who'd sung those heart-pounding lyrics almost fell over from the shock of seeing me there so close and moved as if delivered by the fog.

Ginny, the old man bellowed and he had to lean against his guitar, setting it on the porch to keep himself upright he was so heavy and his legs like two wooden poles. Ginny! he hollered. There's a nigger come in the fog. There's a nigger come to get us.

XII

Old Burlhead Mathers ~ Something else entire ~ Me
as emissary ~ Their own special calling and language ~
The black hole of his mouth ~ The current of his undertaking ~ Mr. Yancey Jakes ~ The thinking of his
eyes and mind ~ Bristol and his scars ~ The names

WELL A.D. DIDN'T EVEN HAVE TIME to tell the old man (old Burlhead
Mathers, A.D. later told me) we was only there to listen and play the songs he'd
already written and given to his own grandson. The man was in such a tizzy
to see me approach through the fog he shut down his merriment and general
demeanor from only moments before. His big white head shook and steamed
up red and hot to find himself so exposed to such a one as me. Then as the
Missus Ginny Mathers strode out, almost as fat and wobbly as her husband,
she handed him a shotgun that the old man cocked and pointed at me, before
squinting into the mist that was fractured and brilliant and stunning to see in
the warm mountain air.

Did you bring him? he growled at A.D. He didn't turn his barrel from me
nor his dead unblinking eye, which was as small and pinched as a raisin in the
doughy loaf of his face.

Sir? A.D. said. He'd stretched both hands upright at the first appearance of
the shotgun and was shaking now as the sweat started to bead in anxious pellets
on his forehead.

The nigger, old Burlhead said. You brought him to hear one of the songs
my own grandson hasn't even heard, when I thought it was just you and me
playing. He spit then, a brown line of juice to the porch from the small pouch
he gnawed in the hole of his cheek. You lied to me, son.

I never, A.D. said. But the gun had swung upon him and A.D. had already backed up as soft and slow as he could, creeping down backwards without ever taking his eyes off the end of that cold black barrel.

Yeah, you never, old Burlhead said. You never heard nothing, and then he wobbled to his door all the while keeping his squinty black eyes on the two of us as we backed up to the edge of the hill before the bright slapping sound of the screen door banged shut. A.D. turned to say something though I never quite heard the words, but could have easily guessed what he meant to mention.

Sorry, I said, and stood there a moment longer watching for he had cocked his head already to take in something else entire, something that was just now rising below the property. But it was always like that with him, wasn't it? You couldn't slam one door in his face nor threaten him at the end of a gun before another something come into focus like a beacon or signal that only he could understand. Because already he was off before I could even say anything for what just happened with old Burlhead.

Tumbling down through jimson weed and tamarack, A.D. followed another muddy trail that wound around to a smokehouse or shack where we supposed some convocation or conjuring was occurring. The voice inside was just as loud and forceful as a gale wind that would have stripped you raw if you were unfortunate enough to stand before it. Of course A.D. was never afraid of nothing like that and inched closer and rubbed his hands expectant like as he looked through a crack in the weather-bleached clapboard and heard a few wooden blocks scratch out a rhythm as a foot stomped the dirt floor. Then he turned to me with only his hand and thrust me forward. You, he said, and I hadn't any idea why I was needed at such a moment as that and was about to remind him of old Burlhead up there with his shotgun. But when I inched closer and saw the face of the voice proclaiming some injustice or other with a tune he carried himself—without even the slightest bit of pitchyness or wavering tone—I knew why A.D. had sent me in as emissary: the man was as blind as any I'd ever seen and as black as me and more. His hair was wild and spotted gray and billowed up into all sorts of knotted fits and starts to which he could never hope to see nor tame. And so he just swayed there on top of a turned over milk crate as he sang. O he was a sight to see. With how he seemed to leak out of the seams of his frayed overalls, teetering over the edges of his worn-out cowboy boots as he continued to work while he sang. For he must have set there often tending the fire dug right into the ground. He had kindled it low and steady with wet alder and hickory that sent up a nice smooth smoke for the strung hides of rabbit and coon and trout and whatever else he'd caught and gutted and tied from end to end in the rafters.

Stepping closer, I waved my hand in front of his face for I hadn't run across a blind one since back in church in Bristol, after the Honorable Reverend Michael Williams took charge. When he'd set up some program that brought in all these blind boys from Stone Mountain and Shreveport and other parts I know not, but where it was told they had their own special calling and language. Something like a secret ordination that could bring the spirit right out in people and speak on divinations and meanderings, and so they were thus revered for their sageness in all things religious and prodigal. So I felt a bit scared myself knowing this one here might have been given that same gift at birth, that knowingness. And yet as I listened to him sing, and stood by his side and truly felt it at first—as all his words and feelings swirled about me as the smoke drifted before my eyes—there was really nothing else to consider. It was so pure and deep his suffering, I didn't have to worry about anything he might have said to me, for it would be cherished, his attention, any I could get. And I was almost set to lean down and introduce myself when he spoke up first from the middle of his singing. Y'all don't have to tend it, he said. I got it.

Got what? I said.

The fire, he said. I got it and you, too, and he swayed toward us as he spoke and smiled to show the black hole of his mouth, with most the teeth worn away to little ivory nubs. I keep it warm, he said. I always do, and he motioned to the flames, before dropping another hickory branch on the pile and starting up again with some other song. Some tune that let his voice rise higher and higher as if the walls of that shack had been busted open and sprawled out so that the mountain air and sunlight were pouring in now—that's how elemental it was and profound. I had to shiver as the sound of it shook through me, rattling my chest and chin with such force I grabbed A.D.'s guitar and set down on another milk crate to start in playing to whatever he was doing. Sure. As soon as I heard it, I felt as if I'd have rode all night in the current of his undertaking just to witness such a thing as that, it was such a supernatural and righteous sound.

Yes, he said when he first heard me riding along with him then, plotting out notes in a fury or ecstasy of arrival. Of arriving—that was what it was. His voice was an arriving as much as old Burlhead's was a renunciation, or departing. This here voice was not diminished in the least. Not at all. And it would never be. No matter the circumstance. No matter the pain. Old Burlhead's was devoid for sure, but I didn't want to think about him no more. Not as Yancey (he told us his name only later, Yancey Jakes) charged on into a territory I had not felt as mine in some time. Not since coming back south so far below the Mason and Dixon to begin with. He sung of a suffering, true, but of a rising up, too, like a dove fluttering in the blueness of the ridge, absorbed almost wholly by the air and space. So that the tears started again as I heard it and knew the wings of such sweetness were for me as well as for him and anyone else who listened and who'd been downtrodden and abused. And for anyone else that had been treated as such. O it was intimate and natural his words, but also childlike, I suppose. Though they ran much deeper than what childhood runs, much deeper than any of the foolishness or trouble with adults. It was a deepness like the woods and streams and hills about us. For when he finished and swayed over to slap my shoulder since he'd liked so much my playing, he moved his long fingers out upon the fretboard and up to my chin and nose for a second to realize my face.

You colored? he said.

Yes, sir.

Then you ain't come down from old Burlhead to hear?

No, sir.

And you ain't come down from his grandson neither?

No, sir.

Shiiiiiit, he said and let the word linger in the smoke as he placed on another branch. I thought for sure you was colored when I heard you play, but I just had to make sure in the touching. I'm real sorry about that. But I had to know for sure to tell you the word so you'd know it was true.

O I knowed it, I said and sat transfixed before him as he swayed and sniffed turning his nose up. Maybe to the scent of the hides strung up in the smoke, ripening and drying into the flavor that would carry him on through the winter of another year. Or maybe just sniffing something else.

And there's another? Yancey said, because he was still sniffing. But he'd turned his otherworldly head in A.D.'s direction and as he stared at him the whites of his eyes turned up inside his skull like hard-boiled eggs. A.D. shuffled his boots once and coughed to announce himself in Yancey's presence.

Yes, sir. There's another here and I liked your song very much. I've heard nothing like it.

No one has, he said. That's new and just come to me last night in the darkness as they all do when there's nothing else to see. Nothing else but the spirit rising in shapes like they say the fire does, rising and falling across the air. Yancey had two sticks in his hands and tapped them lightly as if the rhythm inside him was too strong to contain. For he was moaning now lower in his voice, and tapping with his sticks so the refrain from his new song spun out of him as A.D. sung echoing him as the words reverberated and the guitar picked up the intonation and played itself out on its own. I swear. Even as I sat above it plucking notes and strumming as of a ghost working the strings, I couldn't tell if I'd done a thing to bring the refrain back to its conclusion. Yes, Yancey said. Yes. That's it. That's it and it ain't for Burlhead no, sir. Nor that boy of his.

Why would it be for them? I said.

That one's mine, Yancey said. That one's mine for all time.

A.D. was leaning above the fire and pulled from his coat the whiskey bottle. Then I could see him smiling as he thought a moment longer and got a notion and blinked once before he pulled the cork so that the sweet dark scent cut through the smoke and Yancey sat up as if pulled with a pole he must a known the smell so dear and true. He turned to A.D. and held out his old soft hand and touched the bottle that A.D. passed to him.

Yes, Yancey said as A.D. let go and the brown liquor sloshed against the sides as Yancey tipped it up and swallowed deeply twice, before releasing it as the smell wafted off his lips.

How come Burlhead gets your songs? A.D. said. He was closer and refused the bottle that Yancey offered back. He was leaning to be closer to Yancey's wet lips, and was lost to me in shadow then, his face. His eyes darkened and gone, and the thinking of his eyes and mind gone too, I supposed, as Yancey lifted the bottle again for another pull. How come?

Shoot, Yancey said. You know, and he tasted again another pull before finally setting the bottle into his lap as he rocked slower, ticking like a clock from side to side as he spoke. It's my color, sir. Y'all know about them white folks and how they takes from Yancey Jakes and gives him this last sad plot and says that's it. That's all there is for the sad blind nigger now and for all time. O but they don't see me as I shuffle off through the woods like none of them ever could. Cause I listen to it and stretch my hands out into it and feel it—the dirt and air and wind—and know it's inside me and outside me and all around me, because of that closeness and truth. Even in the darkness I don't fret and hide for the seeing ain't nothing more than I ever had anyways. And nothing more than I need to live and sing and see them by. O I sees them. They know it. Even that old Burlhead knows it when he sends that boy down to pick it all up from me, my sound, to take it away and play it for others as their own. I know. I always did. I know it's mine and that it's always mine and that's why this one ain't for them. Not no more. I'm done with all that to know you two. To know you now and to feel you and hear it so much better than what they could ever play. They ain't got nothing on you two. And Yancey Jakes stood then as he said it and pulled swift and efficient three smoked trout from where they hung. We ate them just like that. Standing without any forks or plates, and they were just as light and sweet and perfect as you could think, and when we were finished he told us more of his story.

He told us about growing up in Bristol and showed us his scars. Almost like gray slugs dripped across his skin they were. The ones from the whippings along his back and legs that he must have got almost sixty-five years hence to tell it when he was no older than a child and the South was still the South. But it didn't stop me none, he said. Not in being who I was nor what I knew I could be. And as he touched his finger to his wrinkled brow, he took us then to the swift deep stream that he fished in a ways down in a hollow, touching expertly the tautness of the strung lines and hooks before restringing some bait. I would have thought he was a young man had I seen him from a distance. Walking along the wood or scrambling along the rocks strewn about remembering and feeling everything with his mind and sniffing the cool mint fern and sharp bright pine as he led us on to his small brick hut down from the smokehouse. Till both me and A.D. were too tired to walk it wore us out so and we heard so much more from Yancey Jakes about so many other names of singers dead and gone or still living, yet lost to Yancey's world, lost to his life. That we couldn't begin to calculate them all and didn't make it back to the car before midnight, and even then, A.D. hadn't spoken in some time. He just sat there behind the wheel looking into the starry darkness and drifting clouds that hung low before being pushed off into their vastness.

What? I said. What is it?

A.D. just closed his eyes and tilted his head against the window to breathe the cool raw air.

What?

The names, he finally said, straightening up and touching his collar, before rubbing his hands along the buttons of his shirt. It was as if he was a new man. That something had been unraveled and removed inside him. That thinking up whatever he'd just thought up had changed him again. Had changed him maybe like how I'd seen Yancey changed and energized by the woods, bubbling like the stream coursing through the stony seams of the ridge as he took us around. Didn't you hear it? he said. The names?

The names? Well, sure, I said. I heard them. So what?

So what? And he looked at me as if I was the most rank and ignorant nigger the world had ever known. Well, I'll tell you so what, because right there's the whole thing. Right there's the names we've got to find.

XIII

A spell to him ~ The wrong end of a gun ~ He touches the
dial ~ The Ballad of Clara May ~ The old Barn Dance hour ~
Some greater angel ~ His song as he called it ~ Runnymede
in the storm ~ The crows ~ The last girl and her glassy skin

THE NAMES WERE ALL, HE REPEATED THEN aloud and to himself,
and were otherwise whispered to the air as of a prayer or incantation that finally
become like a spell. Something that transformed him into something else than
what he was, and so I worried about him and shied away, for it scared me to
look upon him in his mania as we drove the next day and the day after, and into
another week. Always driving farther into the ridge, into towns and places that
were nothing more than way stations or crossroads maybe, and then not even
that once we reached them.

Sometimes rolling in at dusk they might have just one measly little dime store
out front. Or one rusted-over filling station with a single paraffin lamp strung
above a chipped up butcher's block. Or nothing. Just dirt. Places like Whistling
Pine and the Richlands, Busthead and Honaker, Grapefield and The Crows.
And everywhere we went A.D. was determined to find the faces of the names
Yancey Jakes had said because behind the faces were the songs he wanted to get
at so much it burned him up to think they were just sitting out there waiting.
Tucked inside each of those old singers' minds wasting away into nothing where
no one could ever reach them or bring them back to the light of day. O it vexed
him! And so he had to ask around and spend our money freely and coax people
out of their shyness, especially the ghosts of old women and men, dust-covered
and disconsolate, as if in their sad gray faces, deep inside, they hadn't seen
nothing in years nor heard one word about some old nigger bluesmen, let alone

anyone Yancey Jakes might have only dreamt up in his head. And most times, the people didn't want to speak to him at all, at least not with me standing there in the shadow of the train depot or chancery or wherever else we parked. So I'd have to leave or walk around nonchalant and quiet like.

O but the songs are there, A.D. would say, they're real. So when we couldn't find any in this town or the next, or in the house we'd just been directed to, he'd start in again on the names as we left, repeating them, singing them, stringing them all out like the worn beads of some forgotten necklace as we drove through the night: Old Mossfield Churchwell and Clarence Ashford. Pee Wee Woodsman and the Appalachian Mayfairs. Bill & Bella Reese and the New Carrolton Singers. Blind Uncle Vecsey and Sister Mary Patton. The Williamson Trio and Doc Ferry Sutters. Bascomb Teak Nelson and Sleepy John Sumnter. On and on it went, and some days I don't think I got a word in edgewise to redirect him in the slightest. And yet A.D. always stopped long enough to remind me to play the song old Burlhead had given us for it was to be reworked almost immediately and trimmed up into shape.

Shape? I said.

Well, sure, he said and looked at me all queer like, as if I had no notion as to what we were doing, and I knew then that it was to be like that with him. He thought it'd been given fair and square to us by old Burlhead and didn't remember nothing about being held up at the wrong end of a gun. Or hearing the screen door slam shut in his face. Instead, we were to work those lyrics over as he drove. He saw some problem in them and wanted a hook to rise out of the feeling of them. The inclination, as he called it, in the rhythm. Sure, that was a term he coined himself—the inclination—if anything could have been attributed to his process. Though I guess he'd say the songs were his, too, once he worked on them long enough and in the way he did. For there certainly wasn't no one else to say any different, at least not me, as A.D. did most the talking anyways, but that was alright. Even more than alright, as it gave me time to ask around for my Annie and Lucy girl as I saw fit, to follow up on any leads however remote it might be to their whereabouts, to keep asking.

Hold on hold on hold on, A.D. said and stopped in the midst of a dirt road somewhere tucked beneath the overhanging pine and larch as I finally seen the colors start to change in the leaves with autumn rolling in across the ridge. But none of that mattered for the moment, as we'd finally run out of Mr. Ralph Peer's $50 dollars from our initial song and I was glad of it. I was glad because it meant Bristol might be finally pulled back into our sights and I might see the

Honorable Reverend Michael Williams after all this time of running away to finally ask about my family. I was just about to remind A.D. of this fact when I seen him touch his finger to his lips and turn the radio all the way up as he killed the engine. Listen listen listen, he said and touched the dial keeping his hand there as the sound rose up surrounding us.

I'd been slumped against the door a few hours by then and half-asleep for he'd finally stopped repeating the names in the darkness of the road. But now that the radio played, it was as if something had come to us born out of the darkness. Something soft at first, but knowing and able to touch us on the heads like an ordination or baptism. Something of our own making, you could say. O it was biblical and religious in its effect, and I'd never felt nothing like it before nor since, for all at once the air changed around us, too. It had become stretched out and silent, as of the stillness before a swirling storm, and as I inched closer on my seat, all the breath in me about ceased as I realized it was A.D.'s own voice singing to us over the airwaves and my own guitar plucking out the rhythm beneath it. It was our song! The Ballad of Clara May, at least that's what the voice called it when it was done and he played it again for good measure because he said he'd gotten enough requests pouring in from every-where since it first aired two days ago. A.D. and I had to look at each other then to realize what he meant.

Requests? I finally said.

Two days ago? A.D. said and let the idea linger as we listened to the song in the hushed darkness of the car. Only the glowing radio dial shone on us and it was as if a wayward star had fallen to visit us and us alone. For it tore through the center of our ribs and hearts and throats and flayed our hides with its light and warmth, and for all the life of me I couldn't help but feel as if we were inside every single radio in the entire world listening in at that particular moment, to that particular station—for it was a big one out of Nashville across the other side of the Appalachians, and had just started not too long ago broadcasting like this—a station tied into the old Barn Dance hour. WSM or something was the call letters. It was a show that used to sell insurance or whatnot, but had expanded into songs like this and to programming that reached all the listeners up and down the ridge. To all the folks who'd like what we had brewing up for them with our songs that drifted away just slightly from the blues they were used to. Drifting into something more familiar and repetitive with the hook he thought up. Moving Jessico's lyrics around a bit, chopping it up so that they could trust these words a bit more, now that they were tied a bit closer to their own lives and experience. Though of course, I had to explain all of this to A.D. as he sat there dumbstruck and awed by the significance of what we'd done, and as I did, his eyes lit up then and I seen a new direction turn in him finally. A new life.

This radio station plays for real and most the night, I said, and A.D. had to pinch himself to hear it and to know that this was just the beginning for us, just the beginning of our lives. For the car was already rolling from under our feet, barreling down the ridge.

He had the throttle in for sure and the strangest smirk on his lips, so that I had to stare away so as not to be touched by the spark of his madness. For as happy as I was to hear our success plainly spread out and dazzling in the very air we breathed, the blueness was fading from us the more we drove away from it, from the ridge. And as we both watched for hours or minutes (I cannot say for sure) as the light of the world raced up to meet us, and then as the burning gold rays shone down only for us, it was as if a layer of burnt skin was being peeled away from our path, and I thought: Sure. The old skin. The one we've just set aside. It's gone now. The one we've labored under in our ignorance and wandering is gone. There's another world we're venturing into with our souls and sound and suffering. There's another world entire for us to see—until Bristol appeared like a burning spot on the edge of our seeing—and we raced down towards it, singing the whole way the song old Burlhead had stole from Yancey Jakes in the fog of his magnificence.

THE MAN WAS STANDING OUTSIDE my crumbled stone wall when we pulled up. The car was steaming and shuddering and a most miserable sight for we'd rode her hard the whole way back and the man just had to stare at us to see if we'd fall apart ourselves as we rolled up to a chortling stop in that heap. He just touched the waxed ends of his mustache, before shaking his big ten gallon hat, waving away the steam and smoke as he slapped a silly little smile upon his face and watched as we stepped out into the early evening dusk.

You're late, he said.

We're what? A.D. was spying this old boy pretty hard by then and stood slumped against the steaming hood trying not to look like he was sweating too much from the effort for looking so calm.

Just what I said is what I mean. You're late. And here they've called all over the state for you two, and Mr. Tabeshaw from the Mercantile has done set up the stage right there on State Street, and called in the few entrepreneurs from over Bristol, Tennessee of the concessioning kind, and then some of the canvassing sort out of Richmond. And of course the local newspaper hacks—the ones writing up a puff piece for a dollar a shot—and he's even got three other acts to go on before you and one to follow. But all they say is the Hardy Family, the Hardy Family, who's gonna find the Hardy Family? So I says, I am. Benjamin Marks is my name.

Isaiah, I said and shook his hand. He was short. Smaller than me but with a belly as big as I'd seen on anyone, so I guess that's why he looked like he was always riding side saddle on a mule or something when he walked. His legs and belly kind of wobbled all over the place as he moved—with one foot and then the next rounding out like a bowlegged cowboy—I had to laugh to see him like that, but didn't say nothing. A.D. had already got him cooked in the center of his mad blue eyes, so I thought that was enough for the little fellow. That was all that old boy needed. To be centered and fixed in A.D.'s mad gaze, which kind of turned inward then. I'm certain he was wishing he was at that very moment still perfecting the song we'd just gotten from old Burlhead, instead of having to watch or even acknowledge this Benjamin Marks as he stepped closer and smiled, speaking as if he must have wanted something from us—or for us. On that point, I'm still unsure.

He was trying to say something about the set up and general outlay of offered monies. Then he twitched the mustache beneath his wide red nose as he sneezed to scent the wild azaleas blowing just then from some lost farmland tilled under years ago. O he sneezed and sneezed as he watched us, but just wiped his chin clean of snot when he was done, wiping with a red handkerchief before talking on in his slow nasally way about royalties and contracts and such and such legal concerns that I suppose A.D. finally did start to listen, for I seen him nod once and rub his chin. But I certainly wasn't listening. The only thing I could focus on were his hands. He had the smallest red-hued hands I'd ever seen and as he waved them at the end of his stumpy little arms he kind of shooed us on backwards then, back to the car as if we were to follow him out. For he kept checking his brass pocket watch on the end of its long rusty chain, dangling as it did from his vest pocket to see if we could still make it. If we had time.

Time for what? I said.

Well, they're gonna play the show regardless, Benjamin said. But they still want you there.

But what will we play? I finally heard A.D. ask. We had climbed back in and

Benjamin was waving us on, smiling that thin-lipped smile of his that I never could read clear enough, for it was as dark and murky as a mud puddle with how it always hid any intention he had cordoned off in the depths of him.

Play? Play? and he looked at us queer then as he slammed his car door. Well, there's only the one song they want to hear. What the hell else you gonna play?

THE STAGE WAS STREWN WITH CORDS and microphones and a drum set from the previous band, though I couldn't rightly say for sure what was out there. It was as dark as could be as some clouds had since commenced thrashing in their spasms of lightening high above the ridge and would flare up now and then over the spotlights that shone down from the top of the nearby granary. O it was a tangled mess for sure, being the first of its kind in a while of the outdoor entertainment. So that as the lights flashed and intensified with the lightening, and a great buzzing sound filled the air, I watched as the crowd billowed out toward the front awnings and store windows before leaking back up to the line of pallets set up like teepees all in a row to keep space in front of the stage so we could walk to the steps unmolested.

It was considerable loud, too, with them calling and hooting at us. Some of the younger folks in front had even started serenading us with the lyrics of our own song and I never knew such things could happen to a man who'd only ever worked his whole life and didn't know how to take it. So I just watched A.D. for any cue, because he sure was under the influence of some greater angel than I was. He seemed even taller somehow and stretched out with each step, so that the long legs came out of the center of him like he was dancing on polished tile, he glided so soft and easy along the stage's floorboards. That before I knew it, he had his guitar slung around in front of him and was bending down to the microphone with a smile creased across his long thin face.

Howdy, was all he said and a great cry went out that would a drowned your deepest thoughts if you hadn't sense enough to cup your ears to block out the furious noise of it all. He had them all in something of a frenzy just by smiling and being as tall and smooth as he was, and then he turned to me as if we were both in on something and nodded in that cool way to me, and so I knew what that meant and started in straight away on the introductory notes, running along them as easy as could be. And I never once looked up because I knew that would a been it for me, because this wasn't no Mr. Ralph Peer no more in the quiet room of the hat factory. This was the world—the new one we'd been thrust into—and it scared me to death to stand there and feel the rush of all that energy as it surged up toward me as if strung on chords sent straight from their eyes and minds. Even though I knew it was just really A.D. that most of them were watching. For I knew then that none of my worry would have amounted to anything if I'd froze up there or played the wrong note or chord, or even a whole different song.

Shoot, that crowd was just as happy as could be and started singing along as A.D. struck the first word like you wouldn't have imagined a group so large and energized could do. But they continued sing-along style through the whole thing and did it nice enough I can say now that A.D. was even dumbfounded to hear them and to know they'd hung on every last word. He just smiled and said thank you and bowed gentlemanly-like at the end of his song as he called it, and then waved his hand to the crowd that cried and applauded and stomped for more. I was dumbfounded myself to hear A.D. say his song with me standing right there, even though I knew it was old Jessico's anyway. I had a mind to mumble something about it, but that was when Benjamin Marks deemed it necessary to rush up and grab our arms in his small little hands and lead us offstage, because I guess he thought all them newspaper boys wanted him in the picture too. The flashes were innumerable and blinded us, and sure enough, the next day there we were—on the front page of at least three of them—with Benjamin Marks right in the middle and the caption reading Manager beside his name. Lord, lord, he was a one like that, too, to get his grubby little face in everywhere and grab every little bit of attention he could get.

But in that moment, I didn't have to worry about that foolishness yet, for there weren't nobody asking after me once we reached the street and stood outside the local saloon. I was just the colored accompaniment after all, and I liked that well enough myself. But when I looked at A.D. there must a been thirty gals as pretty as could be lined up for his autograph. Autograph? I said as Benjamin Marks reached for the bevy of pens he must of kept squirreled away in the bottom of his drawers for just such an occasion, for he huffed and puffed to keep up with the general commotion of our being in the midst of all them like that.

Sure, he said. Autographs. Don't you know what that is? He smiled and patted my back before he was sucked off into the current. It was like a maelstrom on the ground. Something that swirled around A.D. who was the tall beanpole center of it. The girls giggling and screaming and talking and hushed, too, watching every last thing he did. Signing away with his big loping initials and posing ever once in a while as a flashbulb burst up and another girl scurried off as another took her place. They all might not have realized how close they resembled the storm racing down from the ridge. As I looked back up as the general excitement for the last act started to build, I seen another flash crackle far off but getting closer. Then I heard the first loud booming thunder in the heated clouds rushing down to flutter the hair and hemlines of the girls lined around A.D., before lifting the errant sandwich wrapper and newspaper that fluttered up and danced off as if on strings in the air.

A.D.? I said. A.D.? But he didn't hear. I'd wanted to get him going out of there, but was caught dead by the name of the next act. A man was already introducing him and saying because of the inclement weather they only had time for one song and that sent a loud groan of disappointment through the crowd, but once the loud flashy music started I turned and seen him. I blinked once just to make sure, then shook my head to know it was true. O I knew at once what it might do to A.D., and wanted to tell him about it, and it was easier now, for as I turned the rush of girls had ceased to a trickle and then only to one. The music of the last act had taken away all the attention A.D. had reveled in, and that he'd probably wanted in the depths of him for all time, turning as he did in it like a little rowboat in the rush of all that excitement.

Runnymede, I said, and another white-heated bolt sizzled above the rooftops of the granary and a shriek rose from the crows nesting there. It's Runnymede, I said. It's Runnymede. But he hadn't heard. He was looking at the last lone girl standing before him, the one reaching up with her hand to trail along his long smooth face. And lord, lord, lord if I hadn't seen her, I wouldn't have believed it with my own eyes. As it was I had to blink again and then once more to make sure of it and to think to myself for a moment that maybe there was a god after all (though I'd still like to hold off judgment on a thing like that). But there she was: Ms. Clara May Staunton. In the flesh. She stood before A.D. and had so transfixed his gaze that he couldn't see me nor hear any other thing for that matter. He was already reaching up with his shaky right hand to trace along the back of her neck. To touch with his icy fingertips a glassy wrinkle of skin where she'd stood stock still and been burnt in the fire at the Peabody when we'd left her—when we'd thought she'd been burned up to a crisp—and the tears streamed down A.D.'s face as he watched her.

XIV

Its unrelenting gyre ～ A witch's brew of drumbeats ～
A short quick bird laugh ～ A dozen glowing sparks
～ That singular omission ～ Of what befell old John
Hill Carter and the marks therein contained

THEY STOOD THERE AS IF IN AN UNAPPROACHABLE cloud. The air continued to whip and swirl about them in its unrelenting gyre, as the scraps and ticket stubs and popcorn boxes that littered the sidewalk scuttled to and fro at their feet. But they were beyond all that, buoyed up by everything else and their own remembrances. Hell, by the sheer sight of each other and the circumstance of our fame that had brought us here, and mostly, by her name, Clara May, which was raised as if from the air by our song, and all I could do was watch as they stared at each other and then swayed to the sound of their own bodily murmurings.

A.D. was speechless and limp but soon found the strength to lean down so he could speak to her. But he could not speak. And he knew it. She did too, and just smiled to see him so affected by her appearance that she kept her hand to his cheek even as Runnymede played and the lightning struck bright pinpricks overhead. The crowd oohed and ahhed as if Runnymede himself had called out for the lightshow of the heavens to accompany his latest and greatest song—which had played nonstop on the radio that last week. O he strutted and preened as if to a witch's brew of drumbeats as each subtle movement was taken in and absorbed by that crowd as if a divining rod of pure merriment had struck their souls. As they listened, they seemed to spirit up their laughter and amazement evermore, and even as they did, a tightness in hearing and seeing him act the fool constricted my chest. I could not take much more for sure, and made then as if to point to Runnymede, to point out the obviousness of his ridiculous antics (as I'd never liked him much to begin with), but it weren't no good. A.D. was so intent with touching the glassy skin where the fire had licked her that night, licking almost to her head, that he did not see me, nor pretend to care. So instead, I just watched them. I watched and listened, for when he finally did muster up enough strength to speak, she had to smile at the depth of his repentance. I'm sorry, he said.

For what?

For leaving you. I should have never left you.

You were scared and I could not move, she said. I know it. I should have moved when you reached for me, but I couldn't, and she blinked looking at him and shook her head as if still seeing that moment. I couldn't leave my birds. But I understand. I understand why you left. You were broke and scared and had to run, and as she said it her voice rose quickly, snapping like the awnings in the wind whipping faster above the street.

I just couldn't see you with him no more, A.D. said. Not for all those months and days and it just tore me up to know it. That you were with him.

Well, you don't have to worry about that now, do you? And she touched his lips, leaving her finger lingering there a moment. I always felt you back then, looking at me, feeling me with your heart, and John Hill's nothing to me anymore. Nothing. That's all he was anyway, but I forced myself not to see it, with all the gifts he gave me. With all the attention. But of course when it came right down to it, he was the first one to leave me in that room and the first one to accuse you of lighting it. Well—and she laughed a short quick bird laugh then, something that twittered and jumped from her throat—I put a stop to that right away, when I stepped out of that smoke. You should have seen me. I scared him half to death in the process. Dr. Alpionaire too.

She smiled and that short wan face of hers grew warm in the telling and the laughter buzzed from A.D. as surely the spotlights buzzed now too with the great electricity of the ridge surging closer and closer until . . . *FZZZT* . . . one bright burst sent a dozen glowing sparks dancing in a shower of glass to their feet. Another round of cheers went up because Runnymede had just then pointed to the air on the final drumbeat and bowed as if the whole world could now come to an end for he was finished and off to Nashville where he had his next pressing engagement. You could listen to it by dialing up the WSM. He said it just like that and thanked the other bands before him—all 'cept us of course—and that was the one thing I remember most. That slight, that singular omission (and it was what I would later tell A.D. that would move him finally against Runnymede from then on), though at the time, I held my tongue. For A.D. had no earthly idea what universe he was in to hear this last satisfaction from Ms. Clara May's own lips, about what had befallen old John Hill Carter after her miraculous reappearance.

What? What happened to him?

What should have happened long before, but it just took his final cowardice to bring it all out in me. My wrath, and she raised her hand in front of A.D. shaking her perfect white fist. I held up the bird cage to him then. I still had it, you know. I had walked through the smoldering hallways after the two of you tried to help. I don't know why, but I had to wait for the birds to die. I had to know they were in a better world than what I was and at peace after the smoke had robbed them of their last little breath. Their perfect voices. I was lucky to wait as long as I did. A timber fell then in front of me and sort of cleared the way of that burning rug. I stepped right across the glowing beam and made it to the hallway, and then out into the courtyard, and still I hadn't been able to unclench my fists but I'd felt the heat on my neck, rising, rising all the while as it burned.

You still had the cage? A.D. said as the wind whipped harder and the crowd cried out, dispersing.

There was just something about those birds, she said, and she finally un-clenched her fist to look at her hand, twirling her short white fingers in the rain. They were this perfect thing that he couldn't see. That he could never see. The birds. They were all I had. Their voices. Their music. It all came down to the birds and I couldn't let them go, even as I watched them wither and drop from their perches. Even as their bright yellow wings smoldered on the edg-es, browned by the flames. She became quiet then, remote, saddened by the thought of her birds, of their perfection. Because I thought it would be like that forever at the Peabody. That there would be nothing else in my life but looking at the birds and listening to them sing and singing myself. I don't know. I guess I thought it was my right, of walking through the courtyard each day in the bril-liant sunlight, of sitting with my friends on the benches, of having nothing else to do the whole day but sing, and I couldn't leave them. I couldn't. Don't you see? Leaning up, she scoured his face then, looking into his now rain-soaked eyes, imploring him to listen, to hear her, which he could only do. Because that would have taken it all away from me, A.D., that world, it would have collapsed it. For I kept thinking, if I'd only realized early on what John Hill was, it would have been different. It would have ruined the illusion and dream of it all: of going to the Peabody and meeting a rich boy, of singing for all I was worth and having everything laid out perfect for me so far from Norfolk where Sissy and Clement needed everything I could give just to exist. Just to get by. So when the fire started, I couldn't see it anymore. I couldn't see my dream turn out so wrong. But of course it did, and I know now I can never get it back, the essence of it, that spirit, and so I still see John Hill to this day, looking at you and lighting that goddamn lighter. Then turning and running from me. That was when he vanished forever from my life. When I stepped out onto that smoke-billowed street, he shot bolt upright from a bench and pointed speechless with his big fat mouth drooping open, his lit cigarette falling to the street.

He was smoking? A.D. said.

Even as the Peabody blazed in the night. Well, by then he was already jabbering to Dr. Alpionaire about you two in particular. He spoke about the way you'd busted in, with how you held a lit torch to his face threatening him the whole while, saying that if he didn't leave me at once you'd do it, you'd burn it all down. He was hollering for the constable to track you already. For a posse to be rounded up and munitions to be loaded, as if we were all still down on his plantation and some runaways had just taken off, and yet he stopped his nonsense when he saw me. His eyes narrowed as I stepped closer. Leaning down, he looked at my smoldering skin and sniffed me. He sniffed me! Before holding his palms out as if that was it, some appeasement or gesture that meant we were right again, that he had done everything he could to save me.

It was the boy, he said, watching me close. The boy and that nigger. They did this.

No, I said.

Clara? he said then, and straightened himself up to his full height. As if it might straighten out my own recollection, as if it might influence everything I'd ever thought about him that wasn't true. Clara. He looked at me, his hard eyes imploring.

It was you, I said, YOU, and I must have screamed it for the people carrying their water buckets and hoses turned as if the very night was charged with my voice. They watched dumbstruck then as I swung my fist up to his fat, sweaty face and held the cage there as it seared his cheek and nose and forehead with the thin burned lines that he carries to this day. Marked by his own failure. Marked for all time, and she took A.D.'s hand in her own as she said it, pulling him close. I've marked him for you. I've done that. Even now he walks the streets of Richmond destitute and alone. His own daddy won't see him, she said with a grim smile; he is shunned by those who know him and reviled by those who don't. She was finished, and satisfied with the telling looked up at A.D. who smiled back with a calm leveling smirk that lit his whole face and sent a deep chill down my spine. Turning then, they walked off arm in arm, oblivious to the staccato chorus of the snapping awnings and rain drumming like God's own percussion with not a soul left 'cept the few coloreds who'd been charged with striking the stage and clearing the street. And me.

XV

The sound that so charged her ~ Over a glazier's shop ~
Their courtship begins ~ The Honorable Reverend Michael
Williams ~ Behind the shadows and pews ~ I finally step
forward in the Lord's house ~ The body swinging in the
trees ~ They take what they want ~ Only silence and wind

WELL THE DAYS GREW INTO WEEKS, and the weeks into months, and
the fall weather fell upon us and the world slowed down beneath its cold hypnotic eye. I would go for days at a time without seeing A.D. since I knew it
was his first time being so young and in love. As for Ms. Clara May, she said
she'd heard our song on the radio and stood stock-still to know it was her own
name being sung and revered in such a way and that she knew it was A.D. and
me playing for she'd made a point of straying near our boiler room door at the
Peabody, hoping to gather the courage to knock and ask to sing with us. Or, at
the very least, to sit closer to the sound that so enchanted her. But always another student would walk by or she'd see Mr. Vickers fumbling down the long
stairwell, and she'd skitter off with the hope of one day getting the chance to
ask A.D. about his singing and our songs. But after she'd listened and knowed
it was us, she heard tell we was from Bristol, and so she up and headed south to
find us. She'd even rented an apartment in the middle of town over a glazier's
shop with the money the Peabody had given her for her fire-licked skin (and
other minor injuries, which she'd healed quick enough from; she was always
so strong in that regard), and just bided her time. Walking the streets, she'd
calculated and remembered street signs and such until she'd just seen us (of all
things) take the stage that night. She hadn't taken her eyes off A.D. since. So
I let them be in their courtship for a while, for I knew it was something you
couldn't get in the way of no matter what you tried or wanted for yourself. Any-

ways, it made sense enough for me to see them so joined for what they'd been through, with always missing each other as if at the opposite ends of life—with him right off the street, and her a decorated student—so now they just needed to be alone for their affections to take hold.

In any case, I had my own path to follow in those days, and my own chores to do. Now that I finally found myself alone without A.D. dragging me off on some other quest for names or faces or some lost song, I set to fixing up my broken-down home. I needed to plaster up holes and lay brick and stone to make it habitable before the cold came in and the snows hit hard in the upper ridge dusting it all like stardust and a crystal wonderment. O I did love to walk amongst that magic wonderland at dawn, traipsing through the stillness of the ridge thick with snow as the sun glimmered through the towering tree boughs. Just thinking about all that delicate beauty made me miss my Annie and Lucy girl, and so when I wasn't rebuilding our house, I visited with the Honorable Reverend Michael Williams, and beseeched him and his congregation for any information about my family. I reckon they never in their whole lives imagined they'd see me again, even if the reverend didn't seem too surprised.

ISAIAH HARDY, HE SAID, IN HIS DARK RASPY voice that third Sunday after service. I'd finally built up enough courage to speak to him and to show myself from behind the shadowy pews where I'd hid the past two weeks. O it had been nice enough to find out from Ms. Clara May that they weren't looking for us in Baltimore, not for the arson and general dishevelment of the Peabody. But I still couldn't be sure they weren't still looking for me in Bristol. Not after what I'd done to that old Hackett fellow, the one I'd killed for my sweet Annie, stringing him up in the woods for all to see, and it haunted me. It did. To know I had to leave right after it, as if my own life were ending. Never to see them again nor touch them, nor to lose the feeling of loving them the way I had, and to know that I could not go back for them ever, not for all the world. And then for all those years to feel pursued and lost from them like a dog really, or worse, made me struggle now to speak, to stand up, to find out what had happened to them, and reclaim some broken piece of me. To finally put to rest that past pain.

(Though I should say right here that that old Hackett fellow never haunted me in the least. Not since he'd only got what he had coming. But the ghost of my old life sure did. It was still there in my mind, calling me, beseeching me, because I'd listened to it return each Sunday as the Honorable Reverend Michael Williams sermonized, as the thoughts and feelings rose above me as atop a wave, before carrying me off in their sweet current.) Because he certainly had a way of talking, of shaking his hands in the light of the steeple amidst all the music and thunderous amens of the people crowding the aisles, that it felt as if I'd never left in those moments. That all the intermingled years had been but a blur. A dream. A terrible nightmare that I could finally erase. For the most powerful and vivid memories of my wife and baby girl came back to me in those moments, so that I could still feel Lucy in my arms, holding her in that same pew. Or, I'd recall watching Annie's soft brown profile next to mine: her brown wicker hat atop her head, her round cheeks moving as she whispered her prayers along with the reverend, and it made me shy that first Sunday. And a little bit scared the next. To know what I had to do, to finally change my way of running and hiding after all those years and step forward from behind my long, sad face, which I'd hung like a mask till then before me, wiping it most perpetual with a white handkerchief. Or shading it with my hands, so that the ones who might remember me wouldn't, and the ones that couldn't remember me, wouldn't suspect nothing when I finally did step forward, showing my helplessness at last. After I'd got my courage up and walked out amongst them at the end of service, remembering all the while how I used to be part of it, the community, for I knew then I could ask him about my family, and where they could have possibly gone.

The Honorable Reverend Michael Williams, I said and shifted in my boots. Hello, and I looked at my hands. They were long and hung at the end of my arms, for I couldn't think of any other place to put them or what words to conjure after all those years of running. The pews had hushed to an eerie silence behind me, and as I took another step forward, I seen not a few familiar faces shade their eyes and squint to place me in their minds and then shake their heads to know it was me for sure, remembering at last what I'd done. Though with a soft subtle movement, that was it. He shook his hands, as if doing nothing more than straightening the bone cufflinks he always wore, and the whole congregation stepped out much quicker and quieter into the cold autumn sunshine. Then it was just us—in the lord's house—me and the reverend, eyeing each other.

You're old, he said, and stepped from behind his tall pulpit, a cracked brown Bible in his hand. Much more so than I would have thought.

It's been seven years, I said, and touched my gray stubbly chin and sideburns, before leaning against a pew. Seven long ones.

Seven ones of sinning? he said. Or seven on the bright side, on the side of redeeming?

I have no redeeming in me for that man, sir. Never will.

He looked on me then in a silence so long I thought we'd slipped into a seam of time itself, something held out only for the dead. Something awful and lonesome where life outside had ceased altogether. But then after some imperceptible shift in his mood, or thinking on me perhaps—or maybe just because the light had shone in a brighter burst through the upstairs windows as the clouds raced past—he moved again. Raising his Bible, he set it behind him on the pulpit before turning toward me with a water pitcher in his hand and two small glasses. He motioned for me to come forward, and as I did, I watched him pour the two glasses before handing me one. I was most considerable dry. More so than I thought possible standing before him, seeing his gray eyes and the deep lines in his cheeks reach down and down into his flesh, as if to touch his soul perhaps, marking everything he did inside him with their time. The lines. Lord, I hadn't thought I'd see the lines again, and gulped the whole glass in a rush and then held the glass in my hands as he sipped slow and steady and wet his thick brown lips, before setting his glass back on the pulpit. Hackett, he finally said.

Yes, sir. Hackett's his name.

And his people come to me the very next week after they found the body swinging in the trees, and even the people above Hackett come—the overseer above the overseer. They come unto me and even touched me in the house of the lord. For they said I knew you and what you'd been planning and so they stayed and scared off the congregation on a Sunday when we were all set to pray. Even the men I thought might help me in a time such as that were sent away, and it was only me and them. All those white devils in the house of the Lord talking and conspiring about you. You alone, son.

I shifted in my boots to hear the hurt in his voice. I still had the empty glass in my hand and looked at it, bowing my head. A few last drops still rested in the bottom, and as he waited for me to say something, I shook the glass to make the drops quiver around the edge, but I couldn't make anything budge. Hell. I breathed then to steady myself, but could still feel the shaking in my arms, and I had to move them again just to feel free of the moment and awkwardness and shame. Well, I'm real sorry about that, sir. I never meant to harm you, nor your church.

Not to harm me? he said. Or my church! and reaching out, he took the glass from me and slammed it on the pulpit next to the pitcher. You kill a white man and think no harms gonna come to no one else? To the ones that know you?

But you knew that man, sir. You knew what he done.

Yeah, I knew him. I knew what he was. Everyone did, and he took the wire-rimmed spectacles from his face, wiped his eyes with his big black hand, and set his spectacles back on his face. But you didn't have to hang him, boy. Not after he was already dead.

Didn't they hang enough of us over the years? Didn't they drive us down into the ditches with the hogs?

Lord, lord, he said and bowed his head as the darkness of the clouds slanted in as if to take away every last hint of daylight and goodness. They take what they want, Isaiah. You know that. They always have. Always will. It don't matter what. They take it and use it for their own need and the lesser amongst us be damned. It's been like that forever and always will be. Even if it's not them doing it, it'll be someone else. Someone else to fill the gap. Someone else to do the deed. So I suppose you were the next one to do the deed, taking Hackett's life, even if he was a miserable sonofabitch to begin with. Even if his own people knew it. But that day they come in here, they watched Annie and Lucy as they left the front steps. They were gathered on horses and in a few Model Ts cause I guess they meant to chase after you, even with you having a week's head start. But there must a been something about Annie that moved them. Some quiet sense. That way she had of looking down and never breaking her silent concentration with her beauty. She was beautiful, and I had a mind to follow them, your wife and baby girl, but that woman had a head on her even if you didn't. Some say she'd already used her savings for train tickets and never did say goodbye. Never said a word. I thought I'd hear from her long before you. Thought it would be a letter here, a letter there. Something from her people up in Brunswick, Maryland or Oneonta, New York, but all I got were your letters and that money you sent. All that blood money you thought would a buyed back your soul. He'd stepped within a few inches of my face. The big black bulb of his nose was level with mine. Breathing his sour breath on my cheek. The tips of his boots touching mine. Did you think you'd get it back so easy? And so quick? Well? Did you?

I looked at him feeling nothing but the silence of my Annie, the silence of the words she never spoke to no one, not even to the reverend, and the pain of it all. Annie's pain and shame in having to walk amongst them with her head bowed and embarrassed. Walking amongst those that were her own community, her own people, and not getting anything back from them by way of sympathy or compassion, and it sent a shiver down my spine. I had a sudden icy feeling then for the reverend, too, like he must have had for me, for the words rose cold and slow from me, and even to this day I would not take them back if I had to. I might only add to them and make them harsher and colder. Well, the money was for them, sir, like I wrote. Or didn't you look after that, neither? Hiding away from folks here, making them feel ashamed when all they need is some help from you. When all they need is some—

You son of a . . . He was furious, but caught himself and bowed a moment whispering some invective or curse—I can't rightly say—though the redness of his rage shined in his cheeks and I'd never thought this was how it would go. I never thought a man of the cloth would hate someone so in his own church, someone who'd come before him with the most honorable intention. But he'd composed himself enough to spew at me again. I damn well know what you wrote, he said. I read it, didn't I? You just lucky Hackett's people didn't give a damn about him, neither. O they put up a show. Had too. Couldn't have a town full of niggers running around killing and carrying on. But then of course the company come in and bought up all that land anyways and it amounted to nothing. They still haven't planted it. Supposed to be surveying for minerals. Manganese or something. But then they got bought up, too. I don't know. Don't care neither. He'd stepped back from me. There were steps behind the pulpit, and I could hear him stomping down them, still cursing my name before breathlessly stomping back up with a big white envelope in his hands. An envelope he thrust at me huffing from the exertion of stomping around so furiously, and on the lord's day at that. Then without another word, he pushed me so forcefully in the chest I almost fell sprawling against the pews and rows, but righted myself enough to put my hands to the front doors pushing them aside. Then we were out on the steps in the cold autumn light, the wind scattering leaves and bits of paper at our feet.

But I still have to know about Annie, sir. I still have to know if you've heard from her, if you know anything.

There's nothing to know, he said. She gone. She gone and took that baby with her and you can't come back here no more. Not after what you brought me. Not after all that worry. This here's the last of it and then I will be done.

Done with what?

With you. With it. With all the darkness you brought down upon me. It will be done and I will be free. I know it. Here, he said, and pushed me again, pushing the envelope tighter to my chest before turning with a quickness I hadn't thought possible in a man that old, shutting the doors and locking them, for I could hear the heavy bolt slide in the cold brass slot.

But I'm here alone, sir. Alone, I repeated the word but couldn't hear his loud stomping boots no more, and thought he was still there, still waiting on the other side of those doors. Or praying maybe to be done with me for good—and so I banged on the door and shook the handle just to rile him for what he'd done to me—for throwing me out. For raging on me with his eyes and words and guilt about what had been done to him, when it sounded as if he hadn't even been hurt in the slightest, just inconvenienced whilst all my family and life had been lost, just as much as Hackett's had been lost. Though at least I'd been loved, at least I'd been respected, and had lost that much more in the bargain. Reverend? I said. Reverend, what would your god say about you now? What's in your heart? But there was only silence. Only silence and wind and then my hands tearing open the envelope to find what he'd left me, what he'd needed so desperately to give me. I had to sit down then to see it, to finally realize what it was—the sum total of the ninety-two letters I'd sent in the seven years since I'd left—$538 dollars in cold hard cash.

XVI

The instrument of my music ~ In a halo of windblown
leaves ~ Stitched from the same cloth ~ Just a name ~ The
odd fire that burned in him ~ At Ezra Lee's house ~ Women
of the working variety ~ The entanglements of certain
distinguished gentlemen ~ Pushed into all that abandonment

A SMALL PORTION OF THAT MONEY BOUGHT ME a sirloin steak that
night, with fresh-baked apple pie on the side. While for dessert, I bought a bottle of the finest Scotch I could find, took it home, and drank it to its conclusion.
Cursing to the rafters the reverend's name, I slumped in a beat-up chair in the
den of my broken-down house, watched a fire blaze in the chipped-up fireplace,
and listened to the wind rattle the shutters and boarded up windows. That man,
I said and drank until I could feel my body loosen from its wound-up rage over
what the reverend could not help me with—with what he would not help me
with—even after all that time.

O I sat there for what seemed an eternity and watched the deep red flames
and light-blue essences collapse amidst their endless energies and diverging
paths. And when I tired of that, I watched the shadows of the fire dance upon
the rafters—for I had at least fixed them and most the slate shingles on the
rooftop—so that when the rain and snow did come, it would not touch me
here in the confines of my home. O but I wanted my Annie to touch me here. I
wanted to see her again and look upon her dark brown skin and wide thick lips
as she stood next to me, or over me, as we touched. That she would be there.
That she was here. Yet in thinking on her so long and lost, another pain took
hold inside me. Like the one I'd known in thinking of her bowing her head in
her own church when the reverend and congregation shamed her after what
I'd done to that man—after what that man had done to her!—when those

white devils had shown up to chase me afterwards for it. So I sorted through the letters I'd written to the reverend to give to her, the letters she'd never held, never read, nor knowed I sent, and arranged them all in a row, and then placed them one by one into the fire.

O the paper caught and sent up a bright flare of light and always in the sudden illumination I would see her, standing at the sink washing and peeling potatoes into the bucket. Or swaying on her bare feet, with Lucy cradled in her arms, singing to our child. She was singing to her, and the sound of it was delicate and fleeting and never once seemed to rise into the distinction of anything that words could ever shape, and yet it was a sound that was lovelier than anything the human mouth could utter. It was beautiful and heartfelt with rhythms conjured from the depths of her. So that always in my playing, I'd sought to recreate that sweet perfect emotion, that deep rendering and divestment. Sounds that I'd only heard in my Annie's voice, with that purity and love. Always with her love. And in all my days and years since, there's only one sound I'd heard as perfect and true. It was Yancey Jakes' song for sure, the one he'd sung to us in the smokehouse on the ridge. The one he said he'd never give to old Burlhead or any other, and I got the inkling then to play it, to breach its lost power, to somehow spell me from my sadness with its beauty. Groping in a haze, I reached for my guitar, but couldn't find it, and the shape of myself seemed to bleed away then as a quake of stark panic set in upon the center of me, and I truly felt as if a shadow had descended across me entire. That it had swallowed me up.

Turning, I realized my sight was dimmed from staring into the flames, that the light from the fireplace didn't help me none in searching for my instrument. In fact, the light was washed out and made me touch my eyes to right them, but that didn't help neither. It was as if a milky stream of tears had begun to flow stretching before me into a dark expanse of boards and nails and planks that I could not see the end of, not entirely. Though I knew somewhere along those lengths, somewhere far away, or in another part of the world—in a space left only for them—stood my wife and baby girl. My family, and I reached out for them then. O I reached into the air, and all the thoughts and feelings that had built up inside me since I last looked on their faces came flooding back and my legs gave way and I found myself upon the floor with my ear pressed to the boards to maybe hear my Annie singing again. To hear my wife singing, or calling me back across the world. Was it possible? Could she call me back across the years and ridge and falling night? Could she release me from the pain of failing to find her again and again and again?

Isaiah?

I couldn't move. The voice was raw and scratchy and right on the other side of the door. With the shutters creaking and clanking in each gust, I about collapsed to hear it come so close and so soon after I'd just called out to her in my heart, calling into the world. And yet, as I listened closer, and hushed my beating heart—I could hear it wasn't her, that it couldn't be her. My Annie. There was something short and sharp in this voice. Something that could never be for me, not with its tight jagged-edged boundary, and as I opened the door, Ms. Clara May Staunton stood there instead, in a halo of windblown leaves and dried hay, unwrapping the bright red shawl she'd bundled about her hair. O the world seemed to swirl about her for another second as she shook her auburn curls on my doorstep.

It's you, I said, and still wasn't sure she wasn't just an apparition the Scotch had delivered to me in my loneliness. Stepping aside, I showed her to my fire, eager to do something—anything—to break the spell her appearance marked in me.

You're damn right it's me, she said. Her blue eyes shined like glints of far-away coal in the firelight, and I had to look away and set my hand again on my bottle so as not to suffer under eyes so pure and cold. Wrapping her shawl about her shoulders she said, And here I run all the way out here driving myself silly thinking on him and the shape he's in, and all I find is you're drunk, too. Well, it figures.

What figures, ma'am?

The two of you. You couldn't of been more stitched from the same cloth then if you walked around in one shirt. She shook her head and stared straight at me casting a horrid pall upon me with her blazing eyes. Excuse my curtness, she said finally, you'll find me a much nicer lady under more normal circumstances.

Circumstances? What circumstances? I had a feeling that only A.D. and his predilections could have raised such a fuss in his new love already, but after asking and getting only a mean, pleading stare from her, I asked again. What is it? What's made you so un-normal? I knew I shouldn't have said it as soon as I heard it, but it was out there now and wasn't coming back. Well, almost at once her small wan face scrunched up and her strong white hand set firm on her thin narrow hip and she stared at me with a face full of righteous anger. The time between us seemed to stretch and grow more lonesome by the second. Her jaw tensed up, and her sweet pink lips turned white and nibbled at the air, for she seemed determined to stand like that till the roof caved in and maybe hell froze over, too.

He's drunk, she finally said.

So am I, I said and hiccuped as if to put an exclamation point on it.

But what's worse is he's gone after some other name of his.

Name?

That's what he said—a name—and then he took off walking like a fool with his pants on fire the minute I turned my head.

Then he's close, I said, and closed my eyes to think of A.D. as drunk as I was and out there in the darkness, maybe with just his guitar slung over his back and nothing else. Going after nothing but a name, after something he repeated on his tongue like a prayer or destination. Something to guide him to his deepest and most pressing obsession. Even with her here now, too, he's gone off.

For a name.

After all this time, too, after thinking on her and wishing on her and putting her up on some golden pedestal—this vision, this Ms. Clara May Staunton, this special somebody he'd made up into an impossible perfection—she was flesh and blood for him now and he'd gone off for a name anyways. And now here she was in my den, standing before my fireplace, with all hellfire burning on her tongue.

She'd been burned up by one man (most literally), and finally got hold of another (A.D.), and knew him now as only two people can know each other behind closed doors, and was finally seeing the fire that burned in him, too. And damned if she wasn't prepared to dig in with both heels to stop his smoldering, for she'd certainly toughened up from what I could tell, in never intending to let her world flare up again. Not in the slightest. Not for anything. Even drunk, I could see that, and supposed I could forgive her for her brusqueness.

I turned to the fire again, as I could do nothing to quell the shiver that shot through me from the glare of her purposefulness, and thought I'm just a man alone in the ruin of his life, and look at what I've been called upon to do, to help my only friend, and I must do it. Even if this woman is as alien to me as the anger in the reverend's heart, I must do it. I hiccuped again to see my haggard face reflected in the Scotch bottle. My lips glistened from the drink and tears I'd wiped away when Ms. Clara May had arrived at my doorstep, when it was only my Annie and Lucy girl I'd yearned for. And I wondered if I was really the combustible one amongst us, if I was nothing more than dry tinder set to ignite in my desperation and despair. I shuddered again and stumbled away from the fire, just in case my body decided to catch alight right then and there. I knew that despite my pain and forlornness, I had to go get A.D., if only to keep him and Ms. Clara May from burning up on their own. 'Course I knew it was that way with love sometimes, all fiery and hot and confused, and then, sudden like, all cool and aloof, and who was I to judge between the two? All I knew was I had to bend myself to this task, to do it and be done with it, to go and bring him back so he could right whatever wrong he'd committed. So I turned to her eager now to go after our boy, ready for anything. I suppose you want me to go get him then? I said.

Good lord, she said, it took you that long to figure that out? She shook her head and smiled for the first time since I'd seen her and raised her snow white hand along the glistening skin crinkled on the back of her neck. It was like glass really, her skin, where the fire had been so direct it had changed her hairline for good, and so it would never grow long again in the back. Not after staying for a week in the hospital with them putting ointments and mustard salves on it the whole while, and that was why she kept it as short and trim as she did. To embrace how the flames marked her, to signify this fundamental change in her, and I rather liked it, her short curls. I told her so, too, later on, after the madness of this first incident was finally put behind us, when I learned to watch her neck from then on and gauge her moods by it. For it certainly gave me more information than her face did—though I don't think A.D. ever learned that trick.

He was a curious kind, A.D., but certainly not as hard to find as she'd first thought. In fact, he was only right over the next hill. You sure he said Ezra Lee? I asked again as she drove, even though I knew I'd heard it right the first time. (I just didn't want the silence to stretch again between us like it had in my house, with her cold blue eyes staring into the center of me and my drunkenness.) For I figured this might not be a singular occurrence, me running out to retrieve A.D., even if she didn't know it yet, this pattern of her betrothed.

I'm as certain about it as anything in my life, she said and never once took her hands from the wheel. I'd never seen a woman drive before and it shook me to feel so helpless under her control, guiding us as she did across the darkened land, veering and accelerating with an abruptness a little too irregular for my liking. Women hardly drove back then, but I certainly didn't want to say anything to her about it, for it looked as if she would a done whatever she wanted regardless of what any man could have said. Not least of which was to give A.D. a cold hard knock on the ear for running off from her already. So instead of watching her, I fiddled with the radio. O I worked it and tuned it until I got old

WSM on the dial, that Nashville station. For wouldn't you know it, as soon as I got it, old Runnymede was playing the same song he'd sung when Ms. Clara May and A.D. had stood beneath the gathering storm that night, when they'd found each other alive after all those weeks. And instead of turning to another station, to maybe offset the emotion already running a bit too high in the gal, I kept it there, and thought it an apt backdrop for the trouble we were heading in to, with A.D. already deep in Ezra Lee country, as the locals called it.

It was only 'bout two miles away. Ezra Lee's house. A man known far and wide for the singular distinction of the silver mouth harp he played that had been passed down from his late great-grandfather General Robert E. Lee. Ezra was known to put that harp to his lips in-between reciting hypnotic verses to the bodies he processed for a living. Working with a meticulous artistry and pomp, he had people signing up years in advance just to receive his service— all so he could look down into their souls (as it was reported) and give them the proper showing they deserved when they passed. Sure, I'd known it was a mortuary, and Ezra Lee an undertaker, but it was something A.D.'d just heard before Ms. Clara May showed up, and I figured he'd been counting on paying ol' Ezra Lee and his harmonica a visit. Knowing A.D. as I did, I guessed he'd grown listless after having lain with Ms. Clara May in her love nest so long, for even a day was too much for that boy to sit still.

If I hadn't had to go on account of A.D. running off in search of his names, I would a never set foot on Ezra Lee's property. It was a sprawling Southern-style plantation not only monumental in the old architectural way, but with the added history of keeping my kind as property in a shed row out back in years gone by. The dead bodies only added to its mystique. But it turns out the mortuary only took up the basement floor of the big central house, while it was oft told that Ezra Lee filled the upper rooms with women of the working variety, and that he ran a gambling parlor and cabaret inside the main floor that some of the best acts of Vaudeville, in its heyday, had once graced on a rotating basis. That was when Ezra was just a pup and his father Honus did the mortuarying. So I guess you could say it was a family business.

As we drew close, the air was filled with sound. The place was ablaze with lights set behind two of the tallest oaks I'd ever seen, so it looked as if the treetops were lit with new-fangled stars just come down to roost in the lower reaches of heaven, they shined and sparkled so. O I looked on them and had to blink my eyes and turn away.

And that sound! I scoured the green dial to see if that was its origin, but it was not. Listening closer, and closing my eyes, there was even a moment amidst all this commotion of movement and arrival, when an otherworldly sensation crept over me, that caused me to touch my pocket for I still had a wad of my just-returned reverend money and was worried about it. I tucked that wad further down, figuring the sound was the siren call of Ezra Lee's women and gambling wheel, that there was devilment and temptation in the air trying to reconfigure my body, tuning it to a frequency I had not had to worry about before with my Annie at my side. Back then the oft-told tales of Ezra Lee's place and the entanglements of certain distinguished gentlemen never concerned me in the least. But now those tales did concern me. They did indeed.

Steeling myself, I recalled everything I'd ever heard about Ezra Lee's place, about its illicit depravity and greed. Yet I was in such a sweat to hear that eerie note persist—since it so captivated and removed me from the pressing need of reaching A.D.—that I wondered if I could still do this, if I could go into that teeming house and re-emerge unscathed. For I could see it now, as we rounded the last bend: A bright red bonfire raged outside while a daisy chain of grotesque figures danced about it, their arms raised with sticks and instruments, as the silhouette of some suckling pig or goat roasted on a spit. The front porch was crowded with over a dozen men going in and out, as periodic blasts of rambling music echoed when the door opened and the clinking sound of chips and currency seemed to craft its own underlying rhythm of barter and exchange. While from the higher windows, red-tinted shades wavered now and then, the only glimpses of tenderness and invitation the house deemed fit to offer the larger night.

I looked upon all of this as if in a stupor, held in some strange enchantment. There was laughter in the night. It scattered up over the yard and across the tops of the cars Ms. Clara May parked beside, and I wondered if my Annie was laughing somewhere too now in the world, laughing with my daughter? It was an image I wanted to keep in my mind, if only to save me, or keep me whole while facing the horde of depravity soon to be unleashed upon us. And I began to hum along to that clear sweet note that persisted even as Ms. Clara May turned off the engine and I watched the green radio dim and then blacken on its dial. I tapped it once to be sure, for I still heard that sweet note ringing in my head and could feel my voice intertwine with it as I gathered all my drunken courage to proceed. Even when I stepped out, it was still there, and I passed my hands across my face for the tears began to pour at its sweet persistence. There was a truth hovering in me with this sound. There was something deeper in its naming, in its formlessness and reach, and even as I stood before the blackened untruth of that house, I could feel the harmonious depths of that music buffeting me up in that moment. Buffeting me up for what I had to retrieve—a life—and A.D.'s life at that.

Isaiah? Ms. Clara May said, for she had watched me wipe my eyes twice before stopping as the sweet note ceased as she spoke. What is it? What?

I looked at her then for a long moment, far longer than when we'd stared at each other in my house. It was you, I said. You, and I touched my ear to show her I knew she'd been singing on the way here without even knowing it, harmonizing with Runnymede on the radio. For as she stepped away and scowled into the night, her face scrunched up and tense, she never once denied my suggestion nor pretended to allow it, but just swept her hand along the glassy skin beneath the edge of her hair, and so that was what I watched as she pushed her way right into the midst of all that abandonment.

XVII

The blaze ~ To the darker corners for gambling ~ That mean
midget ~ In their individual fugues ~ Of fire and war and
Man's eternal conflagration ~ Dousing it with ether ~ The
matter of Ms. Clara May ~ The rosy sparks ~ Surrounded by
scoundrels and fire ~ Catullus ~ An otherworldly summons

A LARGE FAT MAN IN A BLACK HAT AND A SHORT STOUT ONE
in a blue coat stood by the bar directing people to different parts of the house.
But before I could stand there long enough to see if maybe they knew me, or I
them, Ms. Clara May had already pushed her way up to inquire about A.D.'s
whereabouts—but I don't think they heard. Or at least, they preferred not to
hear her, not above the din of voices calling and shouting in their ecstasy across
the room. For they thought she was a woman already working for Ezra Lee in
the upper rooms, and were confused by her long suede dress and brown wool
sweater, which was much too demure for that business.

The blaze, the midget said and smiled as I stepped closer. He winked and
made a swift motion like drawing a knife across his neck and it sent shivers
down my spine to think of whatever fiendish purpose he had in mind. I turned
to look at the people streaming past, as if to make some appeal for my safety,
but no one seemed to notice. They just filed on in their blind revelry to the
darker corners for gambling. Or to the wide lacquered bar along one whole side
of the room to drink. Or to the two red doors in back where women and men
and the periodic jolt of some somber singing emerged as they were opened and
closed and swung on their hinges like in some backwater saloon. Send him to
the blaze, Macon, send him.

Macon bent closer to his friend and whispered something pointing at me,
and as he did, I touched Ms. Clara May's arm to pull her away from those two

gentlemen. But she was so determined in continuing with her present endeavor, she just sloughed me off and leaned down to the face of that mean midget to ask him again if he knew where her man could have possibly got to.

His name is A.D., she said. He came here with a guitar. He came to see Ezra Lee.

Everybody's here to see Ezra, he said. The midget's face was greasy and shined in the heat, and for a moment, I thought he might reach up with his fat meaty lips to kiss her, she'd bent so close he might have done it if he'd tried. But he just sniffed her once and turned his face as he struck another cigarette and blew the smoke up to mix with the other emissions drifting about in a fetid brew of stale beer and vomit and spit that made a perpetual smog inside the room like its own shifting weather pattern. O it was something vague and grotesque the air, and acted as a substance that stretched and morphed the vision of most, and transfigured the shapes of others, so that I watched people stagger about in their individual fugues. I waved my hand, as if to waft it all away, and as another rush of people went past, Ms. Clara May and I were momentarily released from the inspection of those two gentlemen, as a line of people separated us from them. To find some distance between us had me breathing a bit easier, and I scoured the depths for A.D.'s tall lanky shape, but didn't have long to ease into any kind of comfort. From the back of some table, I spied something large and wavering and elusive rounding into view. Something that seemed to part the waters of the people milling about in their revelry. I had to watch then closer to believe it to be true. For as if on cue, they stepped from their positions of gaiety and mirth and quieted up considerable as the ritual procession of a man with a high burning wheel, balanced in his hands, walked through their midst.

The blaze. I could hear the midget giggling as the man brought the high wheel forward. It was attached to a platform studded with bolts and nails with various strings and feathers dangling from it, and as he set it on a small porcelain-topped table in front of me, another group of folks were being led across the room by one man in particular. A man with the blondest hair I'd ever seen. Hair so blonde it was almost white, and picked up on its gleaming surface the glinting flames that shimmered and danced and twisted in his short straight mane as of a fire embedded in the broad marrow of his skull. I could plainly see he was a man of much importance, for as he proceeded, the gathered customers swooned and preened and even held up their hands in reverence, as if to convey it was all they could do in their lives to finally touch the red velvet smoking jacket he wore, or the slender gold cigarette holder he clenched in his sparkling teeth. Or to point at the beautiful brown orientals he had attached at either arm. (Though I never did ascertain if they were man or woman or both, the orientals, the haze and stench of the place was such that the burning wheel relegated everything else to ruin.) Everything else seemed to pale in comparison to his high regal arrival, and to those wavering white flames—which stood stockstill now in their oiled positions. So that I knew the man approaching with a wry smile and powdered face would address me and me alone, for I could look at him level now through the center of the wheel and catch his each intention.

You have been called out most particular, he said, and stood there finally, after sauntering for what seemed like ages through the room as people bowed and shuffled away, as if asking with their own humility his final approval. And for that reason alone, I knew it was Ezra Lee, even though I'd never seen him before nor heard but tale and rumor concerning his name—a name which always sent up shivers and an uneasy air through the ranks of all assembled wherever it was mentioned.

I have been called out for nothing, I said.

O but you have, and with a subtle motion he nodded and the two orientals drifted off from both sides and I could see for the first time the black polished holster he wore at his hip—just under the edge of his velvet smoking jacket— with General Robert E. Lee's silver harmonica sticking out from inside it. The top embroidered plate had caught the stunning glare of the burning wheel and seemed to sing in its beauty about fire and war and Man's eternal conflagration. While as if held in stark contrast to the beauty of that instrument, Ezra clutched a blue handkerchief that he brought to his nose and breathed from before sighing and looking back at me as if through a new collection of eyes. Eyes which receded and dulled and brightened again, as he breathed deeper still more, as if tasting the wet cloth more truly. His lips parting deliciously. His shoulders slumping with a soft practiced release. And if I hadn't seen it myself I wouldn't have believed it in a million years, but the wee pink tip of his tongue edged out as he tittered and giggled as a lamb or baby goat might in a high whining dither.

A general wave of laughter rose in accordance across the room, but then fell silent just as quickly, as his body trembled and shook with spasms before he straightened his doughy body again, touching his jacket here and there as if to smooth it all away, his whole deranged self, before looking back at me. (At this point, he'd let the handkerchief fall and one of the orientals had picked it up as if gathering in a holy shroud to revere and esteem, before dousing it again with ether. I'd seen the brown bottle glide out effortlessly from a purse the oriental held before disappearing again as quickly.)

You have been called out for your impudence, he said and trailed a ruby-ringed hand along his pale white cheek. If I was meant to look at him, it worked, for there was nothing else in that room as far as my eyes were concerned. He was so striking in his white greasy face paint and rosy red lip gloss, and yet devilish to behold too, for the surreal profile he evinced in his each dramatic movement. Even the sounds and smoke that had so bombarded me before had dispersed. It was just him and me then, eyeing each other through that ring of fire, gauging what each might do.

Niggers don't walk the floor, he said, after what might have been an hour, for all I could tell. But I looked then to the bartender and dealers at the gambling tables, and even to the attendants at the red doors in back, and saw they were all black like me and in tuxedos that were too tight or uncomfortable for each. But they each to a man looked down after I'd caught their glances and I knew then I'd stepped where none of my color had dared step before.

I'm just looking for a man, is all. Just one. Ms. Clara May was at my side and shivered a bit. Her long thin arms were right up against mine and Ezra must have seen her in the shine of the flaming wheel, for his blackened mascaraed eyes moved from mine to hers as he closed his lips before opening them with a slight puckering sound to behold Ms. Clara May in all her beauty. Even in his condition, he could tell straight away she wasn't one of his girls roaming the crowd for tricks. Nor would she ever be.

You've been to a mortuary before, he told her.

Hesitating, she breathed deeply to see him concentrate on her and to my surprise did not look away nor subjugate him in the least with the quill of her sharp tongue. Instead, she seemed to melt beside me, melting right there into the floor, and dripped from all her previous rigidness. I have, she said.

And in the country like this, he fluttered his long black eyelashes at her. Out in the dark with the tombstones. Rummaging amongst the dead. O how it frightened you, and he shook his sharp narrow head as he watched her.

Yes, sir, it did.

And so you swore never to come back. His voice trembled now a bit from the ether, and from his invocation, and as I listened—as everyone did—we heard his breath rise an octave in accordance with the thin penciled eyebrows outlining his face. So that after he spoke his lips kept moving and jiggled a bit as he shook slightly his head watching her. For your father, he said.

Yes, sir, Ms. Clara May whispered, and kept her head bowed a long moment. For my father who's dead and gone now, sir.

But you're here again, he said and smiled a slight leading smile. Against all asking. Against even the darkness and the fear.

Yes, sir, I am. Even after I swore to him I wouldn't. Even after I promised I would never come back to see the places of the dead.

I watched then as the tears filled the barren spaces of her eyes. She was trembling and as soft as I'd ever seen her, and it was curious that all the sass in her had left at mention of her being in a place such as this, with her reluctance of ever returning for her father. She had opened up to Ezra Lee so easily, as if accepting every notion in his high, lilting voice, and stared directly at him through the brilliant ring not teetering nor blinking nor moving an ounce. Her short curls dazzled and shimmered in the heat as the crowd hushed to hear her confession, moving in that much closer to be near her, pushing almost on top of us so that I feared her being so close to the fire, and it reminding her of her first death, as it were, the one A.D. and I had thought she'd suffered at the Peabody. But now she only seemed tempted by Ezra Lee. It was as if he knew something about her just by looking and waiting. (And maybe that was his game all along, that insight into the shadows of others?) He had a way about him for sure, of focusing his eyes with a depth and deliberation I'd not seen. Something mesmerizing and dark played out beneath his gaze, for even as he performed his prophesying, I could hear my heart beat as Ms. Clara May took another step forward to be near him.

You've been touched by fire before, he said.

I have, and she turned once for all to see the skin on the back of her neck. As she did, and the crowd gasped, it did not stop one of the orientals from grabbing and guiding her head inside the wheel of fire, which was turned now on its edge so that Ms. Clara May stood inside it as the flames ascended around her on all sides.

I know, he said and stepped closer. His blue eyes narrowed in the shine of the heat. His red lips glistened as he licked them. Ms. Clara May was only a few inches from him, the wheel barely separated them, and his breath rich with ether alighted like a soft glimmer in the darkness. The flammable breath of the man. The rosy sparks. Fire, he finally said, so that all leaned in closer to hear. A delicate fire. In the flesh.

Ms. Clara May brought her hand up to her neck and it was as smooth as could be and yet there she was, surrounded by scoundrels and fire and that hypnotizer himself, swallowing whole her body and soul with his voice, and I didn't have the first notion as to what to do, to bring her back. There has been fire on me before, she said, her voice soft, her eyes fluttering in the white shine and then closing of her own accord as Ezra leaned one hand out and touched a candle flame. Trailing his fingers there for seconds and seconds, the crowd marveled to see how calmly he stood as if the flame was his only companion.

O my dear, he said, leaning in closer. I knew there was fire in you. I could practically smell it, and as he sniffed her ravenously the crowd sent up another wave of laughter, even as he hushed them with his powdery face. And yet it is in everyone from the first, he continued, but in you most particular, and as he pulled his hand out finally, he touched his steaming palm upon Ms. Clara May's forehead as a backwoods healer might to the lame and penitent. Everyone close could hear the sad sizzle of her skin and smell the slight acrid burning, like a few hay straws lit by the summer sun, and gaped to know she'd been marked by the great man and auger. So this will be your new beginning, he continued, your true birth. And just so no one can be jealous of us, he said, as he smiled and turned to the crowd that laughed at every little thing he did, he kept his hand there as he leaned even closer to her soft white face and recited some secret verse. His eyes closed now as if consumed by the devilish rite, whispering with his lips to her cheek, before speaking louder as he finished, as if commencing the passage of some prophesy and pact, reciting for all to hear: When he finds out how many kisses we have shared, and we sleep a never ending night.

Catullus? You cannot use Catallus against us! The voice was loud and cut across the ghoulish ceremony, so that all turned to see the red doors swinging wide as A.D. strode tall and otherworldly toward us carrying his black guitar gleaming. His eyes were ablaze to see the crowd so hushed and his own Clara May stranded in the wheel of fire. In truth, I was not sure what he might do. There was an air to him of something invincible, as if he'd been returned to the words and verse he loved most, after drifting these past months since his studies at the Peabody, that to hear them used against his love was a betrayal of everything he was. So, he said, as his long lean face scowled in the light, let us judge all the rumors of the old men to be worth just one penny. And then he was there, standing at the wheel, and as Ezra eyed him, A.D. flicked from his thumb one shiny coin in the air so that Ezra had to stand back shocked and awestruck to see the object hurtling in the room above all the gathered heads before falling in its perfect arc straight upon him until—PLOP—it landed on his greasy forehead and the crowd stared to see it stick there as if glued immortal to the man's hot skin.

You! Ezra gasped, and he made as if to grasp the coin from its firm place but couldn't get hold of it and just smeared the paint into his hair and eyebrows and lashes. You come here to steal songs from me—and then even after what I saw in you—you do this? Usurper! Dilettante! You know she's not yours any longer. She's not even of the same substance.

A.D. had gotten Ms. Clara May out from beneath the wheel before I knew it. Then with one quick thrust, the flames shot up bright and unwieldy as the crowd fell back and the wheel lurched unhinged from its tether, before spinning like a top on the floor. There was a great shouting behind us, as the greasy leather coat of that mean midget caught fire, and the crowd froze in an amused stupor to watch dumbfounded and inert as that short ridiculous man flailed about and twisted in a frenzy of flame. There were only faces then. Hard inquisitive eyes emerged from the dim recesses of the room. A.D. was before me, and I watched as he pulled Ms. Clara May, grabbing her car keys before we even reached the door.

There was no one to stop us. No one even conscious enough to try. There was just Ezra Lee silhouetted in the dark glare of the room. Ezra Lee furious, bending above the smoldering form of that midget, breathing his bright ether breath upon him, the rosy sparks mingling in the air, the shiny coin still wedded to his flesh. As if he'd been paid down for something, paid some otherworldly summons or decree, before leaning back and laughing to the ceiling, then finally reaching down to lick the wheel of fire.

XVIII

From the house of the dead ~ Those red swinging
doors ~ The mark that stayed with her ~ The bleak augury of the man ~ Something sparse and nebulous
~ Our next pressing engagement ~ The black creosote and oil ~ Raspberries and some kind of fruition ~
The taste of memory gone ~ That one divine note

GAIUS VALERIUS CATULLUS. That was all I heard from then on from those
two. Or Sappho. Or Alfred, Lord Tennyson. Or even Rumi and Juvenal and
about the sad, wandering visionaries Arthur Rimbaud and Charles Baudelaire
on the gay streets of Paree! O they poured through their piles of books like they
hadn't in ages and I might not see A.D. lift his head for whole hours while I
tried to get him to pick up his guitar and play.

It was a curious time. Even though we'd escaped untouched as it were from
the house of the dead that Ezra Lee had concocted on that dark-rimmed land, at
night all that week and even for years after, I had visions of those red swinging
doors, of the women I'd seen in their gaudy face paint and skimpy lace stockings
roaming the crowd. I did not think my Annie would have had to succumb to
such downhearted ways to provide for my Lucy girl, but I couldn't be sure, and
so Ezra Lee's greasy white face haunted my dreams. It was no premonition nor
harbinger for his returned presence into our lives, but its image would surface
as from a black lake, or burning pulse of sky. Most nights I couldn't tell if it was
him or not. But then I'd see a line of girls disappear as cattle through a red-tinted maze arranged like sweep chutes where the men lined up to take their turn
branding them with their hot glowing irons, and I'd know for sure he'd come
back to haunt me. I'd sit bolt upright from my pallet and have to wipe my
sweaty brow to remember the single acrid singe of Ezra's burnt fingers on Ms.
Clara May's forehead.

It was a mark that stayed with her for years. Something subtle and off color that you might not have noticed if you hadn't known where to look—almost as if it was little more than a shadow of our ragged collection of lives. Like a smudge she might have gotten from leaning her head against a dusty lintel, or cooking above a woodstove without washing. Or even, from the graceful fall of an autumn leaf, though it was certainly something none of us ever wanted to talk about. Especially not with the smooth way Ezra had with her that night, of speaking right into her fears about her father and the mortuary and the deep sense of fire in her. O the fire! And the bleak augury of that man that still laid somewhere hidden behind his lips, an augury perhaps that Ms. Clara May might have discovered if we'd stayed there just a moment longer, her head burnished in the wheel of fire, the crowd pushing in on all sides . . . Listen to me, going on like Ezra Lee was something sane to behold, something true, with words for everyone. For I can honestly say that that mark might have easily faded from her before anyone could have witnessed it. Anyone but me, that is. For I seen it, and would to this day, I reckon, if she were here.

But I digress, and apologize, for I'd asked A.D. about those red doors and what was behind them on several occasions, and why he'd even been there in the first place and what Ezra had seen in him. But he just looked at Ms. Clara May standing there pretty and unconcerned a few steps away, mixing something in a wooden bowl, or looking on him from their opposite high-backed chairs, where they sat in her apartment reading, and he'd mumble something sparse and nebulous about seeing in person Ezra Lee's silver harmonica, and that was it. He'd stick his nose back in his book as if I'd never asked. O but I knew inside he was hiding something else about his visit to Ezra Lee's, and so I stepped back to consider him and let him ease off a bit from my suspicion. I had other plans anyways that involved A.D., and even Ms. Clara May, plans I'd only recently concocted and hadn't brought up yet with Benjamin Marks. For he figured in them too, I suppose, even though he'd only recently resurfaced. The very next week, after we were still a bit awestruck about our narrow escape from Ezra's wheel of fire, there he was again to prod us about our next pressing engagement.

In Leesburg, he said, and I thought he was kidding since he'd heard us mention Ezra Lee at least once throughout the course of the morning. Though after that we shortened it to just E's on account of the unease it sent shivering through us, quivering like an arrow. Yet when I watched him, I got the feeling there was something more about Benjamin, something in the wrinkles of his tired eyes that made me suspect he'd known more about it than he let on, as if he himself had been there that night. That maybe he was a regular in that house of the dead, trudging into those dank, clove-scented rooms. The little hunchback seeking his pleasure from that carousel of anonymous flesh, indistinct from the others, the depravity and suffering of man and woman alike, who could not quell their desires. For when he stepped close enough to me that morning, taking off his corduroy coat (we were well into January by then and already cold), I caught a whiff of that burning wheel, of the black creosote and hypnotic oil on that wooden rim. The scent rose round me in a vapor, and must have mixed in the creases of his white calico shirt, for it brought out the vision of Ezra Lee upon my eyes. I had to stand then in the small apartment and strum my guitar by the window just to rid myself of it, I was still so uncertain I could ever get that ghastly face behind me. And now that A.D.'s nose was so far in those poetry books of his, I wondered if I'd ever get him to play the songs we'd so loved to find, and if Ezra and those damnable red doors had more to do with his reading then I supposed?

Leesburg? I finally said, looking out on State Street, as Bristol shook off its Sunday finery and settled back into its Monday morning drudge. A thin white veil of snow had fallen, and seemed some abnegation, or wearing away, as if the white bony meal of life lay bare now for all to see.

That's right, Benjamin said and twisted in his chair to watch Ms. Clara May, taking out his ridiculous brass pocket watch all the while. It was a gesture someone must have told him would give him a refined character and high-falutin' air in the music business (though I don't even think the thing worked, since I'd seen the glass cracked in not a few places and the twin hands wrenched). But he loved it so, and snapped the case shut after opening it as if his time was of a timbre and eminence more important than what anyone else could have had. O he had that sort of snobbishness down pat, and that was one of the things I liked about him, since at least I knew where he stood. But I sure couldn't say the same for what he might have wanted underneath it all, bubbling in his soul. He had the beadiest little brown eyes that swung about the room almost continual as he spoke, but which finally froze on Ms. Clara May. For he sure liked watching her, and I wasn't sure, but I wondered if he'd noticed her glassy skin too, he seemed so particular in his watching as if looking for a sign from her only he could see.

Well, what's in Leesburg? I said, redirecting him.

A raspberry jubilee. He smiled and looked up at me. A veritable winter festival. He turned back to Ms. Clara May expressing himself by touching the raggedy ends of his mustache now and then, twirling the thin strands between his fingers and thumb, and as A.D. didn't budge one inch from behind his big dusty book to acknowledge him, I had to be the one to get his attention off her. Someone down at the Mercantile was discussing it proper like, he said, and with the crowds coming in and the bands already lined up, well straight away a telegram come in about the Hardy Family attending care of me, your manager. For a right pretty fee too. So I come out here on the heel to tell you.

Raspberries? But it's January, Ben, and I never liked raspberries to begin with. They get caught in my teeth, and I smiled then showing him my bright white choppers.

Dang it, Isaiah, just forget about the raspberries for a second. Geez. Raspberries? Who cares about the raspberries, for they can jar them can't they?

Yeah, I suppose they can jar them, I said. I hadn't thought of that.

Well, why not focus on that last part instead, about the pay. How about that?

O I heard it, I said, and bent a few notes on my guitar to heighten whatever anxiousness I thought I might transfer from myself about Ezra and his silent auguries onto Ben. I seen it had the affect I wanted, because he cringed up right nice, scrunching his eyes and furrowing his heavy brow so I let the sound linger a while and set the guitar near the window. Now I could look on him all passive and cool and show how much mettle I'd brought to this meeting. Well, as far as I could hear, I said, it all come right after that part about attending care of you and such and such as our manager.

Well, ain't that right? he said and shook his head at me, his fat chin kind of wobbly as his mouth opened a bit and I heard a panting breath escape his round hanging belly. Are you saying I ain't managing you two?

Managing what?

Why work, he said, and getting it! That's what I brung you, didn't I? And here I had to travel clear over Bristol just to find you, too. He was hot. His square little cheeks were red as summer beets and I had to chuckle to see how easy it was to work him into a lather. Here he was calling himself our manager and I didn't even rightly know the man nor how many buttons he had to push, nor if others besides me in the business could push them, too. So I had to feel him out myself, as it were. Hell, I knew A.D. wasn't going to do it. I didn't even know if he was ever going to play again. But I knew Benjamin would have to be on my side for anything involving this here Hardy Family from now on, if we were ever going to get my plan into any kind of fruition. So I eased off a bit on the old boy. I eased off and played more to his strengths, I guess you could say, buttering him up on both sides.

115

Say, ain't raspberries the sweet kind? Not like them blueberries at all. I guess I was thinking about blueberries all along, Ben. Sure. Blueberries.

Jesus Christ, he muttered and looked at me half-dazed to hear my line of thinking and how it had gotten wrapped up with what berry it was. (See, a kind like that always wants to feel more intelligent anyways, so that's what I gave him, that angle over me, and he ate it up with a spoon.) Why that's right, Isaiah, he said now all soft and syrupy-like, condescending now that he knew he was so obviously superior in his way of thinking. Them raspberries are sweeter, and he mumbled something else I couldn't hear, but smiled to see me come around to his line of thinking and rubbed his thin watery lips watching me, for I had his whole attention now. Even though Ms. Clara May had since stood and went to the stove to tend the kettle boiling for tea.

O she had chamomile and rose hips and hibiscus all laid out on the counter and even some little jasmine leaves she'd carried with her from an oriental store in Baltimore that she visited near the Peabody. I had not seen nor smelled any tea like that my whole life and asked her to try some then as she was making her own and lord, when I tasted it, it was as if I was back in my own parcel with my Annie gathering clover. The kind we'd brew a spring morning in the glass pot with a sprig of mint and cinnamon and I had to set down and listen to Benjamin go on for a bit as he was determined to reveal his worth to us and I didn't want him to see the tears dewing my eyes. I didn't want him to see me so wounded by the taste of a memory gone and then returned so easily in that small white cup. My Annie was in there, I thought, and looked back up at him still yakking about contracts and the going concerns and keeping this thing moving now that so many had heard us with the radio blasting out that first big hit every day between Runnymede's other numbers, and I just had to sigh.

Runnymede? A.D.'s forehead wrinkled then. I watched him close his big black book and thought maybe this Benjamin Marks might be worth a damn after all to bring A.D. up out of his funk or whatever else he was in after seeing god-knows-what behind those red swinging doors at Ezra Lee's. Runnymede McCall?

The one and only, Benjamin said. He was standing now, though I wouldn't have known it if I hadn't heard his cheap Sears Roebuck cowboy boots click clacking on the floor. He started to sway and soft shoe now to some song of Runnymede's that must a been circling in his head, for he hummed the same tune I heard Ms. Clara May hum outside Ezra Lee's in the car, when I thought it the siren call of hell itself. Well, I guess it was some good conjuring, because

I got sort of hazy then too in my senses listening to it. Or maybe, it was just because Ms. Clara May had joined in humming, and her voice was of that sweet note again. A voice that rose high in the bright motes of sunlight flashing across the dusty sofa and rickety chairs and bookcases, so that I didn't feel tethered in that moment. I just floated. I felt my body as so much sunlight floating too. A substance unformed and reworked that had just come across the many million miles to find its way and feel the shape of sound emerge from Ms. Clara May's throat as that one divine note persisted. Even sweeter than the sweetest note she sung before, and as we all hushed up to listen, even Benjamin Marks had to steady himself just to hear it.

Clara? A.D. finally said, after she'd been singing in front of the stove for some time, moving cups and washing a bowl where she'd made some egg salad before putting in a loaf of wheat top to heat for jam later that she'd brought out of the pantry. Clara, is that you? A.D. stood from his chair without thinking, and I believe, more importantly, to remember. Sure. He'd set outside her rehearsal room many days at the Peabody when it was just him in the dusty corridor listening to her voice raised with so many others on the other side. And often, when he told me later about her solos and the clear crystal feeling inside him, the emotion her sound stirred in his bones and fingers—as if lifting into the heavens themselves—I thought he might collapse on his cot to tell me for the heat and exhaustion it caused him. So that almost immediately he'd have to go off and search through languages of Italian and German and even Russian to look up the lyrics and translate what she'd sung to get them into words that he might say back to her so she would know he'd been in tune with her from the first. You, he said and just stared at her. When was the last time you sang?

Me? she said, and brushed her curls up past her eyes as she touched the back of her smooth glassy neck, puckering her lips, before looking at us all innocent and sweet. Lips that were glistening and wet from the tea and that all three of us men watched and lusted after then for the sweetness of the aching sound that still lingered on them, in each plump crease. So that in the course of under two minutes Ms. Clara May Staunton had sewn up my own plan for me without me even lifting a finger.

XIX

That perfect counterpoint ⁓ The hook ⁓ The catch
⁓ The worm ⁓ The echoing canyons and chambers
of his mind ⁓ That sharp red flare of ambition ⁓
Descendent from some lost lamp or lantern ⁓ Into
its endless lines of brick and granite indifference

SHE WOULD COME WITH US TO NEW JERSEY. That was it and we wouldn't hear another word even when she said she wasn't ready and hemmed and hawed and said the Hardy Family didn't have that kind of sound yet. She knew we wanted her to join us and give us something that A.D. said even old Runnymede didn't have in his music—that high clear soprano—that perfect counterpoint. O we needed a voice that ached with the sweetness of the ridge, with a depth of innocence that surpassed most any I'd heard before and yet contained the raw pain she'd suffered in that fire. The pain of her skin and what it meant for her appearance and how people saw her and how she saw herself from then on. I'm certain both A.D. and I thought straight away what Mr. Ralph Peer might say when he heard us all harmonizing and playing. For I literally saw the fever spark again in A.D.'s brain as we gathered all breathless and expectant in that dimly lit living room and commenced our first formal rehearsal with Ms. Clara May now officially in the fold.

I shook loose a fat roll of bills from my pocket and spread them out like an oriental fan, soothing my face with the cool air of bright promise, and said, Them raspberries be damned. We're gonna make a record. We're gonna go directly to the Victor Talking Machine Company in Camden, New Jersey, as Mr. Ralph Peer had advised us once we felt so inclined. Well, sure enough that had old Benjamin Marks huffing and puffing to think we'd miss out on all that fine raspberrying and flesh-pressing at the Leesburg festival. But he hushed up considerable when I told him he could come to New Jersey too whenever we were ready to go with a new hit, because A.D. said he had a song he'd been waiting to work on for weeks. All he'd needed was the inspiration, and he had that now in spades as he watched his flighty gossamer of a girl drift and sway beside him in her blue corduroy dress and cotton scarves, dancing this way and that in that soft meandering style she had of stepping in her bare feet to the rug and then back to the cool floorboards. And that was the precise moment we started working on our new song, something like a sequel or reply to The Ballad of Clara May.

A.D. said the song had been in his head all the way back even before the Peabody. That it'd been sitting and stirring in there so long, but had finally only come out at Ezra Lee's when he'd heard that sad singing behind those red doors. For he knew at last where the hook laid in it, as it was an old song from before his father's own house burned down, when A.D. could still remember the faint outline of his mother's soft hand sopping up warm egg yolk and jam with the crust of her day-old bread.

What singing? I asked. What mother? But of course A.D. didn't mention those red doors again, or Ezra Lee by name, or even his own mother. He just mumbled about E's place and something else. But from then on, I gathered he was considering all of these things, and maybe even the psychological state of Ms. Clara May in this new-fangled arrangement of ours, considering her pain and how it made her voice so true and real to touch. Even in her first soft utterings warming up, lilting as if through a grand lullaby or scale, her voice was like an arrowhead that burrowed through your rib cage, quivered into your heart, and buried itself in your bones. It had a sorrowfulness to it, a way of cleaving your soul through and through, opening you up to all the emotion and tender touches and everything else that you just had to fall in love with her and whatever it was she was singing about. You just had to. And as A.D. and I listened again and smiled to know it was really true—her being there with us—we knew this type of music, this brand that was a bit brighter than the blues we took from the ridge, was for women just as much as for men. That adding her to the mix could only help bring in everyone else under our fold, so to speak. For we were singing now for everyone, not just for the sad colored folks and down-hearted, but even for the poor white and rich ones, too. The ones that wanted to celebrate and dance for their good fortune in life.

It was something else to see her now, to see how all the sass had eased out of her just like that, in taking up and playing house with A.D. Not to mention how she felt when she saw how much we treasured and needed her voice. She was as easy and soft as a chamois cloth rubbed over polished teak. She just glided through the room and into her solos, and this ease even spilled into everything else she done. Now she said please and thank you and asked if I wanted honey in my tea whenever she brewed another pot (because she was always brewing more tea for her voice), and she just about fell to the floor when we asked if she'd sing with us a little louder and practice thrusting herself right out there for all to see as if we were onstage and she was in front as the lead singer.

You mean right out front? she said.

Right there, A.D. said, and positioned her as steady as could be to bring her on up out of the daze that come over her after almost every song. All she'd ever wanted her whole life was to sing, to be here in the center of that sound, in that moment, making it together with us—and with A.D. in particular—and for me that all worked out just perfect with the plan I'd devised to get us back on top, as it were. All with Ms. Clara May's help, of course, for I needed to find my wife and daughter again, that much was obvious, and was all I'd ever really wanted.

At first, I thought A.D. was the ticket. That he was the one. Especially after I seen what natural affinity he had in taking a song and bending it, in finding it with me out there somewheres in those backwoods spots where nobody else would go, and by changing it, and molding it to his own degree, all his work brought out the polish and shine in the thing. Until it was almost as if the old song, in its primitive state, had given birth to this new song, in its revised state, a state that he held up and paraded around and sang and that nine times out of ten you'd be singing right along with before it was even finished. And that was all because of the hook he infused in it. The catch, as he called it, when he was a bit tipsy and the whiskey had gotten the better part of him, and he sat there patting himself on the back for finding the infection of it. That sound or lyric that would worm its way into anybody that heard it and would never leave them alone, so that they'd have to like it eventually, after it wore them down and became a part of them, so to speak. So that just to be rid of it, just to shake it free, they'd have to give in to it eventually, to all its magic and rhythm. But even then it could all be called back at a moment's notice—if the light was right, or a certain wind blew a scent of sarsaparilla or sandalwood by, or a dog barked far off and the timber of it reminded you of a particular sound, or one single lyric, or even a slight subtle breath—it would crash back in on you as an avalanche. And in that sense, I suppose it never did really leave you, but just grew inside, or slept for a time until it was called upon again to enchant you again.

The worm, he'd say, and bring his hand up wiggling his big index finger along the top of a worn down barstool, or on the edge of his paint-flecked guitar. Whenever I saw him do that, and could hear he was far away then in the echoing canyons and sound chambers of his mind, I knew he was closing in on it then, on another inflection, and I listened real tight for my chance to lend a note to it, to form an accompanying line, to give that worm the most comfortable and arable soil in which to stretch out and grow.

And that was how we worked. It had been that way since I first taught him in the Peabody, and I thought all along it was fine enough for us. That after playing in Bristol that night when Ms. Clara May appeared, and Runnymede followed us onstage, that would be it, we'd be on our way, barreling off into the fame and celebrity that music now seemed to be making of other stars before us. Like Runnymede as a perfect case. Or even Jimmie Rodgers, that odd fellow who'd been at our same audition, but who'd skyrocketed since, reaching new commercial heights with his yodeling and swaggering brakeman style. The radio had done it all. The radio was starting to hold sway over so many and was reaching further into their lives. So that even their thoughts and needs seemed prescribed by the chiming bells of the station jingles, or the slick advertiser's voicings, and I knew when I first heard it those businesses weren't dumb at all. Hell, they already knew how folks out there in the ridge wanted to spend their time listening and listening some more. Just to forget all the work they'd done that day, or the year past, or their whole life. Just to ease off a bit into the fantasy time the dark words and music spun for them through the night, so that it seemed natural enough to keep proceeding along this same line forever. That it would just build and build, and we'd be on our way. All we had to do was keep tracking down songs and tweaking them with A.D.'s hooks and worms and whatever else he called them—and that would be it—the world would be ours.

But then of course Ms. Clara May and Ezra Lee came into the picture, and with whatever A.D. had seen or heard in the back of that unholy house, everything seemed lost. He'd pulled back, setting down his guitar, reading with her in their high-backed chairs, playing house, and I never thought I'd see that spark again in his eyes. That sharp red flare of ambition—of greed even—that might motivate him to keep going till all was his and every mind on every corner was infected with one of his worms, burning through the world to be heard and sung and held forever. For that was how I was going to find my Annie and Lucy girl, wasn't it? Well, wasn't it?

I was going to be rich. Renowned. And the Hardy Family was going to play all over creation because of it, and eventually they'd hear my voice or see my smiling face on some poster somewheres, or flashing into being above some rusty bulb, and that would be it. I'd finish a last song, wipe the sweat from my brow, and look into some packed house in Omaha or Jessup or Asheville, creaking with applause and beer-stained cheer, and she'd be standing there as pretty as can be. Just hovering in one still beam of light, descendent from some lost lamp or lantern in the ether, as of a halo sent down from some impossible heaven to mark her, and she'd be watching me. Not blinking. Not breathing. Her long narrow hand raised while the other took a hold of the slender figure beside her, the one that would step toward me then from the shadows and transform herself into my little girl. My Lucy. My angel. Grown tall now for sure, but mine, and she'd be standing there as young and fresh as a dream and look on me and smile and I'd know for sure we'd never be apart again. Ever.

And as A.D. put the car into gear after pulling out from a filling station near Carlisle that next week, I thought about it and replayed it a hundred times in my mind as we drove. Until I couldn't even remember standing in the studio when Mr. Ralph Peer raised his hand to me as technicians and assistants scurried about our feet, arranging chords and switches and microphones for us to sing.

Stringing together my medley of notes was as easy as a dream then, and as airy, for I suspect we were all sort of just drifting on the high sweet sound of Ms. Clara May's voice, for it seemed to take all of a second to get another single recorded. (Though I can't rightly say, as there was some trouble afterward with our reservation at the Camden Wilshire.) So that Benjamin Marks had to huff and puff himself up with the manager because I was colored and that changed things and would set us back another $50 bill. Instead it had him shouting down the place and driving us clear up to Trenton for another room in a place as bright and opulent as what he thought we deserved. But then there was something the matter with the dinner there, as we hadn't the proper coats or ties, and anyways A.D. didn't like the place to begin with as he just sat there and seemed calculating something far off in his mind. Reciting a litany of names. Figuring miles and train schedules to boot, because Ms. Clara May had said something dark and furtive in his ear over the appetizers, and then touched my hand as A.D. stood up.

After, he said to her, and then mumbled something else, blinking his eyes as he stalked off. But all I could feel was my wife and baby girl, even as Ms. Clara May held onto me with her cold quivering hand as she watched him leave (so that maybe I wasn't the best help for her as more drinks were poured and passed around, as more plans and hopes were made and toasted). All I could see was them at the edge of my dream, standing in the clearing of all our hard work and fame. I could see them. And the more I drank the more they stepped toward me, winnowing through the crowd as if parted from the swarm of people and years—my little Lucy girl and Annie returned to me. They came striding across that smoke-strewn room and reached out to me as if across the years, and the tears came to my eyes as I imagined it all, for I never in my life thought reaching for someone across an abyss of heartache and loss could be so easy. But there they were, and I knew I'd hold onto them forever now. That it would be easy. That it was how it was meant to be.

But then all of my dreams blew out as quickly as they'd appeared. In an instant, the thunder echoed overhead and Annie and Lucy seemed pulled back from me as if tied to the wrong end of a string. I knew we were moving then, because the bar and hotel changed around me to a train track and tunnel— while in place of my little Lucy girl and Annie—Ms. Clara May and Benjamin appeared at the end of my trembling arm. They were saying something to me with a harsh edict and forceful gaze. I was meant to appease them, she said. I was meant to right whatever wrong he'd already caused. But before I could ask her about it, they were gone, walking through a long dark corridor that seemed to disperse into a plume of smoke and mud-colored puddles. They had left me alone then to chase after something I could not see. To seek something that I could not know. To stalk those city streets as a last yellow taxicab went streaming past and a lone lamppost blinked on and off above me in that vast canyon of steel and abandonment, as I leaned up to see New York City ebb and flow into its endless lines of brick and granite indifference.

A.D. was on the run again.

XX

The open palm of his hand ~ Parting waves of darkness and shadow ~ The Duke in there tonight ~ After the Cotton ~ The true arbiter of movement ~ A side door swung open ~ The saddest number ever ~ Runnymede returns ~ The face ~ The ceiling ~ A bridge ~ On singing the last song

YOU CAN'T GO THAT WAY, BOSS. Ain't nobody go that way but performers and the few white folks don't want nobody to know they come down here in the first place.

A tall colored man stood by the side of an alley. I'd turned down it after spotting a small crack of light beneath a painted door, and thought it was where I'd been directed to go by someone I'd asked a block back. But as he waved a steady hand my way, I stopped and turned to him and had to laugh to think of the route I'd taken to get here. I'd come up (or down or over) from Pennsylvania Station and been turned around so many times, asking folks where the nearest blues club was—getting not a few lean looks in the process—from folks who didn't want to be seen speaking to me anyways, a thin, colored yokel right off the turnip truck. That when I did get some information about a place not too far from where I figured A.D. might have gone, as he was in such a thirst again for songs—for songs and stories and such—I thought it was only natural to sneak in as I'd watched the last few people do. Even if I didn't realize they were carrying beat up cases for trumpets and clarinets, and weren't regular folks at all, but musicians probably getting ready to go on. It's easy, I finally said, and stepped toward him.

What's easy, boss?

To forget I ain't playing. I'm a guitarist, I said, and held up my hand to show the calluses on the ends of my fingers. But I don't think he was impressed.

Well, they ain't too many guitarists down here neither, and he clanged open a gate so I could step inside the sunken doorway smelling of piss and trash and gin. I eyed him slow and steady, for I noticed something peculiar about him as I passed. He was holding out the palm of his hand. He held it there motionless and his sad brown eyes glanced at it and then at me, as if I was meant to know something that I hadn't seen in all of Virginia or Baltimore before—and never between blacks.

A tip, he finally said. (I guess he wasn't taking any chances on me mistaking what it was supposed to mean, his hand, this arrangement, this courtesy.)

For what?

For services rendered, I guess is what they say.

For opening a rusty gate? I kicked the black iron rungs and could hear from the end of a sloping walkway glasses clinking, and the soft murmur of a saxophone parting waves of darkness and smoky shadow. It sounded like a tugboat to me then, drifting through all that formlessness. It was something to wrap your dreams up in, was what it was, sounding so content and mellow, I just had to hear more of it. For just then underneath it, a soft tinkling piano spread out its reach and it was as if it was just rising up then like water for the tugboat to drift on. All the formlessness was made real and elegant and smooth, and the choppiness I'd imagined before, swirling across the sea, eased out and was silent and sweet again. I had to breathe deep to be so close to it, and yet bound up in it already, and was tearful and moved. So I looked up at the small snatch of sky high up and fenced in by some great steel towers so this fellow wouldn't see me cry.

All I could see then was a vast grayness above me. Something vague and electric glittered above all those buildings and clustered signs. It was all so real and immense, it left me dumbstruck—the lights of the buildings and sucked-away sky—that when I turned and touched my head to comprehend it, and to know I was allowed live beneath it and in it—I felt awed again for a moment, and didn't know whether I was here now or not, or what time I'd stumbled into. But I guess I didn't care much neither, as it was all so perfect and true, the music. It took me away from my mind for a moment, taking me away from any care or worry, and that old boy seemed to sense the contentment in me just then. He let me rock there a moment longer on my heels, swaying back and forth, before he touched me, steadying my shoulders. (He'd already smelled the whiskey on me from all those drinks back in Trenton, for he let out a long sigh sniffing me.) But then he just chortled as if we were together in this contentment forever, that we'd always been in on it, standing there for years and years just listening as the world wound around us and then away into its vastness.

You lucky, he said.

Me?

The Duke in there tonight.

The Duke?

Well, sure. The one and only. He come down after the Cotton because he knows we for real down here.

For real for what?

Well, for what he plays, he said, for his voice. His true voice. The one they don't let him play up there at all. Shit, what the hell you think they let him play? And he shook his head pinching his narrow eyes shut to think on it. Ain't nothing but jungle music and dark tribal shit. Because they sure don't want to hear his real voice. Not the one that would make them feel. Never have. Anyways, they only let whites in there to hear, and the whites only want what they already got made up in their minds to begin with. Ain't that right?

I was still drifting on the tide of that tinkling piano. Because he'd caught it, the Duke. I could tell. The spirit of that sound was substance and direction and everything and nothing in an instant. But then it was built up again into a bluster at the touch of a chord, and was made bigger when he wanted it to be bigger, and hotter when he wanted it to be hotter, and it made you follow along close in your mind because of the nuance and nature of it. You had to follow it just to watch it hover there with what it could tell you about yourself. With all the secrets it held. And the mystery. And maybe because of it, I found a question I wanted to ask about all the words he'd used describing us vs them just now, when all I cared about was the music and nothing else, for I knew color didn't have nothing to do with all that, not at all. What do you mean, what they got made up?

When I said it, he sniffed me up and down again, just in case I thought we were on the edge of Andromeda or something, instead of the planet Earth, where any ordinary nigger would have cared about race and sides and such. But I didn't. At least not then. Not with that music going strong. How'd you get down here anyway? he said. This place ain't known by many.

Fella told me, and I shook my thumb back to the street. But it was bare and as we turned to look, the city smoke sifted down like another cold layer of crumbled leaves, and I shook my collar to feel the late winter like a fine metal grit on my skin.

He looked me over again and took a silver flask from his pocket. Care for some?

I swayed watching him. The distance between us and that brown liquor was all I could see. Hell, it was all I could feel besides the anticipation of standing in the swollen beauty of that sound, even if I knew A.D. probably wasn't even inside. (It was funny, I never did ask the man about A.D. or anyone like him. The sound was just too much for me. It was all I wanted to be. It was all I wanted to know. At that moment, I couldn't have cared less about where A.D. was, or where the Duke played before this or what they wanted his sound to be like, for we were here now, and that was enough. It was all that mattered. Anyway, wasn't that what the music wanted to assure us—that we were here? That we'd made it? That we'd somehow survived? And we could never forget it.) Sure, I said and put the flask to my lips. Thanks, and after handing it back, I slapped a crisp dollar bill into his smooth leathery hand and he chuckled low and lean and sung something I didn't know the words to, some spell or incantation as I stepped along the walkway toward the sound.

THE CLUB WAS SMALL AND CRAMPED AND THE PIANO took up one whole wall of it. The Duke sat there as wide and proud as could be, swaying behind his strong dark hands as they pounded the keys till the sound of water pouring out of them was all anyone could hear. There wasn't anything else to hear. The back of the Duke's neck glistened with sweat and shined from the one red bulb swinging from the dusty rafters. Occasionally, the lone waitress would step out from behind the roughhewn plank they'd strung from chains to the brick wall and move from overturned barrel to barrel, touching half-drunk glasses, or picking up errant napkins and murky ashtrays. There wasn't any talking to speak of. Most everyone was already transfixed, watching without hardly breathing, racing inside without hardly moving. Or maybe they had their eyes closed instead, and stared into the dreamy nightscape of their minds. The one the Duke had set to motion and was opening up with all the sad notes he strung together as the other players—on the drums, bass, and trumpet—all seemed to dissolve into grayness as each of us fell into the single enchantment the Duke's music wove.

O we were already lost in the reverie of it by then—the sound—that sad mysterious sound that seemed to rise up from the well of his soul and pour out with its story of loss and forgiveness and truth. So that each of us could craft it then alone and shape it ourselves as he turned and twisted it before us without doing anything more than moving his strong shifting hands back and forth above the keys. Each note seemed a shimmering step unfolding in a world that only we could touch. A world only we could see. Individual was what it was, the effect, but somehow larger, if that's possible. As if each note was a universe set swirling into creation that only we could pluck from the air and hold to our hearts. I know, I know. It sounds crazy. And maybe it was. But I've heard since then that he was only like that there, or in other such hole-in-the-wall clubs, where his voice was free to wander wherever he felt it needed to go, far from the spotlight of his fame and success and the echoing refrain of that other voice of his that gave everything else away. To the people. But this here sound was his alone, and the more I think on it and recover that night, the more I believe every last note from him was as good as any gospel I ever read, or any sunset I ever saw. And maybe better.

Because that was the Duke alright, and I'd never heard anything like it before nor since. For as he went on, and as the faces I thought I knew beside me began to dissolve into something else, as the liquor and music continued to work their magic, I felt the whole world revolve and slow down as he slowed down, or gather up speed again, as he sped up, and it seemed like he was the true arbiter of each movement, of all the living and dying that could happen in the world. His music was so much more than life and death, so much bigger and truer. How else can you say something that's unsayable? How can you know something that's unknowable? You approach it through music, I guess, and magic, which are one and the same to me, and to think on it I had to laugh as he played. So that maybe after another fifteen minutes or so, I shook my head just to rise from the beautiful sadness the Duke had cast upon me and everyone else in that room.

As I did, I scanned the smoky tables and a large white face rounded into focus. And if I hadn't been sufficiently drunk before, well the sight of that face took me even deeper into all the excitement and confusion liquor can bring to a man—for not ten feet away, set against a brick wall, amidst the darkly swirling smoke, sat the spitting image of Runnymede McCall. Singer extraordinaire. Lately of the Piedmont Pipers. And he was smiling! He was smiling his Cheshire cat grin as he slipped another cigarette into his lips and snapped his silver lighter shut just as John Hill Carter had done at the Peabody. Before I could even stand and steady myself to see if it was really him or not, to tell him he was nothing compared to us, nothing for what he must a thought a nigger janitor and white trash vagrant like A.D. could be—he was gone. A side door swung open and I staggered out in my wobbly boots, even as the Duke poured on into the night, touching the soul of the world just to keep it spinning.

AIN'T NOBODY NEVER LEFT WHEN THE DUKE IS ON. And he's on tonight.

I know, I know, I said. My friend from before had somehow found me even though I swore I'd come out the back of the club. But in a moment, he had me turned in another direction because he was sensitive to the gravity that must have brought me out from the sounds that he'd heard and listened to as intently as anyone else inside. For he'd said then to the world and to anyone who cared to listen how it was the Duke's saddest number ever, and that it had been sad before this for sure, but tonight was something else entire. Tonight was of a magnitude that could touch all the way to your marrow and then some went so deep and hot and true, that when he turned to me, a low frown creased his face, and I agreed with him even though I was already looking past him to the street.

I looked and the smooth white face of Runnymede was there at the edge of my vision, floating as if smeared with greasepaint, as if delivered from the night itself. I didn't know if it was real or not, nor how it hovered there as if detached from any physical form—as maybe even Ezra Lee's face still rose in my mind—but it kept rising through the murk and soot of the city, and I gasped deep in my chest to see it. The face was the only thing in the world then that moved me. It had moved me even beyond the reach of the Duke's sad sound, for I could hear his piano fading now as that drum and bass and trumpet started slowly blending their voices in the undertow of what the Duke had spread out for them. For I suppose he wanted us to rise up again now too. He must have even signaled it to the other musicians somehow, with a subtle nod or rise of his shoulder, because they'd started up again, and the sound rose brighter and sharper, building in intensity and tempo, Until it might as well shouted Rise up! to anyone who could hear it, and then I knew it was my cue to move on. That white face implored me. Hell, it demanded me to move. Demanded some action or deed on my part, something that I could not guess nor know, and yet, even as I hesitated to succumb to it, to go, it only seemed to shine that much brighter beneath a lamppost on the other end of the street. I breathed once and blinked watching it, and it shined there as if goading me on to the end of the city, to some other world entire.

Runnymede, I whispered and my friend put his hand out to touch me, to bring me back in to the Duke and his band, but I'd already stepped past him and was off. I was following the face of a man that had vexed me before, and that had reappeared now as if through the very firmament to bring me on into whatever spectral vision or landscape that tortured me. Something I knew not, but that only I could ever be wounded by and forced to visit. For Hackett? I said to the street. Is this for Hackett? For that sonabitch I killed for touching my wife?

But he didn't turn. He never turned nor answered as we went. So I just followed him through street after street, past corners and tenement buildings that rose so high I could not see the air above them nor know if I was still above the ground or had become a thing in some subterranean ward. A grotto of disgust or loss swept down into the dirt. A diminishment was what it was. The ceiling of the city had put its infernal stamp upon me as insignificant, as unwanted, and the feeling immersed me in my pursuit as the slow hard slog of my feet kept me moving. Moving toward water, for I could feel some light turn in the air the farther I went. Some wave of moisture, or humidity, closed in on my face as I blinked and that other face—Runnymede's—disappeared and I had to surge past an overturned barrel set aflame by some vagrants just to keep pace.

I was panting and covered in the amber beads of my whisky-soaked sweat. I licked my lips and looked past a line of taxicabs at the edge of some terminus or port of call. Sails, I said, and sloshed my boots through soot-colored puddles as the sails of ships and creaking beams rose and far off voices echoed over water, rising up as close as my own hideous thoughts just then. For I wanted to wound Runnymede, it's true; I wanted to hurt him for the elusive nature of his spirit and the apparent delight he must have taken in my confusion at his appearance. I could feel him rise up above me like the wind as great precise lungs of wire hummed and pinged, stuttering with a soft susurrus through its web as Runnymede's voice implored me to walk out with him, to walk to the edge of the world.

A bridge. The Brooklyn Bridge and its long span shook beneath me. As I clambered out, the vague shape of people drifted across that stretch of space and time, blurring as they came toward me but were then as quickly gone, sucked into blackness as only the white shining face of Runnymede remained. For he was singing—I could hear—and as I stepped closer, I knew the song, each note. But I also knew it was forbidden to sing this song, forbidden for all time, for it was Yancey Jakes' song, the one from the ridge that A.D. and I would not repeat nor ever play. The one too true to bring to the world of Man and masquerade as our own, for it was the last song was what it was. The last of its kind. Untouched. Unblemished. Forever. Amen. But here Runnymede was singing its first verse as his white glowing head swayed on the platform, and his voice called out in agony, as if to reach something more divine in the air above us. And as I grabbed the back of his shining white head as if to strike him, or throw him forever into the depths—for I knew not what path my rage might take—Runnymede turned to me and his white mask slipped from his sick grin into Ezra Lee's crooked gaze. Before smearing once again, as another gust of wind wavered past, into A.D.'s tortured smile. I choked back a sob and peered into the truth of A.D.'s vast, stunning sadness.

XXI

In the mist ~ Manhattan's myriad blur ~ A magnet
inside us ~ The lights ~ The prophecy and story of the
red doors ~ Three bodies ~ His tale of woe and wonder
~ Tracing a soft circle on his forehead ~ Just a conduit ~
A channel ~ An oiled and floating clock ~ Some other
judgment ~ A child ~ A blessing ~ The wind in the wires

A.D. WAS SUFFERING AN ENCHANTMENT and I had to touch his face
to wipe the demented expression that seemed so eternal, so infernal, as to be
cast in bronze upon his lips. O it glimmered and wove its way there and would
not leave the more I touched and wiped, I had to shiver to see him like that—so
confused and frenzied in his reverie. But I had to persist in bringing him down
from this mania that would have me see both Runnymede in the city, and that
devil Ezra Lee in turn, reflected in his face. It's the lights, he said finally, the
lights, and he took my shoulders in his hands and pressed so hard I could feel
the thin narrow bones in his fingers. It's the lights, is what it is, he said, the
lights. Just look at them like what he said, like what he knew.

Like who knew?

He was pointing with his anxious finger and at the end of it, in the soft
reddening dawn, I seen Manhattan's myriad lights blur and diffuse and shine as
if refracted through a thousand tiny dewdrops. The sight was so revelatory and
absorbing I could feel A.D.'s heartbeat thrumming in his chest. He cast his gaze
about and recognized something so true, something so revealing that surging
out of his person was an energy and force I'd not seen nor felt in any other. I
had to count the heartbeats racing away in his bones then and in my own just
to know it was true, the reason for my wandering through the city to find him.

He has led me to you, I whispered. He has. For as sure as I'm standing here,
the very idea of Runnymede has been set like a magnet inside us to draw us on

toward some desperate conclusion. But then I was hushed at the sight of A.D. and those lights cascading to the water, so that it looked as if the heavens themselves had been ripped aslant from their great milky swathes to touch upon the river and stretch out in it their twinkling, glittering stairway. When I seen it, it made me think of the Blue Ridge in the first dawning shine, or sad aching twilight, when its long smooth shadow, exaggerated and dusky, stretched itself out like that as a creed or truth or something monumental. As if it was something too chaste and pure to be reconciled with or informed of any other idea. For in those moments, I would see the ridge not as it was, but bigger, and all-encompassing, as if it were drawn out then beyond creation itself, becoming something singular and grand to behold in its endless coalescing. And that was how the waters looked to me then, with all the stars scribbled across their depths in an infinite procession of lines and shapes and moods, so that I had to breathe just to know I was living.

Do you see it? A.D. said, for I think he heard my own sucked in cheeks and startled chest. Touching me gently on the shoulder, he whispered, He said it would be like this. Now his voice was as measured and steady as time itself, as if seeing this vision of life had set him in order again, just by the grand structure of it all, in the underlying framework. He said it would be like this at the end of me for sure and now I see it and believe it. The lights, Isaiah, the lights. He'd turned again to the rail and seemed airy a sudden, as a great gust wove up through the rusty girders, before whipping through the wires and walkway, rifling the ends of his brown ropey hair and greasy wool jacket. As the cold air pierced through him and me, touching every part of our eyes and limbs, I had to shiver and twist to warm myself by the lone fire A.D. had become.

O something quivered like electric eels beneath his skin. As I grabbed him, I could not move him from the rail nor know how he might survive the sight of the lights that so beckoned from below, for I felt him inching closer with his body and soul to the void that stretched out then across the depth of that water. It's okay, I said. It's okay to come back to me, to the world again. It is.

No, he said and shook his head furious at me. He said it would be like this for me at the end, and now I believe him and can see it the more I look upon it as on the world itself. But as he spoke the rising wind took his words away from me a moment, before I could hear him continuing as he mentioned what I knew had been hidden in him all along, weighing on him heavily. Because the red doors in his house would never have wanted it any other way. Not for me.

The red doors? I said and knew then the force that had returned somehow to haunt him. Or maybe that had haunted him ever since he'd stepped behind them in the first place. For surely some prophecy had occurred there in that house of the dead for A.D. to be so lost now inside it. To still be so scared and yet elated to know it and to see it come true to life, and I shivered to ask further, to understand the meaning that now turned him into someone else entire. Into someone who would jump as sure as stand there to see the truth revealed and made known to him in the lights of that city, to see it fulfilled somehow, whatever path he had been led to believe was his. So then tell me, I said. Tell me about it.

There is nothing to tell. There is only the end now for me. Like he said.

Like who said? Ezra? About the lights? What did he say?

That they were markers for me. That they were my own special fire as later he saw the fire in Clara May, as it lingered there along her neck. In everyone there is the same visible spark and fire, waiting, patient. He pointed to the lights reflected on the waves and whispered. In time the fire catches up with everything and everyone.

Waiting for what?

For even you, he said, and A.D. turned his cold blue eyes on me and I had to shake my head to see the intensity of his belief in this prophecy.

And he showed you this? I said, struggling to shield myself from the furnace blast of his faith in this lunacy.

He did. But it was already there before I even arrived. It's always been there. It's been waiting all this time. I just needed someone to tell me.

To tell you what?

Why my destiny, of course, he said. The true path. The one I'll take to death for sure, to end all this, and he waved his arms and smiled to feel the wind and coldness against his cheeks, his eyes, gazing all upon it in his wildness, in what he thought was the end for him, the end of all time. We stood above the coffins inside the red doors, Isaiah, and he was singing even before I entered, even before I saw him and knew that he sung for me. That he'd been waiting and singing all that time just for me.

But he called you usurper, a dilettante. He said you were stealing his songs.

That was only after I saw he had my Clara May down in the wheel of fire. Don't you see? That was only after I saw he was watching and prophesying her fire, too. Then I had to act. I had to save her and spoke Catullus to release her, to release his spell, shocking him out of his power, for he did not think anyone else would know it nor use the power of it against him, those words. But still I believe his prophecy. I still believe him from before.

From before what? But he had turned again, had retreated inside himself, wandering the maze of his mind for the red doors in the house of the dead. I could see him remembering and blinking, and as he turned slightly from the rail, I thought I had the first part of him saved. Though I needed the whole part, the other part, the part of his mind and memory that was giving in ever so slightly to the words I kept using, asking, imploring him to remember, to come back to me, to come down from his delusional heights. All I needed to hear now were the words of the red doors that Ezra had spoken to him as if a curse, to make it complete, so that his destiny might be dispelled. So I could help him shake it forever by tearing it apart bit by bit, even if he seemed so set upon believing and making it true. So I waited. And that was how I finally heard the story of the red doors. With all the nefarious reach and influence they had on him, with what he seen that night, and surely, what he could never un-see again to save his soul.

THREE BODIES LAY BEFORE ME IN THEIR COFFINS, A.D. began. The red doors creaked behind me as I touched them—an old cripple with only one leg left and an aged grandmother with a worn down face. I was drawn to that house from the very beginning, after walking clear across town and into the woods toward the rising madness of the voices and dancing faces ringed 'round me ebbing and flowing into their ecstasy, but then dissolving as I stepped inside. It was as if I saw straight away the path parting for me. The people stepped aside as I made my way beyond the bar to where his voice was wafting as of a lullaby. The lullaby of mankind. O something soft and sweet from my past called in its reminiscence, as what a child might hear in the offing of a ship. Or in the sunny inlet of a bay. With what mystery yet to come enchanting me on into the darkness of his rhyme.

He was rhyming?

Very much so, with a voice lilting and true, as if risen across water, you might say. Or half-remembered from a dream. The sound of it was like a dream to me, in all its many paths. Like one you could never forget.

The sputtering smokestack of a steamer trudged beneath us as he paused and blinked. The gray mist had parted so that as we leaned over to look down we could see the fire inside the belly of the engine and the blue-black sparks crackling up like inverse lightning bolts striking against the great cement towers of the bridge. As they did, the wheel of fire from Ezra's house returned and burned its image ever brighter on the veil of my eyelids, even as A.D. himself seemed to push beyond its obvious parallel. For he skittered and flinched a moment, but somehow recomposed himself as that ship passed through. I thought he might dissolve entire into the frightening images and acts the story recaptured, but it only seemed to spur him on that much more as he spoke and wove his tale of wonder and dismay.

Then the third body caught my attention, for it was the one he was administering to with the utmost delicacy. It was a young woman, just a girl really, and the lifelessness of her and the world she left behind moved me. Frightened me. Even now. For she was blue, and her body stiff and naked as Ezra held her thin smooth arms up while he worked. Then he looked at me and touched his lips to her skin, emitting a small sound as he sucked something from her—her soul, her dreams, maybe? Her death? I couldn't say. But I could see the fiery intensity in his sparkling blue eyes as they narrowed the more he set his thin red lips against other parts of her, as he licked and kissed and then sucked her flesh. Her death was the story he wanted, he said, as it is all our stories. For death is a release of fire and sparks, of the inevitable dreaming that spins out into the soil and sky and that was where his intersection was, he said. His house. His work. He thought he was positioned there to catch it all as it moved away from the world and up into the ether or down into the dirt, whichever way it went—after he touched and felt it completely. At least that was what he hoped, he said, and then he held her cold naked body and pressed his ear to her lips listening for the story of her death, his greedy hands cupping and pinching her small hard breasts.

The coffin was a demure cedar box with red velvet lining. The girl's family was of a theatrical sort and imagined she'd like that touch of color, that soft fabric, Ezra explained, as he pawed and sucked and kissed his way to the end of her. And I had to shiver when I seen it, and I shiver now so far removed in retelling it.

It was true. His thin body quivered as if an earthquake shook through each limb. Moving another step towards me, I watched silent but hopeful as he edged away from the railing, remembering the vivid scene of it all, for he must have still seen the small blue-tinged girl so close to him. He must have heard Ezra's thin lips moving along the cold lengths of her as he sucked the death out, sucking out the sex and truth and touch from her. Sucking out everything she could use no more. So did he hear it? I said.

Hear what? A.D. said and looked upon me as the tears pooled upon his cheeks, for he had just then been pressed and bolstered by another shock of wind.

Her death, A.D., her death.

He had to shake his head and close his eyes to understand my question. He did hear it, he said, for it's her song now that haunts me. I did not get to hear the songs of the other two behind those red doors, for he had just ended singing on them when I entered, and anyways at first I was repulsed by his gruesome work. But the longer I stayed, the more I grew accustomed to it, watching his swift practiced movements, listening to his soft religious mutterings. But she remains with me to this moment. She remains.

I touched him then, holding my hand against his arm, squeezing through his wool coat to connect to his pain in remembering her, the youth of her, and the utter waste of it all.

She is still here with me, he said, and he touched his chest before tapping his head softly, tracing a circle on his forehead and shutting his eyes momentarily, thinking on her vision, on her shape. As Ezra finished dressing her, he started singing out her life then, singing out her soul. And it was the most plaintive and saddest tale of desiring I'd ever heard. She wanted to leave that Bristol, to move away with a young boy on a train moving south to Georgia. Just to be gone. Away away away, for as Ezra sang, I listened and had held my guitar quiet till then but swung it around as if on cue and plucked a few notes underneath it as he sang about the ghost of the girl still haunting the farmhouse where she'd died, where a fire had taken her down, like so many before. A fire her brother had set deliberate, bolting her in, jealous of her affection for another, for he'd desired her too, desired to touch her and love her as his own. And when he sung it, it was only then that I recalled seeing the welts and glassy ripples of her flesh as Ezra licked the length of her. But when I looked at her then, after he'd dressed her, after he'd done her up right, those marks were gone, and she was as powdered and beautiful and unsurpassed in her appearance as anyone. He had combed through her long brown hair and swept it up atop her head with two ivory pins. Then smeared careful and artistic his white grease paint upon her cheeks and nose, and then himself. Dabbing it on his face as if in accord to her own unspoken wishes. As he sung her story out and looked at me as he done it, I was so moved by the scene that I remembered my own fire then inside me, listening to him, the one my father burned up in with the house at home. Burned up in the night when I hid, and he knew it.

He knew what?

He knew about the pistol my father had fired into the roof of his mouth. The pistol he'd stole from the merchant in town. He knew about the opium and thick smoke perpetuating for years. The pale blue fog rising through my life, rising as mayflies around a rotten stump of meat. The buzzing of it, too, he repeated, the buzzing of the life whittling away in him, in me, in my daddy as in my mother before. He saw it all and spoke on it and there was no veil between the years or time then, Isaiah. There was no veil before his eyes, nor any lie he could not see through, so that it shook me to hear his vision. It shook me so that I stopped my guitar and knelt before him and clasped my hands for I did not want him to go on. But he pointed at the girl and said it was her. It was all her that said it—through him—and that he was just a conduit, a channel of life and death, and I believed him. I believed him even as the red doors reflected their garish rich claret in the smeared grease paint of his face, and he smiled so sinister and knowing to see me. For then the noise of the outside room had burst up to startle me, even as the walls became an indictment of my pain. I seen clear bottles of liquid and organs harvested and set afloat in formaldehyde. I seen queer instruments of silver and brass arranged and tucked in sheaths of leather. I seen old books and ledgers and packets of iris root and rush and laurel and sandarac and caraway seed all diffused and cordoned off from the harsher chemical astringents stacked in great oak buckets as he moved as a phantom must, hovering in the room. His feet barely touching down as he spoke and pointed to the girl as the live conduit of him shook uncontrolled and alive. His eyes fluttering up as moths opening and flapping their wings and burning in the world, and that was when he told me about the lights.

The lights, I whispered in accordance to his tale, and looked into the mist and was shaken myself as the apparition of a body was upon us before we knew it. The gray wide bulk of it appeared and then dissolved as quickly along the path. The body was on a bike, for it hovered there too and the wheels and spokes of it all made such an eerie ticking sound as of an oiled and floating clock. That when it finally receded, my heart slowed back to the world of the living, and I seen at once the strange color of the mist that had lingered so long, for it was much earlier and brighter above the city. The mist and layers of fog had captured some darker strain of night. Some layer or holdover from the nether hours that had kept the stars spilled and scrawled upon the water so long, but was only now lifting, so that even the stars were retreating and being swallowed into the air. And as I watched it all, I could see A.D. also retreating and shriveling up to recall the words Ezra had spoken in the voice of the girl he'd licked the death from, licking away her soul.

Because the lights are to be my death, he said. The end of me, of everything I mean to hope or do or be. He said it to me like that with his eyes shut and then opened them and smiled for he knew he'd laid his prophecy upon me square and cold. But even then I knew Ezra wasn't finished, for he was touching the girl's dress again, smoothing it down as he touched her hair and pricked his fingertip with a sharp quill he'd retrieved from his sleeve, so that he could squeeze a few drops of his own blood on each of her cheeks, rubbing it into the rouge of her, before rubbing it on her lips. This seals it, he said, and it made me shiver the more to see it and I rose from my knees for he was reaching inside her dress for something else, something hard and perfect that he found, pulling it up. A coin, he said. Gold. He held it out to me then as offering from the departed soul, for her words, and I could do nothing but take it lest I tempt the dead.

You took it? I said. You took it! and I slapped his arm right then for I seen it, the answer for him to tear it all up, this nonsense about prophecies and such. It was right there for him to come back to me, to come down from all this madness. But wasn't it the same coin you threw on his head? I said, remembering the impossible scene in Ezra's house, when the coin had outlined a glistening arc before finding Ezra's white forehead upon which to affix itself. It was hers, wasn't it?

And I gave it back, he said.

Sure, you gave it back, and I nudged him with my shoulder. Don't you see? That means something. Don't you think that changes everything? Changes the power of the lights and your end here forever? He was watching me and touching his face now thinking, shuffling a bit farther from the railing to hear me. When he did, I could see he was swayed a bit by my reasoning, by what he had not been able to see in himself or his actions.

No, he said. I thought about that for a while too. I thought that would be the end of it and that the curse, the words, had passed back into Ezra and the girl. I had hoped that much for sure. Hell, I even told Clara May about it but she didn't want to hear nothing about curses nor lights nor nothing ending in hardship nor death. She'd already had other aspirations entirely, of something she'd been working on for days to tell me and when she did, I finally knew the words Ezra had spoken had been turned around again somehow with the coin and given right back to me ten-fold to hear her. That was why I run out here in the first place.

What? What did she say?

She told me something that struck me down cold is what she said, and all I could do was say to her After. That was what I said, After. This was in Trenton at the restaurant, when I knew it was back with me for sure, the prophecy, from all the way back from Ezra and the dead girl and the coin. But still I told her After, because I didn't want to believe it. Couldn't hardly stand it to be true. But knew it had come down on me so sudden and hard and with me not knowing what to do nor how to act for all the world. So that's what I said. I said, After we get there, honey. After we ride up and down this ridge and find ever last song and name to make my world new. Only then will I be able to handle it, to tackle it for what it is, and fight it off again for sure. Only After.

But she just says no. It's too late already for that, son. She called me son, just like that, and I looked at her in the lamplight and just knew here it comes, some other judgment on me for sure, something old Ezra had cooked up in the last fires of that dead little girl. For Clara just looked on me again, smiled, and repeated her words so I'd know for sure what she'd told me, and I couldn't hardly believe it at first: I'm pregnant, she said. And that was it. My hand went cold and I started looking into the distance and seen all the songs and all the names and all the places I'd never find no more, and it just hit me. The lonesomeness of it all. Of not touching it any more—the music—of not making it my own, of shaping it and leaving it behind to mark me in what I've done and been, so much more so than what my daddy done. So I just had to go. I had to find another song in New York, to hear another name, to move.

Your father, I said, and remembered the burnt up husk of what he'd told me, in that first fire, and what the release of it must have been, and the trauma of seeing and living through it all. After he'd been abused his whole life, suffering unnamed and unwanted.

Sure, my daddy didn't do nothing like this his whole life and never would. So I thought the songs would do it. I thought if anything had the power to change the curse of my life, the songs did. The songs, Isaiah, the songs. But then I seen the lights here, and he turned back to look at Manhattan, as the lights blinked off one by one in the dawn. I seen the lights and knew this was it, that it had to be, the end of me for sure. The end for all time.

When he looked on me again, my own sadness hung inside me as a cold rain or black cloth of soot and rage. To know one so close to me would have what I'd lost. A child. A blessing. That love. Forever. And not to know it nor sense how precious it was, but to see it as a curse instead of a blessing—the one true blessing—set a fire in me, too. And for the life of me I almost threw myself over the railing to think on it and his ignorance. But I didn't. Instead, I put a brave face on, smiled, and touched his shoulder devout like, and together we listened to the wind singing in the wires.

XXII

The Return of Clara May ~ All kinds of funny ~ Nothing about devils nor privies nor ditches ~ To get him down ~ The magic spell ~ Jazz ~ All shifting back and forth and hypnotic ~ Making sand into glass ~ That savage need

THE RETURN OF CLARA MAY SOLD OUT. It was gone in days I tell you and for some reason A.D. and Ms. Clara May were okay with Benjamin Marks handling all the money that rolled in from Mr. Ralph Peer and didn't even ask me none about it in the process. Benjamin said he had savings and checking accounts at the Mercantile and at the Farmers & Mechanics and whatnot, and if we just let it be it would grow with him for sure after he drew us all out a share from the earnings and said there'd be more where that come from as we were all on regular salary now for the remainder.

The remainder of what? I muttered in Ms. Clara May's apartment. But A.D. and Benjamin were counting figures, dividing wages, shuttling between the receipts of some other investments to boot and I had only to look on Ms. Clara May to know how happy she was I'd brought A.D. back to her. Even if she didn't want to let on in her face how much she needed me.

You heard it from him in New York, she said softly, and without lifting a finger, her porcelain-like wrists shifted on her belly where her hands rested, and I was meant to see she was talking about what was growing inside her.

He told me.

Well, you seemed to take it fine enough. Her sharp blue eyes sparkled as she watched me, and it was almost predatory, her look, and I wasn't sure what else was meant behind it. I knew she was happy now, happy as maybe I'd only ever seen her when she was singing and so I couldn't discern then the malice lingering just beneath it. The feeling I got of some shadow hidden behind her shining eyes, for I could tell she just wanted to cut me down, cut me down to pieces.

I smiled and said yes and when he told me my own heart skipped a beat, I tell you. It did indeed, I said as soft and casual as I could for I seen A.D. and Benjamin couldn't hear us none anyways with how they were working their numbers, swiping aside pens and pencils, writing away in their notebooks and such. I took a notion to lower my voice then dramatic-like, as if to exaggerate the confidence I thought we could share now that we were alone.

She noticed straight aways what I implied, and leaned closer and about held her breath she seemed so still and silent there watching me, waiting. But it was funny, Ms. Clara May, I said, as I breathed deep to see the light rising then on the windowsill behind her, outlining her form in golden flossy rays. We'd been back only a few days from New York, riding down on the train after Benjamin and Ms. Clara May had driven on ahead of us that same night A.D. run off, and just by coming south again winter seemed vacated all a sudden. Almost as if it had been asked politely to leave, as how a Southern gentleman might insist, and with it, the early spring was already ebbing in the trees and grass and Blue Ridge of Virginia, and I felt fresher because of it. Maybe fresher than ever before to know we were moving again in the right direction with our music, up to the top with Runnymede for sure, and maybe even beyond him, and perhaps that was the feeling I wanted to ascertain beneath her malice. Was she happy about that, too, about our success? Or mean and downhearted at something because of it?

What's funny, Isaiah? What?

O nothing, I said and looked at my worn boots a moment before looking back into the deep center of her eyes. It's just that something's always in the way, I guess.

In the way of what? She blinked and I seen a little flush rise from the milky depths of her skin, douring her cheeks, before dissolving again into the smooth constrained shape of her. Just say it, she said. Go on. Anything's funny with that fool lunkhead over there doing god-knows-what and running off to god-knows-where whenever he feels like it. When the music rises in him, like he says. Or whenever another name that he just has to track down appears, after finding it scribbled on some old newspaper or on the back of some damn grocery list. Names. Isn't that right? and she nodded her small shrewd head at A.D., and I seen her smile disappear as she touched her belly and set straight up to sip a glass of water she then replaced on the small tabletop beside her. I should think any number of things are out there for him to fall into running off like he does, anything to make us laugh the more. Open manhole covers. Dug ditches. Septic tanks and privy wells. Anything would be funnier than seeing him run off into the black devil night of New York City again. I swear.

But it wasn't black, Ms. Clara May. That's the whole thing. It was full of lights.

O sure, I know all about those lights. The lights, the lights, that was all he said for days sitting with me, hardly reading, holding the book upside-down as much as right-side-up, thinking on it. He was so worried about running into them lights everywhere he went he finally decided going nowheres was the best solution, until you all got me singing again and mentioned Mr. Ralph Peer and Runnymede's success. Always with Runnymede's success. That's what got him. Because then I got to hear all about it and even where it come from, those lights, from that Ezra Lee joker. Though as she said his name, something seemed to ripple in the air around her, some imperceptible shift or mote of dust, a dapple in the invisible string of time, and all the sass that was building up inside her diminished. She had to cough then in her hand and aright herself, struggling to set up against the over-starched pillows stacked behind her. There's all kinds of funny out there, Isaiah, don't you think? So what's your funny? She cocked her head sideways like a little bird and watched me. Well?

I don't know, ma'am, I said and rubbed my chin to think on her fury, the one building inside her. I guess it's not like that at all, is what I say. It's nothing about devils nor privies nor ditches and such. It's just that when he told me about it on the bridge—and I nodded at her belly to signify we were back on that subject—and I heard him name the curse again, I thought it was funny for him to think like that, and talked instead about what life was set to be like with that new blessing coming his way. I talked about the growth of it, too, and the magic of its spirit, with all the anticipation of being a father and how it changes you. How it makes you feel smaller about yourself in what you've always been up to, but bigger in what you've got to do now for the little one, with what you've got to give. But none of that brought him in like I thought it would. None of that moved him down from his heights.

She was silent. Her jaw had unclenched in listening to me and I seen her small pink tongue moving against her neat row of white bottom teeth. It didn't? she said finally, though I swear I couldn't tell from where the words come, for her mouth was as set as cement it didn't move an inch to even show she was breathing let alone speaking.

I leaned in a bit more then shook my head and said none of them words seemed to help. In fact, they only seemed to make him more defiant in the face of them. He just huffed and puffed out a mouthful of cold air and rubbed his hands together contemplating that curse or that gold coin he'd flipped onto Ezra Lee's head, and I tell you I was most lost for a moment on that bridge. I didn't know what to do, nor if I'd ever get him back to see the side of day again, and I looked on A.D. then in the other room. I looked on him as if he were my own son, if I'd had one. He was working and scribbling with Benjamin Marks over another count and the names of some broker Benjamin knew, a cousin or uncle up in Harrisburg, but a good man he said, honest as the day is long, and it was as if me and Ms. Clara May watched them from a great distance, watching from the far end of a telescope, with all the peripherals and room wiped clean from sight. We could only focus on what they were doing, moving silently with their papers, adding and subtracting numbers, reciting a list, and as they did, I wasn't so sure I should tell her what I'd done to get him down. Though I also knew I'd already gone too far into telling it, in giving her maybe this crucial last piece of truth to use against him someday, my A.D., and the thought made me cold.

Maybe it was because she seemed cold to me then, removed from it all with the emotion in her washed clear out for good. For she was looking on me so expectant and tense, I thought I might burst not to tell her what it was that brought him in finally, the magic spell as it were, and shaking my head soft and slow I should have known before this I couldn't never put nothing over on her to begin with. At least not about A.D. and his predilections, and so I just bowed my head, cleared my throat, and told her what it was that saved him. Jazz, I said and looked at her silhouetted face and seen the ends of her thin eyebrows arch up in amazement. Jazz was what it was, and it didn't hurt none neither that all those lights finally blinked out in the sun.

Jazz? she said, and looked on me funny, scrunching up her nose, and I wondered if her glassy neck was all rippled and agitated to have to say such a word as that.

Jazz. And if it wasn't for that and me seeing the Duke do it like the way he did, and then telling him about it, describing it to him, I wouldn't have been able to bring him back in neither. I swear.

The Duke? she said, skeptical now at my mentioning royalty to boot mixed in with all this other nonsense.

Sure, the Duke, and I nodded my head then like she knew him, too. Like everyone knew the power of the Duke and what he did. But of course A.D. didn't know what I meant, so I had to spell it out for him piece by piece, with how the Duke's playing was like the purest water, with how his music was like the blood in our veins. All shifting back and forth like currents on the ocean, in long arcing patterns while at the same time scattered and shifting and loose. And in every sad, swift pass of it, in the melody, in how I wanted to cry out with words for the mood and driving sweep of it, it would all change in the next instant. It would gallop away into some other register, into some higher clime, and there weren't no place nor solid standing for me to swim back to, nothing to hold onto. For jazz was like the city, I told him, and we—and I pointed to him and me then meaning our music and the subject of our music—we was like the ridge, with the brighter hills and mountains raised up from the blues but always tipped with them. Always stained and painted with the pain and sorrow and joy, and A.D. brightened then to hear me because he knew inside himself it was true.

What's true?

That we're not like that wide ocean, but like the country water and streams and lakes. Like even the one near Yancey Jakes, the one he took us to that night, to see the smooth swift flow of it. We're like the river all hemmed in and neat between its banks, our sound. The ones always moving and rushing off the same way you are, for we're always moving with you, not underneath you, nor against you. So it's smooth like that, and aching too in its ease, in its motion. Ain't that right?

Outside a car horn sounded and we could hear the glazier's door below us open as the little brass bell above the lintel tinkled and I wondered for the life of me why we were all up so early and gathered together to begin with. We'd only ridden into Roanoke last night on the train, and then went straight on through darkness into Bristol, and as soon as we knocked on the door Ms. Clara May opened it as if she'd been waiting all that time, even though it had been three full days since A.D.'d run off.

Benjamin was there too with her. His shabby coat and dusty hat were thrown over a chair, and the silly ridiculous shape of the man looked awful comfortable and at home. He was already stacking dollar bills into piles that'd been wired in from Mr. Ralph Peer after the first rush of sales hit. And as A.D. slumped in next to him to start counting it himself, Ms. Clara May gave him such a look I didn't think he'd ever be able to speak to her again, let alone sing nor even say hi to me in the process, it was so hard. So then here we were, waking up with Bristol and the ridge with Ms. Clara May listening to the shopkeeper below, listening to him scrape his boots off and then turn the flue in his stove before pulling the chain as the rat-a-tat-tat of the coal chute opened and filled it out. The great chalky rattle clamored up through the whole building before its echo died away in the silence of her listening and watching the world beneath us. Yet all the while I waited, I knew she still hadn't said what she was holding in for me. Her little pink tongue couldn't help but flicker in and out as if she was testing the air for the preponderance of her thoughts on our music.

Smooth, she finally said, as she held her palm to the floor to feel the warmth of the furnace in the shop catch hold, with it burning anew, making sand into glass.

Smooth like a river. Our songs is, that's what I say.

That's what you say. But she didn't turn to me when she said it. She didn't move neither, but just kept her gaze on the windows and listened to the awakening life shuttling lonesome and slow on the streets below.

Well, it's what we got to keep moving with, ain't it? It's gonna get us where we want to go. Smooth and easy.

Easy? she said, and turned to me with the taste of that word like gunmetal in her mouth. Easy you say? Running around the ridge like fools, barging in on old no-timers shacks and no-count niggers and such, in on folks that have never seen the half-life of a dime in years upon years. That's what's so easy about it? And then to take their songs from them and use them as your own?

I was silent. I'd never heard her call no colored folk nigger before and didn't like how it made her pretty mouth look. How it shaped it like she was biting something out in front of her, gnawing against the air. And so she wasn't so smooth nor pretty to me after that. She had hardened into something else as quick as could be, and as her hand rested on her belly again, I knew why. O she just thrummed her hand there and seen me watching as if to amplify it too, her reasoning, the way the nature of her whole being had turned just like that, as quick as a flash. Though when I consider it now, and think on my own Annie and Lucy girl, and the family I once had, I can't fault her none in that regards. Not in the least. If the man had to change in the coming of the child, then the woman had to change, too. And even if I couldn't remember that savage need in Annie to keep the world safe and close to her, so that everything around her would help make her child that much better and true. Well, with Ms. Clara May, I guess I would see firsthand what it could do to everything that seemed to confront and challenge her with what she meant to have.

Cause when this one comes, she said and smiled devilish and slow, there won't be any more of that grand foolishness of yours—and his—and holding up her hand, as if to wave away that life, I seen for the first time the little diamond ring she had on her finger. Like a small glint of heavendust itself. I glanced to A.D. in the kitchen and seen his ring finger wrapped with a slim gold band and knew they'd been married sometime hence, in some secret ceremony, for they hadn't yet announced it and hadn't seen fit to include me in the event. But I could hear it already in her voice, the new command she had of the room, of the situation, and everyone in it. Her voice was louder, as if our own confidence was through. That the trust between us had left as soon as she'd said it, naming the path A.D. would have to toe from then on.

But you're singing, Ms. Clara May. You sing like no other and love it, too, for I've seen it on your face and eyes and everything else that moves you when it comes out like a shot, your voice. So why would you deny the music to yourself?

Well, I didn't say I wouldn't be singing no more, now did I? She laughed and waved her hand against the flush of heat building in waves and gusts from downstairs so I jumped and pushed up the window to let in a cool rush of air.

You'll still sing with us? I said and shook my head because I thought I'd just heard her say there wouldn't be no more of that.

I said there wouldn't be any more of that ridge running for you two. There won't be any more of that.

Ma'am?

There's already songs, Isaiah. Hell, the whole world is just full of them. Why would you have to go out and find any more?

She said it. I swear. She set right there and said it and nodded her head as A.D. and Benjamin stood as if they'd only just heard our voices and were concerned with the welfare of the unborn child amidst such commotion and quarrellings, even if she was just talking with me. But she took the moment to touch her belly and sigh real loud, wafting her face again for the heat before smiling at me as if none of our discourse or argument had ever happened.

That false cold smile of hers.

The one I would see the more of, and that made her face into a mask I shall never forget. Like the smeared white mask of Ezra Lee's. The one that makes me shiver and recoil every time I recall it, or him, or what Ms. Clara May's decision had me finally resort to in my dealings with A.D. from then on.

XXIII

The days of silence and dread ~ The blueness ~ Burning
to be found ~ Five more like the first ~ The lonely
magnet ~ To keep the blood true ~ Their unfathomable
eyes ~ To my dark side of the room ~ As of a baptism or
ordination ~ Something just audible to the attentive ear

THOSE WERE THE DAYS OF SILENCE AND DREAD. When Ms. Clara
May would be there at the shows Benjamin lined up for us—in Virginia and
West Virginia and even Tennessee sometimes—but wouldn't speak none to me
nor I to her, and that was considered the best solution by all concerned. Since
the tension that still stretched between us about the songs and going out to get
them had gotten so heated that even A.D. didn't know which side of the coin
to come down on.

I would be at my house most times sitting in my bedroom or walking the
property, passing my hands through the tall switchgrass and weeds, watching
the ridge light up in the morning with the dawning. Or, better yet, I'd watch
late in the evening. As the colors of the world seemed to flow into its wan faint
glow and the blueness was the last thing I could see or distinguish, before the
innumerable tracks of stars seeped out one by one, and the mountains were just
a far off paper cutout that seemed to sigh and persist in its resignation as of a
monster nestled and sleeping in the silence of its dreaming.

It was perfect, was what it was. The air was warm to me then, even in the
early spring chill, and I would stand there as if absorbed by the sun's golden
rays and didn't have to think none about my family then, nor about finding
them, nor even about raising myself up with A.D. into some sort of prominence
where my name might be broadcast to the far corners of the globe. There was
just the blueness. That soft sad color, that feeling and mood, a place I could

have stood in all my life just to feel it, to be part of the utter isolation of it. It seems odd, I know, but I don't know how else to describe that feeling other than calling it the blueness, for I have not heard it named nor approached in any other way by anyone living or dead. It was a sort of perfection, I suppose, if you'd care to name it by way of mathematics or books. Though I don't usually go in for all that scientific stuff, and considered the blueness just fine. For I was always real sad when it ended, and watched it for moments and moments even after it ended. Inside then, I'd throw another log on the fire and listen to the blueness fade into its currents and folds of time, and as I stood there and warmed myself in the heat, I couldn't be sure if it had ever really happened, those moments, that suspension I'd just shared with the ridge, even if I looked for it and watched it each day.

A connection, I guess is what it really was, a connection beyond just living and struggling to feel and to be something. O never to worry no more, nor be tired nor striving for anything else. Absolute and devout, as it were. And on some days I kept that aloof blue feeling with me even when I had to see Ms. Clara May or A.D. Or when Benjamin Marks leered at me from the side of whatever stage we were working that weekend, at whatever hayseed venue he'd booked. His face a scrunched up mess of raised lips and gnashed teeth and overblown anxiety that made his small little ears a ruby red, trying to attract my attention as best he could before the first few chords of our last song finally rang out. Or the encore—when I would really be in the moment—and his chance would be dashed for sure. As in Bluefield that next month, or Blacksburg a month later, when I knowed just then that my own last possibility with A.D. had finally come full circle.

Pssst, Benjamin said and I could hear him like a slashed tire he was so loud and insistent. Anyways the crowd had just then hushed to watch A.D., for he was changing one of his broken guitar strings, and it was always otherworldly to the folks to see something like that. I have seen how this worked on them before, fascinating them to see we actually had to work these instruments. That they were just as fallible and meek as anything else, and the totality of it all would throw them into a state of perpetual wonderment. To find out at last there was a fragmentation behind the harmonious whole they'd always heard had never occurred to them, at least not in so obvious a way. And it always seemed to change them into a group of amazed and startled school children as they watched—even if they were all over twenty or even thirty years old—and so of course, Benjamin's listing, leering voice shook the amazement right out of them. I had to play it off like my microphone was staticy and hot. Tapping it once and then twice, I followed the cord to the edge of the stage and knelt down so that I could shake it out and talk to Benjamin even without A.D. or Ms. Clara May noticing.

You gotta stay with him after, and he nodded toward A.D., even though I knew or had a premonition before about what he meant.

Stay with who? I said, just to set him a little more on edge, to see if he really was as anxious as he tried not to let on.

With A.D., he hissed, who else? and he shook his sharp little head as if I was the most ignorant nigger in the whole county.

I blinked at him once playing my part, all innocent and out of sorts like. Then looking straight at Benjamin in the flashing darkness, I seen for the first time that he held the back of a wrinkled hotel receipt and that a name was written on it in the most antique and scribbled script. I knew right away what it was—my chance—even if Ms. Clara May and even A.D. himself wouldn't have wanted me to take it. But I knew my chance was held out to me at the end of his small sweaty hand.

You got to keep him from it, Benjamin said, and waved the receipt before me.

Me? I said, and blinked again, drawing out again his anxiousness, pushing that last little button in him. Why me?

Because you know him, and he averted his eyes as he seen he was leaning a bit too far out and that his fat round belly must have been seen by the crowd for he heard quite a few giggles. Just take it, he said, and puffed on a cigar before snapping shut the broken pocket watch he rubbed furiously as if to satisfy some invisible agenda.

I reached up and touched the paper a second to see the writing on it and seen Benjamin's face too in the half-light looking into the questioning depth of me. The stern consternation of his jaw. His long handlebar moustache twitching now, before his tense little lips snapped shut as he watched me, imploring me to act, to accept it, and I believed him then. I did. I'd drawn out the real him at last and it was all frustration and anxiety and honest indignation. Even though I'd seen how close and comfortable he got when it was just him and Ms. Clara May, with A.D. out of the picture, out wandering or talking to some promoter. Or even reading or maybe working on an old song he'd set aside months ago, re-arranging lyrics and such, trying to make it right. But I could see right through that fat little fellow. If he was playing tough with me, it was all an act. Even if he wanted A.D. at some point to vacate the scene entire, so he could have Ms. Clara May to himself, A.D. was still his meal ticket. And if A.D. went running off looking for some other name, then Ms. Clara May would have gotten real mad at Benjamin for letting him go, and the whole thing might collapse. So I guess he wanted me to track down the songs instead, even if he didn't say so or hint in words to the effect. But I seen his fat red face dangling that receipt that he could have just as easily thrown into the trash or burnt up into ash.

Would you just take it?

There was a rustling of strings then, and as I turned, I heard A.D. strum the first few chords of The Return of Clara May as the cheering and clapping returned like thunder. Shaking out my microphone, I was still engaged in this last bit of playacting before grabbing the receipt, tucking it inside my pocket, and turning to the full force of the crowd, to the sound. For even as I watched them, I couldn't see them no more; I couldn't hear them neither. It all drained away. There was only A.D. now and his face before me—with his long focused stare—for he was intent on Ms. Clara May as she sang, even as I could feel the heat of the name in my pocket burning to be found.

THERE WERE FIVE MORE LIKE THE FIRST. Five more scraps that Benjamin found in the next few months as Ms. Clara May's belly grew and gradually our shows tapered off as Benjamin said he had Ms. Clara May's best interests in mind. He would shrug his shoulders and kind of stare at me as I mentioned we were really just starting to roll again and that maybe we should keep going. But I knew he meant for her health of course, and sure enough A.D. agreed with him all the way down the line, for anyways it seemed the money from the latest record had all but done its business growing as Benjamin had said it would. He'd made a few investments on the side, and as he doled us out our shares the summer sped away till its end and like it or not I seemed to be gathering more and more of the names Benjamin had found and that even I heard and wrote down in my own doings. As if I were magically called to them myself. Or more likely, in the wake of A.D.'s abandoned search of them, the names became my calling. As if I was the lonely magnet that pulled them up out of their obscurity, up from the nothingness and strife they'd become. That just by holding them, by arranging and rearranging them by place and age and distinction, I'd already breathed on them a little bit of life that might bring them back into being.

O there were an intolerable amount of them by then too. And as I stacked each one atop my hearth, I always had the inclination to toss them into the fire each night, when I threw my logs on, after the blueness had faded, and I thought on A.D. and Ms. Clara May's contentment, at their lives spinning away proper and true as she'd always hoped they would. I'd look at the names on each slip and think of the song attached to it and the story, and then imagine A.D. and Ms. Clara May's child soon living and laughing and playing amongst us. A child. His child. With her. Whenever I let the words pass through my lips it tore at me too, I tell you, to know it, to know all that happiness and succor would be theirs soon enough and not mine. Not mine for all these years and maybe forever. That was the hardest part, too. To know my own life was slipping away, even as theirs was just taking shape.

How can I say it? He was my friend. He was more than my friend. He was the only man left for me in the world to know and trust and even I in my weakness did not wish him well. In fact, I took down the names on them papers one by one and touched them, rubbing them together to try and extract from them their own lost secrets, their hidden source or spark even though I knew it weren't no good. The papers just stared at me in the flickering light and would seem as dead and still as stones to my fingers. Only A.D. could truly breathe life into them again. Only A.D. had the fever to retrieve the sadness in each one. Even though I knew Benjamin Marks in all his anxiety had set it in his mind for me to do it now, to track them down and keep our bevy of songs rolling in fresh and new and beyond the power of any other (including Runnymede's recent string of hits), I knew it was not my place to be their interpreter, or conduit, as it were. That was for A.D. alone to complete, because the voice of these songs was my voice. I could no more interpret them in A.D.'s special way as I could interpret my own story. I was so much closer to the source in being black, in being poor and once as much a slave as most the men and women who'd somehow survived long enough to sing and write these songs, that it couldn't have worked for me even if I tried. And I did try. Shoot, I'd look at those slips and names and think about all those songs passed down and worked on in the ridge for no fanfare or money. Just for survival. For the sheer fun of it, too, but for blood most likely. To keep the blood true and the memories true and the world from forgetting it all in its ugliness and blight, in that time when we were nothing more than chattel to be thrown away and used, and it made me immobile almost to think on it. It paralyzed me.

But A.D. hadn't suffered in that same way and that was why he was able to change them, I think, to find in their ancient rhythm and sorrow a speck of brightness, something to build all his burning ambition and hope around. All laid out on his blank emotional slate. Sent out as a child, unformed, untethered, able to bridge some lost divide, bringing them all back into the power of their new form, as he'd always been moving to begin with and couldn't be paralyzed in the least by the emotion, by the grand sad feeling of it all. Besides, it had all sat ill with me from the beginning, if I am truthful. I'd once thought it an abomination what he done, taking credit and not saying nothing about it, but just smiling all the more in his recognition, accepting his success. Even with all those out there who'd done most the work for him and who'd suffered to write their pieces.

Suffered. O A.D.'d had a hard time of it, for sure, but he hadn't suffered like those folks. And the more I thought on it and touched the papers with the solemn and lost names etched upon them, the more I was moved to agree with A.D.'s intentions instead, and slowly understood the stark wisdom of it all. How it was just another part of their survival really. The songs, that is, with the names.

This was how the songs were sustaining themselves, by allowing their voices to be changed, tweaked ever so much, even as the spark of them remained, the truth, buried deep in the blood rhythm. The songs were the ones moving through A.D. to be born again, as if moving through a door as ancient and dormant as hope perhaps? Something with a will and truth beyond me, beyond anything I could ever say or do. Lord, it was too much to even think on, with the mystery of it all, and so the more I thought on it, the more I drank and kept one particular wrinkled receipt in my hand. I began to take it everywhere, this one name. This one name more than any other that gave me pause. That kept me up at night, and generally made a mess of everything I touched from then on.

WHAT'S THAT? A.D. SAID WHEN WE WERE FINALLY ALONE, at the end of another rehearsal. Benjamin had already offered to drive Ms. Clara May to the midwife to go over details as to what herbs or whatnot to use, and which cotton linens were best for the delivery, and how much witch hazel was to be used to wipe out the baby's eyes.

What's what?

In your hand, he said and nodded at me.

My hand?

Sure, he said and smiled at me. In. Your. Hand. Annunciating each word to see me so serious and innocent for once, for he must have seen something as I'd moved away from him. It had become habit to me by then to put the paper back in my palm as quick as lightning after I'd finish playing the guitar. O I'd hold it there in the curve, perfectly molded in the middle of my palm, for it felt right being there; it felt part of me. If it's strange, I know, but it was as if my body sensed its loss when it was away for the few hours of our playing. Or even in the few moments I needed to fix my pants sometimes. Or slip on my boots. Or buckle my belt and any other inconvenience that had me use both hands for an instant. But when I'd slide it back into place, I'd feel such a sense of ease wash back over me, it was as if I'd been out bathing beneath a cool mountain stream, it was so enveloping and easy. All the while it was gone, my flesh was like a gray fire missing its most elemental piece—that name, that source—but the feeling of it, that old smoldering feeling of putting it back in place, would then seem to quell my skins' crying out for this missing and essential spark.

It's nothing, I finally said as I turned from him and looked out on Bristol.

Nothing my foot, he said and touched my shoulder and tugged at me almost playfully. It might have been the first time I'd felt his hand in months, for as I spun from him he laughed and the note fell to the rug so that I had to put my boot out to cover it, but I was too slow. He'd already stepped there—his legs were so damn long—and he just looked at me after he did it and winked something mischievous for he didn't know what it was yet, and I'm ashamed to say I'd already decided to let him see it. O there was nothing else to it. He would hold it up and see it in the dim light and the name would work its power on him like before and we would be back out there moving in the right direction, as far as I was concerned. Racing along the ridge, chasing down each name, each song, chasing our fortune. Even if it meant something awful might happen to him and Ms. Clara May later on, even if it meant that.

Now I'm not saying I didn't care about their relationship. It was just that I cared that much more for finding my wife and baby girl, and maybe I let a little bit of that jealousy seep out of me just then. The jealousy I felt about him having a child and not caring that much for it, in not realizing the powerful gift of it, the magic, for I'd never even heard him speak on it. Not once, and so I stepped back and bowed my head and just watched as he smirked at the dramatics of it all, before groping with his long fingers to hold it to the light. The name. I seen it just as he did and could tell that he knew what it was as soon as he spied it. I imagine he must have felt it in his bones even before he looked, because a soft gurgling left his lips as he focused on it. His head twitched imperceptibly, and a red flush rose in his cheeks as I'd seen it do in Ms. Clara May's before. Shaking his head violently, he held the name out at arm's length, squeezing his eyes shut, saying, No, no, no, no.

Yes, I said, to answer him coldly. Yes, and I heard my voice changing now, delving into some deeper register, into something that coincided with the vague and hazy light outside.

But I don't want it, Isaiah. You know that. I can't no more. I just can't.

Sure you can, I said. You can and you will, and I stepped closer as he held it out, his arm growing limp at the suggested power of it, one little slip, the name. Hell, I said, you already seen it. You already know, and though I can't tell you where the words came from or my dark tone, I imagine I'd become something else in that moment. A shade of myself as another mood crept inside me and seemed to hush and stalk him as I rose up as a cloud or rainstorm to goad him on, tempting him toward his doom. As I spoke, the words came faster and stronger until I was worked up most into a tempest to stand before him, waving my arms, narrowing my gaze, grasping for the weakest part of him. Just look on it, I said. Just think on it. Think what it was like to be that man in that time and to write something to save your soul from the world happening around you, from the death and misery and hatred. Just think on it and tell me you can't no more. Just tell me that, son. Go on. Just tell me that ain't the name right there of the song that saves someone after you change it, after you bring it back to the world new. Just tell me that.

I was all the way in front of him now, for he'd shriveled up with each word. So that I could look straight into his face imploring him on, bringing him over to my dark side of the room, to my dark way of living, now that I needed him to continue. Now that I needed him to rise back up into the fever of gathering in the things that had pushed him on before, and that I knew would push him on still.

I can't, he said. You know that. I can't, and his voice was soft and broken as he collapsed from his own conflicted desire. Still holding the paper in his hand, still touching it with his fingers, he sank to his knees, his head bowed. His long face wet from the tears, so that I could just make out my own dark shape reflected in his cheeks, and had to gasp to see myself like that. Lording over him like some plague or misery, devouring him entire. As I watched him, I seen again the young boy on his first day at the Peabody carrying a sack full of books, just in off the streets, and knew I couldn't no more. I couldn't. For all I could think of then was What have I done to him now? What have I done?

Reaching out, I touched his hot sweaty head, as of a baptism or ordination, before taking the slip and slinking out without even looking back to see the damage I'd done to his frail and crumbled soul. To the one I'd disposed of so easily, with the mere suggestion of a name.

Whiskey was all that allayed me then, whiskey and silence. As I stumbled along State Street, the darkness I'd seen before covered the whole ridge as only bolts of lightning seared the heavens periodically and told me of a story far off in its making. Something eerie and electric in the ether. As of another layer composed and plastered upon the world. A layer I would never see, at least not upon that night, for it was only taverns that reared before me then. As I crept from the first to many, I finally found the lowest of the low where my color was not an issue. Where no one gave pause to see a tired old nigger slumped in the corner with a half bottle of whiskey. Where the music was slow and rumbling, even as I heard the rainstorm and thunder and mumbling crowd dispersed into an eddy of unrelenting rhythm. Ah, the music of it, even in that place—the life of it—something just audible to the attentive ear. I placed the slip of paper by the candle and stared at it, stared at the name that so deterred my A.D., my boy, and knew there was nothing for me to do but cease in this effort of winning him away from his family and comfort and ease, to cease from this sad way of wounding him.

But after another shot and another burned inside my soul, I admit I had not given up entire on tempting him to the names because so much rested on chasing our fame. I didn't know how or where to begin if the names didn't work, if all those precious names didn't tempt him no more. And as I turned to see the latest surge of revelers stumble in, as if drawn to my own dark schemes, there he was, my answer, as if raised from the night itself—my nightmare and curse and command. Come out of the pale blue smoke and beer-piss smell of the place to confront me in all his proper glory: Runnymede McCall. Singer Extraordinaire. Lately of the Piedmont Pipers. Staring me square in the face.

XXIV

This man, this apparition ~ The wide white cream of
his skin ~ Turpentine ~ The true spirit ~ Watching
each by each ~ A turning inside ~ The true and
forever things ~ Our name ~ A puff of black smoke
~ On commerce ~ With the deepest black ink

YOU'RE A HARD MAN TO FIND, he said and I shivered to hear his voice, to smell his subtle, almost minty aroma as he moved smooth as a thoroughbred across the floor. Was he really there? Could it be true? This man, this apparition materialized before me as if to do my very bidding, for my own devices, to maybe even tempt A.D. back to ridge riding again, to get him out there like he should have been?

I held my hand out and had a notion of passing it through the smooth powder-blue coat he wore, but thought better of it as he tilted his equine head back and watched me. His unhurried eyes were dark and unrelenting with nary a spark nor reflection nor impetus of mercy glistening in them—as if the blankness itself was of a seething condition that would rise up out of the center of him and conquer the world.

It's not hard being found, I finally uttered, pouring out another shot and draining it as I watched him. If you want to be.

My, my, he said and grinned down at me. Your homespun bravado, friend, might only be exceeded by your theatrics, and as he slid into the chair across from me, I swear I felt a bolt of heat rise from inside me. A heat not from the whiskey, mind you, but from the very energy his appearance engendered. A supple, slick wave of it rippled through me even as he reached out so elegantly, grabbed my bottle, and held it to his still smiling lips, before turning it up and taking a healthy gulp.

I had a mind then not to say nothing. Not as he set the bottle back down or even when he stared at me while wiping his thin lips clean of every last drop. I could not speak as there was something so regal in his face, in the stunning contrast of it thrown and held and bandied about by the candle flame flickering in a glass jar on the table. I mean, here he was, the man we'd been chasing all these months, and maybe more, in the hidden meaning of our practicing and sweating and rehearsing way back even at the Peabody. Here he was and I had every last chance to smash that thick brown bottle into his pretty white face, and yet I resisted. I resisted even speaking as he eyed me, for my flesh crawled just to think of the wide white cream of his skin. The unnatural smoothness of it all. The perfection.

Turpentine, he said and nodded at the bottle still resting in his thick white hand. Is that what they serve here in lieu of the true spirit? His fingers fluttered on the neck of the brown glass, before caressing the wide shape of the bottle. Then with one powerful gesture, he pushed it out into the middle of the table, back towards me, and I could tell he knew more about me than I could ever fathom. I could see the cruel way he watched me, as if turning through the very pages of my mind, with how his steady eyes never shifted nor blinked nor wavered in the smoky half-lit room. Measuring my every move, I supposed, goading me on to speak, even as I'd hoped to goad A.D. on into ridge riding again. As if life was nothing more than a perpetual round of temptation played out against each other. I tempted you. You tempted me. The wind tempted the rock, and all and all worked backwards on itself to gain an advantage or edge, to come out on top.

What you know about spirits? I hefted the bottle and drained a shot as I watched his whole brash appearance flicker momentarily above the candlewick into nothingness, before flickering back as he laughed thrusting his wide forehead up. As he did, I could see into the black hole of his throat, so deep and endless, opening for a brief festive snort that faded into a silent chuckle that shook his massive shoulders.

Well, I know everything about spirits. I know they live, friend. He leveled his eyes upon me and held up his hand as if to waft aside the cigar smoke drifting in from the opposite table. But his hand never moved. Instead he just held it there, like the sharp mane of a white roan, frozen on a track. And that you've been chasing them all this time.

Chasing who?

Your wife, for one. And your little girl? He leaned forward as he said this last part, lingering on the lilting sound, and I could feel a turning inside me. A pain and wounding to hear it said aloud—that my family was nothing more than spirits to him—that they could have been gone a long time now and I'd have never known it. It was a fact I'd steeled myself for years ago. I'd denied it and forged on instead, relentless in my pursuit. And I would always deny it. To this day, I would. Forever. Amen.

They ain't dead, I said. They can't be.

Why not? he said.

Because I haven't found them yet, is why. Because I still have a breath with which to find them, and a voice, too, and I will do it to the end of me, sir. To the end.

To the end of what? Your memories? This land? This silly business about taking songs from those already passed on into the memory of their own depressing lives. With those niggers you rob?

I rob no one, I said and the words of guilt and accusation shook me awake. I was fresh now with him saying it. I was opposed, too. We're a band, I said, raising my voice and throwing it back on him like a cloak. Like you. We make something from the memories of them and bring it back out. We bring it back out to remember it.

And to change it, he said.

I wasn't sure. Of course I'd thought we'd changed 'em before, but sitting there, in the brash noise of that barroom, and looking into his endless eyes, I couldn't say anything ever changed in the whole damn world. I was still a nigger in his eyes. In so many eyes, I was. The songs we found and saved were the songs of those abused and forgotten and their voices remained even below the surface of the changing words and moods A.D. placed upon them. Had they ever really changed? Had they even moved an inch? Weren't they still the true and forever things we held onto? That was what we were really doing, wasn't it? Bestowing truth again upon the world. Returning it to where it had fallen away. Replacing it to where it had first strayed. Change, I finally uttered, watching him waver in the gray light. They ain't changed none, sir, no. They ain't nothing changed in all the world. Not one damn thing. Not even you.

Hell, he said, and moved his lips to say something, yet no sound came. He smiled just the same and then clapped his hands when he was done and the sound shook the whole room and I wasn't sure what any of it meant or if anyone else had heard, for the room seemed to continue on as before with people drinking and swaying to the staticy singing on the radio. Though as my own general confusion ceased, I remembered why I'd so disliked him to begin with. Then I knew truly why he sat before me either as a living and breathing adversary or as a wavering apparition, for either way he was the same strong urge seeped up out of the drink itself to deny me my strongest desire.

Our name, I said.

What?

Our name, I whispered. You won't say it, will you? and I shook my head watching him. You never have. Not even that night in this same square, in this same town, and I pointed beyond the smoky shapes reflected in the window, out past the striped awning of the Mercantile. On that very stage you stood, even as the storm raced down from the ridge and the crowd raised up even louder applauding you, but you would not say it. Even after you said every other. You would not say our name because you were afraid it was true what we sung. You were afraid we were better.

Nonsense, he said with a smirk. You misunderstand everything. If I do not say your name then you fail to even exist. You fail to even matter. That is all, and he shook his equine head side to side as if to wash away the very suggestion of my charge. I mentioned every other act as a courtesy because they were weak and frail. But for you, and here he paused, the great man, pausing as the light inside his face flickered again before striking back true and steady, I felt something in looking at you and the boy. I've always felt something in looking at the boy. Ever since the Peabody when he spoke to me of Parmenides. You remember. When he said nothing had changed in the whole world just as you have now. And now here you are, and you're just as sure he doesn't change the songs. But I know that's not true, and I will make you see it, too, friend, before I'm done. I will make you see it for yourself. He touched his bright white tie as he said it, straightening it out above his vanilla cream shirt. That is my pledge to you, to make the people see it, too. That they are changing. That it is for the better for them to change, to fall away, and to sing, to forget this burning away of everything, this sad burning of time and taste and love. This whole Earth is changing in every moment and the music is changing, too. This music is moving the whole world, and I thought you of any other would have at least seen that.

I seen it, I said. I seen it, and I sure seen you, too.

Do you? His lips were pale in the light, but shimmery, and as he licked them now with his quick sharp tongue, it was as if the blood between us was boiling up to color his flesh anew in the soft light.

Because I seen the darkness in you, I continued. I seen it towards me and towards my kind. And I seen the fear, too.

Ha! Again, with your bravado. It amuses me, and chuckling he leaned close enough then, ranging his wide chest over the table, so I could smell the sulfurous breath rising from inside his hideous blank depths. Even a puff of black smoke escaped his throat (I swear) as he hovered there. His lips slightly parted and red, his creamy face an endless white pudding I wanted to touch my finger to, to draw in its blank slate some sign or shape of indecency, something to mark him for what he was, and what he'd always been. You change the music and I plan to change you, he said, and grinning deeply, he added, and the boy, of course. I plan to change you two right out of my way. The world is changing and I aim to keep it changing. I don't care about race or creed or time, because all of that falls away beneath my need. All of that can be used to my ends. He moved his hand then in the air purposefully, as if brushing the dust of us aside into a small patch of space that he shook out into infinity. So you see I aim to move aside any impediment. To ease them all out of existence.

O you do? I said, and put my own hand into the air as if to hold up a guitar, twittering my fingers to loosen the strings of life a bit in the face of all his significance. As I did, behind us, a tray of glasses fell crashing to the floor, and Runnymede brightened to hear it, to hear the chaos and changing nature of life raised against the futility of my words.

You are the impediment, he said in the stark silence after the crash, and his straight white teeth came together perfectly with a soft and audible chomping. The ones that want to muck up all the ugliness again. That want to do wrong when it can be made right. When it can all be washed aside like a glaze, washed over the rocks and air and hills, washing it all away. That unpleasantness and strife.

What unpleasantness?

Why the past, of course. If only you'd let it die, friend, you'd see a whole new world before you. Commerce, he said, and his wide white face broke into an otherworldly grin as he annunciated the word, is the new truth, and the sooner you can wrap your rusty head around it, the better. Then maybe there won't have to be any blood in all of this. Then maybe there'll just be you left at the end, walking away from it all, singing unto yourself, strumming for all you're worth.

There was a machine behind the bar working now, heating up oil and kernels and the bubbling noise seemed to diffuse the whole room with the airy scent of a circus or carnival, and I couldn't hear him anymore and what he said for he was mouthing again some words before standing up and grabbing something from beside the candle. He then placed something in it. Something that lit up and flared as sudden as any firework to catch my attention, for I hadn't realized it, but I was close enough to the candle flame to see the name on the slip of paper as it dispersed into smoke. The name I'd carried all that time and had to do right by. The name that had to be remembered for what it'd done, for what it had sung. But it was gone now and I knew I couldn't show him any weakness in losing it, in feeling it drift away. Blood, I finally said. Did you just say blood?

You know I did.

Well, blood don't wash away that easy, and I shook my hand out to show him. It sticks right there on the inside, and only comes out when it wants to show you what is real, and I stood before him then as he leaned back. The minty aroma of the man mixing with the scent of popcorn and roasted peanuts.

No, I suppose the blood doesn't ever leave, he said. It doesn't lie either, and he was rubbing his big beautiful hands together and leering at me in the light. It's just like the lights in that way, I suppose. It's just like the lights all the way through.

I was silent. The room had ceased to exist as the bubbling oil and sugary air faded into nothing. I looked into his endless black eyes, as now emblazoned in them were the lights like what Ezra Lee had prophesized and what A.D. had almost leapt into from the Brooklyn Bridge. The lights I had to draw him away from even as the sun helped me, brightening the world, easing away A.D.'s madness. What lights? I said, even though he knew it as sure as he'd said it, smiling and clapping his hands again so that I had to cover my ears the thunder shook the building so and a soft ash drifted down to settle over everything like a sad winter snow.

Why the ones that will be your end, of course. What other lights could I mean? He was smiling and moving to leave. I tried to block him, but he was already behind me, and as I turned, I couldn't see where he'd got to or where he was going, or if any other had even the faintest notion as to what kind of man walked amongst us and held such sway in what he sung and told people. It's the lights, Isaiah, the lights. It's always been the lights.

The words wavered above the room as I blinked into the smoke. Then another thunderclap rang out, shaking down another rain of ash and soot and when I turned my hands over to shake them clean, all I felt was the hot burning emptiness of the name on my skin. For the letters that had stayed with me somehow, etched into my flesh, written as if by a scalding sharp pen, something eternal and true drawn with lines and drips of the deepest black ink.

XXV

Daisies ~ The sad burning away ~ As meager financier
~ He come to me ~ Some indecipherable pattern
~ A vision perhaps ~ The ire in his cheeks ~ The
monocled man ~ Back from the edge of that window
~ The very metronome of our making ~ A prism of
light and broken geometries ~ Our little Jolie

JESUS CHRIST, ISAIAH, WHAT THE HELL IS THIS?

There were crushed daisies beneath me when I sat up. My house was out in front from where I'd lain most the night, and as I shook my head clear, I could see from the roadway a figure struggling with the gate. What? I said and looked down at my hand as he stood there huffing from the exertion of finding me, because I still remembered the letters and wanted to see if they had remained through the night, if it had all really happened as I'd thought. But there was nothing. Only a small red circle drew its ring where before the name had been, where before I'd held it as my talisman, my charm of sorts, to ward away the sadness. I was forgetting it now even as I tried with all my might to gather it back up, to recall Runnymede and his face and the high flare of that light in the lantern, but it was no use. My head throbbed and Benjamin Marks was peering down into the broken shell of me.

His black mustache was turned out and waxed on both ends. His red cheeks and jowls jiggled as he scoured my worn out and alcohol-soaked form from end to end. Whistling as he done it, he shook his head from side to side, muttering about the true plight of things in the world, about abstinence and temperance and all the other things I suppose he and Ms. Clara May must have preached to each other when they were alone. As he nudged me with the pointy toe of his left boot, I stretched my arms up and could hear his broken pocket watch snap shut and knew that time mattered to him now. Time always mattered to him in some way. But in his agitated movements and sweat-laden chin, I knew there was something more elemental going on here, something tense and ruddy and historic bringing him out here to roust me from my stupor.

It's Clara May, he said. She's at the hospital. Been there all night.

Hospital? And I squinted not understanding the plain arithmetic of his statement.

It's the baby, man. The baby's almost here.

NOW MY JOB WAS TO KEEP A.D. CALM, TO KEEP HIM HOME, as Ms. Clara May had requested. At least, that was what I deciphered from the endless stream of sentences issuing from Benjamin's puckered little mouth. He was a curious man, Benjamin Marks, and I wondered if he'd ever really known love before, if he'd ever really felt a woman's caress. (You can discount, of course, his patronage in those sultry hallways at Ezra Lee's house of ill repute, for in those curtained and red-lit rooms, I'm certain his basest desires had been met.) Because as I watched him drive, moving the wheel back and forth in his fierce little hands, I remembered that fateful night (I'd seen him there stranded in the shadows, I swear) when Ms. Clara May had dipped her pretty little head inside the wheel of fire, when it had danced its brilliant flame of remembrance and regret above her, and I wondered if he'd felt his own regret in not stepping forth to save her, to take her in his arms? For as he drove on and talked, wandering into whatever odd tangent the man was prone to—on moneylending and the current price of tobacco and the yield of a ten-year US T-Note—I could sense the sad burning away inside him and thought he'd finally found it, his love, and it was all because of Ms. Clara May and what he wanted to make for her, in what he'd already built himself up into. Sure, men like that were always trying to outdo others, to set up airs, so to speak, to see in the illusion of themselves some greater good, some stronger hand. I'd already seen him craft himself as meager financier, as stage manager, as intrepid investor, as someone who hoped to put his finger on some wild pulse in the world—if only to break from the dull hand that life had dealt him. And in that sense, I could not begrudge his affection toward Ms. Clara May in the least, nor his worrying on her condition, with the almost doting nature he displayed during her pregnancy.

Now I didn't know how far his affection for her had gone (nor how far it had been reciprocated), but my plan all along had been to let it happen, to at least permit the space for it to happen. I hadn't had the chance to get A.D. away on another trip, going after another song, though I thought this birth might just be the opportunity. Yet as we sped into town, and I watched Benjamin hem and haw over the steering wheel, I felt a certain companionship stretch out between us. The need in him to extend on all sides for some connection or kind of return wavered in the air like an ember. He was truly a wreck to know his beloved was in some sterile room somewheres pushing out another life, another extension for him to love, and he wasn't there to see it, to help. Instead, he'd been charged with the objectionable task of coming out to pick up some drunk nigger, ironically, the same man who held his best interests in heart. The same man who watched now as he wiped another sweat rag across his face. All the nervousness and bluster that had always seemed part and parcel of the man had since faded in light of this new development, with his love, now that he was sick as a dog in worrying on his Clara May.

Clara May said for you to watch him, and I hope you can watch him good, he said again and emphasized this last point by looking at me about as earnest and steady as I'd ever seen. Even as he pulled up on State Street, winking as he said it and eying the closed curtain of Ms. Clara May's apartment. I was all set to appease him, and maybe to even say a nice word about Ms. Clara May, about how tough she was, hinting as I could on his feeling for her and thereby relating in some unspoken way how I was pulling for him in all this, in however it shook out. Yet as I got out of the car and turned to address him, he couldn't have cared less. He was already looking past me to a crowd gathered in the late morning light before the Mercantile.

Some of them were talking to each other and taking their hats from their heads and shaking them out or slapping them against their blue jeans or overalls as the bell above the Mercantile's door continued to ring with a sharp impertinent chime each time another man came out. Then an official in a dark suit and monocle would solemnly let another man in for what I supposed was a promotion or deal with the local Freemasons or Anabaptists, or some such secretness. But all of them seemed very tense and hurried. And as I watched Benjamin take his studied read of the matter—for I knew he had more regard for the world of finance than me—the only thing he could mutter was about Ms. Clara May and the baby, before racing off, his mustache wafting in the breeze. His car skidding against the curb, leaning his pointed head out one last time to survey me and my intentions and the crowd gathering ever larger beneath the Mercantile's striped awning.

A.D. was a mess. He'd never heard of going to the hospital for anything let alone having a baby and set in his high-backed chair reading—or at least trying to—as he fumbled through the pages. Then in the next instant he'd go to the window and tug the curtain as if he wanted to open it, but then thought better of it, for the kettle on the stove was just then screeching out its steamy lament. Off he'd go like a good butler and make us two cups of coffee and then set down a spell himself on a kitchen stool and arrange in a trance the sugar and cream for us, swirling with his spoon for what seemed like ages the mixture. Before finally I had to grab his wrist to get him to calm down into any sort of common courtesy.

I seen him, I finally said to him, as if to jolt him back into some kind of coherence, and I looked into his fluttering eyes as he stood there and swayed in the dim light. I wasn't sure he'd heard me let alone knew the implication, his mind raced so. That I had to spell it all out some more and held up my hand as if the red circle on it would denote clearly and truly the implication of my meaning. Runnymede, I said. He come to me last night at a bar.

What do you mean he come to you? He stepped to the window as he said it and finally took a notion to thrust aside the curtain. As he did, the light come slanting in like daggers and even from my position inside the room I could hear the general commotion at the Mercantile growing louder and louder.

I wasn't sure if I should tell you, I continued, but then I knew the more I thought on it, the more I wanted to get you back out there with me again to find the names of all those songs, and so I knew you'd care about it. I knew it mattered most.

Mattered most? Mattered most? he said and looked on me with all the cruelty in his soul that I'd not seen before. O it was as if a black cloud on the ridge had covered his eyes. His long thin face had so caved in at my words, that all the meanness that he'd always only saved for others like John Hill Carter and maybe old Jessico in Annapolis and even Benjamin Marks when we'd first seen him, come forth in a bluster to confront me. Now? he said. Now is when you're gonna have a go at me with my wife pushing out a little one somewheres in some hospital where you only ever go to die? Now's when you're gonna do it—after I done told you and practically begged you that I couldn't no more—that she just wouldn't allow it. But now is when you're gonna try it all again? Jesus Christ, Isaiah.

I would not bow to his anger then, nor shy away from him in the least. But I just kept my head level and watched him, taking it all in, all the vitriol he had in him to expend. Before I seen his anger finally flush out a bit with his hate, with his exhaustion in waiting on word of his wife, and so I used my lower, calmer voice to counteract all his spite. I just think Runnymede is scared of us is all. I mean, that's why he didn't say our names that night, right?

Jesus! What are you talking about now?

Our names. The night of the performance in Bristol. When Ms. Clara May first appeared again. Parmenides, I said and moved closer to him, my coffee cup rattling on its saucer. You remember, don't you? In the library at the Peabody. The first time you charged him with his falseness, when he said this whole Earth was changing in every moment and you said it wasn't. Sure, you stood right there beneath him in your street rags and offal and told him no as no other had probably ever done, and he marked you for it; I swear. He marked you for sure in his mind, and maybe that was why he come to me then, to tell me.

Come to you? In a bar. To tell you what? He was scouring his reflection and reached out to touch it now as if to trace some indecipherable pattern, some riddle in his long oval face, something that he wanted to get at below the sur-face—an instinct perhaps, a source.

To tell me about how close we are.

Close to what?

Than we've ever been before. Since we first started. Closer to beating him out, is what I think. Goddamnit, you know it's almost been three years since I first seen you. Three years and we've only gotten better. We've only gotten better and can't stop now. We can't stop for nothing.

Not even for my child? he said and stopped touching the glass and slumped so that his wide forehead touched the clean surface. I could see the heat smudg-es of his flesh all spreading in a little mist cloud around him as he looked out, scouring the street.

Maybe that was why I seen him? I said after a long spell of watching him. Maybe that was why he come to me and took a name from me. Because of your child. Because he thinks we're finished. Maybe that was why?

He took a name from you? He'd straightened up at mention of this and wiped the sweat that still clung there to his brow with the glazier's fire below burning brighter and brighter (for we hadn't even heard him come in at all with the commotion building in the street).

He took a goddamn name from me, I said. The same one I showed you. And maybe he wants to take all the names. So we can't get them no more. So we can't beat him out and take what he wants. That celebrity. That fame and success. And all that truth. I held up my empty red-rimmed hand to show him and even I could hear I must have sounded like a madman, that I'd gone beyond the pale, as they say. Though, at least, I was steadfast in my urgency, and didn't waver my hand none and could have walked a straight line with my eyes closed if he'd asked me. Though when he finally did turn to glance at it, to scour my fingers and arm, before giving my overall appearance a general once over, I could hear a loud sigh escape his lips as he rubbed his chin considering everything I'd said. Sure, I was a mess, there was no escaping it, and I'd seen a vision perhaps, and maybe it was my own self that had dropped that paper slip into the candle flame anyhow in my drunkenness. But maybe, just maybe, I hadn't; and anyway, how could he say? How could he know anything about it? As he turned to the window again, shaking his head back and forth, a siren wailed outside and the flashing red and blue lights paused on his face as I watched him narrow his eyes.

Jesus Christ, he said, is this the day, speaking to the windowpane, not moving a breath, not turning an inch. Is this the goddamn day the whole world's gone mad? Out in the street there was shouting that echoed up through the whole building, and as I stepped closer to A.D. to watch, standing beside him, I seen it all but couldn't believe it for my life. Not an ounce of it. A crowd of men had thrown down their hats and were trying to force their way bodily into the Mercantile. Even as a line of police held clubs and batons and beat them back as that one solemn bank official in his black suit and monocle pointed at a few that must have done something awful to raise the ire in his cheeks, for they were flush and blotchy and he was shaking his head he looked so forlorn to inform upon them. But he continued anyway, shouting even as one man stood at some remove from the scrum, and seemed raised into his own invisible buffer of space and time. He was raising his arm slowly at the monocled man and in the late morning sunlight A.D. and I could just make out the tinny glinting pistol and seen the puffs of white smoke before the shots—CRACK CRACK—reached our ears and the pandemonium truly set in.

O the police reached then for their guns and fired on the man who stood out in the middle of the street and just kinda fell over as if he were doing nothing more than laying down to take a nap. The monocaled man had already slumped back against the front window of the Mercantile and was waving his face with his hand for he seemed to be inundated with a terrible heat. He clawed so at his suit and tie as a number of police stood above him and touched their hats, raising them to their foreheads, as one by one they spoke to themselves but could do nothing for the few minutes it seemed the monocaled man steeped and boiled and then ceased to be as a wide wet puddle spread beneath him. That was when the police chief himself, I think, arrived and draped a white sheet from the trunk of his cruiser over the slumped man's head, resting there now for all eternity on the sidewalk with his soul.

Jesus, A.D. muttered, Jesus Christ Almighty, and he watched the same as I as that crowd raged on in their ceaseless fury, before finally disbanding as more police arrived and a fire truck sprayed across the whole lot of them and then an ambulance and even a few reporters scoured the scene with photographers. The streets were filling now with folks gawking and running back and forth and waving their hands as a red police line was strung up and wooden sawhorse barriers cordoned off the sidewalks. But still more folks wanted to get into the Mercantile to continue with whatever business they were so keen to keep at even after all this madness had just occurred.

Here, I said and I handed him his guitar because it was the only thing I could think of to get our lives back from the edge of that window, to get us back into any semblance of reason. With our success over the years, A.D. had since bought a few nice Martin guitars that he kept in his bedroom, and as I strummed across the open strings of one, to hear the true tuning of it, and the sound rang up to reverberate and fill the whole apartment with that angelic sound, it took him another minute to realize he held his own guitar for he was still watching the street. I strummed again, and started a line of notes that I'd been tinkering with for a while, and that got him finally to turn to see me as maybe he'd never seen me before. As someone at the end of the chaos. As someone to raise him up out of the madness. Someone to confide in. Someone to keep. You're right, he said. You're goddamn right. That bastard never did say our names that night.

He never did. My voice was flat and listless, without any emotion, for I suppose most of it had already been drained away in seeing those two shootings, the ones I shall never forget. But the music helped. The music always helped. O it raised us up above everything else, and bandied about inside us then almost as a mysterious presence or cerecloth of intervention. Something to spell and steal away and bleed the hours and take us bodily through a series of upward moving steps into some ethereal delight. Something that only we were ever meant to enter. How else can I say it with words that are not adequate? We were lost then amongst ourselves. Lost amongst our own harmonious divinations and reveries. Lost until the lone echoing footsteps of someone approaching seemed the very metronome of our making.

The streets had since been cleared and as we shook our hands out from playing away the hours and looked at the darkness below, dotted now with the yellow haze of streetlights and the empty storefronts snaking in an undulating line along State Street, a single figure cloaked in some otherworldly blankets and lightness stepped out beneath the window and started up towards us. She was at the door before we could even turn around.

A.D.? A.D.? It was Ms. Clara May. Jesus, but she was strong. She was smiling as she stepped inside the doorway. Her rosy cheeks were clear and shining as she nodded to the wrapped and perfect blankets slumping off her as she came forth. Nodding to the burnished center of her, as the brightest, most astonishing face you'd ever seen stared up at A.D. The little one yawned and made a soft gurgling sound as A.D. fell to one knee to breathe in the sweet warm milk scent of her—his child, his girl—as for moments and moments he touched her soft downy head as he knelt speechless and mute in his happiness. It's your daughter, Ms. Clara May said and smiled as the room refracted into a prism of light and broken geometries for the tears bathed her eyes and lips and chin as surely they bathed mine and even our A.D.'s, for he looked on her and breathed in short quick breaths to hear the news again from her own strong lips. It's your daughter Jolie.

XXVI

Miss Tuesday Staunton ~ From the far edge of the world ~ A burnished pearl ~ The loss and faith of the thing ~ A pantomime or reiteration ~ How it wove its curse upon them ~ That miracle electric ~ Drifting like snowflakes ~ The flames of circumstance and hazard ~ A little more returned

BLACK TUESDAY WAS WHAT THEY CALLED IT, and I would joke later with A.D. that was what they should've named their daughter, Miss Tuesday Staunton, because Ms. Clara May certainly didn't want to use his last name (though if he ever mentioned it to her, I cannot rightly say). But everything pretty much bottomed out after that, considering our funds and the investments Benjamin Marks had been letting glide along easy-as-pie for months had been taken down with almost everything else financial and monetary in the country.

It was a shame and a disservice for certain, cause when he didn't appear that night nor the next, nor the next after that—even after Ms. Clara May and A.D. seemed like they might have turned some blind corner with Jolie, that they might be a tried and true married couple for once—the news of Benjamin's absence was of a trifling matter to them. As of something sad and dispassionate washed ashore from the far edge of the world.

Benjamin went to see his cousin, Ms. Clara May said almost off-handedly, when I finally got around to ask. Not because I worried for our monies and accounts and such (which I never did have any understanding of anyways), but because I'd seen the man when he'd let me out of the car that morning, when he'd needed something—anything—to hold onto and to show his love to and to have his love returned to him. Since I'd also read of the many suicides in New York City after this whole mess started, I felt responsible in a way for Benjamin.

Hell, I needed to know if he was alright, if only for my own conscience. But I'm sure you already heard how it went. What with all those financiers and stock-brokers and bank managers plummeting from the tops of skyscrapers and clock towers and bridges for days and days to come, so that you would a thought a perpetual rain of bodies had lined the streets and oak trees of that darkly nefarious metropolis. It got so that when I looked out the window from Ms. Clara May's, I thought the Bristol streets would have been lined like that, too, with the broken and rotting shapes of the desperately depressed. But of course, my eyes only ever focused on that one spot, where that man had been shot down in the street. My eyes centered on it always, for I still seen the blood stained concrete and had to shake myself free every time from thinking on it in those days, just to move on in my own sad way.

Cousin? I said, trying to parse together her words.

In Harrisburg, she said, he was his investor. But it was no use after that. She had Jolie in her arms, and was swaying side to side and singing in that magic voice of hers. When I heard it and thought on my own baby girl in Annie's arms all those years ago, after the toil of work had been done for the day, with the sun setting low over the Blue Ridge Mountains, dropping like a burnished pearl to flare out with its great dripping colors and ripples of clouds, I had to remember the fair picture of family life. I had to remember how it could fill your whole soul, making you complete, as if nothing else mattered, and left them right then and there and didn't once look back to tempt my A.D. into anything new anymore, into anything at all really. Hell, it was easy. In light of Jolie's sweet and simple face, I'd just decided to quit that plan for good now, to quit it all and to change somehow. To do something else, something free and clear, anything but dragging him back up into the ridge.

I mean, how could I? I murmured as I stepped into the dusky light. It was November already. The town was still on the edge of all that anxiety and need, almost as if it had condensed in the ether like another skin we couldn't get out from under, it was so thick and waxy. That in looking around, you'd have thought nearly everyone had been ground down to dust to know their life savings and earnings were nothing more than empty deposits in a land washed clean of any foundation. It was a phantom world was what it was. Dry husks of people stumbled past. Some dragging behind them shredded bank statements and savings receipts, while others just trailed nothing more than the frayed end of a rope from some pawned wagon or goat. And some didn't even stumble at all, but just sat right there in the street where the news had met them. When they'd realized all was lost, that all was wiped free of any property. That the institutions and implements of success that had seemed as insurmountable and staunch to them as allies in a high-off fortress had left them as impoverished and alone as a severed stump set out to wither in the wind.

It was all gone now. All of it. Just waste and chaff like the powdery smoke a magician might blow from the flat edge of his palm. The more I stopped and looked on them, the more I could see their sad faces hollowed out by the knowledge of it all, by the loss and faith and the end of the thing, of what they'd trusted. This commerce, I said and stood outside the bar that Runnymede had appeared in that night and remembered the cold, calculated way his white teeth had chomped down together annunciating that word, and for some reason I wanted to see him again. I needed to see him again, to hear what he thought of all this.

It gave me a chill to remember him, and to think of his delicious confidence in the elegance of the system, and the change he professed in the things to come. But just the same I slid into the corner table where I'd looked dumbstruck and not a little bit envious upon the smooth pudding of his face. Sitting there, I drained my whiskey scouring the walls and anonymous depths for the man to reappear. I looked at my hand and held it over the same flickering candle flame, but there was no name with me now to burn up into anything. There was no name at all in my mind, as I drank more and thought on the crackling quick shots I'd heard, and then the clean white puffs of smoke when that man had fallen down into a trance of death and sadness where his life had taken him. The empty turn he'd chosen. And I eyed the people behind me and the ones who'd just stumbled in to see how the world was turning, if violence and emptiness was to fill up the remainder of it. If the black iron hull of the world was any indication of the barrenness stretched before us. Much like the barrenness of the smudged window I watched, as each vague shape formed in its murky edge as of a pantomime or reiteration of destruction. Waiting. Waiting all the while for Runnymede to rise up again like the ghost of death itself. The ghost of something long past and yet to come. But there was nothing. No dramatic entrance. No sulfurous odor. No insidious speech.

Music was all I heard.

Turning my ear to the end of the bar, the green radio dial glowed supernatural and queer and from its wooden depths a voice was rising. Fiddles. Guitar. A bass line and some drums combined softly, and then more gradually grew into a much greater marching dirge. Something martial and bright was rising to its heady wave before the first clear lyrics sung out as if writ from a page of the wind itself, and it was Runnymede, I tell you—my Runnymede—singing to me even here, singing for all he was worth. His voice had found me even as dozens of the gathered drunks had started to chime in, following each verse as it wove its curse upon them, as if branding them anew to the pale fire of the world, to the fire yet to come, everlasting, in its commerce of waves and sadness and regret. Amen.

ISAIAH?

I turned to the sound, but there was nothing. Just the mirror's glazed shimmer above the mantle reflected my confusion as I looked upon it. My face. Haggard. Ashy and drawn. The creases of my mouth glinted with the whiskey accumulated from drinking in that sour place, with my gray hair stringy and clumped and spotted with bits of white dust and soot that had fallen down from the rafters as more sad revelers piled in. As more voices called out. As I'd felt the sound and scent and feel of life collapsing upon me to know that Runnymede could be anywhere there was a radio now, anywhere there was a signal or conduit of that miracle electric to beam his devilish charm across the world. That he was connected, attached to some darker current, terrible and true, and that was why I'd had to run straight out of there during the middle of that thing—that song—and waver home.

There was something so wrong in its utterance, something so constrained and vainglorious in the self-pleasing depths of it. That even as I'd wanted to spy Runnymede himself, to stand and confront him about his vaunted commerce and all that it had done for us, I couldn't bear to hear it no more. To hear the crowd in that bar singing along as the swell grew louder, and his voice grew stronger, for even I'd heard this one before. Runnymede had just put out another album and was touring and touting the strength of it and so great long articles were appearing in publications and smart glossy magazines. Even with the country floundering into the hole of its own demise, music and the power of the radio were busting up at the seams to tame the sadness and despair and make a nice tidy profit in the process. Music, I said, and alcohol, and muttered the words, before hefting another log onto the fire. They're the only constants. After all this.

Outside a cruel wind came slanting against the roof to rattle the windows and beams, before leaking in at the chinks of stone to make me shiver to hear the world so thoroughly invested with reaching me even in the hidden spaces of my home. I had to laugh to know my predicament, that I could not claw and tear apart A.D. and Ms. Clara May's union any more. That I could not persist in those designs with that sweet Jolie here now. Not with her face looking at me so precious and earnest that first instant of her arrival. With her simple self without any sin at all to add to the balance of the world, and to this one circumstance—the one with her mother and father and me—with no fault at all to bring us. Jolie.

That's it, I said and looked at the rafters, for I'd fixed them months ago but in the high top span there was a single prism that Annie had hung years ago and which I'd found beneath a decayed birds nest in the rain-rotted debris. That single glass was a gift to her from her father in Boonsboro, Maryland, something she'd kept and held always and had hoped to see in her home shedding peals of light upon the floors and walls she'd made for herself. For her life. With our daughter and me. But I knew what I had to do, and said the words once and then looked into the colors of the prism and then the fire for any reaction from the world, for any remonstration to what I'd said, but could only think of Runnymede then, of his talk of spirits, and the possibility that Annie was one now too. O the thought shook through me as another windy wave raised up outside to howl as that soft faint voice echoed from somewheres close by as a phantom must on cold nights in the ridge. For a moment, I thought it must have been my Annie herself haunting me from whatever spirit world she inhabited, if it was indeed true what Runnymede said. That she was gone. That maybe she'd been gone a long time. And I wondered if the Honorable Reverend Michael Williams had told me the truth all those months ago when I'd asked about her. Had anybody ever told me the truth?

Isaiah?

Yes? and I searched the room, the windows, in the corners and behind the chairs, my voice rising, my eyes imploring into the occurrence of it, of that sad windy resonance. But nothing. There was no answer. Only the shuffling of my boots. The breathing of my lungs. Yes? I said again, as if to tempt the voice into speaking. But only silence returned my call. So that when I finally did spy my face in the mirror, I seen the sadness of thinking on her as gone and gone a long time cloud my eyes, for what would that make of my little girl then? What would that make of my little Lucy? But a phantom herself. A spirit forever born to inhabit the world ceaseless and lost, clinging only to the spectral length of her mother's trailing hand, forfeited to the wind, condemned to drift aimless for all time for what I'd done to that damn Hackett. For what I'd done to set them both loose like that. Out into the void. Without even their home to return to—without even that—and I knew then what I had to say to both of them as recompense for my deeds. I'm sorry, I said. I'm sorry, I'm sorry, I'm sorry, and either with the wind howling, or the alcohol weighing upon me, I grasped the mantle for balance, but scattered instead the slips of the names to the floor. Sinking then to my knees by the flames, I begged forgiveness from the fate that had wrapped the shape of my family up as cold as winter wind in its pure cruel hand.

I'm sorry, I said and bowed my head, whispering as of a prayer. Because I thought these names were it. I thought they'd pull you back up to me from where you were. That you'd be here, and I groped haphazard in a pile of names that had fallen before me so that they spilled again from my shaking hands, some drifting like snowflakes to the floor. While others only seemed crammed like splinters and shivers of ice between my fingers, scrunched into my palms so tightly as to illicit that cold blue spark of truth I knew each one of them to be. I thought this would do it; I thought I'd find you through them. That my name would be broadcast to the four corners and you'd hear it. No matter where you were or what you'd become. You'd hear it and know. And then I'd see you. Sure as Sunday I'd see you here and beside you would be our little girl and it would be like that, like before, like none of this had happened and we'd never had to lead our separate lives. That we'd be put back together, whole, as a severed man is stitched anew with thread. Like to like and piece to piece. That's what I thought. It was what I prayed, too. It was what I hoped for. Annie. Annie?

The fire leapt as if to respond and hovered before me as a wish perhaps, for I knew what it wanted and so held out the first slip and thought in that moment it was an offering to the void then, to the universe, to the darkness dripping down even then upon the ridge to scatter the stars that hung griefless in their nameless tracks. An offering to the flames of time itself, to the flames of circumstance and hazard. A prize made complete to the world, in gobbling up more and more of the truth that had seeped out of its cold dark core to begin with. The truth not yet returned as it must be returned to the center eventually. The truth that knows no end. That is as much a visitation as passenger in its own transience and touch of us. In how it knows us. In how it lives. Because now I would give it all back. I would return it piece by piece, and in that offering, perhaps the world would give me back Annie and Lucy piece by piece as phantoms at least, as wavers or glimmers of light. As a vast assortment of memories—anything to spell the void the years had carved inside me. Anything to rest the emptiness, and salve the piercings of a world that could not see me, that could not stand to hear me, that did not come close enough to touch me, nor love me neither. To love me. Anything, I said, and I shook the name as a recrimination, as a fever to the air, shaking it for all it's worth. Anything that gets me there, I said, I will do. I swear. I will do it, and as I let the first name go, I seen it then, the truth, bursting up in a red hot glow. The slip touched the first bright coal and rose before me in an otherworldly flash. So that when the black puff swirled up, it dispersed into nothingness before my next breath, twisting into darkness, into the vast invisible design of the thing itself. I knew then that a little more had been returned, a little more of the true store of good that could still affect my life, that could still fortify my mind and direct me on, and so I wept to know it, what I'd done. I wept to know there was still more names to do the same with likewise.

Well, he said, I hope that ain't the last of 'em, for we still got a long ways to go and a full tank of gas. He might have been behind me the whole time, how could I of known? But when I turned, I seen him, and he said my name again all whispery and slow, Isaiah, and smiled in the flickering firelight—my A.D., come to me—his hand resting on the doorframe. His long thin face shadowed and still. While outside, as if set in relief below the faraway mountains and jigsaw tops of the indefinable ridge, I seen it, the headlights blazing up on that old car of Jessico's as pure and white as portals in the everlasting night, and knew then that we were the same again.

That we had to go. The names were calling.

XXVII

Some celestial hand ~ On the vagaries and agonies ~ A John B. Stetson hat ~ Always another song ~ The right center of them ~ Hymn after enduring hymn ~ Misericordia Jones ~ The confluence of the Shenandoah and Potomac ~ The absence of himself ~ Casting out for all time into the void

IT WAS A LONG STRANGE ROAD WE DROVE THEN. I set beside him all the while and watched at how accustomed he'd become again to it. With how easy the rhythm of the curves and steep climbs and long sad stretches of just nothing would roll out before us as another roadway wound up up up into the blessedness of the ridge in late autumn with a thousand million colors coalescing and convulsing in the light. It was as if Annie's prism had been hung down by some celestial hand to shed such an immense harmony and resplendence on everything we seen.

O I still had the bulk of money I'd sent to the Honorable Reverend Michael Williams and that he'd given back in his disgust, and so I gave Ms. Clara May and Benjamin half as payment, I guess you could say, for taking A.D. with me, for driving off the way we did. With the other half, we just sort of used it to go. Of course I had a notion as to what Benjamin might do with his portion once he got it, after he reappeared with his usual swagger after visiting with his cousin in Harrisburg and giving him what for with invectives and such that he repeated to us all in full as of a Shakespeare play one Saturday night. O to see him! How he come back on fire speaking most indignant about the vagaries and agonies of human greed, and then on the artifice of Man, and on the duplicity of financial institutions, before lastly expounding on the wayward motions of the irresolute Earth, as if she alone revolved in a sea of unending sin. So of course he never once mentioned all the monies we'd lost and how if you traced it all the way back to the beginning, as if pulling on a dusty string, you'd find him at the end of it. But once he seen what I give him, he shut up soon enough. He just looked me square in the eyes, called me his brother and touched my shoulder, and I had to laugh for I seen how happy he was to hear we were both leaving again—both me and A.D.—driving off into the ridge.

And sure enough, after a few weeks of passing through towns untold and outposts unseen, that not a soul might have visited in months let alone decades—they were such destitute and backward places, with so many still hobbled and blinded by blight, and that might not have gotten over the influenza outbreak ten years before, let alone this Great Depression—whenever we did come roaring into town, it was all I could do to tell everyone how lucky they were with their meager possessions and health, living the way they did. But of course, as soon as I started in like that I'd have to stop once I seen him, and I understood what he could be capable of in those days, even in that general condition of the world, with his outright blindness to the miseries of the human condition.

For Benjamin Marks would have something new on him each week and think nothing of it. Like the new brass belt buckle he paraded around, ordered straight from the Sears Roebuck. Or a pair of polished leather Lucchese cowboy boots mailed in special from San Antone. Or even a new white John B. Stetson hat, one he'd cock to the side as he eyed you and mumbled, saying Yes it was an awful sight what was going on in the world today, and yes, I know all about poverty and whatnot and what it can do to a man. I know clear well, and then he'd spit some fresh chaw tobacco to the sidewalk and off he'd go with Ms. Clara May who weren't none better herself to watch her, and who might have just stared at the two of us as if we were of a nation beyond the likes of Man. Something foreign and benighted from beyond a darker Earth with our traveling ways that she never did forgive A.D. for commencing with again (even though she knew we needed the money). She'd just sigh and wrap tighter the brand new embroidered shawl around her cool leveled head. All the while that soft little Jolie just swayed as sweet as sugar in her cherry wood bassinet, or in her matching new cherry wood crib. Or in the prim Heywood-Wakefield baby carriage they'd just bought, the one with the wicker basket and adjustable hood. So it was all I could do to stand there and laugh devilish to see how happy the family was getting on without A.D., crafting in their own sense an identity even as he was edged further from the picture.

If it was painful to see, it was true, but it was necessary for my own designs. (Though I can assure you it was a picture A.D. held onto too even as he was edged further from it.) Because I seen him do it most nights, after we'd drive off again, after he was intent on following some other name, bursting out of town after maybe only playing one live session of the song we'd found and shaped on the ride in. Stopping maybe only once at a local radio station to play it or to perform it right there over the telephone for Mr. Ralph Peer, who somehow recorded it like that way up in New Jersey. No, A.D. couldn't stand to wait no more. He'd never stood to wait. Not even for his own marriage nor baby girl. He'd just been biding his time really, reading his books, playing house all the while. Because I don't think he rightly saw what Jolie was to him then, or what she'd always be—his all and all—not with the specter of those names stacked up before him and with more accumulating day by day. The names that we just had to find, that we just had to burn ourselves through to get for another few songs.

But how can I describe it? How can I write about his clenched fists, or his pinched jaw, or how tense and indignant his brow got most nights driving, as he turned up from another lost hollow or broken down depot, the moonlight nothing more than a spotlight. A presence echoing behind the darkness of the clouds and ridge as far off and mysterious as an airy gauze painted on with a gossamer brush it was so light and angelic. But always in seeing him, I'd know he was repurposing the picture of his family again. The one he turned over endlessly in his mind and held onto as the last fading strand of his life. Only this time Ms. Clara May and little Jolie weren't besides Benjamin Marks as they'd been, smiling on the front cracked steps of their apartment, arm and arm, a picture of family life and trust. No, for this time it was A.D. and A.D. alone who held the two candied apples for them and smiled his sunsplashed smile, the one he'd set in stone with what he knew he still had to do for them, and what he had to accomplish.

I knew A.D. still loved her, and of course little Jolie, but also that he loved the idea that he was providing something substantial for them even more, that he was in control. I know, I know, how he thought he was in control of his fever was beyond me. But I could see it in him, this pride, this force emanating sometimes like a glowing prominence that stretched and pulled and seeped from inside the very pores of his skin. With that strict focus he had in getting the songs and recording the songs before even reconsidering what he'd done to them, after he'd found the right center of them. Then always there was the way he sealed the brown envelopes afterward. Licking his wide thumb and then pressing along the narrow glue strip at the edge. Before sliding them into the mail slot and watching as all that money we'd made started on its slow journey back to Bristol, back to Ms. Clara May and Benjamin Marks and to little Jolie even. Always to them.

Yet even in all this, I could see the remove in his eyes. He loved something even more than providing for them and that was the movement born in us and in him from the beginning—from before the beginning. All the way back to when he'd first made his way to Baltimore, roaming those dark, narrow streets, straining for sustenance amongst the littered row homes and slums. For in the very next instant of cresting a hill, or rounding a ravine, or backing into some abandoned train offing, he'd see another whole alien landscape beckoning with its rising tendrils of mist and sleek slanting sunlight. And it was as if the land itself was the thing doing the singing then, the thing composing hymn after enduring hymn to decry its blessedness and endurance and pride.

The ridge.

It never stopped giving to us in those days, and it never stopped taking from us neither, bit by bit. Until some weeks, I wouldn't even hear mention of his family in Bristol no more. Nor how old Benjamin Marks had moved in permanent with little Jolie and Ms. Clara May, who didn't even sing now with us when we did stop back in town and record something, but took the money just the same as he sent it in regular as rain.

He spoke on it when I asked him. But of course I had to decipher his answers when he did, for he had a way of talking that wound around a thing, around the substance of his feelings and moods and pain. Instead, he'd mix it all up with the projections of the trees and trains and towns we'd see speeding by as a blur most days, a blur of the most indeterminate design. As if life itself was only composed of one fast speed in those days, one blinding away source of substance and truth that he was determined to find.

Misericordia Jones, he whispered, and I knew it was a name on a slip for I'd seen it and knew it was a woman's name—one that we'd never gone after, at least not yet, and that we might never go after—since she was told to live in Harpers Ferry way up north on the confluence of the Shenandoah and Potomac. And even if we were driving those days most everywhere it seemed, we still come back time to time to see Jolie and Ms. Clara May. For it was something to watch the loud pompous wreck of Benjamin Marks slink off as if he really wasn't living there with Ms. Clara May when we would return. When he thought A.D. was blind not to know it, nor suspect it, and I guess I was meant to be blind too, for no one ever asked my opinion on the matter, and certainly not A.D. He just nodded as Benjamin gathered his coat and hat from the kitchen table, as Benjamin mentioned some business concern or other he had with someone at the Mercantile. A concern that might keep him there all day and into the night, and then he'd snap his new gold pocket watch shut and be gone. As if the absence of him was the thing he was truly meant to meet, the absence and awkwardness that stretched between A.D. and Clara May. The awkwardness never named— except maybe in our car—in its roundabout way, as we drove on.

Yes, indeedy. Misericordia Jones. Revival. A capella, I said and hesitated on the words, looking at A.D. who didn't blink none, didn't show nothing. Who never showed nothing by way of discord in himself or his life—and so I'd always have to nudge him to see what I could get out of him—to see what might show up in the balance. They say she keeps her rhythm with the balls of her feet, I said and watched him drive, kept watching him move through the motions as he listened or thought about something else entire. Another woman perhaps, one who had her own rhythm and code and who he could never quite capture, never quite pin down enough to name. Shakes it down they say, I said. Shakes it down cold and true on the sawn oak boards.

Unaccompanied, he said.

Yessir. Unaccompanied. A capella. I whispered it low and soft.

A capella, he said and whispered the term too for he liked it very much I could tell, with how it moved him. The sense of one voice. Casting out for all time into the void its proclamation, its truth. I heard him whisper it again as he shifted braking into a turn. Yes, indeedy. Unaccompanied, and I watched him, for I knew it was a concept and abstraction so strong and true it needed nothing else but its own raw force to cry out as a beacon of substance, as a pattern of form. As if creating its own past and future with one breath and sustaining charge was its only intent. Its only function. With one throat. One song. Forever. Amen.

A capella, he said, and turned up into the blackness. Though as he drove, I knew just what he meant as he repeated the word: Unaccompanied. Himself alone. Away from all his troubles and family and wife. Hell, maybe even Ms. Clara May had already said as much in one of their private talks behind closed doors. The ones I'd often only hear mumbled refrains from in the living room, as I waited for him and watched half-enchanted as Jolie rolled and waddled across the floor. I couldn't fathom how it had already been six months since we'd been back out on the ridge driving, and her grown so much in the interval.

But still she knew me, my Jolie. Still she watched me, and would always watch me. No matter what. No matter how far we went or how long we stayed away or what sound or strange incantation we might bring back. I would be there and she'd always roll towards me the way that I knew she would. Her soft sweet face rising like a balloon, smiling that sweet toothless smile of hers, when she raised her sticky hand to touch my foot and I knew she was a saint and remembered her always as I watched out the window as the road rose and fell into nothingness. And yet, yet, in the same instant I thought on her and let the image linger before me, I covered my eyes to the blackness of the road, so that I didn't have to think too much of my own self, unaccompanied as I was. Alone. Like some feral animal set loose and disheveled. Lost to the wind and chaotic scent of rain mixed with wildflower and fern, scrub pine and oak. We'd just passed up through Blacksburg, Virginia and were over 230 miles from Harpers Ferry. I knew we wouldn't go there now. No matter how much he muttered her name. No matter how often he whispered Misericordia Jones instead of Ms. Clara May Stanton.

XXVIII

Some ghostly veil of lights ~ One vast blue roan ~
Each nuance and grace ~ The subjugation of my kind
~ Crinkled and greased in the lamplight ~ Dark and
insidious invectives ~ Firewater ~ The dream of their
insect breathing ~ The thin blade of the man

A HEALING IS WHAT IT IS, he said and I shook myself awake in the cold light.

A what?

A healing. Or some kind of force. Something natural and hidden.

For what?

For everything. At least it seems to me. It seems to be the only way now for sure.

The only way for what?

For living, he said and I could see he was livid. Lit up like some grease-sputtered candle. His blues eyes shook as he scanned the road, and I wondered what he'd been drinking.

Here? I said and nodded to the darkness.

He rubbed the black stubble grown long and splotchy along his chin, the grain of which sounded like sandpaper when he lifted his fingers. In the ridge, he said. A sticky whiskey bottle sloshed with a few last sips between his thighs, and the scent of something sugary emanated from his breath. We'd stopped somewheres in the night at some ghostly veil of lights, but then I'd fallen back asleep. Now a few powdered doughnuts rolled in their greasy box as we rounded another corner, and my stomach grumbled in its emptiness. I reached down for one and tasted the sweet wet sugar and jolted up to feel my blood surge another step forward into consciousness.

I'd had a dream while we'd been driving. A dream where I'd seen the ridge as one vast blue roan charging on ahead, a form racing as we drove, moving swift and furious, and yet also as soft and enveloping as the open sky. And as we ranged up through the mist and low lying pine, the faces of women and children and men all around the world watched as we jumped the heights of the world, touching the dipping stars and unconquered night, and I wondered if those stars were really the lights of our demise. The ones foretold all those months ago by Ezra Lee and then again by Runnymede himself, the lights we hoped to outpace.

There was a rhythm to my dreaming in those days, a rhythm that seemed to foretell something larger about the world, about some smooth shape dredged from an inexplicable truth I could never know. Not entirely. And it vexed me, but also made me curious and hopeful. I sensed a vast landscape etched on the very contours of my soul, something dark and nuanced and stained in deep purples and blacks that shined in a kind of internal light. And always when my dreaming self looked to the sky to see what had cast its shimmery rays to lead us on, Runnymede always rounded into being and smiled down in his munificence. Runnymede showering us with his sinister grin set amidst the pale moon of his face. And from then on I would see him as both tormentor and beacon, a force to repel and encourage us in turn. Rolling down the window, I licked the white sugary powder off my lips, and laughed into the wind to cast the image of him away from me as I refocused my mind on the road. The ridge, I said, and pointed to the high rolling shapes that ranged up before us.

That's right. The ridge, A.D. said. It's ours. Always has been. Always will be, and he nodded out the front windshield as if it were an extension of himself. As if the ridge had been composed from the very chambers of his heart and contained everything he thought he was: an artist, a provider, an ambassador. A conduit. He thought he was speaking for the ridge when he didn't even know it. Not really. He only thought he knew it, as far as I was concerned. He thought he alone gave it purpose above all others, granting it an essence and truth. His truth. Alone.

Hell, I said and watched him, and tasted the sourness on my tongue as I heard his familiarity with something I'd spent my whole life watching and absorbing. Something I knew I'd never know all the way. And here his conceitedness about it filled the whole car, before spilling out in a bright brimming wave to cover me, too. We were here now, I knew, in the ridge, and he was intent on taking and taking some more and thinking it was alright to do so. That it was how it was supposed to be with him from then on. That he alone knew what he was doing. That he alone had the insight. That the voices we was finding were really from the people and not the ridge. When all along I knew it was the other way around. That it was from the ridge through and through—always from the ridge—that we took, and we were just lowly passengers on its rising berth, passengers on that blue dreamy roan, the one that could buck us off at any moment and leave us scattered to the dust.

Hell, nothing, he said. It's heaven is what it is. Heaven through and through.

Son, I said, and I shook my head to feel the sugary rush and speed of the road rise to meet us, for he forced the car on as if he meant to swallow the world he went so fast. We don't even know what the ridge is. Listen to me. I know. I've been in it my whole life and know we ain't even tapped it yet, see? Not in the least. Not inside nor outside nor all the way around. We can't even look inside it yet to see what it is for sure, just like in our own selves, and I shook myself out like a dog in waking up more fully to the power of what I meant to say. Did he know what I meant to say? Did he hear me speaking about the voices inside us that we never listened to, that no one ever listened to? Well? Did he? I stopped and watched him to see if anything, a dawning or spark might take hold in his eyes, refocusing them in the slightest. But all he could do was look on me in his silence. He looked and looked and had to laugh to see how serious I was with what I'd said, about what we didn't know inside ourselves, about what everyone living or dying was afraid to see for all time inside ourselves. Then he kind of just nudged me with his hand playful-like, for he could see I had it too now, that I'd been taken over by it already, the fever—his fever—that it had spread to me too. A contagion.

But I'd known that before. I'd felt it creeping over me for months. Felt it even in just talking about the ridge, in thinking on the hidden and gathered spaces of it, in its ancient and budding depths, in each nuance and grace, and knew I had it for good just the same as he did. That it had spread inside me as we'd tracked down more and more names and slept in more and more road-side shacks and ate in broken down pantries and apple carts and wagons and one-bulb diners where the locals eyed me and a grizzled waiter or short order cook always pointed no matter where we were to a single tin sign saying No Coloreds. Or to one saying No Negroes Allowed, and I'd ease myself back out to the darkening sunset with a roasted hambone on waxpaper and a Lash's Orange Drink and eye the blueness edging out above the treeline. And always the lonesomeness heightened by the subjugation of my kind would rush through me and I'd wish for nothing else but to stand there forever and let the blueness absorb me bit by bit. To let it take me up into its essence and be done with it. I needed it to wash away the sins of these people and my own designs of dragging A.D. back out into it all over again.

But the contagion was too powerful. I couldn't no more turn him back nor turn back myself no matter what. Not when he made me furious with what he thought he knew about my ridge. And especially not when I wanted him to go on forever burning to get the songs to make us real to bring my family back to me alive and safe.

SO I DON'T KNOW WHAT I WAS THINKING WHEN I taunted him. Maybe it was for my Annie and Lucy girl. Or more likely for my guilt, at dragging him out into the ridge again, even though I knew it was the only way. Or maybe I was just tired. I'd been waiting hours in the sun and it was dark now and lonesome. So when he finally got out of the diner and was drinking some moonshine or rotgut or something that someone had give him, I looked him up and down and said, she's waiting.

At each stop, he took it upon himself to pump the locals for songs and names, for locations and whereabouts, and whatever else might be mentioned in light of the slip he'd hold up before them, crinkled and greased in the lamplight. That day, he'd been going at it all afternoon and into the evening as the diner morphed into a roadhouse of some repute, as more and more trucks rolled up and fellows rolled out with the dust and dirt of their day's labor still wedded to their trousers. As each one of them eyed me, I stood there as sedate and unconcerned as could be and sipped my soda while they stepped inside muttering dark and insidious invectives my way. But I stood there nonetheless and watched for him. Always for him. And always he'd come back to me.

Damn right she's waiting, he said and slapped my shoulder and spun his hand up to gesture to the tree line as the crunching sound of gravel on some far off backwoods road echoed over the faint clearing. Nearby a few rusted swing sets and see saws creaked and settled and stirred again in their remorseless decay as if meting out some ancient curse on me. Or some raw truth.

She's waiting for you to come back, I said. I didn't mean no real harm by it. I just meant to joke on what was truly real (I thought) in his situation with Ms. Clara May. But I suppose I'd cut too close to the heart, for before I blinked I heard a crunch of gravel, a shifted boot, and then A.D. leaned over me with that pint of moonshine pointed at my eye.

He blinked once watching me, his mouth poised to speak, to refute me, but then stopped as he blew out a long slow sigh before whispering, You're right. You're right. She's been waiting all this time and I didn't even know it, did I? Didn't even know it enough to see nor care.

Well, you can care now, I said.

Jesus Christ, he said and shook his head kicking out his boot. Is this what this is now? After all this? You giving me marriage advice? And he glowered cold and amused then because he knew what I'd done with my own family, disbanding them as I had with my own act of violence. So when he seen how lonesome and sad it made me feel, he snickered low and malicious to himself, and held his glass bottle out as if a sword, something he might thrust through me if given half the chance. Then he pointed with it to the first white cusp of moon rising above the trees, and I looked on it with him, knowing it would be hard to tempt him back into speaking on the life he needed, and that all this drinking and running was just to cover the pain of losing her.

There ain't no marriage if you ain't ever there.

Ain't there? Ain't there? He took another gulp of the firewater that seemed to seethe in the cracks of his skin, sweating out his pores and brow, outlining him in a glistening rain of poison.

You heard me.

I heard you, but don't believe it. Not for a second.

Believe it, I said and he turned on me with his breath a fiery convection of steam and spit and spoke with a voice I'd never heard before. Well, just go on then if you miss her so much, he hissed. Go on back there now if you want to leave me, too.

A door slammed somewheres close by. As I listened, the footsteps died away before a blast of music was thrust upon us, and a bird fluttered off on its soft swift wings. I'd taken it as my cue to fly up then, too, to lighten whatever darkness my line of discourse had already brought down upon us, and turned to him tilting my head, smiling. If I'd a thought it'd done any good, I'd a left a long time ago.

She ain't left me, he whispered. She ain't. He tapped the bottle on my cheek, before tracing it down my chin to rest above my throat. The outside of the glass was beaded with moisture. The cicadas and crickets sang on with their incessant pulsation, so that as I listened, I drifted into the trance of their existence momentarily. As if I'd passed into the dream of their insect breathing and living and dying away. But even as that sound faded, only the force of my heart seemed to remain, rising as a rhythm, rising inside my chest like a song. The constant pleading of which I wondered if he heard, leaning over in all his anger and rage and rancor. The hell with you then, he whispered. The hell.

Just let it out now, son. Let it out. You been inside your head too long now anyways. Too long.

Why you call me that? He pressed even harder with the bottle to my throat, so that the first sweaty drops from my chin trickled down to my belly button. I could feel the warm gleaming trail as I leaned further back and all the burning rage of him reared above me, for he knew I was saying something he could not. That I was speaking about what was inside him all along and touching it so quickly, and easily, as to dispel him, to disarm him, and he wanted none of that. He wanted never to be disarmed against his emotions. Why you call me that, huh? Why? he said, louder, and hotter. Charged by the effort the anger had built in him, I watched as the thin blade of the man blossomed into an anger unseen until that moment. He seemed to measure my very existence with his tongue, licking his sweaty lips to see me as prey, as victim, or as his curse, perhaps. And as if drawn by the thirst and power his blood and cruelty revealed another current rose to appraise us where we stood.

Son, is this nigger bothering you? A man hovered somewheres behind us. I could smell the raw menace of him. The odor of rich tobacco mixed with horseshit and gin.

I ain't your son, A.D. said to me, before turning to that other man, the bottle raised in his fist. I ain't anybody's son. For I seen it then, the power he never knew he held over me. The power he'd never acknowledged with him being white and me being black. It glimmered there now as a spark in his flesh as he looked on that man as if he never seen him, but then smiled just the same, demented like, to know he might have occasion to light a spark into a raging fire. To call over that good old boy and a few more from inside to help beat me down with that bottle and string me up in the trees. I ain't nobody's son, he said softer, after realizing it—the power and the constant force of it—and lurched off as that man eyed me the more when I followed A.D. and touched his shoulder and stood there with him. Behind us we heard the music blare out from the door as the man finally passed inside, before A.D. pointed with his bottle at the pale wan face of the moon, shining as full and untroubled as a midnight sun. She's waiting, he said.

She sure is, I muttered. She's waiting on you.

Then I suppose we shouldn't disappoint her.

XXIX

About his motives and deeds ~ A severance from
his success ~ Our name ~ The dark maw ~ North of
Harpers Ferry ~ The spirit of the voice ~ Above the C
& O Canal ~ That disembodied limb ~ Horses ~ The
track ~ The grandeur and elegance and style ~ The
numbers ~ Like eternal rings ~ They just floated there

THINGS TENDED TO FALL AWAY FROM US AFTER THAT. When
he turned up north I knew where he was going even before he said anything.
Shoot, even when I knew it would take us further from Ms. Clara May and
little Jolie, I kept my mouth shut. I knew we were bound together now in
a way that was much tighter than before, after his sad words in the parking
lot, when he'd said he wasn't nobody's son, leaving a trail of disappointment
behind him. He had slunk off then to the car and just waited for me to climb
in before driving on, and so I just let him.

It was then that I had a premonition about his motives and deeds. For even
then, even with the words he'd said and the miserable way he looked at me
afterwards, as if to say sorry for what he done, holding my throat to the edge
of that bottle, subjugating me to his rage, I could tell he still had a notion
about how to get himself where he wanted to go. To what he always wanted
to be. Raising himself up in standing now after another song come in. After
another hook was pulled up out of the confusion of lines and lyrics we found,
brought back into being by his healing hands. For we were the healing now, I
knew. We were the salving away and the washing over of the wounds and rage
of the past, even as we moved deeper into it, even as we became a part of it
more and more. And as another night passed and another, and still he drove on
and drank and handed me the bottle to wash it all down with, I knew it was
the fever that really had us both tuned together as one. It was the fever and a
burning away of everything that had come before, and everything that could
possibly come next.

Because to burn up like that meant we were getting closer to the truth, to the ridge and essence of it all, wedded as we were to our cause of being the voice for everyone up here and down below. For the ones who only ever heard Runnymede now on the radio, Runnymede singing and spewing out his artlessness. It was our time now. Our time because we were intent on giving him a severance from his success, in removing him from everything he'd gained and what still we wanted. Everything that I felt he'd taken from us by being so opposed to A.D. from the beginning, in deriding his views at the Peabody when A.D. was nothing more than a scared little pup dragged in from the cold. And then for haunting us too—or at least me—with his fame and pride to keep us down, and maybe even more than that in the bargain. But who could say? Who else could keep us down without a name, without the same name he'd never spoken, even as the Hardy Family's songs were still heard on the radio, and The Ballad of Clara May still played regular enough that A.D. sung it out loud as if dredging up all its remaining secrets and stories. For that was perhaps Runnymede's most grievous sin. To deny us our place. Our name.

It was our ridge now. In our time. On the next hill there might be another song rounding into being, or another song rounding out the mystery of our duty—of what we felt obliged to do in our souls and fingers and bones—to find them and to keep them and to give them all out to everyone forever. Amen.

BUT MISERICORDIA AIN'T HERE.

She ain't?

No, suh. Not at all. The voice was low and shaky and come from the dark maw of a splintered doorway as if resurrected from a crypt, and it was a wonder we'd ever made it down here at all. We'd walked half an hour already, heading north of Harpers Ferry along the overgrown banks of the Potomac River, just as the little nigger boy had told us by the bridge after we'd arrived. Keeping the trail, heeding the chunk marks cut slantwise into the trees, we knew we'd headed in the right direction, but never expected this. Touching his head, A.D. pointed as the thicket opened to a clearing leading down to the rocks, and if I hadn't seen it, I wouldn't have dreamt it in a thousand years—a house made of broomsticks, set right out in the current—right in the water.

It was like a fantasy. Or something you'd hear from a child in waking, but would dismiss the next instant. There we stood, dumbfounded and awestruck and sunk too in our effort from sweating and carrying all the things that A.D.

wanted us to carry out here to folks in the hinterland: bottles of whiskey and gin, bags of bread and boloney and smoked beef, real Belgian chocolate and small paper sacks of rock candy and Teaberry Chewing Gum, licorice and caramels, and every other damn thing he thought might tempt them into giving up their songs. Hell, I even had a guitar and portable Victrola strapped to my back and would crank it up and play a record if the person ain't never seen it before nor heard tell the sound of the phonograph and needle in the grooves. So you'd think it was the devil himself come to visit them. The spirit of the voice walking on water almost as airy as Jesus himself.

Thinking nothing of it, A.D. stepped right up to the edge of that bank, shook his head at the lengths he'd had to go already to get here, and looked at the late April dusk, which had a sort of smoky wonder to it. A purple light from the Blue Ridge filtered down, brushing against the high treetops and branches, basking the fern and moss in shadow, the rocks and roots, before he started out on the thin wobbly gangplank. The one they'd stretched from shore to the rickety railing of that houseboat, bobbing as it were on the edge of its chain in the water. Standing there, I could feel my heart race as my neck cooled from the sweat. I hadn't even had time to set down my guitar or Victrola before A.D.'s first question was answered and he'd needed to get his bearings again.

She ain't here?

No, suh. She up at the track.

The track?

Well, sure. In Charles Town. At the racetrack. Ain't you heard? They talking all about it on the line, and a solemn black finger pointed from the doorway to the railroad along the banks on the other side. The B & O Railroad above the C & O Canal. Horses.

Horses?

From all over. They come and bet on anything, the rich, and Misericordia calms them down when she can. She's a walker and a scribe, too, for Mr. Albert Boyle, the owner. But she don't see no one from outside for sure, let alone two, and A.D. and I shuffled on our boots to think on it, that we come all this way to not even see her. She sings to them for luck and gets her money back double betting on the sly.

She sings to them.

Nearly every day.

The horses?

To the horses.

Well, we'll just see if she won't sing to us then, too, he said, or at least me. And that was it. It was enough. A.D. had shook hands with that disembodied limb already and said his much obliges and thank yous. He even left a brand new bottle of gin on the porch for the limb's troubles, and then backed away solemn and steady like before huffing and puffing all the way up the trail and didn't say another word till we were driving the ten miles west to Charles Town and seen that tin sign for the Shenandoah Valley Jockey Club. It was a long dirt road that wound up then. One lined with laurel and cottonwood and elm that swayed in the late evening breeze, so that he just had to whistle low and sonorous to see it. Shoot, he said, and that was all, for there was only the grandeur of it now to consider. The grandeur and style.

There were high whitewashed wooden grandstands along the homestretch of the long dirt oval track. Flags of the state of West Virginia and the United States of America and the Republic of Ireland fluttered as the lanterns were turned low in the twilight and the crackling voice of the announcer came over the loudspeaker with his excitement for the next field of thoroughbreds. As all the spectators turned to look into the ether, the announcer spewed out the line of odds and fluctuating numbers as a short stout bookie walked from end to end below the grandstand with a long notepad that he tore pages from as boys and men trailed behind shouting their questions and implications of conditions, asking the names of jockeys and their experience forthwith. Then another boy would run off from the bookie with the torn pages to the window where a man in a black visor took in the paper slips and money and sent back out stubs for the boy to distribute.

Goodness, it was such a strange assortment of people and movement and proceedings, my head hurt in the excitement and confusion of the crowd. After sidling up to the first unruly edge of it, A.D. had already walked off to look at the faces of the black women in the crowd (if there were any). But then he spied the shed rows behind the grandstand and just knew that was where she was, Misericordia, singing her songs out to calm the ones intent on racing, and so without as much as a parting word or hand wave, he was off. While I watched him leave, I'd kept the whiskey bottle we'd been drinking on the drive and drained the last few sips of it. The whiskey was hot and quelled the pounding in my head, for the sleep had not come easy those last few nights and already I saw two racetracks instead of one stretch out before me blurred and disheveled and locked together like eternal rings that went on and on in their geometry as an ancient rune or tapestry. So that when A.D did step off into the crowd I seen two of him leave as well, swallowed up by the numbers, and had to shake my head.

O the numbers, the numbers! There were so many numbers and money fluttering about, from ticket stub to slip and back again, my eyes hurt to see it all and to know that a general collapse of the country's economy hadn't hit anywheres near this place. But the rich did have a way, didn't they? They could find themselves removed from any of the circumstances of their fellow man as easy as that, and so Mr. Albert Boyle must have done it, too. Setting up this little entertainment here even as the rest of the world floundered at the edges just to hold on, and as I turned to stalk the rail to find out where that boy was with the bookie, to see if I couldn't get in on the action a bit, I give up after only a few steps for I could feel my feet weren't in it no more. The walking along that trail had done me in and as I was about to bend and loosen my laces, at that same damn instant the sharp bell clanged and a great whoop went out and I seen the horses. O the horses charging off as a wave of motion and pageantry, so that my heart went out with them as they run and thumped, and it was all I could do to breathe to see them go. Beauty, I whispered and shook my hands free of the whiskey bottle that slumped to my boots, for I was standing up close to the rail and could see them all going away and even leaned closer to feel the backwards leading draft of the speed careening off them around the first turn.

The lights from town sent up a diffuse halo in the clouds, and with the crowd shouting and applauding in the stands, and the cigarette smoke and cigars swirling and the concession stalls all lit up and electric, somehow, in the mixture of all three—the smoke and light and air—an unusual clarity come over me. So that as the horses raced off, a vision of their movement solidified, and I could see each single leading stride. A big blue roan worked the rail and come along, passing all the rest, and as he turned for the tape I was so close to him I could watch the great long strides from almost directly behind and had never seen anything like it. With his legs stretched out, and the long ribboned mane flowing as the jockey leapt up and up in his stirrups, carrying himself always higher into the blinding draft, it was as if the horses weren't even touching down. Not at all. I looked and saw a few bright specks of dirt fly up, but couldn't tell if their legs ever stopped or started they went so fast. As if they just floated there. Or were held aloft in some ethereal current. Some shifting glitch of space and time. That to hover in the air like that, with their heads moving up and down was a new way to move across the world, and only the horses had figured it out.

It was breathless and immediate and true was what it was, and a white Arabian had overtaken my blue roan to win. It was a sleek stark animal that raised up its fore legs after crossing and then whinnied and shimmied, the sweat frothing from its mouth. Being as the racetrack was still in its infancy, and drawing in more and more spectators, this next race was designated a special maiden race for two year olds, and as soon as it was announced another rush of folks flowed down to the railing as the flash-lamps from the great wide tripods and cameras fizzled and crackled in the air. The parade of animals had started coming in, so that my head was dizzy with the rush of it all.

The speed. It was still in me and I had to wave my hand to quell the force of it to know I was here at such a time as this and could witness such creatures as these. Ones that could roam the whole Earth in the freedom of their movement. As if cleaving the air weren't nothing to them. So that if the rail weren't there nor the betting slips or gambling, nor even the harnesses and bits to keep them in, they would've gone to the end of our knowing and loving them for sure to run as they did. And the thought gave me such a heady feeling, like the ridge drifting up into its blueness, I had to close my eyes and open them again just to feel the wild grandeur of it all. For as if formed from the very air itself, a face of the utmost calm appeared beside me, a face resplendent in the flashing lampshine and chaos and smoke.

XXX

The dance ⁓ The darker order of the world ⁓ Amen
to many things ⁓ The first purchase ⁓ The form
that began the order that initiated the way ⁓ A
great collapsing ⁓ Always toward the lights

IT'S MORE A DANCE THAN A CONTEST, WOULDN'T YOU SAY?

Sir?

Why the race, of course, Runnymede said, when the thrill of watching be-
comes the sport. When we think they might just be able to transcend the rail
and shape and steel and be made free in the running. Free in their choosing. I
turned toward him and as he inched closer, I could smell the sour whiskey of
my breath.

Free?

Why certainly. For I felt it too, he said, and so did they. He nodded with a
swift uptick with his head, as if to encompass the crowd, the grandstand, the airy
masses behind us. I know something more about it, too, he said, and he touched
his chin and held a long finger there. Because it wasn't only for them, friend. The
speed. The force of their going away, the anticipation and arc of their return.
No, for I saw you. I watched the horses and I watched you and was almost as
enchanted with your empathy toward them, with your conjoining in their struggle—with their purchase, as it were—amid the darker order of the world.

Purchase?

Of course, and his face shook across the syllables to think I might question
the veracity of the word. In the order of which they were ordained. In how they
were kept and reared and bet upon. With how they'll be bred and set out to
pasture and slaughtered. As it is with animals, so it is with Man. All is contained

within the purchase of a life—and in the history of each purchase—for that is how it was before the world began, and that is how it will be beyond the world's end. Amen.

My knees trembled. My boots felt slack and limp, as if no flesh or bone occupied them.

But don't you say that too, friend? Don't you say amen? He leaned back to regard me, as if he'd reared up above the whole Earth to sneer down upon me from his heights.

How do you know that? I whispered. How do you know? My chest shrunk at the mention of my own incantation, as my own word was thrust back upon me. I had said amen to many things before, and had prayed before I could even remember knowing what it was to pray and even after I gave up believing prayer would deliver any answers, or deliver my Annie or Lucy girl. Now here he was saying the same thing to me as if he knew inside my own mind and dreams, and the disclosure cowed me. It cut a fear into me I hadn't felt before in seeing him, but which overran me now and defeated me when all I wanted was to cut him down instead. To cut him down to die.

Speak, he said and smiled his soul-chilling smile as the last two year old was led through the wide wooden paddock and gated. The crowd hushed, poised upon the precipice of the charging away, mesmerized by the sheer certainty of the violent motion. As if all was forestalled by the spectacle of the sport.

There was a woman, I said, not looking at him, not hearing or moving, just remembering as I glazed over and could finally see it—the field stretching out to the horizon, in that old heat of cotton. Heat like the very fabric we worked through and which we believed was elemental to our lot, penance for being born black in a world full of whites.

Yes, he said rubbing his big white hands. A woman. When you were young.

When I was young, I echoed and saw her face surfacing from the white palimpsest of his skin. She was black as coal and turned to me as I worked beside my daddy. As we picked tobacco, and she said it to the air she did. Said amen and I didn't know what it meant. Then I heard my daddy say it too and then I said it my own self and they laughed to hear me call out with the word and my daddy hushed me once and touched my lips saying, That is our word, son. Ours. The one that's been given us for all time, a salve for our troubled hearts. And from then on whenever the reverend said it and the congregation repeated it, I would say it soft as if it were mine, too. Mine alone. The word as entrance to the spirit. As entrance to the feeling.

He nodded like an Old Testament sage. The feeling of connection. Of joining and being joined. The feeling without end or harm or fear.

Yes, sir. Without fear.

 But the feeling didn't last, he said. For as sure as I know the number 4 horse will fall on the last turn, I can see it written on your face. You couldn't feel it. Not all the way. Not to your core. The bell rang and I surfaced from the depths of his voice to see the wave of thundering hooves roll off again, rolling across the continent like a rifle shot before I lost myself again in his sound, in his darker examination. For it wasn't what you found, was it? I said nothing, but watched them race on. Not after the world worked on you in the way that it did, he said. Not after all that. This amen of yours couldn't help you after your daddy died.

No, sir, it couldn't. I touched my head to think on it, to think on my daddy and the frail picture of him, the waste of years. The work, I finally mumbled. It was too much for him. Always was. Too much for anyone.

Yet still you searched for it, he said. That feeling. That sense of connection and calming and turning away, and—dare I say—religion. He smacked his lips as he said the word and laughed as the crowd pulsed forward and the horses moved like a raging storm, bringing their truth and beauty to the world. Their truth. Your wife, he said.

Yes, and I could feel my heart beat plaintive and slow in its bloody sludge. My wife believed, I said. Always did. Even after I told her my own doubts and frustrations on the matter. Even after I'd lost my daddy for no reason other than he'd had to work for us to eat. But she took me to church just the same and started in on me, learning me my letters and words in the process, and I fell into it again. After I'd left it behind. After it'd given me nothing of its succor and mystery and charm. Nothing of the promised healing and release.

And ease?

Yes, that great high ease of the thing. Of giving yourself over to the light that is yours alone and all that you'll ever be. Amen, I said and watched him smile to hear the reflex in me, a reaction to my life, to what I'd left behind. For it has stayed with me, I said. The one word I've kept, even if I know it's not true. That it's a falseness and a charming, like what a charlatan and rogue would make together. So instead I looked to the ridge. I looked to the blueness of the ridge for my succor, because it always and forever burned inside me with a knowingness, with a feeling I cannot name, but that I know is good and true and always rising in me. Always rising as something giving back to me more than I could ever know, more than I could ever hope or feel or shape, and that also moves on ahead of me from here. I touched my chest then, and touched my heart to show him what I meant. It moves on ahead of me into something that is free. Finally free from all these deeds, from all these needs.

Ha! He laughed and pointed at the horses across the wide track, at the jockeys' fine colored shirts and boots a slick blur and spray of mud. The crowd leaned closer and shouted at the speed of their passing, but then paused, as if suspended in their revelry. I turned and watched them and it was as if they'd been brought up short before the incidence of the accident foretold. For they all sucked in a final breath, drawing in the very marrow of the night, as the number 4 horse went down in a heap of legs and limbs and rags and the cries went up immediately.

No! a woman howled as the wind of the other horses passed within the slipstream of their speed, and Runnymede whispered what I heard in my soul. The speed, he said, the speed and the freedom of the dance, too. The freedom that had him wagging a long finger in my face. As you can see, the dancer is not free. He never is. The crowd hung on the rail as some even dangled over to watch the tragedy of the downed horse unfold writhing in the dirt and twisted legs of the jockey.

That is the great deception, he said. That the dance and the belief in the dance is a freedom. There are no steps that are free, friend. There is no ease. The steps are prescribed and numbered and mount always to a rhythm that forms a pattern that crafts an intention. Something that pretends to Man on the face of its ceremony. That preens and fawns and fabricates in every instance a freedom that is not there. A foundation that is not true. A form that is not whole. That merely suggests an artful ordination. A shape unbound by sides and geometries, weights and distinctions. Something that gives them hope against the knowledge of the purchase of the event that has already occurred. That occurred years and years before they could even imagine. But it's a purchase just the same. Just as this race was. Just as this dance. Just as your word amen is your purchase on the past. And as he nodded at the track, a man with a shotgun appeared from a wagon and stood inspecting the horse and jockey. The rider had been dragged now from beneath the beast and all looked on as he winced and gasped for we could see his leg split asunder by the weight and awkwardness of the fall. Two jagged bones edged from his pants legs and were smeared with blood that he touched and leaned back from for he was in an agony that would not cease as he screamed and hit fiercely his fist into the dirt.

What will he do? I said and looked at the shotgun and the horse that did not move but watched the man with its bloodstained eyes.

What he would always do, Runnymede said. The purchase of this deed is done. It has been done for years untold. There is a darker order here. That's always been here. An order that keeps us each the purchase of each. That elects one above the other. That offsets heights and weights and weaknesses and measures. That has placed in line the things that weren't in line before and that were left to chance by the universal hand, as if setting sticks to float upon a river. An order that came before money and finance and markets. Before kingdoms and divisions and boundaries. That came before even metal and mineral were raised up as currency. An order that arose from a purchase of power. A purchase of talent and shape. Of substance and idea. Yes, even ideas were purchased. Do not look so obtuse, friend. History is the story of an economy, of buying and trading away lives. All to be pushed and shaped anew. To be forced inside a form ordained from time immemorial. For one purchase does not exist where there is not yet another purchase above it. And still another above it. All in line to the first purchase. The first purchase established the form that began the order that initiated the way, and all others are only subordinate to its condition. Even as this horse and man and gun cannot initiate any other response than the one that began with the first purchase that follows to this day.

He nodded smiling at me, but then as if pardoning both the animal and man who intended to shoot him, Runnymede raised his hand in a benediction, waving it back and forth, and the horse sprang up, as if raised from a pyre. Dazed, it bent gently its front legs testing them and its nostrils flared open like wet holes bored from slate to breathe the night air. I hadn't seen anything like it. Nothing moved in Runnymede's face as we witnessed it. But his lips, his strange opaque lips rose and fell against the smooth white masonry of his teeth, and I felt what A.D. must have at the Peabody in crying out against his logic, in dragging him asunder for his words.

But what of this purchase? I said. The one you yourself proclaimed?

Nonsense. The purchase is still intact. The purchase remains true. This horse was never meant to die this way.

Why? And I pushed closer to him, to the great wide size of him. Because we've all been bought and paid for? Because we've all been divided and apportioned our lot?

Precisely. In the first purchase. The one that initiated the pattern.

The pattern that persists?

To this day and beyond.

Then you were wrong.

Wrong? He turned to me still pristine and calm in his powder-blue suit, unspoiled or touched by the surrounding chaos.

You were wrong when you said change was the only true force upon Earth. In the library. When you said it to A.D. at the Peabody.

The great man touched his chin and sighed. Then as if the wind and light of air had quivered to align in some new way, he leaned down like a shining moon to touch my shoulder. It was a touch so slight, so faint and soft of hand, I turned with him to walk away from the track, and listened as he spoke to me so gently, so hushed and concerned, as if instructing a child in the error of his ways. You misunderstand me. The purchase is always changing, always moving from hand to hand, and shape to shape in its foreordained pattern. Anything that disrupts that pattern is the true hazard. Like your present intention.

My intention?

With your songs, of course. The songs that would unravel each purchase. With what you find out there in the ridge and dredge back up. It's the emotion in the songs that can release each deed. That can undo the purchase. You unfasten the knot that binds, unloosening all that's been cast down and foretold. That's why I'm a great collapsing to you. That's what I do. The world is set for a great collapsing even if it doesn't yet know it, with this radio, and this need for an electric connection. For something to hold fast the hearts of Man in their fear and longing and dread. To collapse them from the songs you find out there that are not songs at all. Those old words and ways that would send them all out again.

Out?

Into the world. You do realize you would send them out to seek their end—or truth—as you might say. Because of those songs, and the power of those songs, the pattern and the purchase could be undone. So that it would be like before if you succeed. A world without order, when chaos licked its delicious lips. Commerce provides the pattern, even if it crashes momentarily now and again. That is why I have to make the music shinier and easier to digest. So the purchase can continue on its way. Where we know the offer and the offered. The taken and the took. Look, he said and pointed as a woman dropped a racing form as another (a servant) carried a bag and drink for her, and then bent to pick up the form before properly placing it back inside her bag. Or there, he said as a man in spectacles coughed and held out his glasses leaning above a vendor who smiled beneath his load. A thick black tray hung from his neck, and as the spectacled man touched and fingered and then released each product in turn, the vendor could see the man's dissatisfaction with the whole lot before moving off on his endless circuit, patrolling the other vendors and products and stalls. Never satisfied. Never stopping, as each transaction was set aside and ranked. As each moment with Runnymede parted a veil to reveal a power I'd never imagined, a power always out there and hovering, braced in the ether, an invisible pattern repeated everywhere as Runnymede pointed and laughed and strummed along the strands of an everlasting web.

Stop it, stop it, I said. It was insidious and gross was what it was. I'd not felt the weave so close before nor felt so oppressed by the revelation and turned away as he placed his powder blue arm upon my shoulder, laughing as we walked.

How can I stop it? he said as the outline of the shed rows appeared, ranging back in an unerring line into the distance. As I said, it is your intention that threatens the purchase.

How can that be?

The purchase of every song is the same as the purchase of every life.

I was speechless and stood cowed as around me the energy of the night seemed drained through an icy sieve. And yet, as I looked back to the shed rows, I could hear a faint singing. Something escaping some shadowed doorway. A lilting pulse I held onto to stand apart from what he'd charged me with—slavery, in essence—of binding the lives of the ones who'd written the songs to the purpose of our success.

By your endeavors, he said. To reap your fame and fortune. By taking those songs and selling them to raise your name up to return—

My Annie, I whispered and shook my head. And my Lucy girl.

For as much as you want them returned to you, he said, and though you may try to change the ideal of this purchase with your intentions, you cannot change the account of its return, no matter what. For love is a purchase, too.

Even love?

Especially love, and he leveled his calm heavy head at me. Consider your own personal receipt.

Of my family? If they return?

If they return, the purchase is intact. You will have won them by your endeavor, by your unsavory peddling of ill-gotten songs. Of songs stolen. Of lives enslaved, bound to the pain of the past.

And they cannot be free? I muttered, even though I didn't know what that meant.

You still don't understand what I aim to do? You still don't see me. He placed his massive hands on my shoulders and spun me around to see the white, perfect plane of his face. Leaning down toward me, he tapped his long white finger against my chest. I aim to change your arrival and your return, the whole dance of your intention. I aim to change your rising up ahead of me.

Our rising?

Into the lights, he said. Always into the lights, and as he turned, a surge of people rushed past. The bell had rung and another race was off and the air and speed were such that sandwich wrappers and errant newspapers swirled up in a vortex above the trampled grass. I had to breathe to not be caught up in the excitement of it, the commerce and change, and searched to find him but he was already gone. His shape dissolving with each word. You're almost there, I heard him say, as he moved back toward the rail. Just keep heading toward the lights, he whispered, before disappearing altogether, ranging up somewhere behind me, moving high into the air. Always toward the lights.

XXXI

An impossible slick string ~ Our run of pure luck
~ The girls ~ His own spectral eyes ~ Just forms –
Some gravitas to the circumstance ~ A fortress of
pillows ~ In supplanting the usurper ~ Nashville

WHEN A.D. RETURNED THERE WAS ONLY MOONLIGHT above me.
A faint airy cloud had risen where Runnymede had been and in the swollen face
of the full moon my head swam to see the world a confusion of compacts and
transactions, of agreements and deficits. Not just on blacks neither, as history
might have told me, but on everyone else besides, and everything. Each invisible purchase was like a static charge that brought up all the hair on my neck. It
was as if each man and woman were tethered to an impossible slick string that
trailed off into the ledgers of a history I could never know. Into a world I could
never see. Not entire.

Guitar, A.D. said and he held my shoulders and seemed inflamed by his
meeting with Misericordia. Percussion, he said and grabbing an overturned
milk crate, he tapped out a rhythm as we started back toward the car. If there
were any chance to tell him about my ghostly meeting with Runnymede this
was it, before he set up in the backseat working on that song, rearranging it
as we went, working his spark of life into it. And yet, as we walked, and the
night unwound into the warmer wind of a spring just settling in, and I looked
back through the soughing laurel and elm to hear the crowd roar as the horses
bobbed in their endless dreamy circuit, I held back. I was in this thing now forever and knew it. Just as Runnymede had said, it was included in the purchase,
and as much as I wanted it to happen, to have my family returned to me, to
find them, I didn't want A.D. to want it as much now neither. I looked at him

as we walked and knew I didn't want him to purchase his life and family with the fame and fortune we sought. I didn't want him to desire to be raised up over another as I'd had to do with that damn Hackett, miserable sonofabitch that he was. I wanted little Jolie and Ms. Clara May to be free, but the purchase of it all had sent me out, had sent everything along its endless course, setting in motion a shape I carried with me to this day.

So I drove, and he worked at that song before the memory of it should fade, and I thought I might have already been too late in extracting him from this agreement. From this purchase, as it were. I could already see the trajectory of his intentions forming as a cloud to hover above us perpetual. Something dense and scalded at the sides, with jagged bits of lightening and a rumbling in its heated core like the rumbling of the horses that had raced off from us on the track. For he'd already pointed us up north, so that Bristol— our Bristol—was but a memory to him. A point receding in the darkness of the land we drove through as he sung his demons in the backseat, and friends, I attest, it was the saddest and most plaintive sounds that ever did come from his throat.

CAMDEN, NEW JERSEY WAS ANOTHER WHIRLWIND altogether. But there was a look in Mr. Ralph Peer's eyes after we recorded Misericordia's song, a look I had not seen that gave me pause. So that when we were done and already on the road, I could still feel his warm handshake and his words saying, This is it, Isaiah. You've finally done it. As we parted, there were tears on his cheeks as the song repeated on a reel to reel behind him, as already the boys in his studio were pressing its magic into vinyl that would change all of it for us and bring Runnymede himself back into the dark trajectory of my dreaming.

O I knew we weren't done with him yet, not by a long shot, even if we drove on in a stupor after that. After A.D. took the wheel and eased off and drove in the wrong direction for a spell spiraling out around Camden. So that we just floated over the road as the lights of the sun and stars shined done on us in turn as we repeated that song of Misericordia's and even worked a new set of flourishes in to boot, and before we'd even made it to Maryland it was on the radio and burning up I tell you. Burning up like fire that could tear away the world it was so hot to hear and to know it was us for all time singing on the air.

You've got your headliner this very same night, if you want it? It was Benjamin Marks on the other end. A.D. had stopped to call Ms. Clara May from a phone booth inside the lobby of the Hotel DuPont in Wilmington, Delaware when I watched him sort of lean in closer to the receiver.

Where's she at?

There was a long silence. Then I could hear Benjamin's loud nasal twang as if it were right beside me, echoing up over the lobby and red vinyl booths, announcing his rank awkwardness in speaking with A.D. on the subject, even if they both knew Benjamin was with her now and A.D. wasn't. She's here, he said, and then there was another long silence before Ms. Clara May came on and A.D. leaned even closer as if to pull her right through the coiled Western Electric wire and frosted copper plates. Closing the wooden door, I watched him raise his hands and describe something before ceasing and slamming down the phone so hard I thought it would break it was so awful and loud that I had to look at the girl behind the counter to see if she'd heard. But she hadn't. We were in a luncheonette attached to the hotel and as I ordered another milkshake A.D. put in another nickel and dialed again and talked again and then slammed down the phone again and that's when I knew it—we were off.

York, he said when I asked where to, and that was it. We were onstage that same night at a theater with all the pomp and circumstance you'd expect befitting our newfound success. I don't think I saw the light of day the next two weeks we were so busy driving after shows to accommodate our run of pure luck. It was a deluge was what it was. The money poured in and the offers built up and everyone remembered: Why yes, those were them boys that sang The Ballad of Clara May. Those were the ones I liked. But now that they had this here Misericordia Blues to consider, it pumped us up even more into an act to take hold of and run clear to the top with. So everyone and many a sundry newspaper ran our story, and I would be remiss to say I didn't offer up my own smiling mug on occasion to anyone who'd care to listen about my long lost wife and baby girl. But it never did make the newsstand. Not with me being black, of course, and that made me drink the more to know our time spent hustling was fruitless in that regard, even if I did get my fair share of attention, for I suppose A.D. got his fair share, too.

There were girls on the road, so many girls you wouldn't of believed it, and I thought A.D. would of burst to touch each one of them after not seeing nor hearing from Ms. Clara May for days and days. From York to Pittsburgh, Cumberland to Pocomoke, Bethlehem to Wheeling we rode and played shows and every time he called back to Ms. Clara May, Benjamin Marks would always get on the line to tell him about the next show he'd already lined up, and the next one after that, but I don't think A.D. ever cared about any of it, to tell the truth. Especially the attention. Especially the girls. For he saw women during that time, I assure you. He saw them and couldn't help but be bombarded by them after a show, as they come streaming backstage or at the side doors of the theaters where we were just sneaking out. O they reared up in their calico skirts and tight cotton shirts just to catch a glimpse of the man who never once seemed to send back any of the flirtations they'd sent his way all throughout the show. Not the way most other front men would a done, I can assure you. Because if they were dancing and swaying and singing in front of his own spectral eyes, I don't think he ever saw them for what they were. At least, not in the way they wanted him too.

They were just forms to him. Bodies drifting past in bars and taverns and on street corners and state fairs. The young and old alike. The curious and grotesque. All the ones who'd found him attractive and desirable and who might have sat rapt and intense staring at their radio all this time. Yet in the flesh and blood of day they couldn't get a good read on him to save their skin he was so dead set on finding the next name, or the next song, or the next spark that might flare us up even higher into the stratosphere of our success. I swear; it wasn't enough for him to know we were blowing up—but we had to blow up that much more so that Ms. Clara May might come back to him. So she'd know, as he finally told me. So she wouldn't be able to help it, with how big we got, she'd have to love him again. Because we'll be bigger than the whole world, he said. Bigger than a thousand Runnymedes and anyone else besides, and she'll have to see me for real again. To remember. To feel it all over again. What we had.

I know, I muttered to him, I know, I know, and touched my head. For I could tell the purchase had been set forth in him for sure and that I'd probably been the one that set it, casting down the economy of his life into scribbles of ink and notes on some unlined page long ago, and it made me weep as we drove. It made me turn to the window and watch the next town drift in and out of focus, the next road fall away into nothingness, the next moonrise appear as if formed from the very cloud and mist of night, it was all so lonesome and useless, the road then. To see that light was such a substance of sorrow and unease to be formed and reformed like that, from the very thoughts and dreams of my resentment, as if none of it had any beginning nor end left a hollowness in me and a regret. So that if we hadn't finally headed back to Bristol after all that to breathe for once, to tip our heads above the overwhelming surface of things, that might have been it for me. I'd have drowned in my own weeping to see him possessed in a way that I'd hoped he'd overcome, but which had only tightened its noose that much tighter around his neck.

SHE'S WALKING, WAS WHAT BENJAMIN MARKS said when we slumped in all disheveled and half-lit with our guitar cases tattered and marked up from all the venues and places we'd been. It wasn't even yet dawning out, it being so gray and formless the light, and with the town stretched out and quiet, and the ridge an indistinguishable blanket draped across the horizon, even I had to wonder at the occurrence of it. Of Ms. Clara May walking with Jolie at this late an hour, or early, however you'd like to call it. But A.D. didn't seem to pay it no mind. He was dead set on seeing her. To see them. To talk about what he wanted from her and what he could give back. But with them not there at the moment, I believe he saw the opportunity to carve out a piece of Benjamin Marks on the side, for I seen him start to lean in and glare at the new gold necklace Benjamin wore. It was a thick link chain with a small crucifix and little gold revolver dangling from it, hanging down Benjamin's hairy chest. So that as soon as Benjamin noticed A.D. glaring at it he touched his stubby fingers to the symbols I suppose he saw in himself. Something about might and righteousness maybe, or worth and reverence. But then he swayed real far back in his seat when he seen A.D. lean in close enough to sniff him as if inspecting a hog set out to wallow in its slop.

Hell, A.D. said, and paused as if to lend some credence to his proclamation, some gravitas to the circumstance. But then pointing real slow like, he leaned down toward that necklace, squinted his eyes as if looking on some premonition, some decree or outlandish edifice he should not have been meant to meet, and whispered then all calm and cryptic. Is that what's supposed to help you then? With all that you've done? Reaching out, he grabbed the gleaming strand of it, so that Benjamin had to lean forward as A.D. pulled on it and the skin on Benjamin's fat neck turned purple beneath the strain.

I suppose, Benjamin said and then he didn't say nothing as he winced and struggled still in the pull of it, before just giving up and leaning in so close to A.D with his chin, I thought the two might kiss. But just as Benjamin ebbed up close to A.D.'s face, A.D. let go and the stumpy man fell back off his chair and rattled the cupboard behind him and a few plates on the table as he groped with his arms and then harrumphed a bit breathing heavy as he struggled to his feet. His gray bathrobe was untied and his silk pajammy bottoms shimmered in the light and he had a face on him meant to strike at A.D. with some blasphemy or insult he probably had stored up inside him for months about A.D.'s behavior. Running around reckless on the ridge. Him losing out on Ms. Clara May and little Jolie. But just then she comes in the doorway and sees them both like that—sort of standing there opposed—A.D. in his ridge-ragged denim shirt, and Benjamin in his silk pajammies—and she just laughed and laughed. I swear, she was a pistol of a woman.

To see them like that must have amused her to no end but she just said, Of course, and then set her keys down on the kitchen table before rearranging the cloth wrap she had on over her dress and wool jacket. Jolie was bundled up in there somehow and as she lifted the little precious girl out, the little one's beautiful pale cheeks were all rosy and chapped and windblown, for the two had been out in the cool brisk morning, and as we all watched entranced then, Ms. Clara May started humming and singing the prettiest little song. Then she set Jolie down on the couch in a fortress of pillows and blankets and kissed her baby girl on the forehead before turning around still smirking at the spectacle of her shabby husband and half-kept beau.

Hello, I said, for I weren't sure she'd even seen me she was so focused on A.D. with all the miserableness and anger still framing his face.

Isaiah, she said and didn't turn as I sort of glided past her to the couch. Whatever else was going to happen in that room, I knew it was going to happen with or without me, and thought I might as well be comfortable. Hell, I didn't even want to be part of it anyways, not since I felt responsible for most of it, but I knew enough to see this was A.D.'s moment. A last chance perhaps to bring himself back into the fold of his family, to be one of them again, supplanting the usurper and fool he'd let in so easy. But I wasn't sure this was the way to go about doing it. I mean, he was mean, A.D. The rage kind of dripped off him in waves and sent up a sulfurous humidity that had Benjamin Marks edging back. So that after a moment, Ms. Clara May was the only one standing there to block A.D. from everyone else in the room, for nobody seemed quite sure how to proceed until Benjamin Marks broke the silence.

Maybe I'll just ease on down to the Mercantile, he finally said. See if they open or something. He was thumbing the torn neckline of his robe and I could see through the doorway behind him to his pleated pants and silk tie and black and white checkered houndstooth jacket, all hung up proper and ironed over the back of his bedside chair. He had been caught unawares as he was, naked and vulnerable without his splendid suit on, and was itching to get somewheres he didn't feel so small or insignificant. They expecting me anyways, he said and turned to go, looking out of the corner of his eye, but he was brought up short before he could even take another step.

You don't have to go anywhere, Ms. Clara May said and raised her hand as if to stay something, to hold it right there suspended in the air. Some momentum or feeling, something I was having a real hard time seeing. As I looked at her, I waited to see if she would drop it. But then a moment went past, and another, and she just kept it there poised in the air as any beacon or symbol, as if to intone to Benjamin that all was well. All was as expected. Then as if directing a marionette upon its invisible strings, she twitched her fingers and he moved beside her, clutching the open ends of his bathrobe before drawing them tight.

Yes he does, A.D. said and he didn't look away. Not at him, nor at anything else in the room. For even as he gauged her, he didn't once shake out any of the anger plumping up his face that looked as if it could a been punctured and released with the smallest pinprick to wobble and whimper like a balloon through the air. And of course she didn't budge neither to see it, and I remembered then how strong she was and looked to see the glassy stretch along the back of her neck, to see if it could lend me any secrets. And friends, she didn't have an ounce of worry in her. Not a one. Her hair was clipped up for all the world to see, and that glassy stretch was as smooth and tranquil as any lake or iced-over pond, and I knew that A.D. was cooked for sure. No matter what he had to say. But I sure give it to him. He still tried. He tried and tried.

This ain't none of his concern, now is it?

Of course it's his concern, if he's around, she said.

Around? Around? And A.D. breathed so deep the tension sort of eased off a bit and his face rounded out at the edges. Listen, he said, a bit more composed, but still boiling beneath the surface. I been around and been around and it's always the same. The world's the same everywhere. Everybody's just looking for a home, for a place to call their own.

And this is meant to help you, she said, what you're saying? With her eyebrows raised, she had the look of someone amused to no end hearing the words of a common charlatan brought before her. Someone bent on assuring her of one thing when the exact opposite was true. You don't have a home right here? she said and shook her hands out at the walls and windows. A home with your own wife and daughter?

I have a home, A.D. said, and I swear when he said it I seen him glance off for the slightest instant to trace in ghostly strides the ridge rising out beyond the window. And of course Ms. Clara May seen it too, for ain't nothing could get by her.

O I see, she said. I seen it from the first but didn't want to believe it, and she smiled then sort of sad and lonely to herself, her lips quivering the slightest bit. Just as long as you keep moving, you think you're free. Well, you ain't. You ain't as far as I'm concerned. Not until you move on from me.

Move on?

Isn't that what you're best at?

As he stepped closer to her, the heat rose up like a furnace between them. Even Benjamin Marks was sweating so that I had to agree with him when I seen him waft the air towards him and then turn his collar back. I was hot and wanted nothing more than to sink my head into the icebox, but I wouldn't have moved an inch when they got going like this. I wouldn't have made a peep neither. I been out there driving for you, he said. And Jolie. Always for you. Like what I thought we needed. And this world, this other world—and he waved his hand then to encompass the window, the street, the ridge, everything— this singing and songwriting and everything, this other world ain't nothing no more, see? For we finally got it. We got what we needed and can spend the rest. Spend it all out for sure now, for we're done with it. Done with it for good.

For good?

For good, A.D. repeated, but then the faintest footsteps you ever heard interrupted Ms. Clara May. She was poised to speak again and strike down this nonsense that even I wasn't buying from A.D., when a slight tap at the door stayed her and was followed by a sliding envelope. It'd been slipped up under the door short and sweet, and as those footsteps pattered away, and all of us turned to see if it had really happened, there was an envelope in A.D.'s hands. He'd snatched it up without even opening the door and frowned as he turned it over to me.

It's an invitation, I said, sent by telegraph this very morning. Tearing it open, I read it just as I seen it. To play at the Hillsboro Theater in Nashville. In two nights. At the Anniversary Jubilee.

Nashville? A.D. said and leaned over toward me and took with his long fingers the invitation to inspect it himself, mulling it over even as Ms. Clara May watched him with her jaw gaping open.

For the Grand Ole Opry, I continued, as the heat flushed my cheeks to say it. In Nashville, I repeated, as the phrase seemed stuck in my mind.

Nashville, Benjamin Marks echoed. Well, I'll be.

We're invited, A.D. said running his finger down the invitation.

Invited? Ms. Clara May had turned to me with a face as scrunched up as a noose before glaring back at A.D. Well, isn't that just like you, she said. Isn't that just like you all over.

What? A.D. said and half-looked at her and half-read the invitation, looking at something he might have been waiting his whole life to hold.

To find a thing that nobody knows about and to take it up like it's God's gospel. You don't know that invitation from Adam and there you are raring to go again even when you just got through telling me you wouldn't. That you're through with all that. That you finally got it and that it don't mean nothing to you no more even if you don't know what day it is let alone the significance that brought you back here like a vagabond blown in with the wind.

What? he muttered. What day is it? and he shook his head to see the opportunity laid bare before us, at the Opry. For I don't think he could see nothing else then in the whole world because of it.

Why it's Jolie's baptism is what it is, she said, or had you forgot? and she crossed her arms then to look on him. As A.D. slunk back from view, he tried to speak, to say something about the chance of it, the great and honored opportunity at the Opry raised before him, before us. But there weren't nothing for him to do but shake his head, close his eyes, and drop that invitation to the floor.

XXXII

The pull of life ~ Of the finest quality ~ The gathering
spectacle ~ The eerie contours ~ A humid skin ~ The
close catacombs ~ Ebbed into a stillness ~ The great
man ~ Those empty seats ~ I aim to sing ~ He's done

FRIENDS, HE HAD FORGOT ALL ABOUT IT, for there was nothing else
on his mind other than being invited to play on the Grand Ole Opry's radio
program in Nashville. In fact, he got so excited the morning before the baptism
that he called up the Opry's radio station just to confirm it, the invitation, and
also to reserve three seats for Ms. Clara May, Jolie, and Benjamin Marks. Sure,
he even wanted Benjamin Marks there to see the grand event, the raising up
in A.D.'s eyes of all our work and ambition and hope. I suppose he thought in
that moment of our taking the stage and hearing our Misericordia Blues, Ms.
Clara May would see the error in her ways and leave Benjamin Marks sitting
right there at the Hillsboro Theater, distraught and alone, opening and closing
his pocket watch for all the world to see.

The Anniversary Jubilee had been trumpeted and advertised constantly on
the radio, and was being billed as an all-out extravaganza for commemorating
the importance of the program going on five years now. Runnymede himself
and the Piedmont Pipers and a host of other acts would be there for three
whole days to ring in this hillbilly sensation taking over the ridge and heartland
beyond. So that at Jolie's ceremony, no matter what I said to him nor how I
tried to stay his feet, he wouldn't stop moving to save himself even in that place
of places. He wanted to get going even though the soul of his daughter was at
stake here—and maybe even his family's—but still he needed to move. To keep
moving. To move eternal, so as not to feel the pull of life settling him down like

what Ms. Clara May wanted and that maybe only Benjamin Marks could deliver. That stability, that sanity, for lack of a better word, even if to see Benjamin Marks at the baptismal font was to look on one of the lowest and most blatant hucksters you'd ever seen.

O he was beaming as the priest dabbed little Jolie on the forehead, and then smiled the more as he held her like she was his own daughter and all the while A.D. was inching closer to the door for he wanted to get going and have an early start and nothing as significant as his own daughter's eternal reward seemed to matter to him. He just looked at me after scouring the whole scene with the priest and choir and attendants and said real quiet like: Hokum, when the crying started and Ms. Clara May crossed herself and the choir joined up with their Praise Jesuses and Hallelujahs. A.D. didn't want no part of that religiousness and was already outside gunning the motor and blasting the horn for he wanted to stop in Knoxville on the way at the John H. Daniel haberdashery. He'd been told to go there to get the finest silk duds and suits in the whole area and he meant to do it up right, even though I told him it was just the radio and nobody could see us anyways. But he just looked at me real serious, cocked his head sideways, and said Runnymede would. He'll see us for sure and will know finally who we are and where we're going.

Where we're going, I muttered, thinking on Runnymede's wish for stopping everything we could become. For as I thought on it, and considered A.D.'s eagerness to get going and outfit us anew for our big moment, I took one last look at the whole place because I never did have that much luck in churches, nor with religion, and as I bowed my head and raised it again who should I see—but Ms. Clara May eying me. She just sort of smirked with her soft pretty face to know what me and A.D. were up to. What we could only be up to—and I suppose that was it for her, even if A.D. had already invited her to come with Jolie and Benjamin after the baptism. He'd even paid their bus fare and everything.

But she just smirked once more and there might have been a telephone line laid direct from her mind to mine, for I could hear ever last thing she said: He's yours now. All of him. So get. Get going. The two of you, before she turned to the choir holding up that sweet little Jolie into the everlasting light and blessedness and munificence, and I wondered all the way on the drive to Knoxville if I'd ever hold Jolie again. If I'd ever see her turn her soft sweet face to mine or touch my knee and coo with that short coddling sound she made, if I'd ever be in her life again. I was pretty sure A.D. wouldn't no matter what he tried or thought to persuade Ms. Clara May with, especially after busting out on this last grand event in the way that he had.

O but to see him in Knoxville, staying there that night and halfway through the next morning, as he hemmed and hawed with the tailors and managers and the proprietor himself, Mr. John H. Daniel. Just to get the right cut and line of suit, and then to make sure all the material was of the finest quality and that even a few bowler hats were blocked out right and the argyle socks starched and ironed—with two new pair of leather wingtips thrown in for good measure—was to see the anxiousness in him for getting everything right. With Ms. Clara May (and maybe himself too), and of course with everything he'd let slide in his life before this. In his thirst for the songs and the names behind the songs that so weighed on him to drag them back out into the truth of day. And yet, when the first lights of Nashville lit up the road that evening, when we hummed out there in the darkness, as if riding down from another land entire, to see the way he slowed that car to a crawl through those streets where the music spilled out and echoed from almost every doorway and window on Broadway and Church Street and 2nd Avenue, was to see him move from his anxiety into an excitement hardly contained. For his eyes—my god his eyes—only seemed to stretch that much wider at it all, to see the gathering spectacle set right there before us as we pulled into the Hermitage Hotel.

Jesus Christ, A.D. said, and whistled as a valet in a red suit stood holding his hand out for the keys. I wonder if she got my message. He looked over at the front doorway emblazoned with lights, decorated with a veritable garden of roses and tulips and daisies. I wonder if they're already here. I didn't have nothing to tell him on that subject. Anyways, I was already scuffling with a bright young bellhop eager to please us with his gumption, for it was all I could do to keep him from grabbing and making off with our guitars. We were already late and had to hurry, but of course a great many people were standing out there to keep us a bit longer. O there were musicians coming and going, and some were smoking cigarettes and cigars and drinking from glasses of whiskey and bourbon and humming the refrains of songs and pledging oaths to the arts and such. And as they did, a harmonica played somewheres far off, and then a mandolin echoed along some muddy cobblestone, and A.D. and I moved then as if through the eerie contours of a dream.

I looked and thought I saw the Piedmont Pipers in their green and white wool outfits traipsing ahead of us, following some dark shape pushing through the crowd. But when I hurried A.D. along to catch up with them, there was only the outside of the Hillsboro Theater lit up like that burning cross those years ago, the one we seen when we first turned down into Dixie, and a shiver ran through me. The entrance was swarmed with people as cars pulled up and more performers emerged and a few great spotlights scanned the night and I could smell the reedy waters of the Cumberland River close by. The water eternal washing past the city. A humid skin alive with the smell of mud and spring and weeds and rot, and it was as if I'd already passed through this trial before, that this instance was raised to a new center of remembrance, for I seen the backstage door then. It was nondescript and bare beneath a red bulb, and it was easy. I just walked towards it. And before I could reconsider the purchase of whatever event we'd already embarked upon, and that had perhaps been written down ages ago, A.D. and I were inside. The close catacombs of the place and the shadow of the mauve curtain moved with a soft rustling, and the echo of the first performer washed over me as elegiac and lonesome as a passing cloud, and I seen him then out of the corner of my eye—Runnymede—moving on the edge of the dressing rooms. Don't, I said to A.D., but he hadn't heard. He'd already wandered on ahead to a chalkboard at the edge of the stage to see the order of performances.

There was a violin then somewhere in the echoing vortex, and the staccato precision of tap shoes working out some timeless rhythm—but then all the other sounds ceased. The refrain of the singing onstage, the clapping and stomping from the audience, even the sad chalky lettering of the stage manager writing our name ebbed into a stillness that washed over me with a presence as close and immediate as what that river would have felt like pressed against my skin. Until only the basic honest core of life remained. This was the core, I knew. I stood at the center of it, and felt a moment arrive like at the track then as Runnymede came closer, walking in a proscribed arc around the backstage props and drum kits and pallets of crated instruments. I looked at the floor and swore he didn't touch down. Not a once. His feet. They just floated now as around him all those other sycophant musicians and agents moved as a pack of horses might around a great white roan, wavering left and right to each of his intimations, before he finally arrived and stood beside me, looking over my shoulder at the chalkboard.

I sniffed once and the scent of ash was close. I made as if to turn, but couldn't. A.D. was watching the act onstage, but then looked beyond the act, to scan the crowd for any sign of little Jolie, Ms. Clara May, and Benjamin. But he couldn't find them, and seemed an anxious mess of a man, shuffling his feet as he strained with his neck to see farther into the dim auditorium. And then, as if made clear above everything else, as if brought out of the entangled code of other happenings, from the inherent living and dying and purchase of the spectacle, I looked at A.D.'s face—at his long, clean profile—and the bright wooden floorboards glowed behind him in all their polished grandeur. Then the great man beside me made a motion, raising his hands in unison as the number finished, and the crowd erupted with applause.

Bravo, he said, bravo, and his minty cologne wafted over me as I turned to his voice and he looked down smiling into my face. A rush of people went past as another act hurried onstage and I found myself pushed up even closer to his powdery blue suit, staring all the while as he smiled and his big barrel chest pressed against the silk edges of my new Western shirt, before the press of people released. I took a step back to appraise him as he addressed me, still smiling. Another moment like that, friend, and we'd have been much more than friends.

I made as if to speak, to deny him my friendship, to denounce him as a fiend or ghoul, but a man appeared beside us with a contract. Brandishing a pen, he turned his back without speaking and bent forward so that Runnymede could place the contract on the flat edge of him and sign it without taking his eyes from me, before the man stood up and was gone. I turned to A.D. as if to show him who was here, to alert him after all our wandering and searching and driving. But he was already absorbed in the next act, absorbed in finding those empty seats filled by his love, by his child, and by his replacement. But there was nothing. He might have been a thousand miles from me then in his mind, even if he was only ten feet.

You don't remember me, do you? I said. You don't remember us.

Friend?

You don't remember what you said? At the racetrack. With what you aim to do to me and A.D.? With what you aim to become?

Runnymede ranged his square chin closer as if calculating the importance of what I'd said, the incongruity, maybe even the need. I aim to do nothing with you, friend. I aim to sing. As always. And to sell records. Then I aim to go forth as before but only bigger, better, stronger. Always stronger, my friend, and more far-reaching, indomitable even. This radio is just the beginning. It's the beginning of all that follows. For the one true direction is the one I'll steer with my own hand. But this much I can tell you, friend, you shall not see it. And as he leaned in closer, one of his dark eyes winked at me as I smelled the chalk white dust of his face, the bitter anise rasp of his breath.

You know you said that to me before. You said you wanted to end us and everything we stood for. That you aim to change our rising up ahead of you. Our path.

And I still do, he said standing back up, brushing the shoulders of his crisp blue suit, whoever you are. I mean to end any and all in my way. That belief has never wavered. It's the one true aim in any competition, wouldn't you say, in any struggle? To those who'd take what's rightfully mine, who'd oppose or run counter to my own true bearing. They will be sent down in turn. All will be sent down in turn.

I'm Isaiah Hardy, I said and stood defiant as the quirk of a smile played at the edge of his mouth. I play in the Hardy Family. We're here to supplant you, sir. To remove you for good.

The Hardy Family? he said and closed his eyes thinking on the resonance and movement of syllable, letting the softness of it tickle his tongue.

The Hardy Family, I said. The Hardy Family. You don't remember me, do you? How the hell could you not remember me? How could you not know my name?

Runnymede laughed then so loudly, I thought the microphones onstage might have picked it up and sent it out, showering the crowd with a rousing chuckle. But another number had ended and the applause rang out and Runnymede touched his chin looking at me. Ah, I know what it is, he said. Of course, you must have dreamed me.

Sir?

Dreamed me. Everyone does. I can tell just by looking at you. Just by what you say. And at your dark shade of skin. Everyone needs an adversary. Someone to blame for their ineffectual lives. To lay rest their responsibility and fate and failings. No, no. No words now. Just listen. I hear it from everyone. At all times. From poets and prostitutes, singers and dancers, businessman and prophets. Bootleggers too. They all want what I have, don't they? Don't you? Then they make me up in their minds as an angel, a devil, as anything they could never hold or know. They all make me up for themselves to treat exactly as they'd like. To manipulate to no end, to extract some certain satisfaction or leveling. So how'd you treat me, friend? How'd I confound you in the depths of your delusion? Did I taunt you? Did I hurt you that much? And was it the truth? That silly old thing. Did I tell you what you couldn't bear to hear?

I couldn't speak. Or breathe. The sense of a shadow loomed above me and was real for I felt it creeping upon my flesh even as he stood there and the music and voices ranged up and reeled in the ether and were sucked back into the voided silence of my throat.

Awww, was it that bad? he said. That you can't even tell me about it, that you can't even speak? Pity. I had so hoped someone might stand up to me one day. To have that strength. That conviction. Because I imagine it was something you couldn't help but hear. Something deep inside that found its way out and honestly, you should be thanking me for giving voice to your fear. To all that desperation. For is it really such a horrible thing to find out now that it was true? After all this. After all the tears and recriminations and trials. That you were wrong. That you were too weak to do anything about it? He was grinning, and leaned down so close, the faintest white sparkle of sugar became distinguishable in the sheer expanse of his face.

It's not true, I whispered. It's not. There's no purchase on life like what you said. There's no purchase on the deeds of man and time forever.

Nonsense, he said. You don't know what I said. You don't know a thing. There are voices divine and decrepit in Man. Voices that hold no limit or edge. That reap and sow and spread their proclivity beyond any reasoning or sense you could know. Beyond even the darkness in me, friend. Yes, I have darkness, and here he leaned close enough that I could feel the raw white heat of each word grace my cheek. You don't know what I've made and broken. You don't know what I've made. You may have dreamed me a monster, a fool, a poison in turn. But let me tell you this, whatever you've dreamed, whatever you've made up and pictured in your mind, I'm ten times worse and before this night is through I swear by god you'll know it.

The Hardy Family? The Hardy Family? The stage manager called our name and as the last act rushed off, I turned from the sheer terror of Runnymede's face to see A.D. already onstage. He was moving out toward the front microphone and had a shiny black guitar around his neck, with his new black fedora inched low enough to keep the glare from blinding him as he stared at those three empty seats in the middle. He then watched perplexed as the tuxedoed emcee must have said something into the microphone for the crowd cheered loudly and laughed as the red neon L I V E sign flashed in the air. As it did, the stage manager implored me with his eyes to follow A.D., and yet—when I looked down, and made as if to step toward the stage—I couldn't. It was impossible. I looked at my shoes and the soft, polished leather fluttered up as I lifted my toes to check if they still worked. Even my fine tailored suit was free of any entanglement. But when I made to move again, the skin of my left wrist felt singed with a slick heat and when I looked to see its cause, Runnymede's steely hand tightened ever closer around my arm. He smiled looking over my shoulder at the stage manager and emcee who came blustering off the stage to check.

Well . . . what's wrong? he said and mopped his brow with a handkerchief he then folded and held as he coughed into his hand.

I don't think this nigger can go on, Runnymede said and nodded toward me. He's done. And as he said it, several fellows who'd walked with Runnymede before as he'd come around from his dressing room appeared beside me and the emcee just watched as they laid their hands upon my shoulders and held me down.

XXXIII

A great echoing stillness ～ Play, goddamnit! ～
With my bondage made visible ～ In the high
dusty rafters ～ Time that's bought ～ A recompense
～ His confession ～ Yancey Jakes returns

I SAID I CAN'T PLAY WITHOUT HIM. A.D. was speaking into the microphone as a great echoing stillness came over the theater. The emcee pointed backstage but his voice was muffled for he did not want to be heard over the microphone and even nodded once to the L I V E sign as he spoke. But as A.D. looked and acknowledged the broadcast, he seemed deadset on what he'd already said. Well, we'll just have to wait until he can come out then, won't we? Because that's all there is to it, folks. He's Isaiah Hardy. It's his family, and as A.D. chuckled to say it, a round of laughter coursed through the theater. The emcee was shaking now the hem of A.D.'s shirt for he wanted him to either start on his song straight away or come offstage for the airwaves demanded it, some movement one way or the other.

I couldn't budge. Runnymede had me and laughed as he whispered in my ear, This is it, the extent of all that you'll do. And all that you'll ever do, and as one of his fellows took my guitar and carried it away, a part of me seemed to go with it and all the strength I'd felt in watching A.D. flowed out of me to him then— for I at least wanted him to play—to rise up ahead of Runnymede, to overtake everything Runnymede stood for. Play, I said and I was surprised Runnymede let me say it. Play! I cried again, but the stillness of the theater had shifted back already to restlessness and then to unease as more people started calling up for A.D. to do something, to play, to begin, to do anything, and my own cry was taken up into the clamor. If he heard me, I can't be sure, for A.D. had to shade his eyes even with his hat pulled down to see where I could be. But it was dark backstage, and as he started towards me, Runnymede stepped forward and then all A.D. could see was Runnymede's smiling face. And Runnymede's blue suit. And Runnymede's large white hands clapping as the crowd clapped too, clapping and stomping for him to play play play, until he staggered back still mesmerized by Runnymede's placid eyes, and turned to the microphone.

I just want to thank you all for inviting us here, he said. It's been our dream to play at the Opry ever since it started, and I'm glad we could make it. The crowd roared then for they would a roared at anything they were so pumped up to hear him play—to hear anyone play—that the emcee sweated and shifted in the wings as he looked from A.D. to Runnymede who towered above the emcee and touched his shoulder whispering in his ear. I began to sweat my own self as I watched the emcee wave with his hand then to the boxes in the mezzanine. A technician was sitting there with headphones on and must have been running and determining the breaks in the broadcast for advertisements, because he nodded back and raised his thumb and I didn't think that was a good sign, for there probably wasn't too much time left for A.D.

Play, goddamnit, I said, *play*, and my voice must have found a break at the end of the applause, for A.D. turned and finally seen me. Runnymede had just stepped aside from the emcee and I was visible. A.D. stared and stared, his mouth agape to see what had become of me, with my bondage made visible, as it were. Those other fellows still had hold of me and never said nothing the whole time, but would a taken me outside at the drop of a hat if Runnymede had given them the go ahead, but he never did. He never said nothing. I suppose he wanted A.D. to see it all. That there was something already written in this moment, some sign or deliberation. For as A.D. seen me like that, bound and held back by the men who would separate us, separate my kind from his kind, something changed in him. Something that maybe even old Runnymede himself hadn't figured. Something not written down in indelible ink as Runnymede's ghost had told me, for a great hesitation come over A.D. Pausing in his breathing (for we could all hear him over the microphone), some final decision must have fluttered up into A.D.'s thinking. Something made real by him right then and there. Looking again to the empty seats for his family, he didn't see them and shook his head to scour his guitar's glistening strings, the brass buttons of his fancy new suit, his polished wingtips and argyle socks, before looking back at me and leaning into the microphone. He never strummed a single note. Never turned a wayward eye then from me after that, but just started in on the names:

Jessico Ayles and Old Mossfield Churchwell and Clarence Ashford. Pee Wee Woodsman and the Appalachian Mayfairs. Bill & Bella Reese and the New Carrolton Singers. Blind Uncle Vecsey and Sister Mary Patton. The Williamson Trio, Doc Ferry Sutters, and Bascomb Teak Nelson. Sleepy John Stack and Mahidabelle Shine. Georgie Black Stevens and the Blue Ridge Charmers. And on and on he went, until the crowd shouted out for songs, or for the next act to be brought on, for something other than this to continue. Of course that had the emcee storming back out as if he might take A.D.'s guitar from him. But A.D. wouldn't have none of that and nudged him away with the end of it and then played a first shimmering chord of the Misericordia Blues and that seemed to quiet the crowd and even the emcee, who retreated to the wings. But as A.D. spied me again, and then seen them still holding me with their thick white hands—as Runnymede himself glared and stood as still as a statute watching him—he played a second chord but only let it ring out and resonate until the bright notes of it were all that buzzed in the high dusty rafters, before starting in again on the names:

Broken Paul Langetree and Carter Shake Daniels. John Grunt Rutterson and the Shenandoah Boys. Robinson White McTell and the Marshall Two-Tones. Joe John Johnson and the Lincoln-Stith Toppers. Walleye Jenkins and the Haymarket Quintet. Obadiah Bagby and the Cleete Hoyt Hubcaps.

What the hell is this? The emcee had moved from the wings over to Runnymede and tried to reach me, to ask me, but Runnymede stepped in front of him again and just pointed at my skin.

He's done, Runnymede said. For all time. Can't you see that? And so is that one, nodding back onstage at A.D.

What the hell does that mean? He's done? The emcee looked up at Runnymede, blinked, and wiped his face with his handkerchief. But that was about as far as he was willing to take it, for he could see Runnymede weren't budging in his assertion of my incompetence on account of my obvious skin color. So he just refocused his efforts on the one of us that was onstage. Doesn't he know he's on air? he finally said, and turned back to watch A.D. still reciting names into the microphone. Doesn't he know we can't just cut out whenever we want? That we got customers? That we got time that's bought.

And friends, I was smiling to hear it, smiling to see the confusion. I knew what it was before this here flesh-and-blood Runnymede ever figured it out. (Even if I knew the one I dreamed of had known it for years and years.) Because just maybe, I'd seen the lines of this purchase a little bit more clearer than he did, that I'd seen them run deeper and farther. There might have even been something in A.D. all along that was fighting toward this end. Some notion or hidden feeling that had turned up in him after all the truth we'd found out there in the ridge had washed over him after all that we'd done, after all that we'd taken. Sure. A recompense, as it were. An absolving, or pardoning away. Or maybe, it just happened because he seen me held back. He seen me subjugated like he'd never seen me subjugated before. Turned into some property, some sad item to be detained and discarded, and it vexed him. Vexed him to no end. I can't rightly say.

But if it was true that he was the most un-white man I'd ever known, as I've said before, I'll be damned if he didn't prove it by what he done next. Because something inside him must have traced back all the names and songs and faces of the folks we'd seen. Across all the lives we'd found on those hillsides and hovels, in those dirty clapboard shacks and shanties, in those old abandoned slave quarters and shed rows, for he just started talking. He talked into the microphone and listed it all out for what he'd taken and had to give back. What we all had to give back.

What the hell is this? The emcee waved his hand now and looked up at the technician in the mezzanine, but his technician wasn't looking. He was just working the dials, working the levels with his headphones so that A.D. could be heard, so that all of it could be heard.

His confession, Runnymede said and smiled as he shook his head.

His what?

His confession.

You mean he came all the way down here to do that? and the emcee waved his arm again at his technician, waving it frantically as he stomped his foot. But he never seen him. Don't he know this ain't no church?

It is to him, I said, and Runnymede looked at me for the first time since I seen him in the flesh and stopped smiling. His lips creased to a thin and vaporous white as he cleared his throat, as if getting set to perform, to set all this nonsense down for good.

Why don't you just have your boy flash the lights at him? he said.

My what?

Your boy, Runnymede said. The lights, and the emcee looked across the stage at where the light board operator stood at his panel of switches, waiting his cue. Just dim the lights and see what happens.

O my friends, the lights. The lights! To hear that caustic phrase spoken so casually and with such meaning took the smile right off my face. As soon as I heard it, I seen Ezra Lee's pale visage surface in the ether, as of a ghost come back to haunt us. And as I watched the emcee make his sign to the light operator, the footlights at the edge of the apron dimmed and flickered and wavered down, and the whole time I thought of the Brooklyn Bridge and A.D.'s wish to jump off it. Then I watched in horror as he seemed shaken from his recitation, and moved toward the edge of the stage still mumbling a last few names as he stood before the crowd.

The lights, he finally said, and shook in his soul to see them and to know after all this time the lights weren't there to lift him up into the promise of his own celebrity, that they weren't there to anoint him some god or king of music. For as he glanced back to see, he knew there was no celebrity without me, no family without the founder. That the lights were now an indictment of all the hatred and prejudice that had shadowed and stalked our trail this whole time, and he'd had enough. Enough of looking out at the empty seats where he'd hoped his family would be in this ridiculous plan of his. Enough of Runnymede's smiling, placid face and my hopeless, pleading gaze. Enough of the crowd howling to see him play something, as all the hopefulness drained from his vision for what this moment—our moment—was meant to be. And as the guitar dangled and picked up the pulsation of the dimming bulbs, and he cried out again—The lights!—with the sharp toe of his fine leather wingtip he kicked the bulbs on the front edge of the stage. One by one, they cracked and burst. The glass sparks scattered and spent, so that only ash and bright blue flames leapt up. While beyond him, with each decisive kick, the great roiling crowd erupted with another chorus of shrieks and boos as they stood and shouted down his life, shouting down his soul, pointing for him to leave, to quit.

There, Runnymede said. The Hardy Family. And with a satisfied air, he touched my shoulder lightly, smiled his awful smile, and faded into the shadows. As if that were their signal, them fellows released their grip and I knew that was it for us for sure. To come into the Opry and desecrate such a ground as this— before a live studio audience, no less—not to mention all those folks listening in on the airwaves, had done it, had cast our name to mud for sure. And even as I was free now and A.D. wallowed on the front of the stage, showered in the hatred of that crowd, and the emcee himself staggered out and tried to drag A.D. off, I couldn't bring myself to go out and help him, to cross that stunning threshold, that last sad divide. Instead, I watched frozen as A.D. stood alone in the darkness, as he rambled on with his guitar, so that finally the bouncers and stagehands had to drag him away. For it was only then, only as he struggled in their grasp singing some last lyric, that it come to me, in-between the swells and curses the crowd cast upon him. That song. The one on his lips. The one in the ridge we said we'd never sing nor sell for all time. The song of Yancey Jakes. The one only now to be sung and heard as never before—the only one that needed to be heard above all else—but that would never be, as he was finally and ruthlessly dragged away.

XXXIV

That urgency and forlornness ~ Out there beyond the ridge ~
Where the music was fresh ~ The City of New Orleans to the
Crescent to the Cardinal ~ The great coincidence ~ Electrified
on Maxwell Street ~ On the Circe ~ Finally, into Asheville

WHEN THE TELEPHONE RANG, I had a notion not to answer it. I was
just setting there in my apartment on the South Side of Chicago, on East 47th
and State Street, if you can believe it (just like the State Street in Bristol), when
I heard it, calling to me with all that urgency and forlornness that I could tell
without answering what it was. Something in the air presaged it. Something I
felt building after all these years had become so open and obvious I just let it
ring and sipped my coffee all the way down and touched up the collar of my
white Pullman Porter jacket before finally stepping over to the counter. I didn't
have to say nothing by way of answering, since she always done all the talking
anyways. It was Ms. Clara May. A.D. was dead. An apparent heart attack had
taken him where he stood in the kitchen of his two room trailer after he'd
moved out of Bristol finally, somewheres closer to Lexington, Kentucky, out
there beyond the ridge.

    I thanked her for her call, of thinking enough to let me know, then paused,
took a deep breath, and said I was real sorry to hear it. I inquired then quietly
about the health of Ms. Jolie, now a mother in her own right, with a baby girl
named Marie and a young fellow named Amos, but got off before she could
even answer. I didn't have time for all that, going down memory lane and such,
for fear of where all those memories might lead. Instead, I just had to set down
and write it all out, scribbling my notes first, before composing the longer studied verse to someone—to anyone—even if it was to my own damn self. I just

had to write about him. About us. The Hardy Family. About all that we done and played and heard. About all that we made and took and gave. And the more I contemplated and put pen to paper, the more I realized what a hard thing it was to think about a life going out like that, like no more than blowing out a candle, and then to make it mean something. But it brought me back to the Opry that night, and to our moment all those years ago, when I never seemed able to cross that last threshold, that one divide, to help my A.D., to reach out to him. O I so wanted to reach out to him, to pull him in closer. To walk back dignified and tall from that stage and never look back at the hatred and rage of all those folks shouting out there in the dark. I wanted to recover him, so to speak, to keep him safe, with me, and I suppose I still do.

It's now November 7, 1960, almost twenty-eight years after the fact, and I'd hoped to find A.D. in much better shape after all this, but knew it weren't no good. It weren't no good from the beginning, not with how we left it. Not with how those lights flickered on the edge of that stage and all them people started hollering in the darkness. When all he could do was stare into the theater reciting the names and lyrics and any last hope he still had of making it through, of rising above it all, was extinguished. Yes. Hope. It's a word I've become accustomed to over the years, and do not shy away from. Because I was lost then, I guess you could say, and have been ever since. Even if I've seemed to be moving in the right direction all along. Even if I've seemed to establish a foothold, or purchase, as it were, in another life entire from what we left behind.

It was the railroad that done it, if you can believe it. At least nobody could say it wasn't. For nobody ever pushed me off from Bristol, as you might have thought. Nobody was ever mean to me nor downhearted about our big flame-out at the Opry. Nobody ever blamed me nor my disappearance, as they called it, from the stage for our final collapse. But I sure felt something hovering there. Some absence or energy in the face of what we'd accomplished and left unfinished seemed to haunt me, shadowing my movements in town, visiting my dreams at night, and so I just had to leave. I locked up the door one day, turned off the lights, and rode the rail all the way to Chicago. I went where the music was, where it was building something fresh, where it was another sound entire from what I knew, but familiar too, and true.

O we still played. We played on many occasions after that night at the Opry, after I bailed A.D. out of the Nashville City Jail, though I can't say any of them were as memorable as that last time. If you'd already guessed, it was the emcee that done it, that accused A.D. with disorderly conduct and creating a nuisance and destruction of property. Even as that goddamned Runnymede swore on the emcee's behalf, writing his account all up with his nice little flourishes and fancy legal speak, commenting the next morning in the *Nashville Tennessean* on the particulars against A.D. and me. Against us. Dragging it all out that much more, with our names included (finally saying our names, though only in connection with our disgrace), so that after all that, what else could we do? We just went further out from where all the noise was. We went all the way to Okie country and Arkansas and even Kansas to play some shows. But eventually our reputation caught up with us there too, with what happened in Nashville. It was only in Del Rio, Texas on the border with the radio stations popping up all over Mexico where we ever got any play, any money. Even that didn't last. O we headlined the occasional benefit then, or a Victor Talking Machine Company reunion or some other event, but mostly we drifted apart. It just didn't seem right no more. Like we were holding onto something that wasn't there, that didn't have no name nor center, so we just had to leave. To let it go.

So when I seen an advertisement to become a Pullman Porter for the Pullman-Standard Car Manufacturing Company, I just had to take it. By then A.D. had already invested in a hardware store right there in Bristol, where I imagined him moving behind the counter like a sad giraffe, reaching up to the top shelves for hammers and nails and half-cent shingles, for I only ever think he did it to be closer to Jolie. But even they moved away not long after. Gone to Ms. Clara May's people in Norfolk, Virginia. So it was only A.D. in the end. A.D. alone and not returning my calls nor letters nor even picking up a guitar, I heard, or turning through the pile of names he kept tucked beneath his pillow. So I had to think less and less of my one true friend until finally he fell away from me entire. Until there was nothing left except what he'd once meant for my family, with that great hope he symbolized. That hope. So that I had to think about the Hardys instead, I had to think about my family, and how I was going to get them back.

O my sweet Annie and Lucy girl were still out there, still waiting to see me somewheres on some billboard or festival perhaps, even if they didn't know it anymore. Even if Lucy had probably forgotten who I was or how I'd touched her cheek in the morning, or placed my hand atop her warm head, kissing her. Even if Annie had gotten herself a new man and lived in a new house in a new life without the echo of my memory no more, of my loving and leaving her still shadowing her. Stalking her, maybe? I don't know. But I still wanted her. I still needed to find them, to know they were out there and safe. My family. My girls. I still believed in them and thought the railroad would see me through. That it would bring me back to them. Or them to me, whichever came first, for I thought it the best way to cover the territory I imagined them to be in. I know, I know, it sounds ridiculous and absurd, and it was. I imagine if you hired some accountant or even first grader, they could have figured the odds weren't on my side by a long shot. But it was my hope, you see. My circuit. The shape I was meant to complete again and again, and I couldn't leave it for nothing.

So riding the Panama Limited (later the City of New Orleans) to the Crescent to the Cardinal (formerly the James Whitcomb Riley) became my life for the next twenty-five years. My route, as it were, my great triangle of becoming and hope. Ah, the trains, the rhythm of it all, the great steady power of the rails rolling beneath my feet, or rocking me to sleep and jolting me back awake. I loved every second of it and wouldn't have quit it for nothing if what came next didn't happen. For I don't know how many of them I rode over the years, nor how many bags and cases I hauled, or the great number of beds I turned down, or the shoes I shined up. But the fear in me was that the one time I wasn't on a train, the one time I wasn't working for all I was worth, would be the one time they'd be standing at some concession stand or ticket booth. Or passing behind some trolley car. Walking out in plain view for all to see, as simple as that, and so it charged me. It made me work from Chicago to Memphis, New Orleans to Carolina, Virginia to Indiana, before finally rolling back into Illinois—it became my journey, my mission, so to speak, year after year. It got so familiar, I could tell the depth of the Mississippi River just by the shadow of the water heading south. Or, I could guess the time of day just by watching the grassy lowlands before turning up north through Georgia. When the Blue Ridge rose up before me as the whole sad dance of it unfolded again and seemed one continuous rolling away, one grand circuit. But it never seemed complete. It never seemed to change neither. Now I'm not saying it never got old or tired. Just that the different faces and mornings and moonlight I seen never once shined on the ones I wanted it to shine on, and so it made me forlorn. It never once helped me craft the great coincidence I was hoping to orchestrate, by following those great centric routes of migration and commerce. My great wearing away and becoming. Yes, becoming, and last sad entrance through the years.

Though I'd be remiss if I didn't speak about the faces I did see back then, the ones that reminded me of my pilgrimage. The faces that kept me company as I rolled along and searched the land and watched for my girls, as all the faces of the black boys and men poured up from the South. All on their way to Chicago or St. Louis or Detroit. All hungry and determined to work, determined for the money and savings they'd send back to the ones they'd left behind in Slidell and Jackson and Birmingham, in Macon and Hattiesburg and Brownsville. All the wives and sisters and girlfriends that the men saw less and less of the more the years dragged on, as their paths branched off and diverged. For it all seemed written down on some great ledger years before, the pain and loss meant for them to suffer. The lost love and betrayal, the anguish and displacement written on our faces and in our dark skin like a mark of our loss. Of our guilt and bereavement at moving forward without the ones we loved, and of then loving others closer to us (who we tried to start the whole bond of family and togetherness with again). But like everything else we'd been through—from the cargo holds to the cotton fields to the sharecropper shacks—-we found our solace in music. The music made us whole again. For however long it played, for however long we remembered, for however long we sang and shifted our tired feet to the sound, the music made it true.

Though as I write this, I'm wondering what I could possibly say that you haven't heard? How the music changed me, how it changed the very air the world seemed comprised of, for it sounded so much like what we'd made in our own day, but different. Electrified they called it. Electrified blues and rock n' roll scattered like thunderbolts in the alleys and juke joints on Maxwell Street. Scattered like lightning in the ears and minds and hearts. Blowing away your eyes. Blowing away your bones and blues. For I played it too, from time to time, with a few fellas who knew me—McKinley and Albert and Jimmy Reed—when it first broke for all of them in the way it must a broke for A.D. and me with our first big hit. They knew what I'd done and revered me in a way that made me a sort of patrician to their lot. Yet in those smoky bars and barbeque joints, in those packing plants and garage stalls, I swear it was like the thing jumped in my hand. Those hot guitar coils. Each reverberating note and feedback loop. Like holding a snake or electric eel out in front of you. Something buzzing and livid and alive. With the soul of the life in it dying to get out, to be free, to rise up ahead like what we always wanted with our music, but which Runnymede stopped plain and cold in Nashville.

Ah Runnymede . . . I seen him again too after all this, after I heard about A.D.'s passing. After it threw me something awful and I got to thinking on all of this again, and just had to go, to ride my circuit again, following it through the land. And even if I can't be sure Runnymede seen me when I did meet up with him again, I know he sure felt me. O he felt me through and through for what I'd become—and what I could only become—but we'll get to that soon enough. For now we've got time. Time to ride the rails. Time to mark the land. For I was working on the Crescent, as I've said, portering on the Pullman named Circe of all things, if you can believe it, if you can allow me such latitude with mythology and coincidence.

If you'll recall, Circe was the Greek goddess of magic, a sorceress who transformed her enemies into animals and grotesque images. She was the daughter of Helios, the god of the sun, and there was a certain symbolism in my discovering Runnymede's location when I seen the poster in Spartanburg, South Carolina when we rolled in. Yes, Spartanburg, as Spartan as my existence was then for sure, for Runnymede was playing not far off that night in Asheville, North Carolina, and I just about jumped at the chance to see him. O friends, I knew it was a sign for sure: Asheville—a smoldering name of a place if ever I heard one—appropriate enough for how Runnymede had burned up our lives. Burning up any last chance I had at making a life for myself with my family. And as I talked with a porter I knew there on the line, and who I'd done a favor for years before, he took over for me in no time, and seemed sympathetic to my case. It was easy. I just stayed over after the Crescent pulled out, bought my ticket on the Asheville Special and pulled into the Biltmore Depot no less than an hour later as the old fire inside me about Runnymede's deceitfulness flared up to boil my resolve anew. And as I started off to see him, I had no earthly idea what I might do.

XXXV

A televised affair ~ Isis ~ A golden ledge in the air ~ Time
and chance and order ~ The jacket and the smoke ~ Some
new doorway ~ A wand of enchantment ~ In different shades
and different times ~ My last purchase ~ Cracks ~ Seams
in the grand scheme ~ Like shivered sparks ~ In the ridge

IT WAS A TELEVISED AFFAIR, IF YOU CAN BELIEVE IT. At the Isis
Theater, if you can further believe it, for now the symbolism and incidence of
the gods stands to swarm my account entire. Isis, if you'll recall, was an Egyp-
tian patron of nature and magic, a protector of slaves and sinners, and also the
goddess of children. Children. No, the significance did not escape me even as
the fire inside me burned to see this fiend banished. This fiend I blamed for
destroying my greatest chance of bringing the Hardy Family's name unto the
world, of seeing my wife and child returned to me, the child I hoped to protect
above any other. And as I bought my ticket and entered the theater, I seen right
away how it was outfitted for the musical performance.

A host of television cameras had been set up for a local broadcast and placed
like great hulking obelisks in the aisles and balconies. So that as I went up and
up to my seat (for I was still colored, after all), I sat in the back row throughout
the whole first act and bided my time. I was calm! Patient even, for when the
emcee appeared and said his piece about what an amazing headliner they had
coming on, I only stood and started down the long spiral staircase, and then the
long center aisle, after taking a deep calming breath, as Runnymede McCall and
the Piedmont Pipers took the stage.

He was as big and brash as I remembered, smiling all the while, waving to
the crowd and grabbing his guitar. He moved as I'd seen him move backstage
at the Opry. I looked and it was as if he never touched down. His feet just

floated like all those horses at the track. He was as mythical and absolute as ever and seemed not a day older nor an ounce weaker and I shuddered as I moved through the throngs of people standing in the aisles to get a better glimpse of the man, applauding after each number as if their lives depended on it. The excitement and appearance of the cameras, mixed with the great man's celebrity, seemed to charge the crowd to no end. Runnymede's prominence had only increased over the years as more albums were put out, as more shrines and tabernacles hosted him, as first the radio and then all the TV screens couldn't contain him no longer. So that even here, in a movie theater, his image was being broadcast to the four corners for his influence had reached such proportion that only the latest and greatest technology could transmit it.

Moving from row to row as a shadow must (just as my race had throughout the centuries), I reached the front stage where the camera stood stock still and centered on the man as he sung. Then before I knew what I was doing, I had my hands on the side of the lens, even as the cameraman still stared into the back hood of it and concentrated his focus on Runnymede as he sang and pranced about. It would have only taken a moment to step out in front and start the harangue building inside me about the fiendish nature of the man. To tell the world about the duplicity and contempt he carried for those foolish enough to purchase his sound, with his false, tinny voice assaulting and deafening me as he sung and preened and then leveled his wide white chin as if resting it on a golden ledge in the air. O I was there now. The moment had reduced itself to a script that seemed etched into time itself. As if I'd stood on this spot before. That I'd touched and moved through the same air in some lost past or revelation, and that even the next step and the next were all ordained and ordered—so that after all this—I'd come to the one conclusion drawn up for me to complete.

Moving out from the camera, I waded amongst the people standing in the front rows and followed a path to arrive at the edge of the stage. Runnymede reared above me and his shadow from the spotlight was thrown and dazzled and loomed ever closer, until I felt its darkness touch upon me even in the dim theater, for there was a purchase now of time itself upon me. A purchase of years too, of the pattern unfolding again and again, for we were one now—him and me, the pursuer and pursued—as time and chance and order aligned. So that as I looked upon him, I could see the pale white veneer of his skin in the footlights. The sickly shine of him. I could have reached up in an instant for his leg, to pull him down into the pit of the world where he'd left me, where I'd been so disposed and put upon for years. Though as I contemplated it, I wondered if this was perhaps his ultimate irony? Had you purchased me and my enmity with your words, Runnymede? Had you purchased this pattern of loss and commerce and captivity that seemed born in my kind, of finding ourselves forever laden to you and your kind, to a world of moneylenders and money-changers and usurpers? To those taken and those who took, from those that were made by the rank dealmakers? Well? Well?

I wanted to shout to him but knew there would be no answer, nothing sufficient to my question. I'd already felt taken myself by the pattern unwinding as all those images and ideas swarmed before me, and yet still he smiled and sang and stepped with a lightness and ease of grace that spoke of its own time-honored dance. Something crafted and knowing. Something orchestrated and ancient, and as I watched, my own hands trembled to perform this one last deed, to cross this last threshold, to drag him down finally as he'd dragged me and A.D. down before. And yet, even as I inched closer, I wondered if this was what he'd wanted all along, for me to lash out at him and reveal the grandeur of his own grace when held to my own ugliness and race? But friends, something miraculous happened. Something stopped me cold and took my breath, and I don't know if it was the silent moment that came over the theater after Runnymede stopped between numbers to dab his forehead with a scarf, or if it was the first strains of the last song he played that brought me from my stupor. But I took the moment to loosen the embossed buttons of my white Pullman Porter jacket, and threw it up on stage.

For I'd seen the footlights, I'd seen them shine on him with a purity anachronous to his making, and I took it upon myself to darken his path. Just as A.D.'s had been darkened by his own boots, kicking out those lights at the Opry. And friends, my aim was true, for it landed at his feet. There it glistened and gleamed and steamed and smoked a bit in the footlights, as if unleashing a spreading, mystic potion—and for the life of him—he couldn't move to see nor smile his soul-stealing smile. As he kicked and flailed with his boots to remove the smoking jacket, I seen the first faint crease and wrinkle in the clean white edge of his face. O the smoke, friends, the smoke! It wouldn't leave him! The jacket and smoke made such an effect upon him he seemed changed by the white blanket of it. As if some older force was only now reclaiming him bit by bit, negating his style and swagger, warping his cold bluster, so that as he tried to stomp on the smoking sleeves, he couldn't snuff it out. And as the brass buttons glared up into his eyes, I like to think the word PORTER embossed upon each circle was all he saw. That I'd finally assisted him through some new doorway of chance, into a greater redemption or rescinding on his part. For as if directed by my own hand, which I raised and moved in the air as if a wand of enchantment, Runnymede and the Piedmont Pipers stopped the song they'd begun and played The Ballad of Clara May instead.

I kid you not.

As sure as I was standing there, the first refrain washed over me and as I stared into the dark unblinking eyes of the man who'd tormented me all those years, I knew I'd beaten him. That though others might rise to follow him, at least he was done if the emotion of these songs—the ones born on the ridge—could course through and guide him, too. He was finished, felled by some darker hand, lost to some true vine or strain of art that had risen, and as I stood there enchanted, I smiled even wider as his encore began and the Misericordia Blues echoed into the rafters. The whole time I couldn't hear nothing but A.D.'s absent voice in the theater. A.D. singing along with him. A.D. reverberating and hollering in the ether. As the tune ended, and I applauded with the rest, and walked out through the buzzing streets of Asheville, my heart burned to know the music had won out. Even if Runnymede had never said our names by point of record. Even if he'd never attributed the songs to us per se. Because I knew that didn't matter anymore. Hell, none of it mattered anymore—for there was no voice—and probably never had been.

There was no one to lay claim to the songs in the end. No one could force them or control their course when the land wanted to sing out, when the land wanted to be heard. As I made my way back to the Biltmore Depot, and glided along as I went, not touching down nor stumbling in the least, I couldn't tell where my own voice started or ended—or where anyone's did, for that matter—and wondered if that was what A.D.'s confession at the Opry had been about all along? His revelation of sorts, even after he'd tried his whole life to make his voice his own. I couldn't say. But only knew that authenticity and distinction were just words we said to delude ourselves, to give some false satisfaction to our deeds. We've only been writing the same thing all this time, all of us, just in different shades and times, moods and forms. And when I rode back on the Asheville Special, and found my way onto the next Crescent—but riding as a passenger this time, as a particular paying passenger—I knew this ticket was my last purchase, the last. Considering I'd paid my dues. I'd served my time, and was moving into something else now, something new and unknown and unending.

Because I guess I just wanted to see the ridge again, to see that blueness rise into the evening, to make another circuit. Always another circuit. I knew enough porters and had worked enough lines to ride perpetual, to ride free and easy and follow the pattern and give up my purchase on the whole idea of buying and of being bought, of acquiring and of chasing fame, now that my moment with the real and imagined Runnymede had put all of that to rest. There was no doubt in me now, not about Runnymede's system of commerce, on that grand purchase of deed and time, for you can't hope to ever beat it working inside it. Shoot, at least not with how they've got it set up—by the same ones who profit the most from it. No, the only way to succeed is to be either very rich or very poor because the middle does all the work. The middle ain't got nowheres to go. But at least there are cracks now and then. Seams in the grand scheme, sending out emotions and songs like shivered sparks along our own weave of sanity and truth. And since the rich have to worry all the time about staying rich, I determined right then and there to be very poor, for the very poor don't have to worry about nothing, except maybe eating. And as far as I could tell, staying poor was about as easy a thing to do in this land—you just had to give up everything you had. So I gave up my books and position and things, and focused on my memories instead, on the feelings and colors and images. Like those lights at the Opry exploding beneath A.D.'s boots. Or Runnymede standing in the camera's piercing gaze, his imported leather boots smudged and scuffed by the white smoking potion of my coat, even as the lights blazed on above him. The lights, the lights. Always the lights. With how they flared and sputtered and dimmed only at the end. Because I can still see them there, even as the Cardinal pulls in with a whoosh of air and steam and smoke and Chicago's lit up like a thousand hovering fireflies above the ridge.

Ah, the ridge, my ridge. Always there no matter what. Always waiting no matter where I wander or roam. Always a memory like a landscape scraped clean of any circumstance or sin. Because it's too big and true to be at fault for anything: the land, echoing up with a sound of stream and sun and stone. Stretching out with a scope and size to recompose my world no matter where the tracks may lead me—maybe even to California to look for them—who knows?

But always I dip back to the ridge. Always I come back to see the high ranging trees and forgotten valleys. I go back and ride the rails and keep the path. Descending along the shadow of the ridge into Roanoke, transferring on the Southern to tip my cap and haul myself to Bristol. To see it all through the window removes me from it to be watchful like maybe I was never watchful before, to go softly and release all the bitterness in my soul.

For Runnymede once said it wouldn't matter none if they returned. That love wasn't enough. That the circuit would still be complete, that the purchase would hold from when I'd sent myself away from them to begin with. And I say okay to that now. I do. For he didn't figure that just to see them again would be enough. Just to see them and to touch my Lucy's head, or my Annie's face, and then to let them go again, would be enough. That even I would abide by the purchase to do that again, that simple thing, to let them go. Because I still wait for them and hope. My girls. I still sing for them and hold my hands together and raise them up to hear the songs like the wind and rain and sky above, and to know that it is all still here, my family. That it is all still true, my life. That everything I've ever wanted and waited for is always hovering and sleeping and dreaming in the echoes of my home in the ridge.

At last.

Forever.

Amen.

THE END

ACKNOWLEDGMENTS

I'd like to thank all the wonderful folks at Blank Slate Press and Amphorae Publishing who made this book a reality. In particular, my editor Kristina Blank Makansi who worked tirelessly to help craft a stronger and more compelling version of the manuscript I plopped (bloated and headstrong) on her doorstep. Many thanks as well to Donna Essner, acquisitions editor, who believed in *Purchase* from the get go and marshalled it on its way.

The Maryland State Arts Council deserves much praise, as well. Without their generous individual artist grants, I would not have been able to carve out as much time as I did for writing, and time is the most valuable variable of all.

A heap of thanks go to my parents for their boundless support over the years. Even though my mother always thought physical therapy was the prudent career choice (and she's probably still right), I gravitated instead to writing and music, and was lucky or stubborn enough to stick with it.

Thanks also to Lesley Riddle, the real-life inspiration for Isaiah Hardy, a man I only ever read about, but whose influence on the Carter Family cannot be stated in words. It takes everyone to make music move from era to era and ear to ear, and it's difficult to call anyone out as more important than any other, but Mr. Riddle deserves more accolades than most.

Finally, I'd like to thank the good folks and towns spread out among the Appalachian Mountains. There is no music without the beauty of the land. Ever. Amen.

ABOUT THE AUTHOR

Christopher Kritwise Doyle grew up in Brunswick, Maryland, a small town nestled on the banks of the Potomac River and Blue Ridge Mountains. After receiving his MFA from the University of Baltimore, he has written about the origins of country music, an embattled elementary school principal in urban America, and the C&O Canal. He lives in Baltimore with his wife, daughter, and bluetick coonhound all in a cramped row house.

CPSIA information can be obtained
at www.ICGtesting.com
Printed in the USA
LVOW10s1929011017

550729LV00007B/7/P